STAR MAGE QUEST

Star Mage Saga

Book One

J.J. Green

INFINITEBOOK

PREQUEL

Sign up to my reader group for your exclusive copy of the Star Mage Saga prequel, *Daughter of Discord*, and the rest of your free J.J. Green starter library at

https://jjgreenauthor.com/free-books

BOOKS OF THE STAR MAGE SAGA

ONE

Carina slung her Jensen 31 across her back and crawled beneath the remains of a desk. She had to bend low to avoid snagging the weapon on broken wood. The door to the room was slightly ajar, and from outside came the whispers and hisses of pulse slugs and the stamp of running, booted feet.

She hated hiding in the middle of a firefight but if she didn't do something soon, it would all be over for her and her merc band, the Black Dogs.

Easing into a spot where she was hidden from view, she bit on the fingers of her silicon mesh glove, pulling it off. She dropped the glove and worked on the other until both her hands were free. Removing her protective gear was reckless, but she needed bare fingers to tell if the wood splinters from the desk were real. If they weren't, the Cast would not work.

Of course, casting brought its own risks. She faced slavery and torture if anyone found out what she was about to do. Not for the first time, she wondered whether being a mage was more of a curse than a blessing. On the other hand, saving her and her merc buddies' lives would be a definite benefit.

The door banged against the wall as it flew open and someone burst in. A pulse fizzed and a body hit the floor. She peeked from underneath the desk. A fellow merc was lying flat on his stomach and facing away from her, a smoking hole at the weak point where his helmet connected to his body armor. The man trembled once then was still.

Though she couldn't see his face, she recognized the dead man. It was the latest recruit, his new career cut short by the suicide mission they'd been sent on.

Another figure ran in. Carina saw the calves and boots of one of the attackers. She shrank backward and lifted her Jensen, resting her finger on the trigger. If the soldier looked under the desk, he would receive a pulse round in his face. But the legs turned and left, and she heard footsteps running up the stairs to the next level. It was a lucky escape, but her luck wouldn't last much longer.

She picked up a splinter of wood from the desk and rubbed it between her fingertips. After peering closely at the fibrous strands, she closed her eyes to concentrate on their texture. The wood fibers were fine but not fine enough, and they were too smooth. The wood was fake. She threw down the splinter in disgust.

Her canister of base elixir was missing only one essential element: wood. The real stuff had proven hard to find on this desert planet. Even if she found some natural wood to add to the elixir, it was no guarantee she would be successful. There had to be fifty or more enemy soldiers in the embassy. She'd never cast at so many, but she had to try.

Crawling out from under the desk, Carina scanned the room. Before it had been blown apart, the place had been luxurious. Some kind of animal skin buffed to a fine sheen had covered the walls, though now it hung in tatters. A delicate translucent mineral, intricately carved, had supplied the window lattices. Broken pieces of it were sprayed over the floor.

The room must have belonged to a high-up embassy official, maybe even the Matahman ambassador—the kind of official to own real wood artifacts.

The sounds of the struggle for possession of the embassy were growing louder. Fighting was going on in the stories above and below. Skirting the body of the fallen recruit, Carina closed the door and went over to a cabinet. The door was secured, but a single pulse from her Jensen melted the lock. She levered the door open with the muzzle.

Reaching inside, she riffled through bottles of the local liquor, beakers, hard copies of documents, expensive-looking jars of some kind of local food or ointment, and boxes of different sizes. She pulled out the boxes and tried to open them, but they were fastened shut in a way she couldn't figure out—possibly DNA or electronic locks.

She had no time for cracking fancy locks, neither through ingenuity nor casting. After a brief glance at the door, she stood and brought the butt of her Jensen down hard on one of the more fragile-looking cases, smashing it apart.

Her luck seemed to be holding. Inside the case was an oblong object. From the complex design carved at one end, she guessed it was some kind of seal or stamp. More importantly, the artifact displayed the finely grained effect of wood. She drove down the butt of her Jensen again, the blow jarring her arms.

She'd split the seal at one end. Squatting, she dug her fingers into the split and ripped the object apart. She extracted a thin splinter and rubbed it into fine strands.

From outside came the sound of footsteps running downstairs. No time remained to figure out if the seal was natural wood and not another clever synthetic. She took out her canister of elixir, unscrewed it and dropped in the strands. She swirled the mixture once, brought it to her lips and swallowed a mouthful.

The elixir was foul-tasting, as usual, but Carina barely registered the taste anymore. Her eyes were closed and she was already writing the ideogram in her mind, willing herself to ignore the steps drawing closer.

Creating the character required the utmost concentration. The Cast was useless unless the strokes were completed perfectly and in the correct order. One after another they appeared in her mind's eye.

Just as she drew the final stroke, someone ran in. Her eyes flew open and she grabbed for her weapon, which was slung over her shoulder, but the newcomer was merc officer Lieutenant Torres.

"Come with me, Lin," the lieutenant said. "Up to the—"

Torres fell forward, the back of her helmet a ruined, burning mess. She squirmed at Carina's feet. Behind her, framed by the door, was the enemy soldier who had shot the lieutenant at point blank range. His weapon was now aimed directly at Carina. She didn't stand a chance. The soldier grinned.

Then the Cast began to work.

As always, the effect wasn't immediate. If the soldier had ignored it and fired, Carina would have been dead, but he was distracted by its sensation. The man hesitated, his weapon still pointing at her, and looked down at his arms in disbelief as they began to disappear.

He lifted his head to meet Carina's gaze, his grin quickly giving way to a look of panic. The next moment, he was gone.

And so were most of the rest of the enemy in the embassy, Carina hoped. She estimated the Cast's radius to be around forty meters, which had to encompass most of the enemy within the building.

She dropped to her knees at Torres' side. The woman was no longer moving, and Carina's stomach turned at the sight of gray matter oozing from the split in her helmet. Gently, she turned the lieutenant over. Her eyes were fixed and still.

Mourning the lieutenant, the new recruit, and whoever else had died on the hopeless assignment would have to wait until later. It was time for the Black Dogs to retreat before enemy reinforcements arrived.

Carina listened hard for sounds of fighting, but the embassy was quiet. Her Cast had given the mercs a little breathing space. She went to find the rest of her platoon. Speeding downstairs, she leapt over the corpse of a fallen attacker and empty steps before running into the embassy lobby. She skidded to a halt. Three Jensens were aimed at her.

"What the hell do you think you're doing, Lin?" barked Captain Speidel, lowering his rifle, "I nearly shot you."

His rebuke stung, though Carina knew in his eyes she deserved it. She had a lot of respect for the captain and hated being the object of his disapproval.

"*Are* we under attack, sir?" asked Staff Sergeant Brown. "The ones who had me and Halliday pinned down vanished. And I don't hear any fighting. Did you see what happened to the enemy?"

"I'm not sure what I saw," Speidel replied.

"Sir, Lieutenant Torres bought it," Carina said. "And the new guy too."

"Shit." Speidel turned away to speak into his helmet mic. As she listened in to his conversation with the mercs on the upper stories, Carina heard their confusion about the sudden disappearance of the attackers. The mercs on the roof reported more enemy forces approaching from every side.

It didn't need to be said. If they didn't get out of here soon, they were screwed.

Two

The mercs crammed into the shuttle that would take them back to their starship, *Duchess*. They laid the bodies of the fallen in sections under the floor. *Sleeping in the locker,* it was called.

No one said a thing while the shuttle lifted into the air and away from the embassy, which was now ripe for the taking. The atmosphere was tense as the mercs waited for ground-to-air fire while they made their escape, but nothing came. The enemy seemed to have lost interest now they'd retreated. Carina guessed it would be some time before the reinforcements realized their associates had disappeared. It would be still longer until the soldiers she'd transported returned from the spot where she'd sent them.

She was mind-weary after such a large Cast. She was also worried about the questions that would inevitably be asked about the unusual events of the firefight. In the two years since she'd joined the Black Dogs, she'd kept her Casts small, personal, and easily concealed. It had been the first time she'd risked doing something so noticeable.

After the shuttle left the danger zone, there was none of the banter and jibes that usually went on among the mercs at the end of an mission; none of the black humor they employed to deal with the loss of friends and even enemies within their band. They'd failed. They'd retreated, and ingrained into the men and women, who were mostly ex-military, was the shame that came along with that.

The mysterious disappearance of their attackers hadn't yet been mentioned, as if no one wanted to risk being thought mad or stupid. Carina was certainly not going to be first to bring it up.

The merc sitting next to her, Smitz, reached into a pocket and pulled out a wad of the foul herb he was addicted to. He bit off a few centimeters of the brown substance and pushed it into his cheek with his tongue before beginning to chew. Carina immediately regretted her choice of seat. She shifted her boots sideways in case he targeted his spit near her feet.

"Bastard lied to us," Smitz finally said, breaking the silence.

The Black Dogs' assignment had been to act as back up for the government force that was supposed to be defending the embassy, only the government troops hadn't shown.

His comment was met with mutterings and grumbles. Captain Speidel, who was sitting next to the exit and gazing out of a small porthole, didn't seem to have heard Smitz's words.

"Can't fight a company with a platoon," Smitz continued, drawing further murmured agreement.

"Quieten down, soldier," Speidel said, finally noticing the man's complaints. The murmurs ceased, and the captain returned to his morose contemplation of the view.

Carina felt for Speidel. He would be the one to take the blame if the top brass decided after debriefing he'd made the wrong call, despite the hopeless situation they'd found themselves in.

He was a good man who didn't deserve the shit thrown at him as the meat in the sandwich between Tarsalan, the company's owner along with commanding officer Cadwallader, and grunts like Smitz. Carina was, and always would be, grateful to Speidel for saving her from persecution and squalor in the slums of a nowhere planet. Though she rarely admitted it to herself, the older man was the closest thing to a father she had. She hoped he wouldn't suffer Tarsalan's ire, though it was unlikely he would be so fortunate. The woman was notorious for her fixation on profits and disregard for the lives that were lost to achieve them.

Still no one was mentioning what was on everyone's mind—that all the attackers within the embassy building and compound had suddenly, inexplicably, vanished.

In the end, it was Halliday who spoke. "Hey, did…er…did anyone see anything weird happen down there?"

The uneasy shifting of bodies was the mercs' only reply. Even Smitz, who was never slow to tell everyone and anyone exactly what he thought, was silent on the issue. From the corner of her eye, Carina could see Speidel shaking his head, no doubt wondering how he was going to explain to his superiors that the only reason most of them had gotten out alive was due to an impossible event.

The micro-gravity of low orbit was taking hold, and Carina lifted from her seat and bobbed against the straps of her harness. They were nearly back at *Duchess*. Soon, she would be able to return to her cabin and safely stash her canister of elixir away from prying eyes.

"Hey, Lin," said Smitz. "You got any water? I'm all out."

Thinking that if he didn't chew his disgusting herb he wouldn't be so thirsty, Carina shook her head.

"Come on, Lin. Don't hold out on me. We're nearly back at the ship."

"Then you can wait," Carina replied.

"Come on, give me some. I know you always bring extra. I can see your bottle sticking out like a third tit." Smitz made a grab for the pouch that held the elixir canister. Carina deflected his arm with her elbow, following through and driving it into his gut. The blow had no effect other than pushing him away a little, due to the man's armor. Smitz reached out with his other hand and Carina knocked that away too. She shoved him into the bulkhead for good measure.

"Smitz. Lin," barked Brown. "Cut it out, or you're both on report."

Smitz relented. Carina's racing heart slowed, and she was glad her face was hidden behind her tinted visor. Her skin was hot and moist with sweat.

It was with relief she felt the shudder that rippled through the shuttle as it engaged with *Duchess'* access hatch. After another few moments she was pulling herself through the short tunnel that led to the ship. As she went along, *Duchess'* AG field took hold and Carina's feet drifted to the floor. She let go of the bars she'd been grasping and walked.

Now they were back at their ship, the chances of reprisals for the mission went down. *Duchess* didn't live up to her name in terms of classy looks, being rather dumpy and squat, but she more than made up for the deficit with armaments. State-of-the-art pulse cannons fore and aft and fusion-rocket long-range missiles were supplemented by turret-mounted rail guns. As well as deterring space pirates with cocky ideas,

Duchess' artillery meant that retaliation from the opposing side after a mission was rare. When it came to Tarsalan's own safety, she didn't skimp.

The same could not be said for the mercs. Carina and the others removed their armor and hung it up in the armory. The protection was flexible, light and tough, but it was showing signs of wear. At the embassy, their attacker's weapons had been able to penetrate it at close range. One of the problems of working as a merc was that levels of technological advancement varied widely between worlds. New weapons were constantly being developed, and they were never quite sure what they would be up against next.

Carina transferred her canister from its pouch into her shirt and went straight to the cabin she shared with three other mercs. It was empty. She slid the canister into the hole she'd dug in her mattress. Then, finally relaxing for the first time since she'd cast, she lay down on her bunk and put her hands behind her head. After around half an hour a comm woke her.

"Corporal Lin," came the message. "Report for debriefing immediately."

Her earlier tension returned. Why did they want to talk to her? Had someone seen what she'd done? Carina wondered how that might be possible, and her stomach dropped as she remembered Lieutenant Torres had been wearing a body cam like they all did. What if it had recorded her casting?

She swung down from her bunk, wracking her brain for an explanation as to why she would have taken a drink and then stood still with her eyes closed in great concentration, just before a horde of enemy soldiers disappeared.

By the time she reached the debriefing room, she hadn't thought of a logical explanation for her behavior.

THREE

"We don't need to know everything," said Lieutenant Colonel Cadwallader. "Only describe exactly what you saw toward the end of the engagement, Corporal. Don't leave anything out."

Standing to attention in the mission room, Carina's gaze flicked to Captain Speidel, who sat on one side, stroking his stubble and watching. Cadwallader and Tarsalan sat behind a desk.

Cadwallader's pale blue eyes seemed intent on piercing right through her, and Tarsalan's full lips, coated in a purple sheen, were set in a line. Neither gave a hint of what they were expecting her to say. Carina didn't know if she had to explain herself regarding Torres's body cam footage or only report on the disappearance of the enemy.

She hesitated.

"We don't have all day, Lin," Tarsalan said, her heavy-lidded eyes drooping lower. The woman drummed fingers bearing thick, bejeweled rings on the desktop.

"Around ten minutes before Captain Speidel gave the order to withdraw," said Carina, "I was alone in a room. I think it might have been the ambassador's office."

"What were you doing there?" Cadwallader asked.

"Checking for insurgents, sir."

"Go on," said Cadwallader.

Carina explained how Lieutenant Torres died. "After the lieutenant fell, the enemy turned his weapon on me," she went on. "He would have shot me too, except…"

Her mouth was suddenly very dry. She swallowed.

"Spit it out, Lin," said Cadwallader, frowning.

"Whatever you saw, or thought you saw," said Speidel, "all you have to do is tell the truth."

Carina focused on the captain. "The soldier disappeared, sir. Right in front of me. One minute he was there and the next he was gone."

Tarsalan gave a huff of bitter frustration. "Just like the others. This is ridiculous."

"We have the body cam vids," said Cadwallader. "They don't lie."

"It was an optical illusion," said Tarsalan.

"All fourteen of them?" Cadwallader asked.

"It makes no sense otherwise," Tarsalan countered. "If someone's invented cloaking technology for individuals, why didn't they use it when they attacked? Why use it in order to retreat, especially when by all accounts they had the upper hand?"

"I don't think it was cloaking technology," said Cadwallader. "I think it was something else."

"Like what?"

The lieutenant colonel was about to reply but he noticed Carina was still there, standing to attention.

"You're dismissed, Corporal," he said.

Carina saluted and left. She guessed her story backed up the testimony given at earlier debriefings. She hadn't been singled out for scrutiny, but Cadwallader's comment that the soldiers' disappearance had been *something else* had her stomach in knots again.

The sound of fast-moving footsteps from behind made her stop and turn. It was Captain Speidel, striding quickly to catch up to her.

"We're going in the same direction," he said. "Let's walk together."

As a subordinate, Carina's compliance was a given. The two continued on their way.

"How are things going for you?" Speidel asked.

"Pretty good, sir."

"You can drop the *sir* for the moment, Carina."

"Okay." Speidel had talked with her in this friendly way fairly regularly since recruiting her to the merc company, and she enjoyed their amiable conversations.

"I wanted to give you a heads up," Speidel went on. He put a hand on her shoulder. "Stop a moment."

Carina turned to him.

The man's expression was serious and pained. "You can't tell anyone else what I'm about to say to you. I can trust you, right?"

She nodded.

"Why am I even asking?" Speidel smiled. "You're tighter than a drum." He checked up and down the empty corridor. "I wanted to let you know, things might be over soon for the Black Dogs. We might be disbanding. So if you come across an opportunity to do something else, you should probably take it."

"Disbanding, s...?" She stopped herself just in time. "Why?"

"Tarsalan's been complaining for a while now she's pouring creds into the company and making no profit. This last job we just did might be the final straw. The client's refusing to pay the balance of the fee because the embassy was taken."

"But they lied," Carina exclaimed. "We were on our own and totally outnumbered. We could never have defended the place. If we hadn't withdrawn, we would have been slaughtered."

"That's not what they're saying at their end. But it doesn't matter what they say. If they won't pay, they won't pay."

"Maybe Tarsalan should send us on a mission to persuade them," Carina said bitterly. Working with the Black Dogs was her life. She didn't know what else she could do. She was damned if she would join the military and get paid a pittance.

Speidel gave a wry smile. "That might be effective one time, but as soon as word got out we'd never work again. It isn't like merc bands are difficult to find these days."

"So you're saying I should sign up with another company?"

"I don't know. Soldiering's a tough life. Maybe you should try something different while you're still young and it isn't burned into your bones. The galaxy's a big place. There has to be some way for a young woman to make a living that doesn't put her life on the line. You aren't dyed-in-the-wool military like most of the rest of us."

Carina shook her head. "Fighting's all I know."

Speidel sighed and resumed walking. Carina went along with him.

"I sometimes wonder if I did the right thing," Speidel said, "breaking up that fight you were in and signing you up as a merc. You might have ended up doing something less dangerous and more worthwhile."

"No. I wasn't gonna win that fight. I took two of them out, but I was five minutes from being beaten to a pulp. If you hadn't stepped in..." Carina's memory of the event was vivid. Though she'd learned her fighting skills the hard way over the previous six years since Nai Nai died, even she was no match for the five boys who had set upon her. Their motive was only to have some fun, it seemed, as she had nothing to give them. It was a heavily bruised, bleeding Carina Captain Speidel had brought back to *Duchess* and patched up. "Well, I wouldn't be here now, that's for sure.

"If you take my advice," Speidel said, "you won't be here for much longer." The captain's comm button chirped. He checked the message. "Looks like my dinner will have to wait. Think over what I said, Carina. It might be time for a change."

As the captain turned to go back the way he'd come, Carina thought she saw a look in his eye that indicated he knew more than he was saying. She felt sick. Had the captain's friendly advice been a cover for a deeper warning? Had he guessed her secret, and did he think that others were also drawing closer to the truth about what had really happened in the embassy fight?

Perhaps it was indeed time for her to move on.

FOUR

None of Carina's bunk mates had returned to the shared cabin, so she took advantage of the rare moment of solitude to meditate. Nai Nai had taught her the habit, telling her it preserved and strengthened one's powers.

The old woman had said that though mage abilities were genetically inherited, it wasn't a fixed thing like hair or eye color. Casting was also a skill that had to be learned, refined, and maintained, and she'd explained that if Carina didn't regularly perform mental exercises, her ability would lessen and perhaps fail. What was more, if she did lose her ability, there was no guarantee it would ever return once she was an adult, no matter how hard she worked.

Sitting in her top bunk, Carina crossed her legs and faced the wall. The steps to achieve a trance state were always the same. She mentally recited and embraced the concepts of the five Elements: wood, fire, earth, metal, water. Following the Elements were the Seasons: spring, early summer, late summer, autumn, winter. This second part of the pre-trance task was not so familiar to Carina. Though she'd visited many worlds while working with the merc band, she'd never encountered a place where the climate followed the pattern laid out by Nai Nai with its types of weather, variations in temperature, and fluctuation of daylight hours.

Next, she mentally wrote the Strokes. Each line had to be written perfectly, each taper and flourish correct. She wrote them separately and then together in the character that meant *forever*. Finally, she conjured up the Map in her mind. Nai Nai had made her draw the 3D image over and over again on her holoscribe while she was growing up. There were more than a hundred stars, and her grandmother would measure the angle and distance between each star carefully when she finished. If anything was incorrect, she had to draw it again.

The Map showed the birthplace of their clan, Nai Nai had said. At the center of the Map was the star system their ancestors had been driven from, so long ago no one knew when.

Carina had once asked her grandmother why they didn't try to return to their original home.

"No one knows where to go anymore, Mei Mei. No one remembers where we came from."

"But we have the Map," Carina had persisted. "Why can't we find it using that?"

Nai Nai had laughed and dipped her hand into a jar of sand she used for polishing the beautiful stones she sold for a living. She scattered the sand across the floor where Carina sat.

"Tell me, Mei Mei, how many grains do you see?"

Carina frowned. Was it a test? "Ten thousand? No. Fifty thousand."

"Probably about five thousand. Look closely, child, and imagine these are stars. In our section of the galaxy alone there are ten times as many stars as there are grains of sand lying here. It would take several lifetimes to visit each and check if the surrounding pattern of stars matched the Map. One would need to look at the groupings from many orientations. And our galactic sector is only one of thousands."

The young Carina eyed her holoscribe drawing, which had taken her over two hours to create. "Then why bother remembering it at all? Why not give up on ever returning home?"

"That is something every mage must answer for herself. But let me ask *you*, little one, do you feel as though this place where we live now is your home?"

Carina considered their two-roomed house, which in truth was little more than a shack. She considered the dirty street outside with its open gutter that kept the local rats well fed. She considered how different she felt from the other children, who didn't know the Elements or the

Seasons or the Strokes or the Map, and who could not cast. She shook her head. "I don't, Nai Nai."

The old woman sighed. "My great-grandparents told me once they'd heard it said our birthplace was the origin of humanity itself—the world where humans first evolved, invented space travel, and journeyed out to colonize new planets. If we could find that place again, it would truly be something very special.

"But more important even than that, the Map gives us hope," her grandmother continued. "we are exiles and our clan has been scattered to the stars. Nowhere are we accepted for being who we are. We live in secrecy, always. The Map holds the promise that one day we may live openly and together again in our homeland. Holding onto that possibility helps us to go on."

Remembering Nai Nai's words calmed Carina's anxiety, and she slipped into a deep meditative state.

Some time later, the sound of the cabin door opening entered the edge of her consciousness. She brought herself out of her trance and turned to see Thyrna Atoi, her bunk mate, bend down to sit on the lower bunk. She began to take off her boots.

"You missed dinner," said Atoi. "Not that you missed much. Chef's on a marine plant kick. Yeuuuch! *It's high in nutrients and protein*, he said whenever anyone complained."

"I wasn't that hungry anyway," Carina said.

Atoi threw a boot at the corner of the room. "Got it!"

"What was it?" Carina asked. "A roach?"

"Yep," said Atoi as she went across the room to retrieve her boot. She picked up the squashed insect by a leg and carried it to the garbage disposal chute.

"That's not a roach," Carina said. "That's a scalobite."

"What difference does it make?"

"Scalobites are good. They eat roaches."

"Whatever. Now it's a dead scalobite."

Carina sighed and lay on her back. The bunk shuddered as Atoi shifted her position. She was a large, heavily muscled woman.

"You missed the announcement too," she said. "Got another mission. Hykara sector."

"Where's that?"

"Don't know. A long way from here. We're fast-burning through the quiet shift."

As Atoi mentioned the fast burn, Carina began to feel the vibration of *Duchess's* engines powering up. She lay down and fastened the safety webbing over her bunk. Soon, the ship would lurch as they switched to FTL drive.

"What's the mission?" Carina asked, studying the rust patch in the corner of the ceiling above her bunk.

"Search and rescue. Kidnap victim."

"Huh? Isn't that one for a planetside control force?"

"You'd think, wouldn't you?" Atoi replied. "Word is, no one local will touch it. *Other mercs* won't touch it. We're only doing it because it's that or disband. Tarsalan says she'll pull the plug otherwise."

Unfastening her webbing temporarily, Carina leaned over the edge of her bunk to look at Atoi. The woman had the satisfied expression of someone spinning out a juicy piece of gossip.

"What else does the word say?" Carina asked.

Atoi smirked. "The boy who was kidnapped is a Sherrerr, and the kidnappers are—"

"Dirksens," Carina finished for her. She threw herself onto her back. "We've bought it."

"Yeah. Everyone's trying to bail but Tarsalan won't let them. Says they have to work out their contracts. No negotiation. After the last mission, people were already pissed. Some chairs got thrown, tables broken. Tarsalan exited at the first sign of trouble and left Cadwallader and Speidel to calm things down."

Carina could imagine the scene. She was glad she'd skipped dinner. Merc bands were mostly made up of men and women who had left—or been discharged from—the military because they were unstable or lacked the discipline necessary for service in the forces. They could be aggressive, anti-social, impulsive, and belligerent.

Her soldier buddies' personality quirks had never bothered Carina much. Surviving alone on the streets from a young age had brought her into contact with many unsavory types. In fact, the mercs' unpleasant characteristics made things easier for her. Superficial friendships and casual hookups were all she could risk in terms of relationships. In her time with the Black Dogs, she'd only ever contemplated something more with one man: Stevenson, the pilot, who was relatively sane. She'd avoided him ever since coming to the realization.

No, mercs were not to be messed with, and Tarsalan, in her usual nonchalant, disinterested manner, had just told a room of them their next mission was to be even more suicidal than their last.

FIVE

As Carina went to the armory to suit up before leaving on the mission to rescue the little Sherrerr boy, she was reconsidering her decision to go along. Speidel had advised her to move on from the merc band, and she had recently come dangerously close to revealing her ability. What was more, the assignment was highly risky. Even if they succeeded—which wasn't likely—the chances were the Dirksens wouldn't rest until they found and punished the people responsible for thwarting their plan. And in the list of possible punishments the Dirksens meted out, the best and rarest option was a quick death.

Despite Tarsalan's threats, there wasn't much the company owner could do to the mercs who refused to take part in the assignment other than fire them. Being let go was a problem that paled in comparison to the potential consequences of defying the Dirksens.

The Sherrerr/Dirksen feud was notorious. It had gone on for so long, the inciting event was lost in time, but the reason for their mutual hatred and constant clashes didn't matter. The Sherrerrs and Dirksens were equally wealthy, powerful, and corrupt, which meant their rivalry to be the ruling clan in that sector of the galaxy was inevitable.

Anyone with any sense had nothing to do with either family if they could help it. It was true that when you were on the inside, you had access to all the luxury and privilege the connection provided, but there was a large drawback: you could never leave. Once you were in, you were in for life and that was that. If you left, you were an unacceptable liability, and you would spend the rest of your prematurely shortened life looking over your shoulder, wondering where and when the blow would fall.

Carina guessed the Sherrerrs had promised Tarsalan rich rewards and lifelong protection for her and her loved ones to persuade her to take the deal. The same recompense and safeguarding wouldn't apply to the grunts who did the actual work.

The mercs who had refused the job were dumped on a remote planet, unpaid. The rumor was that Speidel had threatened to resign, though for some reason he was now coming along. Perhaps his motivation was similar to Carina's. She certainly had no interest in the clan feud or in incurring the vengeful spite of the Dirksens, but she had thought more than once about the little boy they had taken.

According to the information the Sherrerrs had given, he was only six. Carina had been but four years older when she had also found herself alone with no one to protect her, and she hated to think how the ruthless Dirksens might treat a Sherrerr they had in their clutches. No ransom note had been issued, and no other explanation had been given for the kidnapping, so what they were planning to do was unclear.

Someone had to get the boy out. Carina had done some morally questionable things during her time as a merc. If rescuing an innocent child was to be her last mission, it would be a fitting finale to her career.

The armory was already busy with the rest of the mission squad. She took down the legs of her armor and stepped into them, tightening the fit before slotting the torso into place and sealing it. The arms came next. She slipped the canister of elixir into its pouch and adjusted its position so that it wasn't in the way. From the edge of her vision she noticed Smitz watching. She gave him the stink eye and bent down to pick up her helmet.

"Hey, what are you doing, you bunch of useless grunts?" asked Captain Speidel as he appeared at the door. "Didn't you hear the directive? If we go in there dressed like soldiers, we'll be blown to bits before we get within five klicks of the target. You're in civvies for this. And no guns. We don't want to draw any attention when we disembark. We'll buy weapons planetside. Get changed and get to the shuttle. We're leaving at eleven hundred and fifteen."

Half an hour later, Speidel gave them a final briefing as they descended to the planet.

"Listen up," he said to the eight mercs seated on each side of the shuttle, looking uncomfortable in normal clothes. "Orrana's a young world, geologically speaking. Too young to be settled, in my opinion. It's highly volcanic, and while that makes for lucrative mining operations, the effects are pretty much what you would expect on a relatively new planet: regular eruptions, earthquakes, tsunamis, geysers, boiling volcanic springs, and so on.

"The biggest settlement is on one of the most stable landmasses, and it's a pretty lawless place from what I can gather, which suits our purposes perfectly. That sword cuts both ways, however. If anyone gets into trouble, they only have themselves or us to rely on to get them out of it. There is a local civil control force but it's probably either ineffective or crooked. It's unlikely to interfere in any fights and we might find ourselves on the wrong side of it if it becomes known why we're there. If they don't already know what the Dirksens are doing, they probably aren't going to do anything if they find out.

"You're likely wondering how we know where the Dirksens are holding the victim. The simple answer is the boy's been fitted with a transmitter. It's embedded in him, so we have his exact coordinates. We only have to break or sneak through the Dirksens' guard, rescue the lad, and escape with him. *Duchess* will be ready to run the moment we have him aboard."

Smitz said, "You left something out, Captain."

"What's that, Private?"

"What's our cut and when do we get it?"

"What?"

"The Sherrers must be paying a fortune to rescue their kid. What I want to know is, how much of that cred are we seeing? What's our bonus?"

"No one's mentioned a bonus, Smitz."

"We're taking all this risk so Tarsalan can buy another pretty ring?"

"You'll get what you're paid," said Speidel. "Now be quiet."

"Right," Smitz said. "I'll remember that when the Dirksens have me cornered in a dark alley. I'll be sure to give them her home address." He spat into the gully that ran down the center of the small ship.

Speidel grimaced in disgust. "What the hell are you chewing, man? Hand it over."

His face set in anger, Smitz pulled out his packet of herb and gave it to Speidel, who put it in his pocket.

"Take these," Speidel said, handing out breathing masks. "Wear them at all times and never breathe the local air. The atmosphere has enough oxygen, but the CO_2 level will kill you. I'm hoping we won't have to stay the night there, but if we do, change the filter every day. Everyone take one of these too." He opened a drawstring bag containing small electronic devices. "They're comms with high level encryption, as you won't be wearing your helmets."

Carina took one of the small gadgets and pushed it into her right ear. She pulled her hair forward to cover it. When Speidel spoke again, she heard his voice loud and clear.

"Now I know we don't do much plain clothes work," the captain continued, "so some of you might not feel comfortable with it. What you have to try to remember is that, until we're inside the place where they're keeping the kid, you're to try to forget you're soldiers. Whoever's guarding the child will be on the lookout for anyone who seems like they could be ex-military."

Pondering the captain's words, Carina's gaze roved over her fellow operatives. Smitz was the largest of the bunch. He was built like a heavyweight fistfighter and wore a permanent scowl. Brown was as tall as Smitz but more supple and lithe. He moved like a predator. Next to Brown was Atoi, who loved to work on her upper body strength. Her bull neck and biceps were stretching the material of her shirt.

On Carina's left sat Carver. She had a scar that ran diagonally across her cheek and under her nose, permanently lifting her top lip. It wouldn't have been expensive to get the scar fixed, but Carver seemed to like the look. Halliday sat on Carina's right. He had the gaze of someone who had seen enough horror for several lifetimes. Further on from Halliday were Jackson with his prosthetic arm and Lee, who had a nervous tic that made him blink excessively.

They were gonna buy it for sure.

Six

They set up at a hostel for transient workers while Captain Speidel went out to procure some weapons. Firearms of any kind were prohibited on the planet according to the signs at the arrivals section of the spaceport, but it seemed as though no one paid much attention to the rule. Carina had seen guns and rifles carried openly as they rode the transport to the hostel.

Orrana was a dark place in climate and mood. Thick haze generated by frequent volcanic eruptions blocked much of the sunlight. As a result, vegetation was minimal. Deep gray-green, straggly stems covered the black soil to the horizon. Speidel had told them that animal life was at the microorganism stage, so they had nothing to fear from the indigenous species. Carina doubted the same could be said for the Dirksens or their employees.

The locals she'd seen at the spaceport wore sour or suspicious or desperate looks, judging by what she could see of their faces. Their breathing masks covered the nose and mouth and were fastened by a strap on each side of the face and one over the top of the head. The clothes the locals wore were basic and utilitarian and their hair was plainly cut. Fashion was not of any importance on Orrana. Survival was.

The mercs' story was that they were a team of smelting workers. It was a subterfuge intended to account for their rough, burly appearance. If asked, they were to say they were looking for work and were not interested in setting up their own operation. Conflicts over land, mining rights, and raw materials were rife, and the mercs were to expect scrutiny in that regard.

As she stood in the shared hostel room and pulled tight the wide belt she wore, she hoped no one would ask her any awkward questions. She didn't have a clue about smelting.

Atoi stepped into the room. "Come downstairs," she said. Her voice was muffled by her mask, but the comm Carina was wearing conveyed the woman's words. "Speidel's back. We're leaving soon."

Carina caught her reflection in a mirror as she left. She so rarely looked at herself in a mirror, let alone saw herself in civvies, that she paused a moment to take in the sight. She was wearing narrow pants that went down to her calves, boots that fastened with interlacing straps and a plain, open-necked hemp blouse. Speidel had told them to stick to dark colors.

Her figure was athletic but not bulky, and she didn't—yet—have that hard, intense expression that a life of killing had given so many of the others. Of all the squad members on the mission she thought she looked the least like a soldier. Perhaps she could find another way in life after rescuing the little boy.

Did she look anything like a smelting worker? She didn't think so, but her outfit would have to do.

She followed Atoi downstairs to the hostel bar, where the others were hanging out. Speidel wasn't there, and they were drinking the local brew. When Carina sat down at the table, someone pushed a beaker of frothy liquid in front of her. The smell of it told her the drink was some kind of alcohol. When she hesitated to try it, Jackson leaned over and said, "Speidel said it's okay. Just one drink."

For the benefit of eavesdroppers, they weren't to use the word 'captain' in public, nor any other terms that might identify them.

Carina sipped the deep green liquid. It tasted like someone had fermented the local vegetation, which was probably the case. "I think I'll pass," she said, pushing the beaker away.

Smitz laughed. He grabbed her cup and drained it.

Speidel came into the bar carrying a bulging bag. He set it down on the table and handed out weapons. Though the bar was full of the hostel's patrons, no one took any notice. It was as though on Orrana *not* carrying a weapon would be strange behavior.

Jackson held up his gun to examine it. "Where are these from? The last century?"

Smitz snickered and poured himself another drink from the pitcher.

"That's what's available at short notice on the street." Speidel held out his hand to take the gun back. "Unless you'd rather go without?"

"No, no. Not complaining," Jackson replied, pushing the weapon into the back of his pants under his shirt. "No way. Just asking."

After quickly checking it over, Carina tucked hers into her belt.

Speidel said quietly, "I picked up some explosives too. C8 with delay fuses. They weren't difficult to find and they'll probably prove useful. They have thirty-second and two-minute delays. Okay, let's pay a visit to a smelting plant. I've hired one of the local transports. We'll talk more about the job on the way."

He clearly didn't want to risk their conversation being overheard at the bar. The eight mercs rose and left with the captain, making their way outside. As they went to where the transport was parked, Carina got her first close-up look at the settlement. She wasn't impressed. The place reminded her of where she'd grown up.

Like HER birth planet, Orrana was far from the center of the action and way off trade routes, and it showed. No one was planning to settle here, so no one had made any effort to create a proper infrastructure, like good roads or basic public services. From the flimsy pre-fabricated buildings to the dim street lights hung on makeshift poles, everything was temporary.

She pondered the advisability of building a smelting plant on a planet that was prone to earthquakes, but the financial savings of refining the ore planetside probably offset the costs of rebuilding after a shock. The risk to the workers was undoubtedly low on the list of priorities, as it always was in ass-end-of-the-galaxy places.

Carina climbed aboard the multi-person transport Speidel had rented. The heavy vibration when he started it up signaled that the vehicle ran on some kind of organic fuel. Orrana really was about the most backward place she'd ever been. She slid into a window seat and rubbed a clear patch in the grimy window with the edge of her sleeve. Speidel input the destination and the transport pulled into the road.

"The smelting plant where the Dirksens are holding the kid is at the edge of town," Speidel said once they were on their way down the potholed street. "We're going to pretend we're looking for work. Gangs of transients looking for labor are common. The guards shouldn't be too suspicious at first. Don't forget you're supposed to be contract laborers. Low-skilled, boneheaded grunts."

"Sounds about right," Carver said, her scarred top lip rising in a gruesome grin.

"That way, no one's going to expect us to answer any difficult questions," Speidel continued. "All we need is enough of a cover story to get inside the plant. Here are the plans."

He handed out thin, transparent sheets.

"The red dot is the kid."

Carina studied the blueprint of the plant. It felt weird to not see the image on a visor overlay and not to be able to interact with it. The smelting plant was large and complex, and the Dirksens had secreted the boy on a basement level at its heart. As she saw the scale of the complex, the desperate nature of their attempt began to hit home.

The Dirksens had chosen the place to hold their hostage well. Not only was the boy in the least accessible part of the complex, the place was full of people working for Dirksens: tough men and women who had led hard lives. They wouldn't be averse to using their fists or whatever weapon came to hand to do their boss's bidding, and there had to be hundreds of them.

"You've gotta be joking, sir," said Lee, staring at the blueprint. His nervous tic had started up. Normally quiet, the man's outburst signaled the dismay the rest of the troop was no doubt also feeling.

"Lee's right," said Smitz. "They aren't gonna let a bunch of strangers in even if they believe our story, and if we try to fight our way in, we're dead. With our regular armor and weapons, we might stand a chance, but with these antiques, we'll never make it. Stop the transport and let me out. I'm going back to the ship."

"You'll stay right where you are, soldier," Speidel said.

Smitz spat a brown, greasy ball of spittle at Speidel's feet and got up to leave. The captain rose and roughly pushed the man back down into his seat. The soldier scowled and was about to stand again when Carina said, "Wait. What if we try something different?"

Smitz hesitated then buckled under the captain's glare.

"Like what, Corporal?" Speidel asked.

Carina outlined her plan. It would spread the mercs thin, and they would have to sacrifice force of arms to diversionary tactics and speed, but she couldn't see how they could retrieve the boy otherwise.

Speidel listened, his face betraying neither approbation nor disapproval.

"I'll go in to do the rescue," Carina added. "The kid's only six, and I think I'm the least scary of all of us. We don't want to frighten him into trying to get away. I'll need just one other person to come with me."

Atoi said, "I'll do it."

"Okay," said Speidel after a moment's pause, "we'll do it your way, Lin. It sounds like it might work."

Seven

Speidel stopped the transport two klicks from their destination and spent some time studying the smelting plant from afar. One of his eyes was an implant that had around ten times the capabilities of its biological equivalent.

While the captain was studying the processes of the plant and the movements of its workers, Carina checked her weapon over again. It was fully powered, but that was about all it had going for it. Jackson's earlier estimation that their guns were from the previous century seemed optimistic.

Her firearm was single pulse only, and the gauge on its side indicated that it had to build power between each discharge. Great. She hoped it didn't take long. What wouldn't she give for her trusty Jensen 31. Consulting with Atoi, she was relieved to find that the woman had received a better model. Hers didn't require time to recharge unless after rapid fire.

"Okay." Speidel turned around in his seat to face them. "The heap of ore on the right side is fed by a conveyor belt into a press to crush the rocks. Another belt takes the crushed rock inside—I'm guessing to furnaces to smelt it. We need to get some explosives onto the belt that enters the plant. That should mess the place up pretty good. Our second target is a pile of smoking waste on the far side of the complex. Nothing like falling red-hot ashes to rain on someone's parade.

"Another possible target is one of the chimneys. They're wide and they aren't that tall. Seems like concern for the environment is a concept that hasn't arrived on Orrana just yet. Someone with a good aim might get lucky. Anyone want to try?"

"I'll do it, sir," said Jackson. Lee and Halliday slapped the man on the back. With his prosthetic arm, Jackson was the obvious candidate.

"Good," Speidel said. "They've just turned on the lights, but their coverage isn't good. Should be plenty of shadows for cover. Brown and Carver, you're on target one. Halliday and Lee, you're on target two. Smitz, you're with us."

Smitz gave Speidel a surly glance but said nothing.

It was nearing twilight as the transport drew close to the plant. The emissions of its chimneys were dark gray against the deepening sky, leading from a dim glow at their bases. The mercs were well beyond the edge of town, driving down an empty road.

At a dip where the transport was briefly out of sight of the complex, Speidel stopped the vehicle again, and the five mercs who were to provide the diversions got out. They immediately stooped to grab handfuls of dirt. After mixing the dirt with a little water from their canteens, they would rub the resulting mud on their faces and exposed skin, helping them to melt into the encroaching darkness.

Speidel held out his weapon to Carina. "Take this and give me yours."

Carina pulled her pulse gun from her belt. "Why, sir?"

"Never mind why, Corporal, just do as you're ordered."

She took the captain's gun and briefly studied it before slipping it into her belt. His weapon was a better model than hers. He was swapping with her relic so that she could protect herself better.

A few moments later, the transport was on its way again, leaving the five disembarked mercs behind and slowly heading toward the light that glared from the guards' office at the main gate.

The figure of a tall woman could be seen sitting at a desk behind translucent, scratched plexiglas as they drew up. Carina glanced at the gates to the facility, which were large, heavy, and well-secured. There was no way they would be getting through them. Their only way inside was via the guards' office. She could see a shadowy exit at the back, blurred by the degraded glass of the window.

The guard was alone in the small room, her head turned toward a bank of roving holos that showed the activity inside the plant. She looked over as Speidel leaned out and spoke into the intercom. "We're here to see the manager about some jobs."

The woman's brow furrowed. "What's your name? I don't have any record of an appointment."

"You wouldn't," Speidel said. "We're only here to ask."

"The manager's busy," the woman said. "Check the job updates in the town news or make an appointment." She returned her attention to the holos.

"It would only take a minute to comm, ma'am," said Speidel. "We've got plenty of experience between us. Been working—"

"Get out of here," exclaimed the woman.

While Speidel dragged out the conversation with the guard, Atoi, Carina, and Smitz slowly opened the door on the side of the transport facing away from the guards' office and slipped out. Bent low, they crept around the vehicle and took up positions on either side of the window, just below its sill. All three had their gazes fixed on Speidel, waiting for his signal.

The captain raised his pulse gun, and they stood as one and fired at the plexiglas, cracking and melting the panes. Smitz drove his booted foot through the remains of the window on his side and Atoi elbowed out the rest. Carina followed them as they leapt into the room. The tall woman backed into a corner, her face pasty. The weapon she held was shaking. Clearly, she was just an ordinary guard and not one of the Dirksens' hired goons.

Speidel had also jumped inside. He took pity on her and fired a stunning shot. The guard slid to the floor as more appeared through the doorway at the back of the room. These men and women were professionals. They came out firing aggressively, but they weren't suited up. Carina, Smitz, and Atoi picked them off with accuracy, showing none of Speidel's mercy.

The mercs' position was dangerous. They had to avoid being pinned down in the outer office, trading shots with the Dirksen thugs while the local security force made its way over. They had to force their way inside, but stepping through the door wearing no armor would be suicide.

Still, they probably only had to wait a few more moments...

A boom split the air and the floor shook. Klaxons sounded. Someone had succeeded in placing a diversionary explosive.

Smitz and Atoi ran into the rear room, spraying pulses as they went. Carina and Speidel were hard on their heels. Two Dirksen hands were on their backs in the further office, their chests smoking. Speidel hit the arm of another who reached out from behind a cabinet to take a shot and Smitz finished her off. A fourth ran down the corridor leading from the room. Atoi shot him in the back.

They sped out and into the interior of the complex. The klaxons were still blaring, the sound penetrating Carina's skull. Another boom shook the plant. The general employees would be well-occupied at least.

Speidel took the lead as they ran deeper into the building. They fired at anyone who approached. Most of them ran away. The mission seemed to be progressing well, but Carina began to feel a nagging doubt about what was happening.

The captain took them down a set of stairs, along a corridor, and then downstairs once more. The sound of the klaxons grew quieter as they moved away from the busier sections of the complex.

"Okay," said Speidel, drawing to a stop at the top of a third set of stairs and panting. "We're here. Lin, Atoi, don't take too long. We can't hold off a sustained attack."

Carina and Atoi were to retrieve the Sherrerr child while Speidel and Smitz protected their rear. The two women ran quietly down the stairs. Though the klaxons were fainter here, Carina guessed the noise was sufficient to cover the sound of their footsteps. They were heading for a small room—not much bigger than a closet—in the corner of a large basement at the bottom of the stairs.

What they might expect to find, she didn't know. She hoped the child didn't have a large, round-the-clock guard, but it seemed unlikely the Dirksens would station lots of thugs right outside the kid's door.

At the top of the final flight of stairs, Carina and Atoi stopped. They checked their weapons, looked each other in the eye, nodded once, and bounded down the final steps, firing into the basement as they went.

The wide, low room was full of old, dusty, broken bits and pieces of equipment, lit up by the pulse flashes from the women's weapons. Carina couldn't detect any returning fire. The two split up and ran for cover behind separate hulking pieces of machinery.

Carina sat with her back to a machine and waited, listening. The room was dark, but she could see Atoi's position from the glowing dial of her pulse gun. The faint light shining from the stairs to the next level was the only other source of illumination.

No movement nor sound of any guards could be heard. Carina reached out and took a wild shot. No response.

"Atoi," she whispered into her comm. "I think the place may be empty."

"I was thinking that too," came the woman's response.

"Let's head round to the room where they have the kid," Carina said.

"You got it."

Carina crawled cautiously around the edge of the dark room, making her way to the door in the corner. Atoi approached it from the other direction. Carina arrived first. She reached upward, feeling for the door handle. She found it and pulled it down.

The door was unlocked. It swung open easily. Something was very, very wrong.

The smaller room was also dark. Carina stood and brushed the wall next to the door until she found the light switch. As it activated, Atoi arrived.

"What the hell?" the woman said as she saw the room. Aside from a few pieces of furniture, it was empty.

"What is it?" Speidel said over her comm. "Report, Lin."

"The kid isn't here, sir," Carina replied. "I think we're in the wrong room."

"If you're in the small room off the basement," said Speidel, "that's definitely where the child should be. I'm receiving the signal from the transmitter. Are you sure you're in the right place?"

"Yes, sir," Carina said. "But the whole basement is empty. Not even any guards."

Atoi had moved into the room. A couple of overturned chairs and a small, low table were its only furnishings. "I guess it's possible the kid was here but they moved him when we burst into the plant."

"The captain's receiving the signal from here," said Carina. "The kid has to be around somewhere. But where?"

Atoi was crouching down, looking at something she'd spotted on a stained part of the floor. "Aw, fuck." She stood and backed away, the color draining from her face.

"What?" Carina asked.

Atoi raised a hand to her eyes and shook her head. She didn't answer.

Carina went over to see for herself. She picked up the object for a closer look. Her stomach lurched and her legs turned weak.

It was a tiny chip, around the size of a baby's fingernail. Like the floor where it was lying, the chip was stained brown. The stains were dried blood, and the chip was the Sherrerr child's transmitter.

EIGHT

Carina forced down the bile rising in her throat. She'd seen plenty of blood and death in her time, but she couldn't imagine how anyone could harm a small, innocent boy.

As she gazed at the tiny chip in her hand, other things started to add up until finally it all made sense. The whole mission has been too easy. They should never have made it that far with their shitty weapons and no armor. "Sir, we found the boy's transmitter. I think it was put here to lure us in. It's a trap. The Dirksens want to capture us."

She waited for Speidel's reply, but none came. Perhaps he was distracted.

"Captain?"

Nothing.

"Sir?"

A loud *crunch*.

Carina turned to Atoi, her eyes wide. "We have to get back to them."

They flew out of the room and across the large basement, steering around the shadowy shapes of discarded machinery. Atoi gave a cry as she ran into a piece of equipment low down on the floor. She tumbled over it and landed on her face. Carina ran back and helped the woman to her feet. Blood was flowing from her nose and dripping off her upper lip, dark in the dim room.

She drew her sleeve across her face and spat. "I'm okay."

They climbed the stairs together, slowly. Carina hadn't heard a sound from the captain since his most recent words to her, and there had been no sounds of fighting from the next level. But then, pulse fire wasn't noisy and she wouldn't have expected to hear it above the continuing noise of the emergency klaxons.

They crept around a corner in the stairwell and found themselves staring down the muzzles of guns.

The two guards who were waiting for them were kitted out more like Carina would have expected from employees of the Dirksens. They were dressed in full armor and bearing gleaming new weapons of a kind she'd never seen before.

Their order didn't need to be verbalized. Both Carina and Atoi put down their guns in one slow, measured movement. One guard led the way while the other went around behind them. The group climbed the stairs to the corridor, where Carina was relieved to see Speidel was still alive. She even felt a mild satisfaction that Smitz also wasn't dead.

He was facing the wall next to the captain. Two of the Dirksens' thugs were holding weapons to their heads. Carina and Atoi were pushed against the wall next to them.

"Which one of you was it?" Atoi asked between her teeth.

"Shut up," said a guard.

"Which one of you held the kid down?"

Speidel looked from Atoi to Carina, a curious expression on his face. The guard raised his voice. "I said, shut up."

"Who was it that dug it out of him?" Atoi yelled.

The guard fired, and Atoi screamed as a thread of light shot from the weapon and made contact with her back. She fell to the ground, writhing and jerking in agony. The guard kept his finger on the trigger, seeming to enjoy the spectacle. When he finally stopped firing, Atoi lay motionless, barely conscious and covered in sweat. Next to her was the captain's comm, which had been ground to pieces.

"We have orders to try to deliver you all alive," the guard said to her, "but the Dirksens won't mind if we slip up once or twice along the way. I was just playing with you then. Don't make me use the lethal setting."

He nodded at another couple of guards, and they hauled Atoi to her feet and pushed her against the wall once more. She swayed and staggered as she struggled to stand upright, gripping the wall with both hands.

The Dirksen thugs seemed to be waiting for something. From the corner of her eye, Carina saw the one who had tortured Atoi murmuring into his helmet mic.

Tense seconds ticked past. Carina wondered what the new weapons were the Dirksens had. Pulse guns fired bolts of concentrated energy that burned the target or, at a lower setting, shocked him into temporary unconsciousness. The Dirksen guns seemed to emit a continuous flow of power that kept the victim in constant pain. Perhaps the lethal setting would stop the heart. She wondered what range the weapons had.

The men and women guarding the mercs were growing agitated and throwing glances from side to side along the corridor. Something was up. One of the women jabbed Carina in the back, and she gasped as the hard metal muzzle drove into her spine, causing a sharp jab of pain.

"Move," the woman said, jerking her gun to the right.

The other mercs were being pushed in the same direction. It seemed a good time to stage an escape attempt. Once the Dirksen thugs had secured them somewhere, getting away would be a lot harder. But Carina couldn't see how any of them could make a move without being immediately shot with one of the torture weapons.

The klaxons had finally stopped, and the lower levels of the plant were quiet as they went along. Carina was at the end of the line. A muzzle was thrust into her again, hitting her kidney. She bit back a yell.

"Faster," said the guard.

Carina imagined what she would do to the woman if she got a chance.

A *whompf* of detonation came from the corridor up ahead, the explosion deafening her. Cracks appeared in the ceiling and walls. Carina swung her elbow upward into the guard's helmet, toppling the woman. She snatched her weapon from her and fired. The thread of intense light shot out, but the woman only jerked in pain. Her armor seemed to absorb some of the energy.

The guard snatched at the muzzle and tried to stand. Carina pushed the weapon against the woman's chest and fired again. That time, the guard's body spasmed and was still.

"Fire against their armor," Carina shouted, her ears still ringing from the explosion.

An agonizing flame shot through her, but was cut off abruptly. She turned to see Smitz grinning and pulling his weapon away from the helmet of a falling Dirksen guard.

Three of the mercs who had planted the diversionary explosives came running down the corridor, shooting. Carina ran at a Dirksen thug who was about to return fire. She thrust her weapon against his back and pressed the trigger.

Speidel and Atoi were struggling with their captors. The captain screamed. His guard had shot him in the eye. He fell, clutching his face. Brown ran up and body-slammed the guard, at the same time relieving him of his firearm.

"Press it up against his chest," shouted Carina.

The third Dirksen thug died.

Carina was wondering if they should try to take the fourth alive when Atoi killed him. It was the one who had tortured her.

Brown was helping Speidel to his feet. The captain's face was a ruined, blackened mess, but he was alive. The staff sergeant pointed down the corridor, in the opposite direction to the area of the explosion, and the mercs began to run.

Carina's hearing was gradually returning.

"There's a hole in the fence north-north-west, where the chimney exploded," Brown said. "If we get split up, make for it and head back to town. We'll meet at the back of the hostel. We leave for the shuttle at 0600."

He didn't say it, but the implication was clear. Anyone who didn't make it to the rendezvous point in time would be left behind.

NINE

Things were turning ugly aboard the *Duchess*. The five mercs who had set the explosives had encountered Dirksen guards roaming the complex, and neither Carver nor Lee had survived. Brown, Halliday, and Jackson had fared better and headed to find out what had happened to their captain after they heard the fateful *crunch* of his comm.

Setting a small explosion in one part of the corridor provided the distraction to give the mercs the edge they needed to turn the tables on the Dirksen thugs. After escaping over what remained of the fence, the surviving mercs had eventually made it to the shuttle and returned to their ship.

That was where the shitshow really started.

Carina had always known that Sasha Tarsalan was a nasty bitch, but she'd never witnessed the level of fury the woman unleashed on the mercs who had failed their second mission in a row.

The heavily bejeweled woman ranted and raged at the six mercs, spittle flying from her mouth. Speidel was in the sick bay, where the ship's doctor was removing what remained of his ocular implant. Carina and the others stood to attention, facing the full brunt of Tarsalan's fury in silence.

'Incompetent' and 'inept' were among the nicer words she used to describe them. According to her assessment, they were also 'moronic grunts,' who were a 'waste of oxygen' and had 'brought the company to ruin' with their 'pathetic efforts.'

After a while, as Tarsalan explained how 'real' soldiers would have behaved like professionals and done the 'simple job' they were asked to do, Carina tuned the woman out. She watched her gesticulations, red face, and bloodshot eyes but paid little attention to what she was saying. Tarsalan's hair was piled into a tower on her head, and as Carina watched, the tower began to slip and hang at an angle. She wondered if, and when, it would fall down entirely.

The patience and stoicism Nai Nai had taught her from a young age meant it wasn't difficult for her to bear Tarsalan's dishonest, unfair ferocity. The other mercs, however, were not so well-equipped. Though none moved nor spoke, their growing rage was almost palpable.

Predictably, Smitz was the first to snap. He didn't say anything. He strode over to the woman and stood glaring down at her, his hands in fists at his sides and his broad, heavily muscled back tense.

Tarsalan's words dried up, and she seemed to suddenly realize she'd spent the last ten minutes insulting and berating six professional killers, and she was alone with them. She swallowed and looked up at Smitz. Her previously puce face paled, but she said tersely, "What do you think you're—"

Perhaps if she'd apologized, Smitz might have mastered his rage. Even if she'd said nothing at all, there was a chance he would have calmed down and stopped himself from doing something stupid. Though he was undisciplined and often offensive, Smitz had spent so long skirting the line of report-worthy behavior that he knew exactly where it lay.

As it was, Tarsalan's continued arrogant attitude made the man snap. He grabbed her throat, lifted her with one arm, and slammed her against the bulkhead, where she hung, wriggling. The company owner's eyes protruded from their sockets and her mouth was forced open by the pressure of Smitz's hand on her neck. Her tongue waggled wildly but not a sound nor breath left her mouth.

She plucked uselessly at Smitz's fingers while her feet kicked and jerked, suspended several centimeters above the floor.

Carina and the other mercs enjoyed the spectacle for a few moments until, halfheartedly, they tried to make Smitz release his hold. Staff Sergeant Brown gave him an order to drop Tarsalan immediately, and the others tried to open his fingers and pull him away from her.

With apparently great reluctance, Brown finally fired at Smitz and stunned him. As he collapsed, Tarsalan fell to the floor too. She was unconscious but still alive. The marks of Smitz's fingers on her neck were already showing.

"Good one, Smitz," spat Halliday. "Now we're out of a job for sure."

"We were out of a job anyway," said Atoi. "If he hadn't done it, I would have soon enough. He only did what we all wanted to do."

Jackson agreed. "I would've punched her, though. Probably more than once."

"Quit it," said Brown. "Lin, help me get her to sick bay. This son-of-a-bitch goes to the brig. You understand, Atoi? Halliday? Jackson?"

The three nodded glumly. Transporting Smitz to the brig would be no mean feat, whether he was unconscious or awake.

After notifying the doctor they were on their way, Brown and Carina managed to carry Tarsalan to the sick bay between them. She had begun to regain consciousness by the time they arrived. The two of them lifted her by her shoulders and legs and put her on a bed.

Brown quickly left. He might have been avoiding Tarsalan's fury, redoubled after Smitz's attack, but the man's hand had damaged her neck to the extent she could barely croak. The doctor told her to be quiet while he examined her and motioned Carina away. She had hung around in case the doctor wanted to know what had happened, but the evidence apparently said everything.

Carina had passed a curtained bed on her way into the sick bay. She guessed the occupant had to be Speidel. She peeked in. The captain was awake and reading an interface with his remaining eye. A patch covered the place where the other had been.

She opened the curtain wider. "Hi, sir." She spoke quietly so the doctor wouldn't hear and maybe make her leave.

Speidel's smile when he saw her eased her concern for the older man somewhat. He put down the screen. "Come in, Carina. It's good of you to come and see me."

She stepped close to the bed and drew the curtains closed.

"Did doc get all your implant out?" she asked.

"All that was left of it," Speidel replied, pulling himself into a higher position before relaxing on his pillows. "Several thousand creds gone in a single shot. But I was lucky, really. If the beam had hit my real eye, it would probably have fried my brain. Better one-eyed than dead, huh?"

"I'd say so. Are you going to get another implant or a new bio eye?"

"I'm not sure. I guess it depends on whether I continue soldering or take the hint and retire. Have you heard what's happening with the company yet? Cadwallader isn't answering my comm and the doctor won't tell me anything, except to rest up and not worry myself for a while. Like it's easy not to worry when you don't know what's going on."

"Well..." Carina wasn't sure if she should tell Speidel about the incident with Tarsalan and Smitz, but she guessed he would find out soon enough, what with being right next to the company owner.

"Holy shit," Speidel said when she reached the part where Smitz had tried to strangle Tarsalan. "What an imbecile. If it wasn't over for the Black Dogs before, it certainly is now. Tarsalan's definitely going to cut her losses and split after this."

"No doubt about it. Which kinda makes your advice to me earlier moot, doesn't it?"

"Yeah. But it was good advice, Carina. Brown, Atoi, and the rest will find another merc band to join. Even Smitz might find someone who's on the lookout for an insubordinate, aggressive bastard. But... Listen to me, okay? I've gotten to know you over the years, and you aren't like them. I didn't realize it when I dragged you out of that fight. I never told you, but I watched it going on for a while before I stepped in. I watched you defend yourself against those older, bigger street rats, and I saw your skill and strength. But that was all I saw.

"I thought providing you with a safe place to live and a regular paycheck was fair exchange for what you could bring to the band. And you stepped up and did the job, after a little training. It wasn't until later I saw a different side to you. You can fight and kill if you need to, but you don't like it. You aren't immune to it like half of the others, and you don't relish it like the other half."

Speidel half shut his remaining eye, scrutinizing her. Carina began to feel uncomfortable.

"There's something else about you too. Something more than disliking the fight."

Carina felt that familiar wrenching she had whenever she was worried someone might discover what she was. Time to change the subject. She had another topic on her mind anyway.

"What's going to happen now, sir?" she asked. "About the Sherrerr kid, I mean."

Speidel sighed. "Who knows? Now he no longer has his transmitter, it's going to be a lot harder to find him. Whatever happens, we're out of that game."

"Are we? It doesn't seem right to abandon him like that. He's just a little kid."

"He's just a little *Sherrerr* kid. If anyone has the money and influence to track him down, it's them."

"That's something I don't get," said Carina. "They're so rich and powerful, why did the Sherrerrs hire us to do their dirty work? Why not send in their own goons?"

"I never got that either," Speidel replied, "and, for what it's worth, I feel the same as you. I'm not happy about leaving the search to someone else, assuming someone else *is* searching for him. But I don't know what else we can do. He could be anywhere, and the Dirksens sure as hell aren't telling."

"That's the other thing that bothers me," Carina said. "Why did they kidnap him in the first place if they don't want to ransom him? They just took him and disappeared. What's the point of that?"

"Maybe for revenge. Maybe they already murdered him. That room where you found his transmitter, was there...?"

"No," Carina replied. "There was only a small amount of blood. Not enough."

"Whatever the Dirksens did with the kid, we've reached the end of the road. Even if we wanted to continue after Tarsalan disbands the company, we have no way of finding him."

"I guess you're right," Carina said, but inside she was saying, *Yes, there is*. She had kept the child's transmitter. The trace of blood on it held his genetic code—his unique signature in the fabric of the universe —and that meant that she could find him, but she would have to cast.

TEN

The doctor bought the mercs some time when it came to the breaking up of the Black Dogs. He insisted that Tarsalan remain in the sick bay and leave the running of the ship to Cadwallader for at least forty-eight hours. If the company owner had had her way, Carina was sure she would have thrown them all off the ship at the earliest opportunity with no time to pack their stuff or make arrangements.

As it was, after Smitz's attack, no one was in any doubt the band's days were over, and they acted accordingly. The soldiers began to clear out their cabins and pack the items they wanted to take with them. Cadwallader transferred the monies owed to them to their credchips, and people decided where they would go next.

Mealtimes became almost convivial as stories of old missions were recounted, then the mood would turn melancholy as the dead were remembered. Silence would eventually fall as the mercs no doubt inwardly reflected that their fate would be similar.

Captain Speidel was up and about the day following Smitz's attack, looking more than ever the old soldier with his eye patch. The skin on his face glistened with burn-healing gel and only very pink, fresh color remained of the damage the Dirksen guard's weapon had done.

Carina was happy to see him looking not too the worse for wear, and not only for his own sake. The plight of the Sherrerr boy had lain heavy on her mind and heart ever since the failure of their mission. She had made the Cast and found the child, but the knowledge was useless if she had to attempt a rescue alone. The Dirksen force was formidable, and she doubted she could defeat them even using her special abilities.

She needed help, yet how could she convince anyone she knew the boy's location unless she explained *how* she knew it? She would have to reveal that she could cast. The thought of it alone made her break out into a sweat. Nai Nai had impressed nothing else upon her more than the fact that she must never divulge her secret. Even the idea of it felt like an act of betrayal to the woman's memory, but if she didn't do something, she would be leaving a young child to suffer—perhaps even to be murdered.

Carina was glad the captain's recovery was going well because she'd decided that, of all the people she knew, he was the one she trusted the most. He'd also expressed his concern about the missing child and he might be persuaded to help her mount a rescue.

When her cabin was empty, Carina removed the canister of base elixir from its hiding place in her mattress and went to Speidel's room. She found him alone.

"Come in, Carina. I'm glad to see you. Have you come to tell me what you're going to do next?"

She stepped into the man's single cabin and waited for him to close the door before she spoke. "I have, and I need your help to do it."

Speidel sat on his bunk while Carina took the chair. The captain rested his elbows on his knees and clasped his hands. "Would you like me to write you a reference? I'm happy to, but I'm not sure how relevant it will be if you're giving up the soldiering life as I hope you are."

"I've thought about it," Carina replied, "and maybe you're right that I'm not suited to life as a merc. Maybe I will give it up, but it isn't over for me yet. I have one last mission I have to do. I want to rescue the Sherrerr kid."

Speidel straightened up. "I understand how you feel, but as I said, we're hamstrung on that. We don't know where—"

"I *do* know where he is. He's in the smelting plant. He was probably there all along. We were just tricked into going to the wrong part of it."

Speidel's expression was a mixture of confusion and disbelief. "But surely you're speculating. You can't know for sure, and we can't return to the plant on a guess. It's far too dangerous."

"I'm not speculating. I know where he is." Carina took a deep breath, trying to quell her racing heart. "I know because I cast to find him."

"You...?"

"Sir..."

The captain was looking concerned. Carina became even more aware of her flushing face and anxiety. Was she making the worst mistake of her life? Perhaps, but she was committed. "You must swear to me that you will never tell anyone what I'm about to tell you. If you can't make that promise, then we can't do anything about the Sherrerr boy. It's very important that what I tell you remains a secret between us. My life depends on it."

Speidel nodded. When Carina waited expectantly, he said, "I swear."

"Thank you," Carina said. "It's a little difficult to explain, sir, but I can do things that most people can't. Things that I can't rationalize and that don't make sense scientifically, as far as I understand. Yesterday, when I was with you in the sick bay, you said there was something different about me. That's because I *am* different, though I don't know how or why."

Speidel didn't speak. He was giving her the space to finish what she wanted to say.

Carina explained how her Nai Nai had brought her up after her father and mother disappeared, and how the old woman had taught her to harness and hone her casting power. She didn't tell him the details like the Elements, the Seasons, the Strokes, or the Map. Those weren't necessary for the captain to know. He only had to believe what she could do and that the Sherrerr boy was where she said he was.

"It isn't a simple or easy process," she went on. "The reason I was able to cast to find the child was because I had something of his. I had the transmitter Atoi found. I can't find people randomly, or at least I never learned how. Nai Nai died when I was ten, and I was alone after that. I couldn't fit in where I was. Maybe the people in my neighborhood could sense the same thing you can—that I wasn't like them. I used to get picked on a lot."

She stopped. She felt she had said enough for Speidel to take on board for the moment. Oddly, though all her life she'd feared someone finding out she was a mage, she now felt relieved, as if a burden had been lifted from her. It felt good to share her secret with someone else. She realized how alone she had felt before.

Speidel rubbed his stubble. "That's quite a story, Carina." His tone was non-committal.

Carina's heart sank. He didn't believe her.

"I take it you can prove what you say," he said.

"Yes," she replied, her hope rising. "Yes, I can. I thought of a simple Cast I can do to show you, but I don't want to unsettle you."

"I've been a merc for eleven years and in the military for thirteen," Speidel said, laughing. "I don't think there's anything you can do to unsettle me."

She took out her canister of elixir and sipped a mouthful. She scanned the cabin for a handy object and saw the captain's uniform hat on a table. She closed her eyes and drew the ideogram in her mind. The Cast was an easy one.

She opened her eyes to see the captain had an indulgent, disbelieving look on his face. He opened his mouth as if about to say something to mollify her, but then his hat appeared on his head. He reacted as if a poisonous spider had just fallen on him. He threw the hat to the floor and leapt up so fast his legs hit his bunk and he overbalanced, falling comically onto it.

Carina tried to suppress her laughter but was unsuccessful. In all the years she'd known him, Speidel had been the model of self-control. She'd never seen him so surprised or amazed.

Still lying on his bunk in an awkward pose, Speidel blinked his single eye several times. He sat up. "Well, I asked you to prove it, and you did." He straightened his pants and ran a hand through his graying hair. Reaching down to the floor, he picked up his hat and turned it over in his hands. "I guess I believe you."

"You do?"

Speidel nodded. "It's a lot to take in, but to tell you the truth, it isn't the first time I've heard about such abilities. Of course, I never believed the stories before. What else can you do?"

"Quite a lot of things, though some are easier than others. I can move things, as you just saw, and find things that are missing if I have a part of the object—something to link to it. I can heal, though it's difficult and not fast. I can't prevent someone who's been shot from dying, for instance. I can start fires and engines at a distance, open locks, change my appearance—"

"Can you hurt people...kill them?" Speidel asked softly.

Carina looked down and slowly nodded. "But it isn't straightforward. Shooting or knifing is much easier."

There was a moment's pause as Speidel considered her response. "Oh," he suddenly blurted, his eyes wide. "It was you! At the Matahman Embassy. It was you who made the enemy soldiers disappear."

She gave another quick nod.

"Did you kill them? All of them?"

"No. Like I said, that's hard to do. I just moved them about a kilometer away."

Speidel whistled in admiration. His brow furrowed. "I saw you drink from that," he said, indicating her canister. "Is that essential to what you do?"

"Yes. I must take a sip of elixir. And...do some other things."

"So if I drank that, would I be able to do magic too?"

A shadow settled over Carina's heart. Was this what Nai Nai had meant when she'd said that knowledge of her abilities would turn friends into enemies? A change of direction to the conversation was needed. "I don't think of it as magic. 'Magic' sounds like something out of children's stories, like three wishes and wizards disappearing in puffs of smoke. I think my ability is natural, only it's very rare and outside our current understanding of the universe."

She paused. "Even if you had the ability, you wouldn't be able to cast just by drinking the elixir. It takes training and practice and there's a lot more involved besides." She handed him the canister. "Take a sip and try if you don't believe me."

He took the offered canister and lifted it to his lips. His gaze upon her, he tipped back his head and poured a measure of elixir into his mouth. Immediately, the liquid erupted as he spat it out, splattering it across the floor. He coughed and retched for a minute or so. Wiping his eye, he said, "You didn't tell me it tastes like weeks-old piss."

The corners of Carina's mouth twitched. "You get used to it. Are you going to try some 'magic' now?"

Still wiping his eye and mouth, Speidel burst into laughter. "Okay, you got me good. If I have to drink that sewer effluent, I'd rather stay non-magical. What's in it?"

"Nothing that's important by itself. What do you say? Do you believe I'm right about the location of the Sherrerr boy? Will you help me rescue him?"

"I do believe you. How couldn't I after your little demonstration? And I will help you rescue the child. But I don't think we should try to do it alone. I'll speak to some of the others. I'll tell them I received additional intel from the Sherrerrs. Maybe we can rope in some of them to help us. But we'll have to start soon."

"Yeah. I hate to think about that kid all alone among those thugs, especially after what they already did to him."

"Not only that," Speidel said. "I plan on us going in fully armed this time, which means we need to leave before the doctor lets Tarsalan get up."

ELEVEN

Somehow, Smitz got wind of what they were doing, and he insisted he wanted to come along too.

"He's just saying that so he can get out of the brig before Tarsalan recovers," Carina said to Speidel when he told her. "The minute we arrive planetside he'll be gone."

"I don't think so," the captain replied. "There's more to Smitz than meets the eye. I would have kicked him out of the Black Dogs ages ago if I didn't think so. He talks a lot, but he always follows orders in the end. And he came on the previous mission when he didn't have to. He could have bailed like most of the rest did."

"He was expecting a bonus, though."

"And when he found out he wasn't getting one, he came along anyway. I think he wants to help."

"I don't know, sir. I don't like it."

"I've been commanding mercs for a long time. They're a difficult bunch and it's easy to underestimate their better motivations. I think you should trust me on this."

Carina sighed. "Okay, if you say so."

Atoi had also quickly volunteered when approached, and Stevenson was happy to fly the shuttle.

Scans of the smelting plant showed the explosions had put it out of operation. The damage the mercs had caused was extensive. There was little movement and the furnaces were cooling after being shut down.

According to the results of Carina's Cast, the Dirksens had the Sherrerr boy in what seemed to be a staff locker room on the first floor. The room was central, which meant another deep infiltration from the perimeter of the building. Approaching the front entrance was out of the question. They had no reason to be there as the place had closed down for repairs, and they would be recognized immediately.

Carina's idea was to approach at night from another direction and enter the site through a breach in its fence.

"They won't be expecting us," she said. "They won't think we'll return to the same place."

"They might if they find out the intel about the kid was leaked," said Atoi.

A look passed between Carina and Speidel. "I'm confident that won't happen," the captain said. "But I have another proposal," he added. "I don't doubt that the Dirksens will have alerted the planet authorities about us. If we land at the spaceport, we'll likely be arrested on a trumped up charge. Instead, we'll catch them by surprise. We tell Stevenson to fly us right onto the plant roof. We fight our way down to the room where they have the kid, grab him, and fly right out again. They don't have any spacecraft on site to pursue us. If we're fast enough, it might work."

"What about ships orbiting the planet?" Smitz asked. He was chewing his disgusting herb again.

"If the Dirksens had a starship in the vicinity that stood a chance of defeating the *Duchess*," said Speidel, "we would have been under attack by now. I'm guessing they didn't want to draw the Sherrerr's attention to Orrana by stationing one of their better ships here for no obvious reason. But that isn't to say one isn't on its way to force us out of the area after our escapade."

"Will the roof withstand a shuttle landing on it?" Carina asked.

"Enough to not collapse," Speidel replied. "And that's all that matters for our purposes. We'll be suited up, so we'll have some protection from the heat."

No more questions were forthcoming, and time was of the essence. Within quarter of an hour, they were in the shuttle and descending to Orrana's surface.

The descent was rapid. Stevenson swept them in at maximum speed. Carina and the others gripped webbing above their heads for extra stability as the ship tilted at a forty-five degree angle. The speed lifted them out of their seats, then they were thrown forward as the pilot employed reverse thrusters hard. The shuttle dropped precipitously to the smelting plant roof.

Before the shuttle had fully touched down, Stevenson opened the ramp, and the mercs ran out onto the smoking hot roof. The door to the building was locked, but in a heartbeat Smitz burst through it and led the charge down the stairs.

The mercs' attack was so fast, the first Dirksen guards they met were taken completely by surprise. Concentrated pulse fire from the mercs' Jensen rifles was sufficient to penetrate their armor, and some weren't even suited up.

By the time they reached the second floor, the news of the attack had arrived, and they met stronger resistance. Turning a corner on the stairs, Smitz ran into a shot from one of the Dirksens' advanced weapons. He was thrown back and lay unmoving on the steps.

His chest plate bore a melted patch from the glancing hit. Carina lifted his visor. Above his mask, the man's eyes were open. "M'okay," he said. "Just gimme a minute."

While Atoi sprayed pulse fire down the stairs, Speidel started the twenty second delay on an explosive. Through her comm, Carina heard him counting down. As she helped Smitz up the steps, away from the blast zone, she mentally counted with him. *Six. Five. Four.*

Speidel set the explosive rolling down the steps and sprinted up them with Atoi.

Three. Two.

The explosion roared up toward the mercs, sending a cloud of smoke and debris with it. Having no choice but to abandon Smitz for the moment, Carina, Atoi, and Speidel hurtled down the stairs and into the blast area, which was thick with a smoky haze.

Unable to see where she was going, Carina collided with a Dirksen guard and found herself sprawling on the floor. A muzzle appeared in her vision and she grabbed it, hauling the guard on top of her where the close quarters would prevent him from firing. She tried to wrestle the gun from him.

Letting go of the weapon, she jumped up and kicked it from his grasp. The gun went skittering down the stairs, and the guard tried to go after it, but Carina jumped on his back and wrenched open his visor.

She ripped off the man's breathing mask and tried to throw it, but he tackled her from behind, grabbing her around the knees. Carina's helmet hit the edge of a step. The cushioning absorbed most of the blow but she remained tightly held as the guard fought to free his mask from her hands.

She was lying face down, head downward on the steps and her blood was rushing to her brain. She held the mask and her Jensen under her and was kicking backward to force the guard away. Suddenly, she felt the man's full weight upon her. She wriggled out from underneath him. He was dead, his face a melted mess, and Smitz was standing over him.

They continued to the bottom of the steps, where Speidel and Atoi had their backs to a corner wall. They were at the corridor that led to the locker room and the Sherrerr child.

Speidel lifted his weapon. Carina, Atoi, and Smitz nodded, then all four ran simultaneously around the corner, laying down suppressive fire as they went. Two Dirksen guards were in the corridor. The mercs' pulses focused on the first, penetrating his armor. He fell. The second guard fired at Smitz and hit him, the shot sent the man spasming to the floor. Speidel, Carina, and Atoi turned their weapons on the remaining guard and killed him.

Speidel lifted Smitz's visor. He was dead.

His voice strained, Speidel said, indicating a door, "The kid's in there."

They burst through, expecting to meet more resistance, but the room was empty save for the Sherrerr child. A sound from the corridor drew Speidel and Atoi outside again, leaving Carina alone with the boy.

Twelve

The child was smaller than Carina had expected, or maybe it was only that he was hunched in the corner of the room, his head bowed and turned to the wall. He was visibly shaking, plainly terrified.

Carina realized she was still holding her weapon ready. She slung the Jensen over her shoulder and went over to the kid. He shrank against the wall and squealed at her approach.

"It's okay," she said. "I'm here to rescue you."

The boy didn't seem to hear. He pressed himself harder into the wall and moaned in terror. He was wearing a child-size CO_2 filter mask. She suddenly realized how scary she had to look to him, suited up in armor and with a tinted visor covering her face.

She put down her gun and unsnapped the locks on her helmet. Lifting it off, she squatted down a short distance from the boy and held out a hand. "Don't be scared. We're here to take you home."

This time her words seemed to penetrate. The boy peeked at her from underneath an arm, and for the first time Carina saw the child's large, deep brown-black eyes.

"Carina," Speidel said, bursting in again, "what are you doing?"

The captain's abrupt appearance undid all of Carina's work at calming the boy down. He flinched and turned away again, sobbing and moaning.

"Grab him," Speidel said. "We have to get out of here."

"Okay, I'm coming." She put on her helmet and picked up her gun. She also scooped up the child, who wriggled and fought and bit her armor. With horror, she saw the cause of his terror. The boy's fingernails and toenails had been ripped off. The Dirksens had been torturing him.

Holding the struggling child firmly over her shoulder, she ran down the corridor, following Speidel's echoing footsteps. In her other hand she held her Jensen, muzzle up. The hiss of pulse rounds came from up ahead. Speidel and Atoi were in a firefight.

She brought down the smelting plant's blueprint on her helmet overlay and searched for another escape route. She didn't want to abandon Speidel, but taking the unprotected child near weapons fire would be insane. The blueprint was complex and she had no time to figure it out. Spying what appeared to be a different route to the roof, she turned down a narrow corridor on her left. She followed the next turning too and the next, going deeper into the complex.

The boy seemed to have gotten the idea that she was trying to help him. He'd ceased struggling and hung like a limp rag over her shoulder. He was small for his age and Carina hardly felt his weight as she ran.

She turned another corner and abruptly stopped. She was at a dead end.

"What the...?" She checked her visor overlay. She was sure she'd seen another corridor leading from the one they were in. Her heart sank when she saw that what she'd mistaken for a corridor was an air duct. Spinning around, she saw the access point: a square wire grid in the wall, behind which a fan whirred.

The sounds of battle were drawing nearer.

"Carina," Speidel said through her helmet comm. "Where'd you go? We have to leave. Stevenson heard from the *Duchess* that Dirksen ships are on their way."

"I'm making my way to the shuttle," she said. "I didn't want to take the kid within range of fire. Give me two minutes."

"You've got it," Speidel said. "Don't keep us waiting."

"I won't," Carina replied, wondering desperately how she was going to make her way to the roof in time.

Her gaze returned to the wire grid. She could melt it and the fan behind it with a pulse from her Jensen, but that would leave the metal too hot to touch, and the kid had nothing to protect him.

She put the child down and pulled her knife from its sheath. At the sight of it, the boy took a breath as if to scream. She clamped her hand over his mouth. "For the last time, kid. I'm not gonna hurt you. I'm here to take you back to your family. Now can you be quiet?"

The boy swallowed and nodded. She removed her hand and went to the grid. She pushed the knife blade behind it and prized the cover away from the wall. The fan was only slotted in place. She lifted it out and peered into the dark tunnel. The boy could fit in, but it looked impossibly small for her. She had no choice. She had to try to squeeze inside.

Hastily, she began to unclip her armor. "Get in the tunnel," she said as she worked. The boy looked from the dark opening to her. He shook his head.

"Get in," she repeated. "It's the only way. If we can make it up to the roof, we have a ship waiting for us, but they're leaving soon."

The boy still didn't move.

"Come on," she said. "Please."

He hesitated but then finally padded on his wounded feet over to the square, black hole. With a final look at her, as if checking she wasn't tricking him, he climbed inside. She had nearly removed all her armor. She unclipped the legs and stepped out of them. Crouching down to enter the shaft, she rued the fact that she had no way of reattaching the wire grid once she was inside, nor of making her pile of discarded armor disappear. Where they had gone would be glaringly obvious to anyone trying to find them, but it couldn't be helped.

She picked up her helmet and put it on. The internal gel that molded around the back of her head would hold it in place, and she needed it for light in the tunnel and comm with Speidel.

The soles of the kid's bare, dirty feet were all she could see of him. He was moving fast. Was he trying to get away from her?

"Hey," she called. "Wait up."

The feet paused. She was relieved. The kid seemed to trust her after all. His resilience impressed her. He'd been taken from his family, kept hostage, and tortured—tortured! What kind of sick fuck would torture a six year old? And why? Did they think a little kid had secrets worth telling? Or had they done it for kicks?

She blinked the blueprint into view again, overlaid on the inside of her visor. "Helmet," she said, "shortest route to the roof." A red line threaded through the mass of green ones. An arrow pointed at the next turn. "Go left," she called.

A flashing clock on the helmet display made her heart sink. Estimated time to destination: 10m 23s.

"Shit," she breathed. She stopped crawling. "Hold up," she called to the kid. Going faster wasn't going to help. She needed to think.

Somehow, the boy had managed to turn around in the narrow tunnel. His dirty, tear-streaked face, topped with shaggy hair came toward her. He hadn't yet said a word to her, she realized. He was probably too traumatized.

She was on her front, facing him. She knew there was only one way out of the situation for both of them, but still she balked at it. If the kid blabbed, she would be at extreme risk. But if she didn't do what she had to, she would be captured and killed by the Dirksens, and the boy would have lost his only possible chance of escape.

She debated trying to explain away what was about to happen, but decided to just do it. Later, she would figure out how to deal with whatever interpretation the kid made of it.

She reached into her shirt and brought out the elixir canister, which had been painfully squeezed between her and the metal floor of the tunnel. The boy's eyes grew round.

"Just wait a minute," Carina said. "I need to take a sip of this."

She swallowed a mouthful of elixir. "Hold my hand," she said. "You're coming with me."

Thirteen

Carina appeared in a corner of the roof at just the point she'd aimed at according to the blueprint. She was relieved to find that the boy, his eyes wider than ever, was still holding her hand tightly. The shuttle was there, and Speidel was pacing impatiently in front of it.

"Quick," Carina whispered, "come on."

She ran out a little way onto the roof. "We're here, sir."

Speidel turned. "Where have you been? And where's your armor? Never mind. Get aboard the shuttle."

He cried out and collapsed to his knees before falling forward on his face. A guard had emerged from a doorway behind him as he was speaking and shot him in the back. Carina leveled her Jensen at the guard and fired off a round that hit the man's visor. The plexiglas darkened and sagged from the blast, and the guard dropped his weapon, yelling with pain.

"Go up the ramp," Carina told the boy, who was frozen, staring at the guard who was clawing at his melted visor. She gave the child a push, and his trance broke. He ran aboard the shuttle. Carina tried to haul Speidel up, but his body was heavy and entirely limp. Turning him on his back, she opened his visor. The captain's face was still and peaceful. Her heart stopped.

Sounds blurred and her vision swam. Time seemed to slow down. He couldn't be dead. Carina blinked away hot tears that were dropping onto her visor and scanned the older man's face for any sign of life, but there were none.

"Lin, get aboard." It was Stevenson, the shuttle pilot. His words pulled her out of her frozen state. In the corner of her vision, she saw movement. More Dirksen guards were arriving.

With a terrible wrench, she let go of Speidel's body and ran up the shuttle ramp. As she reached the top, agony exploded behind her knee. Her legs collapsed. She'd been shot.

The ramp closed, and pain tore through her. Without her armor's pain-suppressing injector system, she felt the full effects of her wound. She lay on her back, trying not to scream. All she could see were the ceiling lights and the concerned face of the Sherrerr boy hanging over her.

What seemed an age later, Atoi appeared, staggering in the shuttle's rocky flight. She pressed an anesthetic gun to the inside of Carina's wrist, and the cool feeling of relief flooded through her. The drug made her groggy and confused too. She said to Atoi, "Where's the captain? We forgot him. We left him behind. I have to go and get him."

Atoi placed a gentle hand on her stomach. "Stay right where you are, soldier. An auto-gurney's waiting for you."

Carina's head flopped to one side. "Where's the kid?"

"He's right here," Atoi replied.

The child was sitting on his haunches against the bulkhead, watching her. He had an inscrutable look on his face. She wondered vaguely what he was thinking. What had he made of their impossible transference from the cramped tunnel to the rooftop? He was only six. Hopefully, his young mind would find a way of explaining it away.

A low hum signaled the arrival of the auto-gurney. They seemed to have made it back to the *Duchess,* though to Carina only moments had passed. Atoi stepped out of the way as the device lowered to the ground and secured her neck and spine before lifting her onto its base. The hum started up again as the vehicle moved away.

She could see only the corridor ceiling as she was carried along.

"Hey, kid," she heard Atoi call. "Come back here."

"I want to go with her," the boy protested. They were the first words Carina had heard him speak. The pain relief was clouding her senses, and she didn't hear if Atoi relented and let the Sherrerr boy accompany her.

The next thing she knew, she lying on a soft medroom bed surrounded by curtains.

She tried to sit up, but her right leg was restrained somehow. Her memory of the mission came flooding back, along with the knowledge of Speidel's death.

She lay down and wept, her tears running down the sides of her face and into her hair. After a long while, she lifted her head and looked down her body. A cylinder of transparent plastic encased the middle section of her leg. Restorative gel filled the plastic, working on the wound she'd received. Her nerves in that part of her body were numb.

On the edge of her vision, she noticed the Sherrerr boy sitting down nearby. He came closer when he saw her notice him, and a pair of large, brown-black eyes stared into hers. The kid had been cleaned up and his hair was a little less shaggy.

"I saw what you did," the boy said.

Carina's chest tightened. Through a gap in the curtains, she could see the doc on the other side of the room. He didn't seem to have heard the child.

She tried to signal the boy with her eyes and lifted a finger to her lips. To her great relief, he seemed to understand the need for secrecy. He nodded solemnly and moved his chair until it was right next to her bed. He watched her face.

"We should have you back with your family soon," Carina said.

The doctor heard this. "Carina, you're awake? How are you feeling?" he asked, parting the curtains. He bent over her leg to look at it closely through the transparent gel. "Should have you back to normal in ten hours or so, and no scarring. This latest gel we picked up is very good. Stimulates your own stem cells to replace the damaged tissue. Your new skin will be as soft as a baby's bottom."

"And your little friend is still here," he went on. "I thought I told you to stay in bed," he said to the boy. "Plenty of vidgames on the system to keep you occupied."

The child lifted his hand and placed it gently atop Carina's. The hand was encased in a glove of healing gel.

"I want to stay here," he said.

The doctor grimaced as Carina lifted her gaze from the kid's torture wounds toward him. He looked as though he wanted to say more but was refraining due to the child's presence.

"I don't suppose it will hurt for you to remain with your rescuer for a little while. But if you feel odd or dizzy, it's straight back to bed with you, and you must let me know. Do you understand?"

"Yes, sir."

The doctor smiled. "You can call me Harvey, son." He addressed Carina. "Keep an eye on him for me, will you? I need to report to Tarsalan on how you're all doing."

"Is she up and around now?" Carina asked. "Has she recovered?"

"She hasn't fully recovered, no, but that didn't stop her from getting up and telling the Sherrerrs of your success the moment she heard about it. We're on our way to one of the planets they control right now."

"What's happening with the Black Dogs?" Carina asked. "Did she say anything about that?"

"You've been through a lot, Lin. Just take it easy for now, okay? I'll be back in an hour or so." He left, pulling her bed curtains closed.

"What's your name, kid?" Carina asked, realizing he'd only ever been referred to as the victim, the target, or the Sherrerr child.

"Darius," the boy replied. He leaned forward. "I saw what you did," he repeated.

The familiar, horrible clenching in Carina's chest returned. The boy's words also reminded her of something else she needed to be concerned about. She craned her neck to scan around for her belongings. Her clothes had been folded in a pile on the shelf next to her bed, and the metal elixir canister was on the top of the pile. A little relieved, she sunk back into her pillows.

She had to divert the child's mind to another subject. "How are you feeling?" she asked.

"I'm okay now." Darius's gaze shifted to his injured hands, and the shadow of a painful memory crossed his features. "Thank you for rescuing me."

"You don't have to thank me. I was only doing my job. Your family paid us to bring you back."

The boy's expression turned sad, and Carina realized her words sounded harsher than she'd intended, as if she didn't care whether they'd succeeded in their mission. "But I'm glad we found you and got you out of there."

Darius's expression brightened. "When we were stuck in the tunnel, I was scared. I didn't know how we were going to get out. I thought we would die in there. But I didn't mind too much, just so long as I was away from the people who were hurting me."

"But we did get out, right?" said Carina. "And now you're safe. So don't think about that anymore."

There was no stopping the child, however. "You took out your bottle, and you had a drink, and I wanted some because I was so thirsty, but I was too shy to ask."

He seemed hell-bent on going over how they'd ended up at the shuttle. Carina resigned herself to the fact and was grateful nobody else was around to hear him.

"Then you told me to hold your hand, and you closed your eyes," Darius continued, "and the next thing I knew, we were on the roof next to the starship, and I didn't remember how we got there."

"It doesn't matter how we got there, does it?" Carina asked. "We got where we needed to go. All that matters is that you're safe now."

"I guess so." The boy looked doubtful.

"So let's not talk about it anymore," Carina suggested. "It's only going to confuse people. You probably fell asleep while I carried you up to the roof, only you don't remember."

Darius's brow furrowed. "No, I didn't fall asleep. I know how we got there. You cast."

Fourteen

Carina almost—but not quite—swallowed the gasp that rose from her throat. The shrewd look on the little boy's face as he watched her reaction told her she had severely underestimated him.

Though she felt guilty at lying to someone so young, she made another effort to maintain her subterfuge. "What do you mean? We went up to the roof together. Don't you remember going through the vent tunnels?"

The boy giggled. "It's okay. You don't have to pretend with me. I know it's a secret. I won't tell anyone. I promise."

Carina was so deeply conflicted that, for a moment, she was lost for words. Her grandmother's warnings sounded in her mind as strong as ever. She felt an almost physical revulsion at the idea that the boy knew her secret, not least because the only person she'd ever revealed herself to was now dead.

Yet the temptation to speak freely again to another human being about her mage ability was strong. Telling Speidel had been a sweet release after her years of isolation and loneliness.

Adding to her emotional turmoil was a burning curiosity. How did this kid know about casting? Nai Nai had told her that her family were scattered across the galaxy. Could it be possible this child knew one of her long-lost kin?

She was reclining on pillows, but now she pulled herself upright. "Would you please open the curtains?" she asked the child.

He dutifully hopped down from his seat but then realized he couldn't do as she directed. He held up his thick-gloved hands.

"I'm sorry," Carina said. "You sit down. I'll do it."

She got out of bed and, hopping on one leg, she pulled back her bed curtains to the wall, checking the room was entirely empty and the door was closed.

She returned to her bed, settled herself once more, and looked into the child's eyes.

"Darius, please tell me what you meant by what you said. How do you think we got to the roof?"

The little boy rolled his eyes. "I already told you. You cast. You drank some elixir, and you closed your eyes, and I guess you thought of the right picture, because after you told me to hold your hand, we went to the roof together. I know that's what happened because I've done it before. I wished so many times I could do that when the bad people were hurting me. Only I didn't have any elixir."

The boy's chin trembled and his eyes swam with tears. Carina reached out and laid her hand on his shoulder.

"You can cast too?" she asked.

Darius nodded, teardrops running down his cheeks. Then suddenly he stopped crying and turned pale. "You aren't going to hurt me, are you? Mother told me I mustn't ever tell anyone what we can do. But you rescued me, and you seem so nice. I thought it would be okay to tell you because you're a mage too, so you know the secret already. You *are* going to take me back to Mother, right? You aren't going to keep me and do bad things to me like the other people did, are you?"

"No one's going to hurt you, Darius," Carina said, "and yes, we are going to take you home. But you and I have to keep this secret between us. Do you understand? You can't tell anyone else what we can do or say anything about casting except when we're alone. Nothing at all. You were very strong and brave to not give any secrets away to the people who hurt you. Can you keep quiet for a little longer? It's very important."

"Sure I can." Darius smiled. "I get it. No one else here knows you're a mage. I can keep your secret as well as mine."

Smart kid. "Thank you." Carina squeezed the boy's shoulder.

Her head was swimming with the implications of what the child had said. She had many questions for him but she didn't know where to start.

"Darius, is everyone in your family a mage?"

"Mother can cast, and Parthenia, Oriana, and Ferne. Castiel and Nahla can't, though, and they hate it," he added, somewhat gleefully.

"Are these people your brothers and sisters?"

"Yep."

"You have five? That's quite a lot. And are you the youngest?"

Darius nodded. He didn't look too happy about his position in the family hierarchy.

"How about your father?" Carina asked. "Can he cast too?"

At the mention of his father, the little boy's face clouded over. "No, he can't." His lips thinned to a line and he looked angry. Since his father was clearly a sore subject, Carina decided not to continue on that line of questioning. Something else was puzzling her anyway.

"Do you remember how you were kidnapped?" She was wondering how it was that, if Darius had mages in his family, the Dirksens had succeeded in capturing him.

The little boy's face clouded further and his cheeks flushed. His eyes filled with tears again. "It was my fault. I was naughty. Mother told me I must *never leave the garden.*" His voice became singsong as he mimicked his mother and wagged a finger at an imaginary Darius. Carina bit back a smile at the adorable imitation.

"She told me that bad people would take me, and she wouldn't be able to get me back because she couldn't give away our secret. But I so wanted to know what was outside. I wanted to see the city and all the different people, and no one would let me go with them. I made a hole in the garden wall and I went out. I was stupid. Outside, everything was boring. There was hardly anyone around, and no trees or flowers or anything like that. I walked away from the house. I was trying to find the city. Not long after, bad people found me. They took me away just like Mother said they would." His head hung low.

"Darius, it's okay," said Carina. "It isn't your fault. Everyone does stupid things every once in a while. You're very little. What happened is the fault of the people who kidnapped you. Besides, we're taking you home now, and you'll see your mother and all your brothers and sisters again. Aren't you glad?"

The child's easy smile quickly returned. "I'm very glad! I can't wait to see them! Except Castiel. I'm not happy that I'll see him. He always teases me. Or...maybe I'm a little bit happy that I'll see him." He finished in a rush, his eyes shining.

Carina was deeply interested in finding out more about the mage members of the Sherrerr family. It sounded like the boy's mother had married a non-mage and had passed on her ability to only some of her children. She wanted to know if there were any more mages among the Sherrerrs, and if they were part of the ancient family or newcomers, but she also wanted to distract Darius from the whole subject.

Now he knew he was safe, the boy's resolve to keep the family secret had obviously weakened. He'd already brought it up with her, only afterward thinking of the possible consequences. She needed to divert his young mind to other things.

She asked Darius to tell her about his home, and a wellspring of information gushed forth from the child's lips. He told her about his bedroom—he had his own and so did all his brothers and sisters—from which he could see the city. He said he hadn't realized how far it was. He also told her about the garden that surrounded the house, which was full of trees as tall as the roof, and lawns where he and his siblings played, and fountains and pools where they cooled down when they were too hot.

The children all had pets they could ride and that would fetch things for them. He described the animals, but Carina didn't recognize any. The pets would climb trees to bring the children fruit when it was ripe. Each child also had his or her own private tutor, who would teach them mathematics, reading, family history, leadership, charm, oration, deportment, and other subjects they would need to run Sherrerr businesses when they grew up. Only Mother taught them to cast, the boy said.

Carina steered him away from the subject of mages again with more questions about his lessons, though the boy clearly thought that was the least interesting aspect of his home life. She noted the comment about casting tuition being left to his mother, however, and filed it away for later reflection.

Darius was in the middle of a delightful impression of his tutor lecturing him about dignity when the doctor returned. "You two aren't still talking? And why are your bed curtains open, Lin? Back to bed with you, young man. That's plenty of chatting for today. The more rest you get, the quicker that gel will work. Come on, off you go." He shooed the little boy back to his own bed.

The child went happily, and Carina also felt better for their conversation. It had lightened the dark shadow that Speidel's death had thrown over her heart.

Whether or not Tarsalan had changed her mind about disbanding the Black Dogs now they'd fulfilled the assignment, Carina's time with them was over. She knew she wouldn't be able to remain where her memories of the older man were so strong.

Before, she'd had no idea what she could do or where she would go, but Darius's revelation had opened possibilities she could never have imagined.

FIFTEEN

Carina's heart beat fast as, holding Darius's hand, she walked with him from the city toward the Sherrerr estate. Behind them, Tarsalan waited and watched in the shade of a tree at the city outskirts. The Sherrerrs had insisted on a simple handover, much to Tarsalan's apparent chagrin, judging from the bitter tone she used when she informed Carina. Perhaps she'd hoped for a chance to meet members of the powerful clan—an 'in' to the exclusive Sherrerr world.

If an introduction wasn't on the cards, the Black Dogs' owner wasn't going to put herself in any danger by performing the handover. She'd noted the boy's attachment to Carina, however, and had ordered her to accompany him.

Despite the risk that the Dirksens might launch another attempt to capture the child, Carina wouldn't have had it any other way. This was her chance of a glimpse of Darius's mother, who might be able to tell her much about their mage clan. Carina also clung to a sliver of hope that the woman would be interested in meeting her too, once she heard what Darius had to say.

The Sherrerrs had told Tarsalan they would be watching while Carina brought the boy to them. Did they fear a trick? Carina didn't know. She was only uncomfortably aware of distant eyes on them as they went along. She also felt vulnerable out of her armor and with her face uncovered, as the Sherrerrs had requested. But it couldn't be helped.

They were nearly halfway down the dusty, empty road that led to the vast Sherrerr mansion, having walked around eight hundred meters, when Carina glanced down at Darius and remembered the child's feet were bare. His toes had healed up, though his toenails hadn't yet regrown, but the *Duchess* carried no child-sized shoes and Tarsalan had clearly been so eager to return the child she'd been in too much of a rush to do anything about it.

"Don't your feet hurt?" she asked him.

"Only a little."

"Let me see."

She squatted down to look at the soles of Darius's feet. Sure enough, as she'd suspected they were red and blistering. He wasn't a child accustomed to going barefoot.

"Darius," she said, "why didn't you say you were in pain?"

"It doesn't hurt much, and we only have a little way to go now."

She tutted. "Hop onto my back." She turned away from the boy and as he climbed onto her, she tucked his legs under her arms. The strange, misshapen shadow of the two of them stretched out long. It was nearing sunset, and the insect life in that region had started up its twilight song. Razor-backed beetles the size of small cats crawled out of holes and rubbed their legs along their serrated backs. Carina watched them with interest. She'd always had a thing for bugs.

Feeling the boy's body tense at the sight of one of the beetles flying across their path, she reassured him. "Don't worry. They won't hurt you." At least, she was pretty sure they wouldn't. A local had told her they were harmless.

The tall, wide, metallic gates of the Sherrerr estate drew nearer. She adjusted the child's weight on her back. She felt no strain carrying him but the movement eased her nerves a little. She scanned the high, blank wall, which glowed yellow in the rays of the setting sun. It was smooth and solid, unmarked by windows or patrolling guards along the top.

Darius wriggled. "Can you go faster, Carina? We're nearly there. I bet Mother is waiting for me at the gatehouse."

"I'm sorry. They told us I had to walk slowly. But it won't be long now."

They had only another couple hundred meters or so to go. Carina turned and looked back to where Tarsalan waited under the tree. The woman was barely visible in its shadow, but she hadn't left. She would wait until she saw the handover take place, she'd said, before returning to the ship. She wouldn't hang around for Carina, who had left the *Duchess* for the last time, having said all her goodbyes.

Parting from Stevenson had been particularly hard, and she had the impression he felt the same, but it couldn't be helped. Her life lay in another direction now, no matter what happened when she returned the Sherrerrs' child.

A clanking sound came from the gate, piercing the insect drone that surrounded them. They were less than a hundred meters from their destination. A small door at the base of the gate opened, and an armed guard came out.

"Stop," he called. "Wait there."

Carina did as he asked. The guard's armor was entirely black, as was his visor. She couldn't make out the man's face at all as he approached. She felt Darius stiffen.

When the Sherrerr guard was twenty meters away he said, "Put the boy down."

She squatted down, expecting Darius to slide off her back, but he didn't. He clung tighter. "You have to get down, Darius. This man's going to take you home."

The boy buried his face in the back of her neck. Reaching awkwardly around, she gently extracted him from her back and set him on his feet. His head was down and he crossed his arms defiantly.

"What's wrong?" Carina asked. "Don't you want to see your family again?"

He nodded but didn't raise his head. The guard had reached them, and Darius turned away from him, presenting the man with his hunched over back.

"Come with me, Darius," the guard said, holding out a black-gloved hand.

The boy made a grunt of refusal.

The guard sighed with exasperation. "Give me your hand, Master. You must come with me."

Darius repeated his grunt, adding, "I want Carina to come too. She's a—"

"I can't come with you," Carina interrupted before the dreaded word could leave the boy's lips. "That wasn't in the instructions, remember?"

The guard's blank visor turned in her direction, and she could feel the man's curious gaze burning into her.

"Please?" Darius asked, lifting his head, his eyes pleading.

"I'm sorry, I can't. But do you remember what we talked about?"

"Oh yes! I forgot." The returned memory lit up the boy's eyes. "Okay, I'll come with you," he said to the guard. Still refusing to take the man's hand, Darius skipped off, heading for home. The guard quickly followed him.

Carina stood and watched Darius the whole way. When he reached the small door, he turned around and gave her a wave. She waved back, smiling at the young boy's happy face. Then the door closed and he was gone.

She looked toward the spot where Tarsalan was waiting and just made out the figure of the woman leaving.

Hugging herself, Carina began what she feared might be a long wait. She went to the side of the road and sat down next to a small boulder. She didn't know how long it would take for Darius to tell his mother about her. She'd made him promise to wait until they were alone together, and that could take a while. The Sherrerrs would probably want to have the boy medically assessed after the joyful reunion, and who knew what else.

She passed the time watching the large bugs sing their song and perform their mating dance. She'd been to many worlds in the two years she'd spent as a merc and seen many strange sights. The giant beetles were another to add to her list. She relaxed against the boulder and watched the night's first stars appear.

So many suns, so many planets, she mused. *Life in so many varieties, sapient and non-sapient, vicious and peaceful and everything in between.* In her eighteen years, she'd seen both so much and so little of the galaxy. *Was one of those stars the sun that shone on the home planet of her clan?* Maybe one day she would find it and mages could return from their exile and live together again without fear.

The temperature was dropping fast now the sun had set. She shivered and rubbed her upper arms. The wall to the Sherrerr estate was dark gray, unlit by any external lights. From within the compound arose a glow that had to come from lights within the gardens Darius had mentioned. She imagined the lush grounds, with their trees, shrubs, flowers, and fountains, and the little boy playing happily within them, safely home again.

Darius, have you spoken to your mother yet? Have you told her about me?

The night wore on, and Carina grew colder. The beetles retired to their underground burrows, and silence fell except for the occasional animal noises in the darkness. In the city, movement in the streets diminished. She began to think about where she might sleep that night. She had held a faint hope that it might be within the Sherrerr mansion, though that was looking increasingly unlikely.

The garden lights went out. She was tired and stiff with cold, and her dreams of companionship with other mages were rapidly fading. It was so dark, she could barely see the road. The Sherrerr estate walls had become black and forbidding.

It was time to leave.

She stood and stretched her aching muscles. Finding the road by feeling with her feet as much as by sight, she began her return to the city. She had her wages from Tarsalan—any bonus for rescuing Darius noticeably absent. She should be able to find a hostel that was still open, and a hot dinner. And then...she would think about that tomorrow.

It was at that moment she missed Speidel the most. What wouldn't she have given for a word of advice from the older man?

The clank of the Sherrerr gate door opening sounded behind her. She paused and turned, her defeated heart lifting in hope. Through the gloom, she spotted a guard walking over. Was it the same one who had escorted Darius inside? She couldn't tell.

"You," said the guard. "What's your name?"

"Carina Lin."

"Here, this is for you."

He held out a pouch about the size of a large man's fist. She took it and pulled it open, but in the darkness she couldn't see what was inside.

The guard had already turned to leave.

"Excuse me," Carina said. "Do you have a light I can borrow?"

The man hesitated.

"Please?"

His black visor remained enigmatic, but the guard pulled a small flashlight from his belt, turned it on, and handed it to her.

She shone the light into the pouch. A handful of glinting gems were the first items she recognized. They looked valuable. She drew in a breath. The objects that had made her gasp were less impressive than the gems: a tiny transparent box of metal filings, a vial of water, a small container of dust, a tiny firestone, and a bundle of wood splinters tied with a thread: the base ingredients of elixir. Meaningless to an outsider, they were a sign that whoever had sent the pouch knew what she was.

The guard was shifting impatiently. She went to hand his flashlight back when its beam caught another item. This one made her knees go weak. It was a simple, almost valueless object, meaningless to an outsider, but to Carina, it meant everything. It was a pebble, polished to a fine shine to bring out its beautiful colors. It was exactly the kind of pebble her grandmother used to sell for a living.

She drew the strings on the pouch to close it and returned the flashlight to the guard. "Was there any message?" she asked.

"No. No message. I'd get into town if I were you or you'll be sleeping on the street tonight."

He marched away, leaving her alone in the darkness.

She took a final look at the Sherrerr estate. Somewhere inside was a mage who wished her well. Perhaps it was even someone who had known Nai Nai and understood her connection with the woman, but for some reason would not or could not talk to her.

For now, the Sherrerr fortress was impregnable and she couldn't see a way to change that, but in a way she didn't care. She was no longer alone.

Sixteen

Carina was too young to be so drunk. She stared morosely at the rough tabletop, blinking it into focus, drew her dagger from its sheath under her arm, and drove the tip into the wooden surface.

"Hey," shouted the barkeeper. Carina turned. He was watching her, but he took his objection no further. The tavern was a down-market place, and the cut her knife had made only added to the many others that scored the ancient table. Nevertheless, she pulled the dagger out and returned it to its home. Her glass was half full of the strong local liquor and she didn't want to get thrown out before she'd drunk it.

Stabbing the table hadn't eased her frustration anyway. A few coins were all that remained of her wages after quitting her merc job three months previously. She needed another source of income, quickly. She was at a crossroads and whichever way she turned the road looked either unsavory or obscure.

Across the tavern, in a corner the dim lighting hardly penetrated, a pair of eyes met hers. It must have been the fifth or sixth time that evening. She had lost count as she'd downed more alcohol. They were dark eyes, belonging to a dark, slim, coltish figure.

She took another sip of the numbing alcohol and looked away. She had enough problems. A casual hookup would probably add to them, not solve them. A burst of laughter came from behind. She grimaced and ignored it. She'd already checked out the mercs who were responsible for the loud merriment.

Their behavior was dissuading her from signing up as a professional soldier again. If time had dimmed her memory of working with mercs, the bunch in the tavern was a great refresher. Scarred, loud-mouthed, and fond of throwing their weight around, the soldiers were almost exactly like her previous band, the Black Dogs. Only her impression of these wasn't softened by familiarity.

Could she really become a merc again? She didn't think so, but there didn't seem to be any alternative. Bile rose in her throat, and she didn't know if it was due to the liquor or her train of thought.

Her mind strayed to the pouch in her pocket and the angular edges of the objects inside that pressed into her thigh. Among the objects were precious gemstones. If she sold one, the proceeds would buy her another two or three months in this town, but to what end? If she hadn't seen any results from her efforts in all the weeks she'd been here, what advantage would more time give?

Her thoughts moved on to the other items in the pouch, and the familiar ache that crushed her returned. A small vial of plain water, a tiny bundle of wood splinters, tied up with thread, a thumb-sized box of metal filings, a minuscule firestone, and a container that held nothing but dry dirt. All inconsequential and worthless, yet when combined they created the base elixir that allowed mages to Cast.

The moment she had received the pouch was burned into her memory forever. After rescuing a kidnapped boy and returning him to his wealthy family, someone had sent her the pouch as a gift. It had been a thank you or a reward, but to her, the elixir ingredients meant so much more than the gems. They were a sign that the giver knew what she was, and that perhaps that person was a mage too.

For three months, she had clung to that hope.

Yet everything she'd done to try to enter the family's mansion or meet the sender of her gifts had failed. They were Sherrerrs: members of the clan that controlled that region of the galactic sector, which meant they were powerful, aloof, and unapproachable. Yet somewhere behind the tall imposing walls enclosing the estate dwelt someone who either knew the closely guarded secret of mages or was a mage and a member of the long-lost, scattered clan to whom Carina also belonged.

What would she do if she were ever introduced to that person?

What she would say? She'd never been able to decide. Just meeting someone like her would be enough. She had kept her ability secret most of her life to protect herself from harm, but keeping the secret had isolated her. Always being alone was hard.

The dark eyes flashed again. She blinked. How had she happened to be looking in that direction once more? In her drunken state, her gaze had roamed. Her glass had also somehow emptied another quarter.

She took another sip, though she was forcing the liquid down. Maybe she should quit while she could still hold onto the contents of her stomach. Finding her way back to her hostel would also be useful. She tried to stand but her legs wouldn't obey. Pushing the nearly empty glass away, she watched the marked tabletop as it shifted and swam in her vision.

The pockmarks and lines seemed to coalesce into a pattern. She squinted and tilted her head. The pattern was familiar. It was the Map. The one hundred stars surrounding the birthplace of mages and perhaps of humanity itself. If she could find that set of stars, she would be home. She shook her head. It was impossible.

Suddenly, she found she was resting her head on her arms. If she took a little nap, she might feel better in a while. Not more than a few moments after she closed her eyes, however, a hand grabbed her shoulder and shook her so roughly she almost fell off her stool.

The barkeeper's face loomed, close and ugly. "Where do you think you are? A hotel? If you're in no fit state to drink, you're not welcome here. Get out."

The man's words echoed around her skull. She didn't have the ability or the will to argue about it. He was right. She should go back to the hostel. If only her legs would do as they were told. She stood up, wobbling.

"Awww, don't be like that, chief," yelled a merc. "Let her stay. We'll look after her. She's with us. Isn't that right, sweetheart?"

She gave the noisy soldier a dirty look, causing his fellows to shout with laughter. She swallowed saliva that heralded an eruption from the grumbling volcano of her stomach and, concentrating on putting one foot in front of the other, made her way to the door. Her path took her past the mercs' table. One stood up to intercept her, his arms spread wide. "Let's have a cuddle, darling. You'll feel so much better." She side-stepped the man, but as she passed him, he leaned in and planted a sloppy kiss on her cheek. Though she was heavily inebriated, she reacted by reflex.

She punched the merc hard on the side of his head.

What happened next was hazy. She heard raucous guffaws. She was shoved to the floor and a heavy body landed on top of her. Then the body was gone and the barkeeper grabbed her upper arm. "Let me give you a hand," he said sarcastically and half-supported, half-dragged her to the front door of the establishment before pushing her out into the night. "Thanks for your custom. You're very welcome to return—when you're sober."

The door banged shut.

Much to her surprise, she found she was able to stand. Maybe it was the cool, dry night air reviving her. Outside the noisy tavern, her head spun less and her stomach quietened its protests. Perhaps she would be able to walk the short distance to her rented room.

She checked she still had her pouch and knife and that the barkeeper hadn't pick pocketed them when he threw her out. Their bulky shapes under her hands reassured her. She put one foot forward, and then another. Wobbling a little but keeping her balance well enough despite the motions of the ground and surrounding buildings, she went down the street. Tomorrow she would regret her over-indulgence, and she still had no idea what she should do next.

From behind her came the sound of the tavern door opening and an accompanying explosion of noise and laughter. The door closed and the sounds were muffled once more. Resting a hand on a wall to remain upright, she looked back. The long, lithe figure of the stranger who had sat in darkness was following her.

Seventeen

Carina pushed herself away from the wall and continued on. Ordinarily, she had few problems defending herself but at that moment she wasn't feeling her best. She had no friends or family anywhere, let alone in that town, and there was no enforcement agency to call upon. If you weren't a friend of the Sherrerrs here, you were on your own. The only people who would give a damn about her if she died tonight would be the ones who had to remove her body tomorrow.

She put one hand on her dagger and rested the other above the pouch in her pocket. She would happily kill with the first item to protect the second. Hurrying her pace as well as she could, she walked on.

The footsteps of the stranger grew faster and nearer. "You," a voice called. "You with the black hair. Stop a moment."

You with the black hair? Considering the street was empty but for the two of them, the definition was overkill. Maybe her pursuer was as drunk as she was. That would be useful.

"Don't be afraid," the person continued. "I just want to talk to you."

Ha! That's what they call it on Ithiya, is it? She didn't slow her pace. Triggered by the threatening situation, a rush of adrenaline was running through her veins, sweeping away the numb alcoholic fog. She wasn't about to answer the stranger. Answering only gave encouragement.

"Hey, come on. Stop, won't you?" The footsteps were running, and before she could get away, the person had caught up to her. She gripped her dagger's handle in a fist and spun around as she drew it. Bringing up her other elbow under her pursuer's throat, she pushed him up against a wall and held the tip of her knife below his breastbone.

"Whoa," said the man, the quick pallor of his face noticeable even under the sparse streetlights. He held up his hands.

"What," she said between her teeth, "did you want to talk to me about?"

"I only..." He swallowed. "I only wanted to..."

They stood frozen in their positions, eyes locked.

"You aren't really going to kill me, are you?" the man asked.

She blinked and peered at his face. He was very young, probably her own age if not younger, and he looked genuinely frightened. Maybe he didn't have any ill intent.

"I didn't mean to startle you," he went on. "I called out to you. Didn't you hear me?"

"Of course I did. That doesn't mean I have to stop. Now, what do you want?"

"You know, I actually forgot. But if you put away the knife, I might remember."

She studied the youth's expression. Life had thrust her into many dangerous and harmful situations in her eighteen years, and she'd become a fairly good, quick judge of character. This person wasn't setting off any warning bells in her. She stepped back and sheathed her dagger. "Whatever it is, I'm not interested."

Released of her hold on his throat, the young man collapsed. She turned and left. The encounter had cleared her head even more. She was tired and despondent. All she wanted to do was go to her room and sleep.

Her pursuer, who she'd begun to think of as more like a hanger on, didn't give up. He ran to her side, his footsteps matching hers. "I remembered what it was I wanted to talk to you about."

She rolled her eyes and didn't deign to respond.

"But I need you to stop."

She marched on.

"Just for a second."

She sped up. She was nearly back at her hostel. She hoped this exasperating person would have the good manners to not follow her inside.

"Please."

She halted and spun around so they were nose to nose. "What the *hell* is it you want?"

"To be honest," the young man said, "I only wanted to check you were okay and to walk with you wherever you're going. I saw you had a little too much to drink, and after you punched that merc, I was worried he might come after you for revenge. But now I'm not sure you need any help."

Her anger dissolved. She broke her stare and stepped away. "No, I don't need your help. Now please leave me alone."

"And I wanted to ask you something," the man said quickly as she was walking away from him once more. "Could I stay with you tonight? I don't have anywhere to sleep."

As she was about to say no, he went on, "I did help you with that merc. I know it's a lot to ask, but I was hoping you might be willing to help me in return."

"What do you mean, you helped me?" In truth, she barely recalled anything of the encounter.

"After he shoved you, I punched him. He fell on top of you. Don't you remember?" The young man smiled ruefully. "I hurt my hand." He showed her his knuckles, which were grazed and reddened. "It turns out it hurts to punch people. Who knew?"

Guilty at her misreading of him and the entire situation, Carina said, "Look—"

"How old are you?" the man asked.

"Not that it's any of your business, but I'm eighteen."

"I didn't realize. You look older."

"Right. Er, thanks? Look, I'm really sorry, but..."

The youth nodded. "It's okay. I understand."

She continued walking. After hearing his story, she wanted to help him. She knew exactly what it was like to have nowhere to sleep, but she couldn't risk it. She couldn't risk sharing her life with others, even if only for a short time. No matter how desperate they were.

Carina sighed. She halted and turned around. The man was walking away slowly in the opposite direction. "Okay," she called out.

He didn't need any more of an invitation. Immediately, he came running up. "Thanks. I'll be gone in the morning, probably before you wake. I promise."

"Yeah," she said, "you will."

Unperturbed, he said, "I'm Bryce. What are you called?"

"No names."

"Whoa. Okay."

In a few minutes, they'd reached the hostel. It was dark and silent. She led him up the outside staircase to her door, unlocked it, and went inside. The room was as dismal and bare as it had been when she'd left it. Strangely, the man's presence made her feel her isolation more strongly. "This is it. You sleep on the floor."

"Sure," Bryce said, but he didn't move. He was watching her.

She also remained still, watching him.

He reached up and touched her upper arms. She raised an eyebrow, but she didn't protest. He leaned toward her, his face coming close. To her surprise, she found she did nothing to stop what was about to happen.

The kiss was soft and warm, and she didn't think she'd ever been kissed so well in all her life. When it stopped and Bryce drew back, a pregnant pause hung in the air.

"You sleep on the floor," she repeated.

"Sure."

She took a blanket off her bed and gave it to the young man, who spread it across the narrow space between the bed and the chest of drawers that sat below the room's only window. She pushed her pouch deep into her pocket and, tucking her dagger in its sheath under her pillow, she lay down.

"You really don't have anywhere else to sleep?" she asked as Bryce stretched out on the floor.

"No, I really don't."

"You can't get a job?"

"I've got a job. It doesn't pay enough for my needs."

"You can't get a better one?"

He sighed. "It's a long story, No Names. Maybe we should go to sleep."

Complicated, shrouded backgrounds were something she could understand. "Okay." She closed her eyes and tried to sleep, but her alcohol-induced languor had given way to alertness. The kiss had awakened something in her—a need for closeness. She felt a compulsion to share something with this stranger, even if it wasn't her bed. "I'll be going offplanet tomorrow, so this really is just one night."

"Where are you going?"

"I'm joining that merc band. I just decided."

"What?" He sat up on one elbow and gawped at her. "After what happened?"

"That guy was just fooling around. As soon as I put him in his place, he would have left me alone."

"What makes you so sure?"

"I was a merc myself for a couple of years. That's just what they're like. They'll push you, but if you fight back you'll earn their respect and they won't bother you."

"Mercs don't sound like the best people to have as workmates."

"They aren't, but, like you, I don't have a lot of choice."

"Well, it's your life. But if you want to join that band, you'll have to leave early in the morning. I heard them say they were shipping out tomorrow."

"Right. Thanks. Good night."

"Good night."

Now she'd made her decision, she felt calm. Putting it into words had strengthened her resolve. It was time to give up her efforts to connect with another mage and accept that of her few options in life, the best one open to her was returning to the military.

Eighteen

It must have been around three in the morning when Bryce made his move. Carina wasn't sure how long he'd been awake. Perhaps he hadn't slept at all and had been searching her room for anything valuable, or waiting until she was deep in slumber. She only realized he was a thief when she felt his fingertips at her side.

Disappointment and frustration at her own stupidity were her first reactions. She wasn't afraid of what he might do. Her dagger was under her pillow and her fingers rested on its handle. It was how she'd slept for months. But she was bitter and disillusioned at his betrayal of her trust and she cursed herself for being so gullible.

Never again, she promised herself. She must learn to never trust others' better natures.

His fingers were slowly inching into her pocket, the one that held her pouch. He was taking his sweet time, understandably wary of waking her. The fact he'd chosen that pocket meant he knew something valuable was in there. He must have watched her push it in deep before she lay down. He'd been setting her up to steal from her right from the start. Maybe he'd even deliberately punched the merc who hassled her in the tavern, *if* he punched him at all.

She mentally cursed again. It served her right for drowning her sorrows.

She debated whether to kill him. It would be easy enough. She could yank out her knife and draw it across his throat in one move. It had to be only death or kick him out. If she wounded him he might fight back and things would get loud and messy. Then again, killing him would be messy too, and her landlady would charge her extra to clean up the blood.

Bryce's fingers worked their way steadily deeper.

Decisions, decisions.

The fingers hooked around the drawstring of the pouch and the bulky shape shifted. She also moved, as if she were about to wake up. Bryce froze.

He was stuck now, she realized with a modicum of pleasure. If he moved his fingers again, he might wake her up fully and be caught red-handed. But he had to move his fingers at some point because she would wake up eventually anyway.

After a minute or so, she tired of the game. She was still suffering the effects of her drinking and really wanted to sleep. "Yeah," she said, "I'm awake."

He snatched his hand away and jumped to his feet.

When she sat up and turned on the light, his face was a red beacon.

"How dumb are you?" she asked. "After I nearly killed you tonight, you pull a stunt like that? What's wrong with you?" She rubbed her eyes.

"I'm sorry," Bryce replied, hanging his head. "You were kind to let me stay. I guess I should leave."

"Yeah," she said, "I guess you should, and be happy you're leaving with your throat intact."

Avoiding her gaze, he opened the door and went out without another word. Though she regretted her poor decision-making, she couldn't help but feel a twinge of guilt as the door closed. It was the middle of the night, he apparently had nowhere to stay, and judging from the thrum of rain against the window, it was pouring outside.

She turned off the light, thumped her pillow into shape, and thrust her head into it as she lay down. She couldn't afford to care about others. Look where that had led just tonight. If she hadn't had her wits about her, she could be dead.

On the other hand, if Bryce had seen where she kept her valuables, he'd also known about the knife under her pillow. He could have gone for that first. If he'd been quick she wouldn't have stood a chance. He might have oh-so-gently slipped her knife from its sheath and inserted it in her back.

He hadn't, though.

She turned over and stared at the ceiling as the rain steadily pounded the window. She couldn't shake the young man from her mind. She wondered what was wrong with her. She hadn't done anything to feel guilty about, yet she did. Was it something to do with the fact that, despite what he'd done, Bryce seemed intrinsically good?

She sighed and sat up. It didn't look like sleep would be returning to her. She would meditate, as her grandmother had taught her, to refresh and retain her powers. She crossed her legs and closed her eyes. First came the Elements: earth, air, fire, water, metal. Next came the Seasons....

Five minutes later, her eyes opened. She couldn't stop thinking about Bryce.

She climbed out of bed and walked to the window. A river of rain was running down the glass, obscuring her view, but she thought she could make out a figure standing in the scant shelter of a wall. Was it Bryce? She couldn't tell.

A small Cast was needed. She picked up her plain, battered metal canister from the table and swallowed a mouthful of the contents. She closed her eyes and wrote the character, Clear, in her mind. When she opened her eyes, a circle of glass was repelling the rain so it ran around the sides, leaving the center open and transparent.

She looked down into the street and confirmed the figure was Bryce, looking wet and forlorn. She debated telling him to come inside. She would have to remain awake but it seemed she wasn't going to sleep again tonight anyway. It wouldn't hurt to give the man shelter for a couple of hours.

Just as she was about to go down to tell him he could come back in, he pulled a metal box from his pocket and opened it. He pushed up his shirt sleeve, took a syringe from the box, and pressed the end of it against the inside of his elbow.

She changed her mind. Now everything made sense. There was no reason a fit, healthy young man couldn't find a job that would support him. He was an addict. *That* was why his job didn't pay enough to meet his "needs". It also explained why he'd been so desperate to steal from her that he'd risked his life.

She returned to her bed. She wouldn't invite an addict into her room. That would be madness. Who knew what lengths he might go to for a dose of whatever local drug was his habit?

This time, meditating came more easily to her. She mentally went through the steps. Elements, Seasons, Strokes, and finally the Map. The Map was the most complex item of all to remember, and she wondered if she sometimes got it wrong. Perhaps she always did. Since Nai Nai had died eight years ago, she had received no feedback on her efforts. She had nothing to check her memory against. Like all things to do with mages and Casting, no physical record of the Map existed.

Perhaps even Nai Nai's Map had been wrong. After all the millenia that mages had been lost, the Map could have changed as the memory was passed down the generations.

By the time she finished her meditation, the rain had stopped, and the sun was rising. Bryce had disappeared from his spot under the street-light, probably wandering off in a drugged-up haze. She looked out over the town, thinking it was her final view of it.

Her gaze shifted to the side and alighted on the Sherrerr estate. Little Darius, the boy she had rescued, lived there and it was within those walls another mage also lived—the person who had sent her the pouch and its precious contents.

For three months, her attempts to enter the estate had been unsuc-cessful. The Sherrerrs never hired people without checkable back-grounds and the place had airtight security. No one from there except non-corruptible servants and guards ever came into town, though she had spotted shuttlecraft leaving from within the grounds.

She took out her pouch and spread its contents on the table. More tantalizing even than the elixir ingredients was a simple pebble, pretty and shiny but lacking the luster of the gemstones it lay beside. It was the most humble item of all, yet to her it meant the most.

Up until her death Carina's grandmother had made a meager living by polishing and selling beautiful stones they found in the wild lands around their slum settlement. Had the mage in the Sherrerr estate included the stone because that person had also known Nai Nai? And if that was so, why hadn't the mage come out to speak to her when she'd returned Darius, their child?

All the time she had been trying to meet the mage in the Sherrerr mansion, she'd nursed a secret hope that the person would seek her out.

It wouldn't have been too difficult to track down a strange ex-merc in that town. The fact that the mage hadn't seemed to imply they didn't want to. Maybe they didn't think she was important.

Whatever the reason, it was time for her to move on. But after her broken night, tiredness was assaulting her. She needed more rest before she left the hostel. She went back to bed and fell asleep.

By the time she woke, queasy and her head aching, it was already mid-morning.

Nineteen

After handing her last few coins to the hostel owner, she swung her small bag of belongings over her shoulder and went out into the street. She squinted against the sun's eye-piercing, blue-white glare. The star's unusually intense light was something she had never quite gotten used to on Ithyia, and she looked forward to leaving it behind along with her hopeless quest.

Not too long ago, a dear friend and father figure had advised her to give up the soldiering life. He'd told her to get out before she developed the mercs' tough skin, which allowed them to kill impassively and then forget. Well, she'd tried to leave. She'd spent all her cash searching for another path in life, trying to connect with her own kind, and she hadn't gotten anywhere.

She set her jaw and turned in the direction of the spaceport. Bryce had said the merc band was shipping out this morning. With some luck, she would catch them before they left.

She began to jog, her bag bouncing on her back, annoyed at herself for going down to the very last of her currency before deciding to leave. If she had only a little cash or some local credit she could take an auto-cab, but all she had left were the gems. Exchanging them for money would take time she didn't have.

The route to the spaceport took her through the center of the back-water town. The street was already busy with shoppers. Eating establishments were putting tables out on the narrow sidewalks ready for lunch, forcing pedestrians to step into the street. The narrow electric autocars that were the most popular form of transportation swerved around the walkers and gave out their alarm jangles. Children ran recklessly between the vehicles, which went slowly and braked within a heartbeat. At each interruption to their journey, the cars' occupants would open their windows and rage at the kids.

She had become familiar with the businesses, shops, and services that crowded the main thoroughfare, and no doubt the owners had gotten used to seeing her. Small towns were like that, as she knew well from having grown up in one herself, though her home planet was an ass-end-of-the-galaxy place.

Ithyia, on the other hand, was at the center of a Sherrerr-controlled region of the galactic sector. A bustling capital city of millions was a two-hour shuttle flight away, though she had never been there.

Working as a merc, she'd visited many planets. Though climate, location, and population created differences, she found they held some things in common. Humans—and most non-humans, too—had essentially the same requirements: food, drink, clothes, gadgets, entertainment, items for decoration and ornament, and places where they could gather to socialize. Then came the specialisms of the area. In this town it was splicing. The place was apparently known for its splicers, and that was what drew most visitors.

The results of splicing treatments had given her some idle interest while she had tried to find a way to contact the mage on the Sherrerr estate. Splicing to fix a medical condition was heartening to see. Someone with a horrible disease could enter a splicing center one day and emerge the next week or month entirely cured.

Yet splicing for body modification was more interesting. The least adventurous went for changes in their skin, hair, and eye colors. Others let their imaginations run riot, resulting in what appeared almost impossible and possibly painful adaptations. In her time in the town, she had seen plenty of examples. Some customers emerged from a splicer's shop with scaly, hairless skin, slit pupils or bifurcated tongues of lizards. Others sprouted soft fur and had their fingernails modified to claws, while yet more had skins with the smooth, metallic sheen of star grubs.

Carina wondered if the splicers could also confer a star grub's ability to survive in deep space. The creatures were known to float for thousands of years on the mysterious dark matter streams from system to system. If the splicers really could engineer that ability, did the people with those modifications ever attempt an outsystem journey? She'd concluded that, yes, some people really were that crazy.

She was nearly at the spaceport. Passing one of the larger splicing establishments, she gave an involuntary shiver. As a mage, she had a visceral fear of the places. She could never risk having anyone analyze her genes. Whatever it was that gave her her abilities could be discovered, and no splicer would be able to resist the prospect of the riches that would follow if he or she could give others the same talent. Her cells would be priceless, and her freedom forfeit. Splicing presented risks she would never take. She would have to remain a plain human, which was in fact exactly how she liked to be.

A shuttle was taking off. She held up her hand to shield her eyes from the glow of its engines. It was late morning. She began to run faster. If Bryce had been correct about the merc band leaving today, she didn't want to miss them. There was no telling when another troop might arrive, and her other options for escaping the planet were few.

Five minutes later, she arrived. Only a handful of spacecraft stood in the bays and none of them looked like typical merc vessels. One was the domestic carrier that left twice a day for the capital city. Another was a luxury ship, sleek and spotless. There were also some single-seaters for system cruising. Then she spotted one shuttle that looked promising, but its hold doors were closing. It was about to take off.

She ran over to it. "Hey," she shouted to a figure inside. "Are you mercs?"

"What? No, we're on a cargo run. The mercs left this morning." The doors closed with a hiss of compressed gas and the thunk of metal bolts slotting into place.

She cursed and put down her bag. She was out of breath from running. As she panted, she also cursed Bryce. If she hadn't helped him out last night, she would have woken up early and probably caught the mercs' shuttle.

An alarm horn sounded. The cargo shuttle was about to take off. She walked from the field, wondering what she could do next. She rued the fact that she hadn't asked about work on the cargo ship while she had the chance. It might not have paid well, but she would have been offplanet, and maybe even outsystem. Now, she didn't know when her next opportunity might appear.

As she returned through the spaceport building, she took a detour to the booking offices, but inquiring there brought her no solution. Nothing was scheduled to arrive from outsystem for the next week. She would have to sell a gemstone to get the funds to eat and sleep while she waited for her passage.

On her way out of the booking office, she stopped. "When does the shuttle to the city leave?" Her chances of finding a working passage to deep space would greatly increase at the capital's spaceport.

"Fourteen fifty," the clerk replied.

"And how much is a ticket?" The clerk named a sum that made her wince, but she could raise it. She had time. "And are there seats available?"

The man smiled. "There are always seats available. The flight isn't cheap, and after the visitors spend their hard-earned creds on splicing, a lot of them opt to go home by road."

"Great. I'll be back soon." She went out and through the waiting area before returning to the street and the bright midday glare of the sun. A familiar figure was leaning against a wall. It was Bryce, apparently waiting for her. When he saw her, he came over, his expression hopeful. "Did you change your mind about leaving?"

"What are *you* doing here? Have you been following me?"

"I remembered you said you were going to join the mercs this morning. I was hoping—"

"Forget it." She pushed past him and marched away.

He trotted beside her. "Have the mercs already left?"

"Not that it's any of your business, but yes, they have. Thanks to you I overslept and missed them."

"Well your loss is my gain I guess. You need a job, right?"

"No, I don't. And even if I did, I wouldn't take one from you. Not after you tried to steal from me. Besides, I won't have anything to do with addicts."

"Addicts? What makes you think I'm an addict?"

She didn't bother to answer as she sped up her pace. She needed to find a jeweler who would give her cash for a gemstone. Then she would return to the spaceport to buy her passage out of town.

"I said," Bryce reiterated, "what makes you think I'm an addict? I've never been addicted to anything in my life."

Narrowing her eyes as she glanced at him half-walking, half-running beside her, she said, "You know, you have a really bad habit of not taking no as an answer."

He grinned. "Guilty. Now, why would you...?" His eyes widened. "Wait. Did you see me take a dose of medicine in the street last night and think it was drugs?" When she didn't answer, he went on, "I don't take drugs. I'm sick. I have to self-medicate to keep my condition under control. I would show you a syringe, only I don't have any left."

This last comment caused her to slow down. "What's wrong with you?"

"It's a blood disease. Don't worry, you can't catch it."

She paused, trying to decide if he was telling the truth. Her first impressions of Bryce had been that he wasn't a bad person. If he really was sick, it would confirm her instincts and go some way to explaining his behavior.

"You don't believe me, do you?" he asked.

She didn't reply. He went on, "I can show you." He turned and lifted up his shirt, exposing his bare back. It was covered in light purple bruises, yet they didn't look like the marks of a beating.

Suddenly, it all made sense. "You have Ithiyan Plague," she exclaimed.

Passersby, hearing her words and seeing Bryce's exposed back, hurried away with horrified backward glances.

He let his shirt fall and turned around once more, looking down. "That's what they call it, but it isn't a plague. Like I said, you can't catch it."

"My landlady would put a pill next to my breakfast every morning," she said, "and tell me to take it to ward off Ithiyan Plague. She said it was a disease endemic to the planet. Something to do with radiation. How come you caught it? Why didn't you take the preventative?"

His jaw muscle twitched and he still wouldn't meet her gaze. "Like I said last night, it's a long story."

"Can't the splicers fix it?"

"They can, only I can't afford to pay right now. I've been sick with it for a while, but the medicine to keep it under control is expensive. So expensive I haven't been able to save up the money for the permanent fix. I'm kind of caught in a trap. If I don't take the medicine, I'll die. But paying for the medicine means I can't save enough money to pay a splicer."

"So you turned to stealing," she said, "and hanging around in taverns, looking for likely victims."

He nodded. "I really wouldn't have hurt you—"

"You got that right."

"But I was getting desperate."

"Look, I'm sorry, but I don't have a lot of money myself. I'm just about to sell something so I can buy a ticket to the city."

"That's okay. I don't want your charity. But I could use your help, and you're looking for work, right? That's why you were going to the merc ship? I have a job offer that would pay for my treatment, but I need another person. You'll get half the payment of course. I need someone who's handy in a fight but doesn't look it. Someone like you."

She began walking again. She needed to cash in a gem if she was going to catch the afternoon shuttle. They crossed the street behind a multi-person autocar with tinted windows. It was a luxury vehicle bearing the Sherrerr insignia of three stylized blades. She looked back thoughtfully. The car must have come from the Sherrerr estate.

But she'd made her decision. She wasn't ever going to be able to approach any of the local Sherrerr clan.

Fifteen minutes ago, she had thought she was going offplanet. Five minutes ago, she'd been planning to travel to the capital. Now a third possibility had opened up. If Bryce's story were true, it wouldn't hurt to help him out. *If* his story were true. She guessed she could find out more. "What's the job?"

He grinned again. "It's simple. We just have to find out some information about a place way up in the mountains. It is a little risky, which is why I thought it would be good if you came along. The client especially wants two younger people so we won't look suspicious."

A recon job. She had done plenty of those. It shouldn't be hard, yet she wasn't particularly interested. If she didn't do it, Bryce could probably find someone else. It wasn't up to her to fix his problems. She was about to refuse when something made her ask, "What's the place?"

"A Sherrerr stronghold."

Twenty

Faye Sherrerr delicately held her napkin to her nose and then waited until her husband momentarily glanced away before slipping it beneath the table. During another brief lapse in his attention on her, Faye risked a peek at the napkin. Two bright spots of blood were vivid in the snowy whiteness. She slid the napkin into her pocket.

She placed her eating utensils side by side on the plate. It was a signal to her husband she had finished eating and wanted to leave the table. She could never state her intention or even ask Stefan out loud. Requesting permission gave the impression he was in control of what she did, which was absolutely true. It was just that over the previous ten years or so, Stefan Sherrerr had liked to imagine otherwise.

Faye wondered what his warped inner view of their relationship was like. He seemed to nurse a vision of a loving, respectful, equal partnership. Yet that existed nowhere except in his head. Whenever she said or did something that contradicted his vision—like asking his permission to do something—it would anger him. Yet acting without his prior approval would send him into an absolute rage.

Finally, Stefan paused in his lecture to their children long enough to notice her plate. He gave a slight nod.

She said, "That was delicious, but I think I've had enough. I'll see you all in the garden later."

As soon as she'd left the room and was alone, she snatched the napkin from her pocket. She was just in time to catch the blood that threatened to drip from her nose again. She went quickly to a bathroom, locked the door, and held her head over the basin, removing the napkin. For around a minute, blood slowly dripped from her nose before it finally stopped.

She washed the red puddle away and cleaned up. Her reflection in the mirror was pale and tired, and she wondered how much longer it would be before Stefan noticed she was ill. A lot longer, she hoped. So long it would be too late for the local splicers to do anything about it and her husband would be forced to take her to a hospital in the capital, where it would be much easier for her and the children to escape.

Someone tried the handle and a knock sounded at the door. "Who is it?" she asked.

"It's me, mother," her six-year-old son, Darius, replied.

She unlocked the door. "I've finished. You can come in."

"I don't want to use the bathroom. I was looking for you. I want you to play with me in the garden."

Though the boy was getting a little big to be carried, she scooped him up. "I'm too old to play with you. What about Oriana or Ferne?"

Her son had been understandably clingy for the three months since he'd been kidnapped, but she wanted to encourage him to be less dependent on her. If her ruse didn't work, she might be leaving him sooner than she wanted.

Darius's little arms were wrapped around her neck and his face was buried in her shoulder. "I don't want to play with Oriana or Ferne or Nahla or Castiel or Parthenia. I want to play with *you*!"

"But I'm an old lady," Faye replied. "I can't play with you." She lowered her son to the floor. "My joints are stiff, my bones ache, and I can't see farther than the end of my nose."

Darius giggled. "Oh yes you can. You're looking at me right now."

"No, I can't. I'm only looking in the direction of your voice."

"Oh Mother, you're teasing. You can see me. I know you can. You can see me here." He ran a short distance down the hall. "And you can see me here." He ran to the end of the hall. "And you can see me here," he said, waving his arms.

"Darius," Faye exclaimed. "Where have you gone?" She lifted a hand over her eyes as if to look a great distance. "You've disappeared."

The little boy came running back, chuckling. "Here I am. If you really can't see farther than the end of your nose, I'll have to lead you to the garden." He grabbed her hand and pulled her.

Faye allowed her son to drag her down the hall to the stairs. On the way down, they met Stefan coming up. Instantly, Darius fell silent and looked downward. He dropped Faye's hand and held his own together in front of him.

Stefan tutted. "What's wrong with you, Darius? Don't let me stop your fun." When Darius didn't move, Stefan said to Faye, "This is your fault. You're poisoning the boy against me. Don't think I don't know it." He turned to his son. "Hold her hand as you were before." Darius didn't respond, and Stefan shouted, "Do it!"

Darius said, "Yes, Father," before softly taking Faye's fingertips in his own.

"Now," said Stefan. "Continue downstairs."

Both mother and son obeyed, and Stefan said, "That's it. Have fun." He stumped upstairs, muttering to himself.

As soon as Stefan was out of sight, Darius perked up. "Come on, Mother." He pulled harder on Faye's hand as he led her into the garden.

She marveled at the small child's ability to shrug off his father's domineering behavior. One of the few happinesses in her life was the fact that the children her monster of a husband had fathered upon her seemed relatively stable and healthy, despite one parent's harsh, cruel treatment of them.

The girls and boys had the afternoon free after completing all their lessons that morning. As always, most of them were playing in the garden. Only Parthenia, her eldest, seemed to be absent. Perhaps she was in her room. Faye hoped that Stefan was not forcing her to practice her Casting.

Over the years, she had tried to limit the skills she taught her children, knowing the more they could do, the closer Stefan would bind them to him. In the beginning, she had even tried to pretend that Parthenia didn't have the ability. Then one day Stefan had said he would slit his daughter's throat if she was of no use to him.

Thankfully, her husband had softened since then and when it turned out that the child who came next, Castiel, really could not Cast, he had spared his life. It was to Stefan's own benefit, it had turned out, for Castiel grew more like his father every day and was now his favorite child. Ferne's mage abilities didn't attract the same good opinion, and neither did Oriana's, Ferne's non-identical twin. The same pattern was now playing out with Darius. It seemed that Stefan saw his mage wife and children as little more than chattel and tools to further his business schemes. While he saw Castiel, and Nahla, who also could not Cast and was Darius's elder by two years, as like himself: true Sherrerrs.

"What are you thinking about, Mother?" Darius asked. Faye had sat on a bench that gave her a good view of the garden, and Darius had contented himself with looking for fish in the pond at their feet, but now his young gaze was upon her.

"I'm just thinking how fast you're all growing and how well you're doing."

Darius got up and climbed onto her lap. He barely fit anymore. The little boy looked into her eyes. "I messed up my oration this morning and Tutor Peverel scolded me."

"Well, oration is quite difficult when you're six. I wouldn't worry about it."

"And I can never remember my family history. I get the people confused."

"There are certainly a lot of people to remember." Faye wanted to add, *you have another family too, somewhere,* but she dared not.

Darius gave a heavy sigh and squirmed around until his back was lying against Faye and his legs were dangling on each side of hers. His soft hair tickled her neck. Faye wrapped her arms around him.

"Mother," Darius said, his tone remaining sad.

"Yes?"

"I know you told me never to talk about her again..."

Faye's heart froze and she quickly checked that no one was within hearing distance.

"...but I miss Carina."

Faye hugged her son tightly and bent down to whisper in his ear. "Darius, please. You don't want any harm to come to Carina, do you?"

"No, I don't."

"Then...I know it's hard, but you really can't mention her ever again. Not even to me. Do you understand?"

"Okay. I won't."

Faye exhaled. She hoped with all her heart that her son could keep the secret. Stefan had nearly everyone she loved within the grip of his unrelenting fist. Their children lived within a glorious, luxurious prison, their mage abilities chaining them to him. She could not risk him finding out about the one child she had who was free.

Twenty-One

The next day, at breakfast, Stefan seemed pleased with himself. The children had all turned up on time, looking clean and neat, and the cook had made his favorite dish of lightly poached fish roe, but Faye detected there was something more responsible for her husband's uncharacteristically good mood. As always, she couldn't question or remark upon anything to do with him, so she remained silent and waited for him to explain, if he chose.

Parthenia announced to the table, "Tutor Peverel complimented me on my deportment yesterday. He said my posture and bearing were fit for the Assembly."

"Well done," said Faye.

"Yes, that is good to hear, Parthenia," said Stefan, "though perhaps you need extra lessons on charm. You won't endear yourself in company if you go around boasting about your achievements."

Parthenia flushed. "Yes, Father."

Faye felt for the girl. In her fifteen years of life, she'd never once received a word of praise or compliment from her father that hadn't been followed by a rebuke or criticism. Yet despite his ill treatment of her—or perhaps due to it—Parthenia seemed to crave her father's approval. Hence her tactless declaration.

Faye said, "Nevertheless—" Stefan turned cold eyes on her. She left the sentence incomplete. The only noise in the room was the scrape of Darius' spoon as he ate.

Stefan finished his roe and signaled to a servant to take away his plate. Immediately, everyone put down their utensils. Breakfast was over. Two more servants began to clear the table. Stefan removed his napkin from his lap and wiped his mouth. "It seems like a fine day today, don't you think?"

No one answered, unsure whether the question was rhetorical.

"Yes," Stefan continued, "there's no sign of rain or even a stiff breeze. I was thinking to myself, this might be a good day to take a trip into town. What do you think?"

The children gasped. Even Faye's heart skipped a beat. Ever since Darius had been kidnapped, no one in the family but Stefan had been allowed to leave the estate. The Sherrerrs had been purging Ithiya of Dirksen spies and associates. Stefan had declared that until the job was done, it wasn't safe for them to step outside the walls. Was he saying they could go out once more? Or was it one of his cruelties? Was he implying that meaning but then he would declare that *he* would be the one taking a trip outside?

"I think that would be a nice idea, Stefan," said Faye. If she kept her response neutral, it might encourage him to be kind. Or at least not sadistic.

"I'm glad you agree, darling," he replied. "Well then, go and get ready, children."

The children yelled with happiness and scraped their chairs on the floor as they jumped up.

"Quietly, please," Stefan said sternly. The noise immediately stopped.

"Yes, Father," said two or three of the children before leaving the room.

Her husband hadn't yet mentioned if Faye were to be included in the excursion. She handed her plate to a servant and waited for him to say something that would indicate his permission.

"Do you have anything to do in town?" Stefan asked, his light eyes twinkling in his enjoyment of her plight.

"I do, but nothing urgent. If you would rather I didn't go..."

"No, no. You and the children have been cooped up here long enough. Chief Sherrerr's report says they've swept the place clean. It's safe to leave, or I wouldn't allow it. I insist you go and enjoy yourself too."

"I will then," said Faye, avoiding *Thank you* out of habit. Thank you meant he had given permission, contradicting Stefan's self image as a benevolent, loving, indulgent head of the family. It was bitterly ironic. She knew first hand what he was capable of, and she would never—could never—forget. But she stood and went over to her husband as he wanted her to, bending to kiss his cheek like an affectionate wife.

He turned and pulled her head close to his, kissing her fully on the lips. She fought down her revulsion. She tried to act as if she didn't hate what he was doing, though through the long years she knew Stefan had never believed her. She wondered if that made it better for him. She suspected it did.

When he finally released her, a hunger was excited in his eyes she knew he would sate tonight. She forced a smile and went out. In the empty hall, out of sight of the breakfast room, she wiped his saliva from her lips. It was a futile gesture but it brought her some small relief.

The children were already bounding down the stairs dressed in their expensive jackets and hats. Sherrerrs only wore the very best money could buy, and Stefan was sensitive about his family's appearance in public, even if they were only seen by the local townsfolk. Faye hurried through them as she went upstairs. If she wasn't at the front door quick enough, Stefan might decide to leave without her.

She opened her closet and took out a richly embroidered coat. It fitted her perfectly and suited her coloring, but she had never enjoyed the wealth belonging to the Sherrerr clan conferred. She had been so much happier when all she had in the world was Kris and Carina. Her heart was heavy with remembering the little girl as she put on the coat and fastened it.

How in the world had it happened to be her daughter who had brought Darius home? Her secret, hopeless dream was that one day she would be able to tell Carina it was her half-brother she'd saved.

"Mother," a voice called from downstairs. They were waiting for her. She hurried out of her room, but as she left, she coughed. The warm, iron taste of blood flooded her mouth. She ran back to pick up a handkerchief. In another minute she was downstairs just as everyone was leaving to walk to the gate.

A glossy multi-person autocar was waiting for them outside the main gates. Faye climbed into the plush interior with the children. Stefan had taken his seat at the front next to the servant, Nate, who would input their destinations. The doors slid closed almost without a sound, sealing the family inside a cocoon with tinted windows. They would probably visit a store where the children could choose candy and toys, and other places where Faye could pick plants for the garden or ornaments. The shops would be empty of all other shoppers, of course. Nate would call ahead to make it so.

Stefan loved to pretend they were a normal family. Faye doubted he knew what normal was. He must have grown up in the same way as his children, almost entirely cut off from the people who labored to generate the Sherrerrs' massive wealth.

"Look at those bugs," Darius exclaimed, pointing at something on the side of the road that leading the estate to the town. Beetles the size of cats were rubbing serrated legs along their razor backs.

"Urgh," Oriana said, "they're horrible."

"Run them over," shouted Castiel. "Kill them."

"No, don't, Nate," said Darius. "They don't hurt anyone." He went to say something else but stopped himself just in time. He gave Faye a smile. She got the impression he was heeding her earlier request. Had Carina told him something about the bugs? She'd liked bugs, even as a toddler.

Nate didn't drive over the insects as Castiel had urged, and they soon arrived at the edge of town. Stefan did suggest a candy and toy store to the children, and they so vigorously demonstrated their assent, the vehicle bounced on its suspension. Faye relaxed a little. Darius seemed to be remembering her warning never to mention Carina, Stefan was happy in his fantasy that he was a good father and husband, and the children were finally spending some time outside their gilded cage.

After the children had taken what they wanted from the store— Sherrerrs never paid for anything—everyone returned to the autocar.

"Now it's your turn, Faye," said Stefan, leaning an arm over his seat to look back at her. "Where would you like to go?"

She named a plant nursery on the far edge of town. Though she loathed stealing from the town's proprietors, she could at least lengthen the trip by requesting they go somewhere a fair distance away.

"Hmmm." Stefan checked the time before nodding to Nate, who input the destination.

The route they had to travel took them along the busiest street in town. The fact didn't slow them down too much as all the other autocars automatically moved aside as they approached. The town's traffic control program overrode other vehicles' drive systems when Sherrerr transportation was on the road. Faye's children had plenty to gawk at, however, as they went along. They pressed their faces against the windows and stared at the stores and other establishments that were ordinary to less important folk.

A little hand gripped Faye's arm. Darius had grabbed her. He was staring, open-mouthed, at something in the road. Her gaze followed his.

Her heart stopped. It was Carina. Though it had been fifteen years since she'd last seen her, Faye knew her daughter immediately. All her faint doubts that another mage with the same name had rescued Darius were wiped away.

Carina was crossing the road with a thin young man, busy in conversation. Faye thanked the stars their vehicle windows were tinted and Carina couldn't see Darius. She might have approached the vehicle, and Stefan was as observant as he was evil. He would have noticed Carina's resemblance to herself in a split second.

"What's wrong with Darius?" asked Castiel. "What are you looking at?"

The little boy struggled for a moment. His gaze turned to Faye. "I didn't see anything."

"It was just a big bug in the street," Faye said. "It's gone now." She had torn her gaze from her daughter and was facing forward. What was Carina doing still in town? She regretted her decision to send her daughter things that would tell her someone knew she was a mage. She should never have included that polished pebble either. Carina had obviously stuck around hoping to find out more.

She should have only sent her a little money and a thank you note, but she had wanted so badly to show her daughter she wasn't alone. If what she had done had put Carina at risk, she would never forgive herself. She had to get word to her that she must leave Ithiya and never return.

Twenty-Two

That evening, when Faye was finally alone in her room, she let her mask fall. Maintaining the facade of something resembling normalcy for her children's sake had become her habit, but the strain was almost unbearable at times. In her mirror, she daily saw the ravaging effect on her features.

She mulled over how to communicate with Carina in a way that wouldn't put her daughter in extreme danger. The simplest method would be to Cast. She could Enthrall a servant to find Carina in town—a visitor who had hung around for three months for no apparent reason shouldn't be too hard to locate. The servant would pass on the message without knowing what they were doing and would retain no memory of their action afterward.

But Casting was impossible. Stefan had made it brutally clear she was never to Cast without his permission. The safeguards he had put in place to prevent her were extremely tight. She had rarely even thought of attempting it.

Stefan knew she needed earth, metal, wood, water, and fire to create the elixir. Entirely removing the first four Elements from her environment would have been difficult, but it had proven easy to control her access to fire or anything that could create it. The region's climate was warm, so indoor heating was not required. Stefan had ensured a fire was never lit and electricity was never used anywhere on the estate except the kitchen, which was always kept locked even when in use. For lighting, the household used lamps filled with bioluminescent algae that absorbed the sun's rays during the day and glowed at night.

Faye could have created sparks for fire with a firestone, but Stefan had thought even of this and had all of that type of stone removed from the garden's soil. Only once, in many years of surreptitious searching, had Faye discovered a firestone in the garden. It had been a tiny fragment, too small to use. She had placed it in the pouch she sent out to Carina. To Faye, it had been symbolic of the freedom withheld from her but still available to her daughter, though she knew Carina couldn't have guessed the meaning.

The sun was setting. Olivia, Faye's maid, brought in a lamp and set in on her dressing table before leaving without a word. Faye looked out of the window, which gave a view of the road that led into town. If only she could walk through the garden, out of the gate, and down the road to find her daughter. She wondered how far she would get before she was stopped. Probably not even as far as the front door. It had been so long since she'd had that kind of freedom, she'd almost forgotten how it felt.

If she could not Cast, what could she do to contact Carina? Dare she risk bribing a servant to carry a message? The bribe wouldn't be a problem. Stefan enjoyed decorating his captive bird with expensive jewelry. But she pushed the thought aside. The servants and guards were fully aware of the long, excruciatingly painful death they would suffer if they betrayed Stefan. Even if one had been willing, Faye couldn't ask them to take that chance.

The door to her room opened again, and in her dressing table mirror, she saw Stefan come in. He never knocked, of course.

"Good evening, darling," he said. "Did you have a nice time today?" He began untying his cravat. Her stomach twisted so violently she thought she might vomit, but her face had resumed its usual amiable expression.

"Yes," she replied. "Going on an excursion into town is always pleasant. The children had a wonderful time."

"Yes, they were happy with their new toys, weren't they? But what about you? Did you enjoy yourself?"

"Oh yes, dear. Very much."

Stefan put down his cravat on the nightstand and unfastened the top buttons of his shirt.

Faye felt imaginary spiders crawling up her back. She wanted to scream. She wanted to jump out of the window and fall the three stories to the flagstones below.

Her husband pulled off his boots and lay down on her bed with his hands behind his head, resting on a pillow.

Mechanically, Faye unpinned her hair and brushed it out. Night had fallen and, with the lamp's glow on the window, she saw nothing outside but pitch black.

"You look very beautiful tonight, darling." Stefan patted the bed beside him. Faye got up and began to change into her nightdress. Stefan watched. "You look young for your age. I find it hard to believe you can no longer bear children. Yet Darius is six years old now and no little brother or sister has come along." He sat up. "What's that on your side? Is it a bruise? How did you get it?"

"I don't know. Maybe I bumped into a table." The disease assaulting Faye's body was beginning to show clear outward signs. She needed to be more careful. Perhaps Stefan would allow her to undress in the dark if she told him she was ashamed of her aging body.

He pulled his shirt over his head as she turned out the light. She joined her husband in her bed.

"Perhaps we will be lucky tonight," He breathed in her ear. "Perhaps your body has one last fruit to bear. And if not, don't feel bad, my love. You're useful to me in other ways. I have big things planned for you and our children. Very big things."

TWENTY-THREE

"Are you hungry?" Bryce asked. "We could eat, and I can tell you more about the job."

"I am hungry," Carina replied, watching the Sherrerr vehicle as it drove away, the other autocars parting before it like retreating waves. "But I don't have any money. Do you?"

Bryce shook his head.

She sighed. "Okay. Wait here. I'll be back soon." She headed up the street toward the market where the gem dealers plied their trade. It looked like she would be financing Bryce's expedition. She would claim back the outlay from the fee, assuming they were successful. With the money she received for one of the gems, she could buy the supplies, equipment, and clothes they would need to survive in the mountains. Bryce clearly didn't have a clue. If he'd set off without her, he would have died along the way. She wondered if he was dumb or desperate and concluded it was a little bit of both.

She hadn't gone far before a crowd barred her way. People were gathering around some kind of spectacle and blocking road and foot traffic.

It was hard for her to make out what was causing the disturbance—not that she really cared. She only wanted to get around or through the throng and be on her way. She forced herself between a couple of the gawkers and began elbowing into the ranks of jammed bystanders, all craning for a better view.

From the center of the crowd came the sound of a man yelping and pleading. A few of the audience laughed, though awkwardly as if embarrassed.

"Please stop," cried a voice. "I'll give you your money."

"First correct thing you've said all day," said another. "You're right. You will. After we have our fun."

She could see an open space ahead holding two large men. She pushed farther in until she made it near the center and whatever it was attracting all the attention. Unwilling to attract attention herself by traversing the open area, she tried to go sideways, but the people were packed shoulder to shoulder and they were unwilling to give up their prime viewing spots to make room. The path she'd cut through them had also closed up behind her.

She forged ahead and burst into the first row of people, drawing many disgruntled objections. She'd been mistaken. There weren't two men in the center of the crowd, there were three. The third had been invisible because he was down on all fours, his pants around his ankles. One of the men had a foot on his hands, pressing them together on the ground. The other held out a splicer's pole—a double helix of thin strips of steel—ready to strike the man's bare behind.

"What's going on?" Carina asked the person next to her.

"He's new around here," replied the well-dressed older woman. "Set up a splicing center. When the Sherrerr men came for their protection money, he wouldn't pay."

Carina grimaced. The splicer was either very cocky or a fool. Probably the latter. No one could be so arrogant as to think they could avoid giving the most powerful clan in the region a cut of business profits. Judging from the state of the man's face, the beating he was about to receive wasn't the first of his punishments today.

Though she pitied the poor splicer, she didn't want to interfere. She doubted she could take down both the Sherrerr men, and even if she could, she would only transfer the wrath of the Sherrerrs onto her own head. She wasn't *that* dumb.

All she wanted to do was get past the disturbance and reach the market. She began to edge slowly sideways across the front row, annoying the onlookers. A crack sounded as the first blow landed, followed by the howling sob of the splicer. "Please. I'll give you double. I'll give you everything." The men laughed and another blow struck loudly against skin.

She felt sick. She'd done plenty of fighting in her time, both hand-to-hand and fire fights, and she was used to people getting hurt, but there was something especially nauseating about the strong and powerful ganging up on the weak and helpless.

Another blow landed. The man shrieked. The splicer's pole would be cutting his flesh. Suddenly she wasn't so sure she could bear to pass by the splicer's punishment without trying to do something. She'd made it halfway around the inner circle of the crowd before she looked toward the group of three.

She found she was gazing into the splicer's face. It was a bruised, sweaty, bloody mask of agony. The thug who was standing on his hands had also grasped his hair and was pulling his head roughly backward, arching the man's neck. His partner raised his arm, ready to strike again.

"Don't you think that's enough?" Carina asked, before she was even aware she was about to speak. Instead of sneaking past, she realized she was standing upright and looking the man holding the splicer's pole in the eye.

His eyebrows lifted. "No, I don't." He landed a blow so hard it caused him to stagger backward. The splicer screamed long and loud. Some of the people who had been watching with morbid interest looked shocked. Some covered their eyes or began to back away, pushing against those behind them, trying to leave.

She took a step forward. If the men had been average citizens, she would have tried to reason with them. But she knew this type well. They enjoyed what they did and hated whatever came between them and the fulfillment of their pleasure. She knew in their eyes she was already the enemy and nothing she could say or do would change that. Only a response of equal violence could make them deviate from their path.

She ran at the closest one, feinting left then driving her right shoulder into his stomach. He fell into the crowd, who hastily stumbled away so that he hit the ground. She heard the whoosh of the splicer's pole and dived to one side, hoping she had guessed right. The pole smashed into the ground beside her. Before the thug could lift it again, she grabbed it and twisted it out of his grasp.

She whirled the pole into the first man, who had gotten to his feet and was drawing a weapon. The blow knocked the gun from his grasp and sent it flying into the rapidly dispersing crowd. She continued to swing the pole around, connecting with the second thug who was coming up behind her. But the blow didn't topple him. He grabbed the pole and tried to wrest it from her grasp. She gripped tightly and resisted, but she was no match for the man's superior strength. The pole began to slip from her hands, tearing her skin.

She ran to one side, forcing the thug to pivot on the spot. Behind him, his friend had found his gun and was raising it to take aim. She ran forward, forcing the man holding the other end of the pole into his partner. He was knocked down again. She continued running until she had pushed the pole-holding man against a shop wall. The pole was digging into his chest. He let go momentarily to adjust his grasp. She ripped the pole away from him and struck it against his temple.

His head bounced onto the hard stone wall and his legs collapsed beneath him. She stepped back, colliding with someone behind her, who grabbed her hair. She elbowed her assailant in the stomach, causing a whoosh of expelled breath. He ripped out of some of her hair as he went down. When she turned to finish him off, she found the person she'd toppled was the splicer, who had probably been seeking her protection.

The first thug was rising again, his gun in his paw. She kicked the weapon out of his hand and punched him in the jaw. He dropped like a stone.

The stragglers of the crowd were giving her frightened glances as they hurried from the scene. No one wanted to be involved in an event where someone had stood up to the Sherrerrs. Even the splicer was shuffling away, holding his pants around his thighs.

"You're welcome," Carina said sarcastically. She cursed. What had she done? After that stunt, the Sherrerrs would be after her blood. She probably had only ten or fifteen minutes before the men she'd knocked out would come around and tell their friends a face-saving story about a nasty woman who'd defied the Sherrerrs.

In fact, they were already coming around. Carina ran. She headed for the market. At the first gem dealer she found, she stopped and pulled out her pouch. Slamming a gem down on the counter, she said, "How much?"

The dealer, sensing her haste, offered her less than half the jewel's worth. She slammed the counter again with her other hand and glared at the woman. Entirely unfazed, the dealer only repeated her offer.

Barely controlling her anger, Carina said, "Give it to me then."

After the dealer had counted out the cash painfully slowly, Carina snatched it from her and went in search of supplies suitable for a mountain trip. She picked up water bottles, thick coats and boots, a backpack and two blankets. Scant provisions for the expedition, but they would have to do.

She raced back to find Bryce waiting patiently where she'd left him.

"You were gone a long time. I was worried you were never coming back. Why did you buy all those things? We could have gotten them after lunch."

"We don't have time to eat. We're leaving now."

Twenty-Four

"Are you sure you know the way to this stronghold?" Carina asked Bryce when they'd been walking about an hour.

"Yeah, I know the route. I would have known it even if the client hadn't explained. I've lived around here all my life."

"You've been to the mountains before?"

"When I was a kid we'd go there to see the snow. By autocar. It was a little faster."

They were walking through farmland. Carina had judged it safer than going by road. Sherrerr goons would probably be looking for her. They would have to make an example of her to discourage others from standing up to them. The trip would give her the chance to lay low.

Giant plowers and seeders were working steadily across the fields. Unmanned, low intelligence machines, they presented no risks providing Carina and Bryce kept out of their way. The machines moved so slowly it was easy to do. What concerned her more was the water situation. She hadn't noticed any streams along the way, and she couldn't see the glint of water anywhere between them and the white-peaked mountains ahead.

"We would stay at a little resort," Bryce went on, "and go snow-gliding."

"Snow-gliding?"

"You never heard of it?"

"There wasn't any snow where I grew up."

"Snow-gliding boards melt a very thin layer of snow beneath them. Makes them almost friction-less and super slippery. You can go very fast downhill."

"Sounds like fun."

"It was. Was it hot where you grew up? What planet was it?"

"Nowhere you ever heard of. Yeah, it was hot. Hotter than here anyway, though I've been to hotter places since. It was a dump and I'm never going back." There was nothing for her to go back for. When Nai Nai had died, she used the tiny amount of savings her grandmother left behind to pay for a cremation. She had scattered Nai Nai's ashes in the wildlands outside town where the two had spent many happy hours searching for beautiful pebbles to polish and sell.

"I'd leave here too if I could," he said."I want to get out of the Sherrer/Dirksen controlled area and see what the rest of the galaxy's like."

She laughed. "The rest of the galaxy's a pretty big place, you know. I traveled a lot of it when I was working as a merc, and we were never in any area where the Sherrerrs or Dirksens didn't have some influence. You'd have to go pretty far, and you'd have to be rich to do it."

He sighed. "Crush my dreams, why don't you? I didn't say it would be easy. I just said I'd like to do it."

"Sorry. I'd like to get out of this sector and see more of the galaxy too. It's just that I found out first hand how hard it is." If she could, she would love to find the birthplace of her clan, but that was an impossible fantasy.

"If we had our own ship, we might do it," he said."We'd only have to find money for fuel."

Mildly alarmed about Bryce's casual insertion of "we" where he'd used "I" before, she replied, "Do you know how much even a single-seater deep-space cruiser costs? Those vessels aren't cheap. On my wages as a merc I couldn't have afforded to buy one with a lifetime's savings. There's a reason everyone isn't system hopping for fun."

"I bet the Sherrerrs and Dirksens have plenty of cruisers. One each, probably."

"Yeah, probably. Bryce, do you know anything about the Sherrerrs who live in the estate just outside town?"

"Not a lot. That place was built around fifteen years ago. Everyone thought it was odd at the time. It seemed strange that Sherrerrs would build a home in a back-of-beyond place. The only thing the town has going for it is the regional spaceport and the splicers. It isn't pretty or interesting. You would think Sherrerrs would want to live in a city, wouldn't you? Or at least some place where there was more to do than watch the crops grow."

"It does seem strange." She had thought the same when she'd brought Darius home after rescuing him. She hadn't thought of the Sherrerrs as small town people. "Have you ever seen anyone who lives on the estate? They don't seem to come into town often."

"No, I haven't," he replied, "but they used to come out more. Every few weeks the family would arrive in their chauffeured car. I heard they have six kids and they take what they want from the shops. The kids might not even know they're supposed to pay for things. That's the only time they leave home, from what I hear. Unless they fly out. They have their own shuttle."

His words chimed with what Darius had told her. This branch of the Sherrerr clan had to seem weird to the local population, but she could understand the reason for their isolation. Some of them were mages. It was natural they would keep to themselves.

"Are you sure you're okay with doing this job?" he asked, perhaps misinterpreting Carina's silence as second thoughts.

"We're on our way now," she replied. "It's a bit late to be asking me that. But anyway, I don't have much choice." She explained what had happened outside the splicer's shop.

"That was you? I heard a commotion but I didn't know you were responsible."

"I wasn't responsible," she objected. "Those Sherrerr thugs were. They were torturing that poor guy."

"Okay, but you didn't have to step in. It isn't like what you did is going to change anything. They'll probably come down harder on the splicer now."

"Well thanks a lot."

"It's true."

They stopped as a seeder trundled across the path ahead of them. When the machine had passed, they continued in silence. The going was easy over the rough, soft dirt of the fields, and the mountains drew steadily closer. By the time the sun was setting, she estimated they must have covered around fifteen kilometers and have roughly twice that to go before they would reach the mountains' foothills.

When they arrived at a ditch that was relatively dry, she suggested they stop for the night. Bryce seemed grateful for the opportunity to rest. They wrapped their blankets around their shoulders to keep out the evening chill, continuing the silence that had persisted between them for the previous three or four hours. She wasn't bothered by it. She was used to taciturn mercs who saw no reason to indulge in meaningless conversation.

After a few more moments, however, the absence of speech appeared to get to Bryce. He blurted, "All right. I'm sorry, okay? I'm sorry about what I said about the splicer. Now can we please go back to being friends? We've got a long way to go and I don't want you to spend the whole time not speaking to me."

Carina, who had been reaching into her backpack for her water bottle, paused and said, "Er...okay. Do you want some food? We should eat now before it gets dark."

"Yes. I'm starving. What did you bring?"

She retrieved the dried meat strips, dried slices of fruit, and grain crackers she'd purchased, which had worked their way to the bottom of her backpack. He chewed hungrily on a meat strip.

"So what exactly do we have to do when we get to this Sherrerr place?" she asked.

"We have to find out as much as we can about their security arrangements. How many guards, what routines they follow, when they change shifts, and what defense systems and weapons they have. The guy said he asked me because he wanted people who wouldn't look too suspicious if they were spotted hanging around. We can pretend we got lost in the mountains or something like that."

From what she'd seen of the Sherrerr thugs' treatment of the splicer, she didn't think they would balk at punishing whoever they caught near their stronghold, no matter how innocent they seemed. They would have to be extremely careful.

He drew his blanket tighter. "Should we light a fire?"

"We probably don't want to attract attention."

"I guess so," he said, "but it's colder than I thought it would be."

"Just be happy that it isn't raining." She hadn't thought to bring fire starters because she could Cast to start a fire. If she'd been alone, that's exactly what she would have done, but of course, creating a fire by Casting in front of Bryce would be madness.

Twenty-Five

By the time they found the rivulet running down the mountain foothills, they were parched. They'd walked the entire day on only the last of the water they had drunk from their bottles that morning. Carina had been seriously concerned about the situation. The snow line lay a day's climb above them. She might have made it that far, but she wasn't sure about Bryce. He'd slowed down a lot over the last few kilometers.

They sat on the bank and took off their boots before cooling their feet in the water. Bryce filled his bottle on the upstream side and took another long drink.

"Take it easy," she said. "Or you'll vomit it up."

He let out a sigh of satisfaction and lay back, his arms over his head while his feet rested in the water. The tiny stream was icy. It was melt water from the snowy peaks that now towered over them, taking up half of the dusky sky.

She took her feet out of the water and inspected them. The boots she'd had to buy without trying on were too big, and she'd stuffed the gaps with dry grass. Her feet were sore in places and her soles were blistered. Bryce's feet also didn't look too good. If she got a moment alone to herself, she would Cast Heal on both their feet. She would Heal their heels. She chuckled to herself.

He sat up. "What's funny?"

"Nothing." She wiped most of the water from her feet with her hands and pulled on her socks.

"Tell me. I need a laugh after that brutal march you made me do today."

"*I* made you? This was your idea, remember?"

"I know. I didn't say how fast we had to do it, though, did I? We could take more time about it."

"Only if we can survive on grass. I don't know about you, but I find it kinda hard and chewy."

"Ah. Good point." He lay down again.

"Where do we go tomorrow?"

"There's a pass, away over there." He gestured vaguely without looking.

"Where?" She was looking in the direction he'd indicated. They were in the shadow of the mountains, and darkness was creeping down the slopes. The place he seemed to mean was already in deep shadow. She took the evening's rations out of her backpack and tossed Bryce's half onto his stomach.

"Is that it?" he asked as he sat up again. "I'm skinny enough as it is. I'll be a ghost by the time this job's done."

"If you don't end up a real ghost, count yourself lucky," she replied. "What we're doing is crazily dangerous, you know. I take it the person who gave you the work is linked to the Dirksens?"

"He didn't mention them, but I guess it's obvious."

"No one else I know would be interested in security at a Sherrerr stronghold." She was getting drawn into the Sherrerr/Dirksen conflict again. It was a deadly place to be. Yet, despite the peril, she was feeling more lighthearted than she had in a long time. Perhaps it was because she finally had some kind of purpose after months of inactivity.

She also enjoyed spending time in Bryce's company. For the last couple of years, all the people she'd known had been mercs. They didn't exactly make agreeable companions. She'd discovered that if they weren't out-and-out psychopaths, they had other personality problems or were deeply psychologically scarred.

"What are you thinking about?" he asked through a mouthful of dried fruit.

"Some people I used to know."

"Before you came here? Who were they? Were they friends?"

"Not exactly. The men and women I used to work with."

"How did you get to be a mercenary?"

"By invitation. It isn't a very interesting story. How about you? You said you used to come to the mountains to snow-glide when you were a kid. What happened? How did you end up on the street?"

He paused a moment and then looked up into the darkening sky as he replied, "A couple of years ago, my dad had an accident and my mom lost her job. Both in the same week. It was months before either of them could work again. We all had to stop taking the preventative medication. It was either that or starve. If you don't take the pills, you stand a one in five chance of developing the disease. Out of my parents and brothers and sisters, I was the unlucky one. My mom and dad didn't have the money to pay for the cure. They could only just afford the medicine that controlled the symptoms. Then they couldn't even afford that any longer.

"They abandoned me. I woke up one morning and the house was empty. They'd left during the night. While I was trying to figure out what had happened, the landlord came around and told me I had to get out—that the rent was overdue and my family had been seen boarding the city shuttle. I don't know where they are."

She sucked in air through her teeth. "Harsh."

"It's okay. I don't blame them anymore."

"You don't?" She stared at the young man, his face dim in the half-light. He seemed to mean what he said.

"I don't think I could forgive anyone who did that to me, especially not family."

"The way I see it," he said, sitting up to look at her, "they had an impossible choice. They didn't have the money to pay for my treatment, and the cost of my medicine was bleeding them dry. They had to choose between sticking around while all of us ended up destitute, and when we couldn't afford my medicine anymore, watching me slowly die; or saving themselves and my siblings and sparing themselves the sight of my death. The end would have been the same. It was only a question of who I brought down with me and how long it took. The way they left spared us all a painful parting."

His revelation raised him in her eyes. Nai Nai would never have abandoned her in the way Bryce's family had, but if she had, she wasn't sure she would ever have been able to understand or excuse it. Whether his take on what his family had done was compassionate or only an attempt to protect himself from a grim truth, she wasn't sure, but it told of a depth to his character she hadn't imagined. "I'm sorry."

"You don't have anything to be sorry for. You didn't give me this damned disease. Anyway, it's okay about my family. I was angry at first, but I got over it when I saw their point of view."

She wondered if her gems were worth enough to pay for Bryce's treatment. She was young and healthy and could find work if she needed to. Though she'd only known him a short time, she felt like he was a friend.

Fear gripped her. What was she thinking? She was a mage. She couldn't afford to have friends. Nai Nai had told her she must never trust anyone, that the knowledge of her powers would turn the nicest, kindest people into selfish, grabbing devils.

"What's wrong?" he asked.

"What do you mean?"

"Your expression suddenly changed. You looked okay, but now you look angry about something."

"You like studying people, don't you?"

"It's a useful habit when you depend on others' generosity for your survival."

She pulled her blanket out of her backpack. "Nothing's wrong. We should get some sleep. We have a long climb ahead of us tomorrow."

He also got out his blanket. They wrapped themselves and lay down, putting their backpacks under their heads as pillows.

"How about you?" he asked.

"What about me?"

"Does your family know you became a merc? Are they still living on your home planet? Do they know where you are?"

She paused before answering, "My family all died a long time ago." Her history was a story she could never and would never tell him. "Good night."

Twenty-Six

The Sherrerr stronghold looked impregnable. Carina and Bryce were lying on their stomachs, peeking over a ridge that looked down on the fortress.

"Here, suck on this," she said, passing him a handful of snow.

"Why?"

"Just do it."

When he'd stuffed his mouth with the snow she explained, "It'll stop our breath from fogging and giving us away." Then she did the same. The guards patrolling the stronghold's walls would have been trained to look for signs of watchers.

Her gaze inched across the building and its surroundings. The fortress stood in a high valley, and a single, narrow, winding road led up to it. The main access to the place seemed to be by air. Most of the roof space was taken up by a shuttle landing pad. She glanced at the sky. They would need to be careful they weren't spotted from overhead if a shuttle arrived or left.

One vessel stood on the pad already and it could hold another three. The craft was black and carried no identifying insignia. It had arrived that morning, judging from its clean, snow-free exterior. Snow had fallen during the night, and the shuttle had melted a neat circle when it landed. Tiny footsteps of three or four passengers led to a closed door that had to be the stairway entrance.

Guard boxes stood at two corners of the roof, and the guards would no doubt be watching the airspace as well as checking arrivals. Solid stone, windowless walls made up the rest of the fortress. The only above-ground entrance other than the roof was a double door that fronted the road, though Carina didn't discount the possibility of a drainage tunnel that opened into a stream somewhere farther down the mountain.

She touched Bryce's shoulder, gesturing that they move down from the ridge. They went to a group of boulders. On one side of the massive stones, snow had piled into a drift. On the other side, only a light dusting covered the ground. They crouched in the sheltered spot.

"My mouth's frozen," he complained, spitting out the remains of the snow.

"That's the idea," she replied. "So we need to stick around for a few days and watch what happens. We'll do it in shifts. We can't stay up here the whole time or we'll freeze to death. We'll make a camp a little farther down the mountain and take it in turns to watch for a few hours."

"I'd forgotten how cold it is up here," he said. "And snow seemed a lot more fun when I was a kid. I was thinking, maybe we should just, you know, make up something to tell them. We can hang around somewhere warmer for a while, then I'll go back to my contact and give him a story."

"Are you crazy? If the Dirksens figure out you gave them false intel, your life won't be worth living. Anyway, I would never do that. We're being paid to do a job, so let's do it, okay?" She had seen fellow mercs die due to bad intel. She wasn't going to be the source of it herself.

They climbed one hundred meters or so down the mountain until they reached a shallow cave they'd passed on their way up. It wouldn't provide much protection from wind or snow, but it was better than nothing. The best thing about it was that it wasn't visible from the track —Bryce had discovered it on a quick trip to answer a call of nature. She expected that Sherrerr guards would frequently patrol the area around the fortress, looking for people who were doing exactly what they were doing.

They had a cover story if they were picked up, but she didn't have much faith in it. They had to avoid detection while they scoped the place out. If they could only remain here for the next two or three days, they could return to Bryce's Dirksen contact and pick up the reward. Then she would have to find a way to get to the capital that didn't involve leaving via the spaceport. She had no doubt the town was still hot for her after her escapade with the Sherrerr men and the ungrateful splicer.

When they had secreted their bags at the back of the cave, she said, "I'll take the first shift. You stay here and rest. Use both blankets to keep warm, and eat your ration if you like. I'll be back in a few hours."

He protested that he should watch the fortress while she rested, but she argued successfully that she'd done recon many times before and knew what to look for. She left him wrapped in both their blankets.

Before returning to the ridge, she stopped at an unusually shaped boulder. It looked like the head of a plains beast, a long-snouted animal that had lived in the wild lands on her home planet. She took out the pouch that contained her remaining gems and the elixir ingredients. If she were captured, the jewels would contradict their cover story. She put the pouch down next to the boulder and covered it with stones.

Soon, she was near the ridge and taking great care to move quietly and look around corners before proceeding. The way was clear of Sherrerr guards, however, and soon she had stuffed her mouth with snow and was peering down at the fortress once more.

It felt a little strange to be doing recon without the benefit of the devices she used to have as a merc. Having no scanning, recording, or special vision instruments made her feel not very useful. She could see the advantage of carrying no technical equipment of course. It meant they wouldn't have any items to incriminate them. It wouldn't be immediately clear the Dirksens were planning an attack. The downside was the true reason for their presence in that place was held only within their minds, and the Sherrerrs might stop at nothing to retrieve the information.

She gave a shiver, partly at the thought of interrogation and partly due to the cold that had begun to encroach into her bones. The fortress looked the same as before, except the shuttle had departed, leaving a bare patch of melted snow.

She wondered what it was the Sherrerrs held within their fortress that warranted such efforts for its secrecy and protection. It had to be something of great importance. The place looked newly built of manufactured stone. They would have had to haul the massive blocks and everything else required to build the fortress all the way up the mountain.

Were the Sherrerrs building a new weapon? That might make sense. It was difficult to keep activities like that under wraps. If they built the weapons at this highly defended location the Dirksens would find it hard to blow up the construction site. If that was what the Sherrerrs were doing, it didn't bode well for the citizens of that galactic sector. Weapons development meant war was coming.

The crunch of a foot on loose stone sounded from somewhere behind. Had Bryce come up to speak to her? It seemed unlikely. Carina couldn't think of anything he might have to tell her that couldn't wait until she returned to him. She eased down from her position overlooking the fortress. If someone was coming up the path, she needed a place to hide, but the only possibility was a low protrusion of the mountainside.

But anything was safer than meeting a guard face to face out in the open. She slid down behind the protrusion, cursing the very obvious trail she'd made in the snow. She searched her mind for a Cast that would make the snow look untouched. Obscure would do it. Her canister of elixir was inside her shirt.

Another soft crunch of a boot on stones.

She sipped the elixir, which was warm from the heat of her body. As she screwed on the lid and returned the canister to the safety of her shirt, she closed her eyes to write the character. But she had only completed four strokes before another *crunch* sounded, very close by. She had no time left. She opened her eyes just as a man in armor appeared around a rock.

Though he was facing away there was no point in hiding now. The minute he turned around he would see her. She leapt up and flew at him from behind. His armor and helmet protected him, while she wore nothing but a heavy coat and hat. Her only hope lay in taking his weapon. Before he even hit the ground, her hand was around the grip and she was pulling the gun from the holster.

She was the first on her feet. She aimed at the guard and was about to shoot when she heard another sound. Her last thoughts were, *Damn. There are two of them.*

TWENTY-SEVEN

Carina woke up inside an interrogation room. She was sitting down, her hands were tied behind the back of the chair and her ankles were tied to the chair legs. Two burly men stood over her and from the looks on their faces, she wasn't about to experience a warm welcome to the Sherrerr fortress.

Before she even had time to speak, one of the men slapped her, snapping her head to one side. Then the other struck—a full-on punch to her jaw. She saw stars. "Pleased to..." She spat blood. "Meet you too."

This drew a chuckle from the corner of the room. A figure who had been standing in shadow stepped forward. She wore a gray uniform and appeared to be a superior officer, judging by the blazes on her collar.

"They said you were the tough one," the woman said. "Your companion whimpered and gave himself up immediately."

Carina's heart sank. Bryce wasn't built for what was about to happen to them. She just hoped he would be able to stick to their story nevertheless.

The woman turned to the men. "Soften her up. I'll be back in a while."

They grinned and nodded, one rubbing his knuckles on the palm of his other hand.

Carina had been beaten up enough times during the years she'd spent alone after Nai Nai died that she didn't fear what the men were about to do. Though she couldn't Cast without taking a sip of elixir, she'd learned the mental discipline of shutting off signals from her nerve endings. Still, she also knew she wouldn't be able to shut out the pain forever. She just hoped they wouldn't break any bones.

What seemed like a long time later but was probably only half an hour or so, the female officer returned. Carina's eyes were nearly swollen shut and, with her hands tied, she could only try to blink the blood away. So the woman looked blurry, but from the sound of her voice Carina could tell she was the same person.

"Not too pretty now," she said. "Quite like your friend, I have to say. The boys are having a wonderful time with him."

Carina winced.

The officer drew up a chair and turned its back to her. She straddled and leaned her arms on it. "So, my dear, now that we have the pleasantries out of the way, I'm ready to hear your story."

Speaking through puffy, bloody lips wasn't easy, but Carina tried her best to sound genuine as she explained that she and Bryce were friends who had hiked into the mountains with the intention of working for the Sherrerrs. Lies were most effective when they were nearly the truth, so that was the only deceit Carina uttered. Everything else she told the officer was true: that she was an ex-merc whose band had dissolved and she'd left the ship. She'd met Bryce, who'd told her he'd heard of the Sherrerr stronghold and suggested that they went there to sign up. He needed the money because of his disease. She needed the money to live, and she was already a handy fighter. They'd been trying to find the stronghold but Carina had gone ahead while Bryce rested off the track.

The officer studied Carina's face in silence as she listened to her story. When Carina reached the end she said, "It all makes sense, except for one fact. If you were so intent on joining us, why did you attack the guard who found you? Why not give yourself up?"

Carina swallowed. It was a good point. "I wanted to show you how well I could fight. I wouldn't have shot him. I planned on making him show me the way here. I thought, if I defeated one of your guards, you'd be impressed."

"Ha," the officer exclaimed. "If they didn't patrol in pairs, you might have succeeded too."

Carina managed a half smile. "I might have."

The woman stood up. "You're certainly a resilient young thing, and you know how to take down a man. Maybe you are an ex-merc looking for a job as you claim. If you can make it through Basic in your current state, you can have one. We're in need of new recruits so I'll take a chance. Don't doubt that you'll be watched closely. One suspicious move and you're dead. Even if the story you just told me isn't quite the truth, things are happening that'll soon show you the benefit of working for the Sherrerrs."

She went to the door. "Put her in a cell overnight. No food or water. We'll see what she's made of tomorrow."

Though the officer hadn't given them permission, the men allowed their fists and boots to become more acquainted with Carina before they finally untied her and dragged her to a cell. When they closed and locked the door, she lay on the bare, cold stone floor. The first thing she did was to feel for her elixir canister, but of course it had been taken.

She curled on her side, resting her battered head on her arm. The officer hadn't said what they would do if she didn't make it through Basic, but Carina guessed she hadn't needed to. The fortress was in an empty, lonely area of the mountains. No one would notice the body of a young woman thrown from a high place.

Now her beating was over, the resulting pain was overcoming her mental barrier. She wasn't sure which place hurt the most, but she didn't think the men had done her any lasting damage. If she had her elixir, she could heal herself overnight, though that would make her captors suspicious. Without her elixir, she would probably heal in a couple of weeks. Only she didn't have a couple of weeks.

Carina closed her eyes and tried to shut out her pain, hunger, and thirst. She needed to sleep if she was to survive the following day.

Twenty-Eight

All she needed was a firestone, Faye reasoned as she wandered the garden. That was all. One insignificant rock, useless for anything except striking sparks. Then she could Cast Locate to find Carina, and Send to her to warn her to leave Ithiya. She wasn't sure that Locate would work. She'd been separated from her daughter so long, it would be hard to make the connection. If she had something of Carina's it wouldn't be a problem, but she had nothing. It couldn't be helped. She would have to try.

Faye had already scraped minute filings from an iron banister, gathered splinters of wood, and a pinch of dirt. She'd hidden each of the ingredients in a separate place—if Stefan came across them together he would know exactly what she was up to and would punish her severely. As time had gone on, she'd been persuaded that her efforts to create elixir were hopeless.

Until now. The sight of Carina still hanging around after returning Darius to her had sparked an inner rebellion that wouldn't rest. Faye had to get a message to her by some method. Any method. Stefan had six of her children under his control. He would not have a seventh.

Her husband was locked in his study, probably speaking with his Sherrerr relations via comm. The children were at their lessons. Faye had an hour or more to herself. She'd told her maid, Olivia, that she was tired and would take a nap. After the woman had left, she'd sneaked out and down the back staircase, hopefully unobserved. The servants all spied on her and reported to Stefan.

In a section of the garden that was obscured from the house by tall shrubs, Faye bent down and turned over the stones in the soil, examining them. Next she looked at the low wall that held the flower bed. It was made from larger stones, cleverly stacked so they stayed put without mortar. Small gaps had been filled by pebbles, wedged into place. Nothing. Faye sighed and stood up. She went farther from the house, her pulse quickening. She wondered if her maid had checked on her and found she was missing.

There were no rules that said she couldn't do exactly as she pleased within her home. No rules except the unspoken ones.

Water was so easy to procure she could leave it to last. But she had to have fire or all her efforts were worthless. Faye fought down the rising tide of hopelessness that threatened to overwhelm her. In the early days, she had searched endlessly for something with which she could make fire. The times Stefan had caught her and guessed what she was doing, he had beaten her so badly she was in pain for weeks.

It was around the time he'd threatened to beat the children instead of her that she'd finally been persuaded to entirely cease her efforts. She couldn't bear to be the cause of her children's suffering. The cage was sealed shut and in all the following years, she had never dared to try to prise it open. It was also around then that Stefan had begun to cultivate a veneer of decency and respectability, an ironic counterpoint to the reality of his nature and evil exploitation of his family.

Over the years, Stefan had used Parthenia, Oriana, and Ferne to give Sherrers the edge in business deals. He had taken them to the capital and made them Enthrall competitors in meetings so they agreed to unfavorable terms, or the children had performed other Casts that confused or wrong-footed adversaries.

Perhaps Faye couldn't prevent Stefan from treating their children as tools but she could save Carina, with a firestone. When the flame she would create was applied to the other elixir ingredients for the correct duration, it would prime the mixture.

Though she'd never made a fire in that way before, she knew it could be done. Before she and poor Kris had been captured by the Sherrerrs, they'd lived with Kris' mother, who used to be a geologist. She knew every stone in the wildlands that surrounded their town, and she'd spent many evenings showing them examples and explaining their origins and properties. At the time, Faye had found the explanations boring, but she did vividly remember the night the old woman had demonstrated making fire with a firestone. She'd said it was a skill every mage should have.

Little had she known how right the old woman had been. Faye hoped she was still alive, but she doubted it. She'd already been old when Kris and she had been captured. Also, Carina had gone outsystem. She'd loved her Nai Nai so much, she would never have willingly left her.

Carina. She had to Send to Carina.

Faye squatted down next to another flower bed and began to examine the stones. Again, she found nothing. She clenched her hands into fists. Firestones were commonplace, though few knew their special property. The gardeners had been digging the beds recently. Perhaps she could find a stone they'd unearthed. Then she saw it. An edge of the stone so precious to her protruded from the dirt.

"Faye," Stefan said quietly.

She shot to her feet. He was only meters away. How had he crept up so close without her noticing? Caught unawares, Faye was too flustered to put on her mask. She felt her face flushing crimson.

Her husband's features were hard, yet somewhere behind his eyes, Faye could also see the glee of an evil child who has been given an opportunity to freely act out their deepest desires.

"I'm so disappointed in you, my dear."

"But—"

He held up a hand to stop her. "Please don't insult me with lies. I know exactly why you're here, but I must say that it comes as somewhat of a surprise. After all our years of marriage, after our love-making last night, I'd thought that I'd come to mean something to you. That *we* had come to mean something to you."

He approached her, waves of evil intent emanating from him and washing over Faye like a tsunami of horror. What would he do? When and how would the punishment fall? She hoped desperately he would take it out on her and not the children.

He stood so close, their noses were almost touching. "Look into my eyes, my dear."

She unglued her gaze from his neck with its silken cravat and fixed it on his pale blue irises.

"Have I not been good, kind, and generous to you? You want for nothing. You have the very best of everything. Think back to the state you were in when I found you. Skinny, poor, and wearing clothes that wouldn't be fit for rags in this home. I've given you more than you could have even imagined. And this is how you repay me."

Thwarted in her efforts to warn her remaining non-enslaved child, Faye's frustration and rage overflowed. She worked her saliva into a gob and spat in her husband's face. "You bastard," she yelled. "You captured me and the only man I ever loved. A man whose shoes you weren't fit to lick. You raped me. You made me give up my secrets on the promise that you would spare my husband's life. Then you murdered him in front of me. I don't care how many jewels you throw at me. I don't care how many dresses you buy me. I don't care what fine foods you give me to eat. One day I'll make you pay for everything you've done. One day I'll have my revenge on you, Stefan Sherrer, you evil, perverted freak."

The color drained from Stefan's face. He grabbed her hair and marched through the garden, dragging her along. She screamed and fought, but his fury leant him extra strength. When she scratched and bit him, he dropped her, hauled her to her feet, then slapped her so hard she fell down. He pummeled her face, gripped her wrist so tightly it cut off the sensation from her hand, and pulled her toward the house.

As they got closer, Faye glimpsed the heads of the children appearing at windows then swiftly disappearing as their tutors or a sense of self-preservation told them it was wiser not to look. Despite her earlier bravery, Faye's courage was deserting her. The sight of her children reminded her of the punishment that lay ahead.

Please, please don't hurt my children. She couldn't speak the thought aloud. It would only fuel his sick satisfaction at meting out whatever it was he had in store.

No servants appeared when they got to the house. When Stefan was in a rage, they were wise enough not to show their faces unless called. He hauled her upstairs and threw her into her room, then closed and locked the door.

———

When he returned, hours later, she was in the same position she'd fallen when he'd thrown her to the floor. She had sobbed out her ages-old grief for poor, dead Kris and her despair at her predicament. She was lying motionless, only hoping that somehow it could all end.

"Get up," Stefan said.

Like an automaton, Faye rose to her feet.

"Come with me."

She followed him downstairs to the breakfast room, which was odd because it was late afternoon. When she went inside, her heart stopped. Darius was sitting at the table.

"Mother," he exclaimed, happy to see her. He went to get down from his chair to run over and give her a hug, but his father said:

"Stay where you are."

The little boy looked down and remained in his seat.

"Sit down, Faye."

Trembling, she did as he told her. She hardly dared to think what Stefan had in mind, but if he harmed one hair on her little boy's head, she would throttle him where he sat.

A dish of shaved ice and sweet pudding sat in the center of the table, just enough for one person. It took Faye a moment to understand what this might mean. When she did, the hairs stood up on the back of her neck.

"Darius," Stefan said, "you've been such a good boy recently, I've arranged a small surprise for you. I know how much you love Cook's desserts, so I had her whip one up especially as a reward. I invited Mother along so that we can both watch you enjoy it. Here you are."

He lifted the bowl and placed it in front of the boy. Faye gasped. It was poisoned. The dessert was poisoned. As her punishment, Stefan was going to murder their child.

Darius wasn't stupid. It was clear from his expression that he knew there was something very wrong with the situation.

"What's the matter?" Stefan barked. "Don't be an ungrateful child. Eat up."

Darius' gaze was locked with Faye's, reading the terror on her face. His lower lip quivered.

Stefan shouted, "Darius!" The child started and snatched up his spoon.

"Don't," exclaimed Faye. She turned tear-filled eyes to her husband. "Please." She swallowed. "Please. I'm sorry. I'll do anything."

Stefan folded his arms. He rubbed his chin. "Really? That's very interesting. Anything?" He said to his son, "Darius, you don't seem to want the nice pudding I had made especially for you. Is that correct?"

The little boy nodded.

"I see. Well, it would be a pity to allow it to go to waste. Shall we ask Mother if she would like to eat it?"

Darius turned questioning eyes to Faye. Before he could speak, and forever remember that he was the cause of his mother's death, she blurted, "Yes, I would like to eat it. I want to eat it. Do you mind Darius?"

"No, I don't mind. You're welcome, Mother. I hope you like it."

Faye took the bowl and spoon quickly, before she had time to think about what she was doing. She ate the dessert in large mouthfuls, forcing the sickly sweet substance down between gasping sobs. When the bowl was empty she sat with fat tears rolling down her cheeks, waiting for the poison to take effect. She kept her gaze on her sweet child so he would be the last thing she saw.

Darius had begun to cry too, though he couldn't have understood what was going on. For several minutes they sat, looking at each other. Just as Faye was thinking she should have left the room so Darius wouldn't see her final moments, Stefan burst into laughter.

"Aren't you two a pair of sad turtles? Look at you both. Crying over a silly dessert. How funny you are." He chuckled and shook his head, then got up from the table.

Faye nearly collapsed with relief. The dessert hadn't been poisoned. He'd only wanted to scare her.

"Darius," Stefan said, suddenly serious again, "go and play."

The little boy jumped down from his seat and ran out of the room.

"Faye, you really are a fool if you think I would hurt Darius. He's a mage and from what I can tell a very good one. With Parthenia, Oriana, and Ferne, I have four mages under my control, which makes *you* rather surplus to requirements, don't you think? I know exactly what you were doing this afternoon, Faye. If you ever attempt anything like that again, what I'll do to you will have you begging for a quick death from poison."

TWENTY-NINE

S tefan's sick punishment was turning out to be a watershed in their relationship, Faye realized a few days later. He had ceased to focus on her and instead began to show Parthenia much more attention than he had previously, usually within Faye's presence. When their eldest daughter wasn't looking, he would throw Faye a malevolent smirk, making clear his statement that now that Parthenia was growing into womanhood and her full mage power, Faye was indeed 'surplus to requirements.'

The idea that her husband was grooming Parthenia into his willing servant sickened Faye to the depths of her stomach, but she didn't know what to do about it. The poor child, who had craved her father's affection for so long, blossomed in happiness whenever Stefan spoke to her kindly, praising her efforts in her classes or her appearance. She began to decorate her hair every day with a ribbon or ornamental combs and pins, and every evening at dinner she would speak at length about what she'd learned, encouraged by Stefan's enthusiastic nods and smiles.

At such times, Faye could only listen and watch, wishing she could have given her daughter a better father, someone who truly loved her for who she was and would never have manipulated her young mind and heart—a man, not a monster.

One afternoon, in the garden, Stefan stooped lower than even Faye had thought he could go. He'd been away since the previous day—flying off to a clan meeting—and the usual sense of relief and calm had settled over the estate as it always did while he was gone. Faye was in an elevated spot that gave her a clear view of most of the expanse of manicured greenery and flowers, and so also of her children as they played.

Parthenia was teaching her pet tricks. She had a tarsul, a long-limbed, tree-climbing animal dappled pale green and brown—a camouflage that worked effectively when it was up among the leaves and branches. Tarsuls lived only three or four years, and Parthenia's had died a few months previously. One of Stefan's recent kindnesses to his eldest daughter had been to surprise her with a replacement. The animal arrived already house-trained, but Parthenia was teaching it to pick and bring her ripe fruit from the garden's trees. There was always something fruiting, and all the children loved to eat the freshly picked produce.

Oriana and Ferne were playing hide-and-go-seek, Castiel was bouncing a ball against a house wall. Nahla stood at her brother's side, begging him to play with her, but he was acting as though she didn't exist.

The children had, as usual, quickly and instinctively diverged into their two groups. The ones who had inherited her mage abilities and the two who hadn't—Castiel and Nahla—stayed subtly but distinctly apart. Oriana and Ferne would gladly have allowed Nahla to join in their game, but she preferred the company of Castiel, even though he was cool and dismissive toward her. At thirteen years of age, he was also five years older than her, while the twins, at twelve years old, were closer in age to Nahla. Yet still Faye's youngest daughter never gave up on her unrequited affection for Castiel. And though he rarely gave her the time of day, he was more often than not neutral in his attitude, whereas he clearly despised the others.

Of all her children, Castiel was the most like Stefan, Faye was forced to admit. In that regard, it was just as well he hadn't inherited mage power. She suspected that if he had, he would have been a dark mage, drawing energy from the unseen matter of the universe and using his ability to cause pain and create havoc.

Though she didn't know how to perform the test that would confirm her intuition, she guessed that Parthenia, Oriana, and Ferne were star mages like herself. Darius, however, she suspected was a spirit mage who relied on the power generated by living things.

Spirit mages were sensitive to emotions and the waxing and waning of the life force. On more than one occasion, Darius had shown himself to be highly receptive and responsive to the feelings of those around him, most recently during the horrifying episode in the breakfast room. He had picked up on both her terror and his father's fury.

Spirit mages were delicate beings who were happiest when protected from highly emotional states. Pushed to an extreme, they could lose their abilities, yet Faye could not explain that to Stefan. He would only be interested in what Darius meant in terms of how he could use him. Affecting the emotions of others at will, sometimes even being able to read their minds and speak to them without words would, to Stefan, only be an extremely useful weapon.

As if by thinking of him Faye had summoned him, Stefan appeared at the open double doors into the garden, back from his trip. She felt a chill like the sun had gone behind a cloud, though the sky was its usual clear, rosy blue. None of the children had noticed their father. They continued to play, and Parthenia continued to praise and stroke her tarsul to reward it for bringing her a fruit.

Stefan saw Faye watching him. He gave her a sarcastic nod and moved from his position of leaning against the door frame to walk toward his eldest child. She had crouched down to pat the tarsul. Stefan stood over her, his hands on his hips.

"How is he doing?" he asked her. "You seem to be doing an excellent job of training him. What did you name him?"

Parthenia said a name Faye didn't catch and stood up, brushing dust from her pants.

"It isn't as pretty as your name, my dear," Stefan said, "but I like it. What does it mean?"

Parthenia smiled in response to her father's compliment. "It doesn't mean anything. I made it up."

"Oh, well, it suits him. What have you taught him to do?"

Parthenia instructed the animal to perform various tricks, including standing on its head, playing dead, and walking only on its hind legs. Finally, she made it go and pick a fruit for her father, which it presented on open palms with a bow.

"Wonderful," Stefan said, laughing as he took the offered fruit. "What a clever animal, and what a clever mistress to train it so well."

"Thank you, Father,' Parthenia said.

Faye grimaced at the grateful tone in her daughter's voice.

"What's wrong, Mother?" Darius asked. He was lying on his

stomach with his arm in the pond, trying to catch a fish. His dark brown hair had flopped over his face and his cheeks were flushed.

"It isn't anything important," she replied. "Have you caught a fish yet? Remember to be gentle if you do."

"Oh, I'm always gentle. I don't want to make them feel bad, because then I feel bad too."

Faye looked down on her youngest child. His ability was growing stronger by the day. She would have to prevent Stefan from finding out the truth about his six-year-old son.

Though she'd discovered a firestone in the garden, she hadn't been able to collect it. Stefan had ordered the servants to watch her around the clock. Her maid even stayed with her when she bathed. If only she could make her own elixir. She could warn Carina and perhaps she could even Cast to effect an escape for her children and herself. She wasn't sure how they would survive outside the estate's walls and avoid detection by the Sherrerrs, but perhaps they could do it.

If she couldn't Cast, her only hope lay in the other ruse she'd planned. The symptoms of her disease were growing more pronounced. Perhaps in another few weeks she would be so sick she would have to travel to the capital for emergency treatment. There, surely the greater freedom would give her more opportunities to escape. In the capital they would stand a better chance of getting off the planet.

She would have to allow herself to become seriously ill to do it, but it was a risk she was willing to take.

Faye had been watching Parthenia and Stefan as she weighed her options, then her husband did something that snapped her to attention. He put his hands on the waist of his adolescent daughter and regarded her figure.

"You're filling out most pleasantly, Parthenia. Becoming a young woman. We must see about getting you some new clothes more suitable for you. Some dresses and things not quite so childish. Would you like that?"

Parthenia was blushing. She looked uncomfortable and a little afraid. "Yes, Father, I would."

"There's my good girl. Perhaps you and your mother can go on a little shopping trip, as mothers and daughters do. Pick out some cloth and have a dressmaker sew you the latest fashions. But you must promise me you won't go flirting with anyone while you're in town.

That wouldn't be at all becoming, would it? You mustn't forget that you'll always be my little girl."

He pulled her close and planted a kiss on her cheek. It wasn't the fond peck of a father to his child. Stefan pressed his lips closely against her soft skin and took his time.

Faye stared in disbelief. Stefan's eyes were closed, but then he opened them and, turning, gazed directly into hers, giving her a broad wink.

"Mother," Darius said, "what's wrong?"

Thirty

As Faye prepared to go into town with Parthenia, her mood was low. She couldn't shake the image of her horror of a husband giving her daughter that intimate, inappropriate kiss. His shameless wink had seemed to convey only one message, and it was one Faye could hardly bear to contemplate.

Stefan had commented recently that her childbearing days seemed to be over. She knew how little he truly loved the mage children she had provided him, while at the same time he wanted more due to the power they gave him and his clan. Now she'd borne him all the offspring she could, was it possible he planned on committing incest with his daughter? Faye's stomach turned at the thought. She hadn't been able to eat since the previous day.

Parthenia came down the stairs in the hall of the grand mansion, buttoning her coat. What Stefan had said was true, she was growing into a young woman. She was a head taller than Faye and she'd lost her child's figure over the recent few months.

She seemed calm and collected, as if she had forgotten or gotten over the embarrassment and confusion her father's embrace had caused. She gave Faye a quick smile as she reached the bottom of the stairs.

Faye couldn't remember when it had occurred, but at some point in her adolescence, Parthenia's attitude toward her had changed. She'd become distant and reserved. Faye had never figured out if it was because she saw her as competition for her father's affection, or if it was only a natural consequence of her growing up.

Some days, when the ache for the loss of Carina was particularly bad, she would imagine her first daughter wouldn't have been the same way. Then she would feel guilty and resolve to never again compare her children's displays of affection.

They went out together and climbed into the smaller, four-seater Sherrerr autocar. Two servants sat in the front. Nate was their chauffeur as usual, and another servant called William had come along. Both servants were Faye and Parthenia's guards and captors.

Nate input the destination and the car set off. He had been with the family for many years, and Faye had sometimes suspected he didn't approve of what went on in the household, but of course he couldn't say or do anything about it. The only people who worked for the Sherrerrs were either foolish or had little left to lose. Faye suspected Nate belonged to the latter category. Everyone knew that though the working conditions were good, employment with the Sherrerrs was a life sentence. Only idiots or those who didn't have another way of feeding themselves or their family asked for a job.

Faye and Parthenia sat together in silence as the car drove smoothly toward the town. Faye wished there was a way she could speak to her daughter out of earshot of the servants, but she might as well have wished for the moon. She wanted to reassure Parthenia she would do everything in her power to protect her from her predatory father, weak though her power was. Perhaps it was best she could say nothing.

Nate turned around and asked for confirmation of the textile merchant's shop he had input into the autocar.

"Yes, that's the one," Faye replied. "Do you remember it, Parthenia? I think we went there last year."

"Yes, I remember, Mother. Will you be taking some fabric too?"

"No, I won't. This trip is for you."

"That's right. Father didn't say you could, did he?"

Parthenia's face was half-turned away as she spoke, and Faye thought she saw an odd expression flit across it. An intense emotion had affected her daughter. If Darius had been there he would have picked up on it immediately, but Faye didn't possess his powers. She only knew her daughter was feeling something deeply.

"That's right," Faye replied. "This day is all yours."

Parthenia nodded, not removing her gaze from the wide, dusty plain outside. She didn't seem particularly happy about the trip. Faye guessed that perhaps the meaning of her father's actions was weighing heavily on the child after all. She reached over and took her daughter's hand, and the two sat hand in hand all the way into town until the autocar stopped outside the textile store.

The general shoppers were in the process of leaving. The owner was shooing them out the door, concern in his eyes as the Sherrerr car drew up and parked. A few pedestrians gazed curiously into the tinted windows, unable to see the occupants. Faye waited until the textile merchant had chased the people off before leaving the car and going into the store.

She always felt bad about taking things from the town's shopkeepers, but she had to. What was more, she had to take the best of what they had to offer. Stefan would be angry if they returned with anything second best.

Parthenia had gone over to look at a bolt of thick, rich purple fabric. Faye joined her and ran her hand down the material. It had a faint sheen.

"A very good choice, mistress," said the textile merchant. "That's a rare one. Comes from offplanet. Made from a plant that won't grow here. That's its natural color. Can you tell?"

Faye looked closely at the material. Its color was indeed a little uneven and not a single block of one shade, indicating the material hadn't been dyed in a factory. "It's very beautiful," she said to the store owner and then to her daughter, "It would suit you, Parthenia." She was speaking the truth. Parthenia had inherited her olive skin and dark hair and the deep purple complemented her coloring.

"Okay," Parthenia said. "I'll take this one. What else would you recommend?" she asked the merchant.

Nate, who had entered the shop with them while the other servant remained with the car, lifted up the entire bolt of material and took it out. Faye saw him placing it inside the roof box, ready to take to the dressmaker. It was a seemingly innocuous act, yet it was odd. The textile merchant would normally send over the fabric himself. That was how they'd always done it before. Was it possible Nate intended to give her and Parthenia a small break from their constant surveillance?

The merchant was busily showing her daughter a crimson fabric that would also look good on her. Faye went to the shop window and looked out into the street. Two small crowds had gathered on each side, a respectful distance away.

"I have a new previewer, if mistress would like to try it," the textile merchant was saying to Parthenia.

"I guess so," she replied without enthusiasm.

The man escorted her into a back room. Faye could hear him explaining the instructions. The machine would allow her daughter to see herself in any of the fabrics and styles she selected. For a moment, Faye was alone in the shop.

Then the owner returned. "Can I interest you in anything today, ma'am?"

"No, thanks. We're only picking up things for my daughter." Her heart began to race. Did she dare ask him what was on her mind? She had to take the chance. It would be the only one she would get. "I guess you must have heard about my son's kidnapping."

"Oh yes, of course. It was terrible, terrible news. Everyone was so relieved when he was returned home. I trust the young master is well?"

"Yes, he's very well, thanks. But..." Faye took a deep breath. "The person who brought him back... I didn't have the opportunity to thank her. I wanted to give her a reward. Is she still in town?"

"Do you mean the owner of the merc company, mistress? No. She left immediately after the young master was returned."

"No, not her. I meant the young soldier who brought him back to our estate."

"Oh, the merc," said the merchant. "Yes, she stuck around for quite a while. No one seemed to know why. But she's gone now. Got into a fight with..." He blanched and swallowed. "She was highly disrespectful toward some employees of Mr Sherrerr, ma'am. After they beat her thoroughly for it, she left town."

Relief and sadness intermingled in Faye. Though she was pleased her eldest daughter was out of immediate danger, she was also sad to hear she'd suffered at the hands of her husband's men.

"Though oddly enough, she left a part of herself behind," the merchant went on. He had the look of someone with a juicy piece of gossip.

Faye gave him the prompt he was seeking. "What do you mean?"

"Well..." The man edged closer. Outside, Nate was leaning one elbow on the roof of the autocar and chatting with William, who was sitting inside. "The altercation the soldier interfered with involved a splicer, ma'am," said the merchant. "Although your husband's men beat her in the end, of course, she put up a very good fight. The splicer grabbed some of her hair, and he's planning on selling her code for conception treatment."

"He's what?" Faye exclaimed. "He's going to use her code to engineer embryos? Surely that isn't legal."

The man made a dismissive gesture. "We don't tend to pay a lot of attention to what is and isn't legal around here, ma'am." He made a face that said, *As you know too well.*

It was a good point. Faye was, after all, stealing from the man's shop. "What splicer was it?" she asked.

"He's just over the way, ma'am, but I hope you won't tell him it was me who informed you. I was only chatting. I didn't know you would take it further."

"Don't worry," Faye replied. "I'm not going to have him prosecuted, but I would like to talk to him."

Parthenia came out of the back room. "I'll take those three." She pointed at the red fabric she'd been looking at earlier and two others, a green and a velvety black. "Do you think that's enough, Mother?"

"Yes, I think so. We have to go to the dressmaker next. But I have another errand to run first. Would you mind waiting here for me for a few minutes?"

Parthenia looked shocked. Doing anything other than exactly what they were supposed to do while in town was strictly forbidden. In front of the textile merchant, however, she could say nothing. "Okay, Mother. I'll wait."

Faye had no choice. If the splicer had Carina's code, whatever child he helped create would be a mage. The child's ability would be traced back to her daughter, and Carina's freedom and possibly her life would be forfeit. Stefan would make Faye pay dearly for an impromptu visit to the splicer, but it would be worth it.

Thirty-One

The news of what Faye had done arrived at the estate before she did. Stefan was waiting for them on the steps.

"What's Father doing?" Parthenia asked as soon as she saw him. "Why is he standing there?"

"I'm not sure," Faye replied, though she knew exactly why.

The autocar drew up and they got out. Faye stared unflinchingly into her husband's eyes, not disguising her hatred. She'd already defied him. Whatever punishment he had in store, she would suffer it whatever she did.

"Go inside, Parthenia," Stefan said quietly. "Dinner will be served in a moment. Your mother and I will be eating alone."

Her daughter's gaze flicked between them before she obediently did as her father instructed. As soon as she'd gone into the dining room, Stefan gripped Faye painfully around her upper arm and pushed her ahead of him. He took her to the rear of the house to an open door that, despite her earlier bravery, made her quail. It had been years since she'd passed through that door and gone down those steps.

The cellar was where she'd spent her first few months in the Sherrerr mansion, tethered to the walls, beaten and raped day in and day out. For months, she'd remained defiant, refusing to give up her secrets, until Stefan had finally broken her by preying on her love for Kris. She'd told him everything in the foolish hope it would save Kris' life. Even then, she hadn't understood how truly depraved and evil Stefan was. Even then, she'd imagined he would keep his word. Right up until that final moment...

Faye gasped and shook her head, holding onto the door frame. Tears welled in her eyes.

"Not so courageous now, are you, my darling?" Stefan thrust his shoulder against her back, forcing her through.

She stumbled and fell down the steps, hitting her head at the bottom. The next thing she knew, Stefan was hauling her to her feet and pushing her into a cell. Restraints were fixed to the walls, and he slammed her wrists and ankles into them before marching back to the door and closing it.

"Think you can defy me and get away with it, you bitch?" he yelled. He grabbed her face and pushed her head against the wall. He ground his lips into hers, pressing the weight of his body against her. When he pulled away, Faye felt a trickle of blood run down her chin.

"Why did you go to the splicer? What did you want from him?"

Faye turned away her head.

"Never mind. I'll find out soon enough. The man may have packed up his business and left town, but my men are on his tail. They'll soon catch him and he'll tell me whatever I need to know." Stefan began pacing up and down the cell, his rage working higher. "I tried, Faye. I tried so hard with you. Those things I had to do in the beginning were unfortunate, but they were necessary. Afterward, if you had only allowed yourself to move on, everything could have been perfect between us. I wanted it to be perfect. But you were too stubborn and unforgiving. I hate it that you bring out this side of me. I hate it that you make me do this to you. But it's the only way. It's the only way to make you understand you must obey!"

"It isn't me who does this to you, Stefan," Faye said. "You like to think you're wonderful, don't you? You think giving me and our children this luxurious lifestyle means something. That all you ask, all I do for you when I Cast, is just payment for all you give me. But this life doesn't mean a thing because I didn't choose it. You treat us like your slaves and playthings. But we're people, with feelings and opinions of our own, though they might as well not exist for all the notice you take of them. You use us and control us, and when we don't do as we're told, you throw a tantrum like a five year old. Only you're a grown man. A grown man who's evil and out of control. *I* don't do this to you, Stefan. This is who you are."

He ran at her and punched her in the stomach. Pain radiated up, and Faye slumped against the restraints. Her mouth flooded with saliva. She vomited, and the vomit ran down her dress.

Stefan curled his lip in disgust. "You're revolting. Do you know that? Look at yourself." He grabbed the neckline of her dress and ripped it from her. Then he tore away her underclothes until she was naked. If he noticed the bruises her disease had created on her body, he didn't seem to think anything of them.

He kissed her roughly again and undid his belt.

———

When Stefan had finally exhausted himself by taking out his anger on her, he undid the restraints. Faye collapsed to the floor of the cell. She lay still, waiting for him to leave. But he hadn't quite finished. He squatted down, grabbed her hair, and lifted up her head so he could look her in the eyes.

"I haven't decided what I'll do with you yet. I may tell the children you've taken ill and are being treated at a clinic for a couple of days. Perhaps I'll allow you to resume your role within the household. I'm sure you still have some skills to impart to our offspring. I hope tonight's lesson will encourage you to give up those final secrets. On the other hand, I may just leave you here. The room is soundproofed. No one will hear you, and none of the servants will dare to interfere with your slow, agonizing demise."

He abruptly let go of her head and her skull hit the cold flagstones. Stefan stood and straightened his clothes. "In a way, this is so unfortunate. I sometimes wonder how different things might have been if only you had listened to reason in the very beginning. Imagine the life you could have led if you had consented willingly to join my clan. You would have been adored —no—worshipped for your powers. A far greater Sherrerr than myself would have claimed you as his own and there would have been nothing I could have done about it. And, floating high on the success afforded by your abilities, the Sherrerrs would have risen above all our competitors.

"But you chose a different path. Everything you've given me has been in tiny, niggardly doses, won at great effort. You made me work so hard for it all, Faye. Why? What was the point? So that you could end up back here again, where we began our time together? Such a shame. What a wasted opportunity." He went to the door. "But, never mind. I got what I wanted in the end. And you know what, my dear? When you say this is who I really am, I think you may have a point."

He smirked and left.

After several minutes, when she was sure he wouldn't be back for a while, Faye slowly moved into a sitting position. She probed inside her mouth with her tongue, working it up between her swollen gums and her teeth. The hairs she'd demanded from the splicer were still there. She pulled them out. Three long, black strands. All she needed was elixir. If she could only get that, she could Cast. She would Cast Locate to find out where Carina was. If she was still on the planet, she would Cast Send and tell her to leave.

Then, if she had enough elixir, she would Transport all her children far, far away. Perhaps she could Transport them to a remote place where they could escape recapture by the Sherrerrs.

And then she would kill Stefan.

Thirty-Two

From where she was standing, Carina could see the ridge she and Bryce had peeked over when they were watching the Sherrer stronghold. It was white with snow against a cloudy white sky and obscured further by grayish snowflakes swirling down. She would have given a lot to be up there again and not freezing her toes off working for the Sherrerrs.

She'd only just made it through Basic, receiving the dubious reward of recruitment into the Sherrerr forces. Still bearing the marks of her beating, Carina had been put to work at the lowest tier of the clan's military wing.

It was a bizarre conclusion to her and Bryce's effort to reconn the Sherrerr stronghold. As she stood on sentry duty on the fortress shuttle pad, Carina struggled to wrap her head around it. If the clan hadn't been undertaking their massive recruitment drive, she doubted the two of them would have been so lucky. As it was, she guessed their youth and lack of any military equipment had counted in their favor. Raynott, the officer who had overseen Carina's interrogation, might not really have believed their story, but she probably thought they were young and poor enough to quickly switch allegiance on the promise of a job, shelter, and a steady supply of food.

Which wasn't so far from the truth. Carina had no loyalty to the Dirksens. They had mercilessly tortured the little boy she had rescued. However, neither did she bear any love for the Sherrerrs. As far as she was concerned, both clans were as bad as the other. The sooner she could escape her accidental employment and go offplanet—preferably outsystem—the better.

She had only one problem: Bryce. She couldn't bring herself to escape and leave him behind. She wasn't sure how long he could survive without the medication that kept his disease under control but it certainly wasn't forever. The Sherrerrs would probably work him until he was too sick to go on and then put him outside the gates. If she left without him she would always have his fate on her conscience. She had to find him and Cast Transport to get them both out of there.

The only information about Bryce she'd managed to glean was that he'd been put to work dealing with slops and garbage somewhere in the bowels of the fortress. There could be no sneaking off during her long work hours to visit that area—she was certain that Raynott had given the order that she was to be closely watched—and when she wasn't working, she wasn't allowed to visit the men's quarters. Male and female soldiers were kept strictly segregated during their brief hours of downtime. She could only hope to find him while he was working and she wasn't.

New recruits were arriving at the fortress every day. Her guess that the Sherrerrs were developing a new weapon had been incorrect. The stronghold was for military training. No one said so, but there could only be one conclusion drawn from the fast, large increase in numbers of troops: the Sherrerrs were preparing for a conflict of some kind. Perhaps they were expecting an attack, but it seemed from the training they were planning an assault.

She stamped her feet. The sentry box on the fortress' roof provided only a little protection from the falling snow. Her boots had created a puddle of icy slush that had penetrated the leather. Her Sherrerr uniform was warmer than her civvies, but standing still for hours meant a chill had inevitably set in. She guessed she had only ten or fifteen minutes of guard duty remaining, but the seconds were dragging past.

When the comm in her helmet chirped, Carina's mood brightened, thinking her replacement had arrived. But the message was only to tell her and her fellow sentry to step below for five minutes. A shuttle was coming in.

They waited in the stairwell until the roar and vibration of the shuttle's landing ceased, then went out onto the roof once more. The air was noticeably warmer from the burst of energy from the shuttle's engine as it landed. A sleek, expensive vessel had arrived, a domestic model, bearing the Sherrerr insignia on each side.

The portal slid smartly open and the ramp extended. A tall, handsome, elegant man cloaked in furs and wearing a cravat and a haughty expression appeared, followed by a man and woman who looked like servants. Without a glance at Carina or the other sentry, the man paused a moment to allow the security scanner to confirm his identity, then he disappeared inside the fortress.

He was probably a high-ranking member of the Sherrerr clan, Carina mused, though not of the military arm. Still, his arrival added weight to her earlier assessment of the situation—the Sherrerrs were planning a big event of some kind. Their extensive extended family was involved.

She received the notification she was waiting for. Her replacement took over and she went down into the stronghold, making her way to the mess room. There, she grabbed a hot drink to help her warm up before setting out to find Bryce. If she could only touch him, it would be enough to anchor the Transport and she could whisk them both far away. Not off the planet, but hopefully somewhere they would be safe from detection.

The garbage processing area was in the basement of the fortress. Free passage through the building, even to such unsavory areas, wasn't allowed for lowly grunts like her. But though Carina didn't have the authority to go to Bryce's work site, she thought she would try. She went down the curving stone stairwell, sipping her drink and appreciating the feeling that was returning to her fingers and toes.

She patted the bottle of elixir at her side to reassure herself she hadn't forgotten it in her sleep-deprived haze when she suited up that morning. She'd made the liquid in the early hours. If she could only see Bryce for a few moments she was sure she could Transport him. The Cast might work with only her mental image of the young man, of course, but it wasn't worth the risk.

The last time she'd used Transport was to rescue the boy the Dirksens had kidnapped. She'd moved enemy soldiers a kilometer away from the scene of engagement. With one of the soldiers in front of her, it had been easy to fix on the others through the common factor of their uniform. Transporting an individual who was out of sight was much more difficult.

She turned the final bend in the stairwell. Her heart sank. There was no human guard at the waste processing zone for her to persuade to let her in for five minutes. The door was locked and unmarked except for a window the size of a human face. She looked through it but she could only see darkness. On the wall next to the door was an ID scanner. She guessed it was worth a try.

"Private Lin," she said into the mic while the device scanned her face and retinas.

A warm female voice said, "Entry denied."

Carina cursed. She was all ready to get them both out of there. She only needed a couple of minutes. Should she wait around? Maybe someone else would arrive and allow her to sneak inside with them, though she doubted anyone would risk being disciplined for her. She looked through the window again. This time she could see a light. A door was open, illuminating a dark hall. Someone was coming out, and as the figure entered the hall, motion-activated lights flickered on.

A burly soldier was walking toward her. It was one of the men who had beaten her up.

She hesitated. He was one of the last people she wanted to meet, but he was also the only person who could help her right now. The man's lip curled when he recognized Carina's face in the window. Pulling open the door he said, "Hello there. I heard you made it through Basic. I was surprised. I should have roughed you up better."

"You roughed me up well enough, thanks," Carina said as she tried to side-step the man and slip past him.

"Wait a minute," the soldier said. He raised his arm, blocking the gap. "Where do you think you're going? Off to see your boyfriend? You don't have authority to go in there. But I don't want you to go away unsatisfied. Why don't we forget what happened and be friends? Maybe I could scratch your itch for you."

"No thanks," said Carina. "Your version of foreplay doesn't do a thing for me."

The soldier laughed. "And here I was thinking you were the type to like it rough. We can try a different style if you want. Come on, you must be desperate for it to try to sneak in here. The smell's bad enough to knock you out better than I did. I'm not so off-putting, am I?"

The conversation was taking a turn Carina had no interest in or time for. She was about to tell the man where to go and give up on her attempt to see Bryce when another of the doors in the hall opened. Carina glimpsed a familiar face. "Bryce," she called.

"Carina," Bryce said, coming through the door with a large sack on his back. "It's great to see you. Are you okay? I was worried about you."

"Yeah, I'm fine," she replied. She'd finally found him, but she couldn't Transport them both with the obnoxious bully looking on.

"What a touching reunion," said the burly soldier, "but if you don't want *me*, I'm not going to let you have *him*." He pushed her roughly out of the way and slammed the door.

At the same time, Carina's comm chirped. "Private Lin, report to the shuttle pad in fifteen minutes with full equipment, ready to ship out."

She looked through the window at Bryce. It was hopeless. She couldn't Cast in front of the Sherrerr soldier. She had no choice but to leave, not knowing when or if she could return to rescue her friend.

THIRTY-THREE

When Carina arrived at the shuttle pad, the domestic vessel that had arrived earlier had left and in its place was a craft occupying the entire rooftop. Along with the other soldiers who had been ordered to board it, she went up the ramp and inside the vessel. She stowed her equipment and took a seat. The craft was military style and reminded her of her merc band's shuttle—bare bones inside but solid and tough.

As she fastened her harness, the soldier in the seat next to her held out his hand. "Mandeville."

Carina shook it. "Lin."

"I haven't seen you around. You new?"

"That's right. I started a few days ago. You?"

"Six months in. First time I've gone into space, though. What's up with your face? Did you fall down the mountain on your way over?"

"Ha, no. I accidentally walked into some fists. Do you know what this mission's about?"

"I haven't heard anything. I'm guessing they'll tell us when we're aboard ship."

The shuttle was quickly filling up, and the vibration through the floor signaled that the pilot was warming the engines. A female soldier took the seat on the other side of Carina. She was a well-muscled woman who reminded her of a former fellow merc and bunk mate, Atoi.

Raynott, the officer who had ordered Carina's beating, entered the cabin. "Helmets sealed everyone," she said. "Taking off in two minutes."

Carina put on her helmet and sealed it. Now anything she said would broadcast to everyone, so she stayed quiet for the trip up to the Sherrerr ship.

When they arrived and the soldiers filed out of the shuttle bay, Raynott ordered them into formation. She addressed the group. "In four days we'll arrive at our engagement site. Until then, you'll do exercises aboard ship. You'll also be issued with new firearms and receive training on them so you know which is the mean end. Wait here until a crew member arrives to assign quarters."

As Raynott left, the soldiers broke ranks and removed their helmets. Carina guessed there were about a hundred and fifty of them, but as she looked around, the Sherrerr ship seemed large for such a number. The shuttle bay they had just left had been massive. Going by its size, she guessed the ship had a capacity of two thousand or more. She hadn't known the Sherrerrs possessed such large warships.

Over the next couple of days, Carina slotted easily into the ship's routine. Even more so than at the fortress on Ithiya, the lifestyle took her back to her merc days. She knew the ropes, but she wasn't happy about re-familiarizing herself with them. Though she didn't have a problem with fighting if she had to, she didn't feel like a soldier anymore. Her short time working for the Sherrerrs had really brought home to her the fact that she'd moved on.

Yet even as she was adjusting to her new view on life, she had an idea that would involve behaving like a good soldier for just a little longer. If she could distinguish herself in whatever conflict they had coming up, perhaps she could exploit the favor she might receive from Sherrer higher-ups for special permission to visit Bryce.

When the troops performed military exercises in the emptied shuttle bay aboard ship, Carina kept her head down and worked hard. Experience had taught her that among the average group of soldiers, even such simple behavior helped you stand out. Or at least it helped you avoid the ire of the commanding officer, which was just as beneficial.

On the day they were to go into battle, Raynott assembled the soldiers in a briefing room. She brought up a holo of a moonscape. It was a large ice moon with a thin, unbreathable atmosphere. The holo zoomed in, and an installation became visible. The place had looked like it was just another part of the rocky, icy surface until the camera got in close.

"This is Banner's Moon," said Raynott. "We stumbled across the place during part of a general surveillance exercise in Dirksen territory. The building you see is invisible to scanners and only visible to the naked eye at close range. The Dirksens clearly have something to hide here, though what exactly, we aren't sure yet. Not that that's going to stop us from storming the place and fucking their shit up." She smirked.

"Seriously," Raynott continued, "we're guessing they might be developing a new weapon or something similar. Whatever it is, we want it. So don't go blowing up anything unless it's absolutely necessary. Feel free to kill as many of the enemy as you like."

Raynott went on to explain what their company's role would be in the assault. They were to attack the facility from the spinward side. Theirs would be the first assault wave—in some ways the most dangerous, but they also had the element of surprise on their side.

When she'd finished laying out the finer details of the assault, she said, "Questions?"

Mandeville raised his hand. Raynott nodded at him.

"Do we have any clues about what we might be looking for?" he asked.

"If it is a weapon, even if it's only at the prototype stage," Raynott replied, "you can bet they'll be using it on you. That's probably the biggest flag you'll see. Other than that, follow the path of most resistance. Whatever they seem keenest to protect, whatever area has the strongest defense, go for it."

A small amount of chatter started up, which Raynott silenced with, "There's something I forgot to mention. We're blowing the place from orbit forty-five minutes after the first assault. We think we have about that long before the nearest Dirksen ship arrives. You'll see the countdown on your visor overlays. Get in, get what you can, and get out. You better be back here on time or you're not going home."

Some of the soldiers shifted uncomfortably. Even Carina with her experience of the callous attitude of her merc band's owner was a little shocked. The Sherrerrs weren't messing around. They would try to take whatever the Dirksens had on their moon, but if they couldn't have it, they were going to make sure the Dirksens wouldn't either. For many of the soldiers, it was their first live engagement. She hoped it wouldn't also be their last.

The briefing was over. The soldiers were told to go to the shuttle bay and into a waiting shuttle. Carina strapped herself in, secured her helmet, and checked her weapon. The firearm she'd been given was a new type of pulse rifle. It produced concentrated fire designed to penetrate the latest designs of armor, though they'd been warned it would only penetrate in one shot at close range.

Always the military tech race continued. Armor was developed to resist the current level of firepower, so more effective guns were designed, resulting in better-designed armor, and so on. Carina wondered whether the Dirksens were developing a weapon that pierced the armor she was wearing.

The shuttle lifted and carried them out of the Sherrerr ship. Mandeville gave her a thumbs up and she nodded. They'd become better acquainted over the previous days of training. He was a nice guy. In fact, most of the soldiers were just regular people. None were seasoned veterans like the mercs she'd previously worked with. She wasn't used to her fellow troops being normal. Some of them looked scared, reminding her of herself at her first engagement when she was sixteen. Her mentor and commanding officer, Captain Speidel, had gotten her through it safe and sound. She no longer needed the poor, dead captain, but that didn't stop her from missing him.

Suddenly, they were dropping out of the sky so fast the shuttle's artificial gravity drive couldn't compensate, and Carina found herself lifting out of her seat. From somewhere to the right came the whine of a soldier's armor sucking up vomit that had erupted into his helmet. She wasn't so far from upchucking herself. She'd spent so long planetside she'd lost her space legs.

Only moments later the shuttle hit the ground. The doors snapped open. Carina undid her harness and ran out with the rest of the company into a barren, icy moonscape. They were a minute from a low mountain—no, that was the Dirksens' facility, and those dark spaces that looked like cave entrances were windows.

She was running. Get in, get what she could, get out. Weapon fire burst from the installation. The defenders had realized they were under attack. She zigzagged randomly. Soldiers began to fall. One hit the ground right in front of her. She jumped over the squirming figure. Was it Mandeville? With tinted visors obscuring their faces, it was hard to tell and her visor didn't bring up a name. She hoped it wasn't Mandeville.

She was at the window. Others who had reached there before her had broken through and the site was depressurizing fast. She jumped inside, vaulting with one hand on the window frame, her hybrid silicon armor impervious to jagged shards at the edge. She was inside. The Dirksens had killed the lights, but her helmet beamed out its own. Sweeping it around she saw hand-to-hand fighting, a jumble of bodies. Her visor overlay tagged the figures as friends and foe.

Someone lunged at her. She swept her rifle around and cracked the butt against her attacker's helmet. As he fell, she fired point blank into his chest, breaking the atmosphere seal. Gas poured out, condensing in the frigid air. Blood also sprayed from the opening and instantly froze.

A pulse round hit her from behind. Her suit's sensors flared, the repair mechanism triggered as she spun around, firing. The shot had come from a now-empty doorway. She ran through it, showering the hallway with fire. She hit two enemy soldiers but didn't cause them much damage. They fired back. More of her company poured through the opening. The two Dirksen soldiers turned to run but were quickly mowed down.

The corridor was clear, and she ran down it with other soldiers from her company. Her helmet was scanning and mapping the place, sending a real time positioning readout to her as she ran. The installation was vast. Much bigger than it had looked from the outside. It had to go underground too. They were heading into the heart of the building, but it was so far from the entrance, she doubted they could make it out in time before the Sherrerrs blew the place.

Then things went crazy. Everyone around her dropped to the ground. Screaming from her helmet comm was piercing her ears. It was the screaming of her fellow soldiers. Yet when she looked around, none of them seemed hurt. Their suits were intact and their bodies seemed undamaged, even if they were writhing around.

She turned down her helmet comm to its lowest setting so she could only just hear her fellow soldiers' shrieks. There was nothing for it but to continue the mission alone.

Thirty-Four

Carina jogged along the corridors, following the route the enemy soldiers had attempted to escape along. It led to a large space that looked like some kind of production facility. She figured this was her best bet for finding the reason for the installation.

Enemy units were ahead according to her visor overlay. She stopped dead. Approaching the next corner slowly, she peeked around it. Three enemy soldiers were in the corridor, but they were squirming on the ground as her own company's troops had. Their hands were over their heads as if something unbearable were happening to them.

She imagined if she could hear them, she would hear their screams. They were clearly too incapacitated to cause her any harm. She ran around the corner and right past the prone figures. After several similar encounters, she arrived at a grim sight. Scientists who hadn't been able to reach environment suits in time when the site depressurized had died. Their bodies, pop-eyed and frozen, were lying near a rectangular object the size of a large piece of luggage.

The device was resting in a steel cradle but it was half lifted out, as if someone had been trying to move it. Whether the instrument was important, Carina wasn't sure, but it could be and that was good enough for her. She grabbed its handle and tried to lift it, but the object was surprisingly heavy.

As she dropped it to adjust her hold, she noticed three small lights pulsing at the top corner. Out of curiosity, she touched the lights and found she could push them in. She pushed one home and the light went out. She pushed the other two until they clicked into position and became dark too. Unsure what she'd done, if anything, she grabbed the handle with both hands and lifted out the device.

Even in the moon's low gravity, she struggled to carry it. If she'd attempted to do the same on an average planet, she would never have been able. Stepping carefully past the splayed bodies of the scientists, Carina went out and began the journey back to the shuttle.

She'd lost track of time, she realized, and checked her visor overlay. Fifteen minutes until the countdown to blow the moon was due to begin. She was already sweating with the effort of carrying the device. Should she leave it behind? If the device was important, delivering it to the Sherrerrs could be just the kind of act that would win her a lot of favor. Carina struggled on.

What wouldn't she have given for an a-grav trolley? She'd heard such things existed but were insanely expensive. Or a powered exoskeleton. Her armor doubled her physical strength, but it was barely enough. She wasn't sure she would make it.

Her visor flashed. Three enemy units ahead. She dropped the device and walked forward. Hoping the enemy soldiers were in the same state they'd been when she'd passed them, she quickly stuck her head around a corner to assess the situation. The soldiers were up and walking, and they were heading her way. One of them had seen her.

A pulse round flew by so close to Carina's face it hurt her eyes, despite the deep tint of her visor. She turned and ran, but the corridor was straight with no cover. It was also so long she would be shot in the back before she reached the end of it. The only protection she had was the device.

She threw herself to the floor behind the block and rested the muzzle of her weapon on top of it. Not a moment too soon, for the barrel of a gun appeared and a barrage of rounds sprayed out. Carina ducked behind her cover. A second later, she raised her head just in time to see all three soldiers racing toward her.

She fired, hitting one in his thighs, which slowed him down a little but didn't seem to do much other damage. She hit the second square in his chest, but the round dispersed harmlessly. The soldiers ran on. She didn't stand a chance, but she continued firing.

Soon, she wondered why she was still alive. She should have been dead, if the soldiers had been firing at her, but they weren't—they were firing too high. Their pulse rounds passed over the device, as if they were trying to avoid hitting it.

She shot again, this time piercing one of the enemy unit's armor. The woman was down. Two more to go, but they were nearly upon her and she wouldn't have the protection of the device. Her heart in her mouth, she fired again. Her last shot. This was it.

Then one of the soldiers slumped forward, a hole in the back of his suit. His fellow turned, confused, and was met with concentrated weapon fire. Soldiers from her company came running up.

"What's that, Lin?" a voice said over her comm. She recognized it. Mandeville. He was still alive.

"I don't know," she replied. "It seemed important, so..."

"Move it, soldiers," came another voice. Raynott. "Shuttle's leaving in two minutes."

Two minutes?

"Can you help me with this?" Carina asked her rescuers. "It's very heavy."

With the help of the three soldiers from her company, Carina carried the device down the corridors while the seconds on her visor ticked down.

"Captain Raynott," Carina said into her mic. "We've found something. I don't know what it is but I've a feeling it's important. We're bringing it out, but we might not make the shuttle. Can you give us an extra minute or two?"

"Negative," came the reply.

"Let's leave it," said Mandeville.

Carina was torn. She wanted to bring the device to the Sherrerrs so she could save Bryce, but she didn't want to endanger her fellow soldiers. "You go. Leave me. I can make it."

But the three men didn't reply, and they didn't leave. The room where they'd broken into the facility was in sight. It was empty except for the bodies of those who hadn't made it. The shuttle was visible through the destroyed window.

The distance to the shuttle was around a minute's run, Carina remembered. She checked her visor. They had forty-five seconds.

With a supreme effort, they got the device out the window. Each soldier holding one part of the long handle that straddled the top of the device, they set off across the icy stone moonscape. Carina's lungs burned and her visor fogged as her suit struggled to clear the condensation of her hot breath on the frigid plastiglas.

At the top of the shuttle ramp a figure stood, beckoning them. Raynott.

Five seconds to go. It was too far. They weren't going to make it. Yet not one of the soldiers let go of their hold on that device. They wouldn't abandon the others to save themselves. The shuttle ramp began to rise and the air around the exhaust ports shimmered as the engines began to fire. Raynott stepped back.

They were at the ramp.

With a grunt of effort, the four soldiers lifted the instrument onto the rising ramp and leapt up. Carina didn't make it. She fell back and hit the ground. With horror, she watched the ramp rising out of reach. Just then, a head and shoulders appeared over the side, reaching down to her, telling her to jump.

She had only one chance. Carina jumped for her life. The soldier's hands caught her wrists. She found herself being hauled onto the closing ramp, rolling down to the access hatch. The ramp snapped closed. The shuttle took off.

There was no getting up while the shuttle pulled away at top speed, escaping the moon's gravity. Even Raynott was forced to the floor.

Carina lay still, listening to the sound of her ragged breathing, looking at the strange instrument that had nearly cost her and her fellow soldiers their lives. She hoped it would prove worth it.

Thirty-Five

Carina's palms were sweaty as she knocked on the door to the commander's office. It had been highly presumptuous of her to even request an audience with him, but the fact that he had granted it lent her courage. The door clicked and swung open a little. She pushed it the rest of the way and went inside.

The commander was speaking with a holo of the head and shoulders of a woman. He held up a finger to her to signal her to wait. The holo woman's hair was tightly groomed into a thick spiral rising from the top of her head. Her shoulders were bare, and she wore a sapphire-blue top that looked like the upper half of a dress.

Was this woman the Sherrerr mage who had sent Carina the pouch? She ached with frustration that there was no way she could find out. She had to give up on her dream and move on.

On the journey back from Banner's Moon, Raynott and the other officers aboard the ship had examined the device Carina had taken from the Dirksen installation, but as far as she knew they hadn't come to any conclusions. She explained that she'd pressed buttons and the lights had gone out. No one wanted to find out what happened if they turned the lights on again.

From what Carina could tell, turning off the lights had coincided with the lifting of the effect that had incapacitated the other soldiers. They hadn't been writhing in pain, she'd discovered, but terror. Everyone but her had been overcome with fear so intense they could do nothing but scream. Carina hadn't suffered any effects at all, but she hadn't told anyone that. They just assumed she'd managed to fight through the emotion, and she didn't correct them. Her natural immunity was odd. She wondered whether it had something to do with the genetics that gave her mage powers.

The fact that Carina, Mandeville, and the other two soldiers had managed to bring out the device, and at such a risk to their own lives, earned all of them plenty of credit among their peers and the higher ranks. Carina was hoping to exploit this.

The commander said goodbye to the woman. The holo faded.

"Private," said the commander, finally turning his gaze to her. His name was Calvaley and he was in his late middle years, but that was all Carina knew about him. She guessed as he wasn't a Sherrerr himself, he had some other close alliance with the clan.

"Sir," Carina replied, saluting.

"Well, what is it?" Calvaley said. "My time is precious."

"I was wondering, sir, if I might ask permission to visit the men's quarters. In daylight hours, just to talk to a friend of mine."

"And what makes you think you deserve that special privilege?" Calvaley's eyes were coal black and as hard as stone.

"I believe the device I helped remove from the Dirksens' moon will prove extremely useful to us, sir."

"Maybe it will." He stood and placed his hands on his desk as he leaned forward. "That doesn't mean you deserve any special recognition. You only did as you were commanded. Don't you think that's rather presumptuous of you, soldier?!" As he spoke, his tone grew louder, until by the time he got to the end of his sentence he was yelling, his face turning pink from the effort.

"Perhaps, sir," Carina replied coolly. "However, it doesn't hurt to ask."

The commander's anger fell away in a moment. He laughed. "Not easily intimidated are you? What's your name again?"

"Lin, sir. Private Lin."

He nodded as if filing the information away for later use. He sat down and drew his chair closer to his desk. "Yes. Permission granted." He flicked his hand at her, shooing her away. "Have fun talking to your friend, Private Lin."

Carina quickly left before Calvaley could change his mind. Finally, she could see Bryce. All their troubles would be over, or most of them at least. She bounded down the stairwell leading to the men's quarters. Mandeville had recognized Bryce from her description and told her where to find him when he wasn't working.

This time when she spoke her name into the scanner, the door lock clicked open. She went through. The hallway lights flicked on and she could read the signs next to the doors. She quickly found Bryce's dorm.

Before going in, she double checked she had her elixir with her. It would take only a moment to Transport them both away. She hoped her dumb luck would hold out and Bryce would be alone.

The door to the dorm opened and someone came out. It was the burly soldier who had beaten her again, of all people. She seemed fated to constantly run into the unpleasant man.

"Come to see your friend?" The man leered. "He's all yours."

He held open the door so she was forced to go under his arm to enter the room. When the nasty soldier didn't leave but stood in the doorway, his sick smile still decorating his face, she shoved his arm out of the way and closed the door.

"Urgh," she said, seeing Bryce sitting on a bottom bunk. "Does this thing have a lock?"

"Carina," he exclaimed. He came over and hugged her. "Thanks for coming to see me. I'm going crazy in here. It's nice to see a friendly face."

"How are you?" she asked. "Are you okay?" She thanked the stars the rest of the dorm was empty. He was alone.

He shrugged. "I've been better. How about you?" He reached up and touched the fading bruises on her face. "Looks like they roughed you up a bit too."

She grimaced. "Yeah, a bit. But I've had worse. What about you? How are your symptoms?"

"As good as I can expect. I need another dose of my medication, but the doctor says they don't supply it, only the preventative. Anyway, I'm glad you've come because I wanted to say I'm sorry I dragged you into this. It was all my idea. It was lucky they didn't kill us."

"Don't worry about it. I could have refused if I wanted. You didn't force me to come along. That's all behind us now. What we have to do next is get out of here."

"That's not possible," Bryce replied. "Believe me, I thought about it. The only way out that isn't via shuttle is through the main door, and that's guarded around the clock. Besides, I don't think I could make the journey back in my current state."

"Bryce," Carina said in a serious tone. "What if I told you I could get us out of here, but it would mean we could never meet again?"

"I'd say, that's great. And then I'd say, wait, why can't we meet again?"

"I can't even tell you that. Believe me, the less you know, the better for both of us."

"Now I'm really intrigued, and a little bit scared. Is what you're proposing dangerous?"

"Only for me. And it'll only be dangerous for you if the Sherrerrs catch you again. Then it'll also be dangerous for me."

"Huh?"

"I know it sounds crazy. If you don't want to take the risk, that's fine. I'll go now. This is the only chance I'm giving you. Take it or leave it."

"What'll happen if I say yes?"

"You'll end up somewhere near where we left the town."

"*What?*"

"Bryce," Carina exclaimed in frustration. "I can't explain. You have to decide now, quickly, before someone comes in. Whatever you choose, whether you say no and I go by myself, or you say yes and I get you out too, it's goodbye."

It was only as the words left her lips she felt the significance of what she was saying. Once Bryce knew what she could do, she couldn't risk being in his company again. She couldn't trust that he wouldn't betray her secret. She'd known that when she'd decided to help him. What she hadn't expected was just how sad it made her feel.

"I don't understand," Bryce said, "but you're saying this is it? I'll miss you."

"I'll miss you too. So you'll leave?"

"Why would I stay? Can I bring anything with me?"

"Yes, whatever you can hold."

He scanned the room. "Actually, I don't have anything."

"Me neither." Carina hadn't wanted to risk attracting suspicion by bringing a bag to the dorm. She took a breath. "Okay. Turn around." The less he saw of what she was about to do, the better.

Bryce gave her a quizzical look, then faced away from her, sitting sideways on the bed. Carina took out the bottle of elixir and sipped a mouthful. She placed her hand on Bryce's back. She didn't need to touch him to Transport him, but she wanted to say a final goodbye. The young man had been the closest thing to a friend she'd had in a long time. Forever, in fact.

She recalled an area between the mountains and the town they'd traveled from, where the countryside was empty of people. Next, she wrote the Transport character in her mind. The next moment, her hand was empty. Bryce had disappeared.

Carina looked sadly at the indent on the mattress where he'd sat a moment before. She sighed. It was her turn.

Thirty-Six

As Faye sat in the garden after breakfast, she pondered a paradox. Mages could create fire, but only when they had elixir to make the Cast, but to create the elixir, they needed fire. Thinking of such things focused her mind on the task that lay ahead. The mental activity also helped to distract her from the pain of seeing the shocked looks of her children when Stefan had let her out of the basement that morning.

The everlasting tension in the household had tightened to screaming pitch. No one spoke a word when she arrived at breakfast. Oriana had gasped and clutched her hand to her mouth. Ferne began to exclaim something but was cut short when Oriana elbowed him. Nahla said, "Father...?" but failed to finish her sentence when Stefan glared at her. Parthenia had studied her mother gravely before returning to her meal. Even little Darius seemed to understand the importance of not remarking on what had happened. When Faye had appeared, after taking one look at her he'd only stared down at his plate as he ate. Castiel had smirked.

After breakfast was over, the children virtually tiptoed away.

From Faye's viewpoint, the only good thing to have come from Stefan's most recent behavior was her new understanding of his feelings. She knew now that she was all-but valueless to her husband. He only hoped to glean what little she might have left to teach, then she would probably 'disappear' as a warning to their mage children of what would happen to them if they disobeyed.

What Stefan probably didn't guess was that this revelation gave her new power. His usual method of controlling her was through threatening the children's lives. Now she knew he wouldn't harm them. Only her own life was at risk—which hung by a thread anyway—and she had lost all fear.

Rather than making her give up her attempts to defy him, Stefan's actions gave Faye new strength and determination. She was going to Transport her children away from him if it was the last thing she did. Of course, they would all remain in danger of recapture. Stefan and the rest of his clan would leave no stone unturned in their search for them, but when they were all free to use their mage powers, they would have a chance of escape. It was a much better alternative to living in that miserable hole with their jailer father.

As she watched the garden, Faye became aware that she herself was being watched. Olivia hovered just out of sight through the open doors behind her. Stefan had departed early that morning by shuttle on one of his ever-increasing business trips, taking part in whatever big thing was happening with the Sherrerrs. If Olivia wanted to sneak to him to betray her, he wouldn't be back until the evening at the earliest.

"Olivia," she called. When her maid didn't immediately reply, she said, "For goodness sake, woman. I know where you are. Come here."

Olivia stepped out, not looking particularly shamefaced about being called out on her spying. Faye wondered if Stefan was dallying with her. If he was, she pitied the woman. "I want to have a bath. Please prepare one for me."

"A bath?" It was an odd time of day for the request, and puzzlement showed on the maid's face, underlain with suspicion.

"Yes, a bath. Have you suddenly turned deaf, or stupid? After what your master did to me, I want to try to ease my aches. Does that make sense to you?"

Olivia finally looked abashed. "Yes, ma'am."

"And ask Cook about herbs that help with healing. She may have some in the kitchen." It would buy her a little more time.

As soon as Olivia left, Faye went out into the garden. She walked directly to the spot where she'd seen the firestone, right before Stefan caught her. It was still there, in the exact same place, half-buried in the soft soil of a flower bed. She thanked the stars that her husband hadn't spotted it.

Her hands trembling with haste, Faye took out the bag she'd secreted under her skirt. It contained everything she needed, each item gathered from its individual hiding place. She set down the bottle of ingredients that needed only the final addition of fire to their mix to be transformed into elixir. She made a pile of thin, dry twigs on the stone path, then picked up the stone.

Faye didn't waste time checking she wasn't being watched. She didn't care anymore. She had this one opportunity to get her children out of that terrible place and she was going to take it. She took out the knife she'd slipped into the bag at breakfast and the fluffy tinder she'd hoarded for so long. After putting down the ball of fluff, she struck the stone against the steel knife blade.

It took her several tries, but eventually sparks flew onto the tinder. Three or four strikes later, the surface of the tinder glowed and black-ened in a few spots. Faye picked up the precious stuff and blew gently on it until it smoked. A slender tongue of flame rose, and she put the ball into the center of the kindling. Crouching close to the ground, her head on one side, she blew steadily into the piled sticks. They caught fire.

Faye place the metal bottle on the little fire. She cursed as she realized she didn't have any tongs to lift the hot bottle out again. She pulled down the sleeve of her dress to cover her hand. It would have to do.

After brewing elixir all her life and often in front of Stefan when teaching the children how to Cast, Faye knew within a heartbeat how long the mixture needed to warm. When the time was up, she reached into the flames with her covered hand and lifted it out. The thin mate-rial of her dress was poor protection from the heat, but Faye mentally blocked the burning pain of her fingers.

Gripping the bottle, she glanced around. She'd been lucky. The garden appeared to be empty.

She would normally allow the elixir to cool. It would be too hot to drink yet, but she couldn't waste any time. The process had taken so long, Olivia would have filled her bath and already be looking for her. She had only a few minutes at most.

Faye took a sip of the scalding liquid that sent fire down her throat as she swallowed it. First, she would Locate Carina and Send to her. Of all of them, she had the greatest chance of getting away and surviving.

She took out the three hairs she'd taken from the splicer and gripped them.

Faye closed her eyes, steadied her breathing and her mind, and Cast Locate.

If she was in the planetary system, Faye's Cast would mentally take her to her daughter. And when she knew exactly where she was, she could Send. It had been many years since Faye had used Locate. The business dealings of the Sherrerrs rarely required that Cast. Her mind lifted up into the sky and ballooned out over the landscape. She could see/feel the positions of her children directly below her. They were in separate rooms of the mansion, having their lessons.

Faye wrenched her mind from them. The Cast wasn't working well. It was confusing Carina with her other offspring. It had been so long since she'd seen her eldest child, aside from that glimpse of her from the autocar.

Had she already left the planet? Or maybe she'd gone to another region? It would explain why Faye was having problems finding her. Maybe she should make the Cast wider, though it would need more time and energy than she had. If she couldn't find Carina within the next few moments, she would have to give up and simply Transport the other children out.

Then she detected a tiny glow in the gray, shady landscape. It was deep within a mountain range. Faye's mind flew to the spot. The glow strengthened in brightness. It was her. She'd found Carina. She'd found her first born.

Now to Send. Without opening her eyes and losing her daughter's position, Faye took another sip of the burning liquid, which seared her tongue and throat once more. She wrote the character in her mind and formulated her message.

"Mother," a voice exclaimed.

Someone grabbed the bottle from her hand. Faye's eyes flew open. Parthenia's tarsul had the elixir in its paw. Parthenia was running down the path toward her, a look of terror on her face.

"You mustn't," Parthenia hissed. She took the bottle from her pet and tipped the contents into the soil. Faye knelt before her child, utterly dumbfounded.

"Ma'am," called Olivia. She appeared. "Ma'am, your bath is ready."

Olivia didn't give voice to the suspicion dancing in her eyes. Faye was in a ridiculous position, kneeling on the stone garden path for no reason whatsoever. Parthenia was rigid as she stared at her. Faye got up. "Thank you, Olivia. I'll be along shortly. I want to speak to Parthenia for a few moments."

"As you wish, ma'am," the maid said and left.

"What the hell did you think you were doing?" Faye asked her daughter as soon as Olivia was out of earshot. "Do you want to live under the control of that monster for the rest of your life? You've spoiled the only chance I had of getting us out of here."

"You mustn't defy Father," said Parthenia, a tremble in her voice. "You mustn't. He'll be very angry." She spun around and left without another word. Her pet loped along in her wake.

Had Faye not been beyond weeping, she would have wept. But she'd cried a lifetime of tears for her children and herself. She had none left. She could hardly believe she'd come so close to their escape only to be thwarted by her own daughter. Stefan had starved the girl of attention and affection so effectively, he'd turned Parthenia against her. The child would do anything to make her father like her.

But Faye hadn't given up. The firestone remained where she'd left it, undiscovered. Only Parthenia had seen the remains of the little fire she'd made. Olivia's view of it had been blocked by her daughter. Faye quickly buried the charred sticks under soil. Although Parthenia had taken her metal canister with her, she could find another somewhere and gather more elixir ingredients.

The next time she had the opportunity, she would Cast again. Eventually, she would succeed.

Olivia was approaching again. *Damn the woman.*

"Sorry, ma'am, but your bath is getting cold."

THIRTY-SEVEN

Stefan had sent a message they were all to wait for him before dinner was served as he would be late getting home that night. The dining room was silent as they waited. It was like the wake after a funeral, Faye mused. Only less convivial.

Parthenia was refusing to meet Faye's gaze. Whether it was out of anger, shame, fear, or another emotion, she couldn't tell. Her second eldest child had always been difficult to read in that way.

Time passed. The sky through the glass double doors darkened to starry blackness, and still Stefan didn't arrive.

Darius finally broke the silence. "Mother," he said, "I'm hungry."

"I know," Faye replied. "Father will be home soon, I'm sure. Then dinner will be served. Just be patient a little longer."

The small child kicked his legs and tapped his knife on his plate.

"Here he comes," exclaimed Nahla.

Out in the night sky, the glowing lights of the family shuttle approached. An almost-inaudible sigh of relief sounded in the room. Though she hated the very sight of her husband, Faye's stomach was empty and aching. She wished he would hurry up.

The family waited another quarter of an hour for the shuttle to land and for Stefan to arrive in the dining room. When he did, he seemed in unusually high spirits. He told Nate, who was attending, to be quick. "It's been a long day and I'm starving. Tell Cook to get that food in here fast, and it better be hot."

The servants also brought glowing lamps along with that night's dishes. The room had become gloomy, but to Faye the artificial lights didn't seem to push back much of the darkness. She wondered what had so invigorated her husband. She feared it was something involving them too, or else why had he wanted to gather them all around him?

The food arrived, and the children pounced on it until a sharp rebuke from Stefan made them behave more politely. They helped each other to portions and, when everyone's plate was full, ate in silence.

The cook had prepared a thick meat stew heady with spices and served in the upturned shell of the animal the meat had come from. It was an exotic species from the polar region, where the sun only rose for an hour or so per day. Along with the stew, there was a basket of leaves and herbs from the vegetable garden, picked that day. Homegrown, tiny nuts had been stirred into the leaves, and the oil they exuded had lent the foliage a soft sheen and savory flavor. The starch of the meal was supplied by the boiled, dried, and ground roots of a locally grown biennial plant that produced delicate, lilac flowers. Side dishes included pickled crustaceans and flower buds.

Over the years, Faye had gotten used to the food eaten by the locals, and whatever the family ate, it was always cooked to a rare perfection—the cook had worked at the most expensive restaurants in the capital city of the region. Yet often the meals tasted like cardboard, when she could bring herself to eat more than a few mouthfuls. Despite her hunger, that evening was one of those occasions. The chance to free her children and herself from bondage to her monstrous husband had come within her grasp, only to be snatched away. And by one of the very people she had been trying to help, the second child she had brought to life through pain and blood and deep sorrow.

She found herself chewing mechanically, the food moving around and around her mouth. She forced the mouthful down and took another.

Faye's thoughts on Stefan were also distracting her. Clearly something important had happened and he planned to make some sort of announcement at the end of the meal, or he wouldn't have made them all wait for him to return. Usually on such nights when he didn't make it back in time for the evening meal, Faye would be able to slip away to her room and avoid him while he ate alone.

She waited and watched as the family ate. It was almost comical watching them. Stefan was hungry after his long day, which made him eat faster than usual. The children knew they couldn't take another mouthful after he was finished, so they were trying to shove the food down their throats as quickly as they could, while at the same time trying to avoid attracting Stefan's attention and accompanying wrath.

Finally, her husband put down his cutlery and signaled to Nate. Castiel risked another forkful of stew, but the rest of the children's cutlery clattered to their plates. Darius looked sorrowfully at a lump of ground root he hadn't managed to eat in time.

The servant who had been waiting just outside the door with the pudding immediately entered. It was Olivia, doubling up on her duties. The strain of holding the heavy dish while she waited for the main meal to be over showed in her sweaty, creased forehead, and Faye was glad. It was a small revenge for the years of spying and betrayal, but she would take it.

Olivia lifted the lid from the dish, drawing a barely audible collective groan from the children. The cook had prepared a mousse made from the sweet flesh of a river fish, tree sap, and tiny black seeds that fizzed on the tongue. The pudding was a favorite of Stefan's. The children hated it, yet none dared to express their opinion. Like most of the food that evening, Faye took no pleasure in it and didn't register the taste strongly. She was waiting to hear what Stefan had to tell them and wondering what it would mean for her and the rest of the family.

After slowly eating small portions of their dessert, the children's torture was over and Nate removed all the dishes while Olivia cleaned the table.

It was late evening. Darius looked as though he might fall asleep at any moment, and the other children were tired and impatient. Even Parthenia, who had watched her father with affection throughout the meal and eaten all of her pudding, was looking as though she'd had enough. But no one could leave until Stefan gave permission.

"Nate," he said, "please bring wine, and also something special for the children to drink."

"Yes, sir."

Olivia took the hint and got out the rock crystal glasses kept for special occasions.

"Have you got some exciting news for us?" Castiel ventured.

"Yes," said Nahla, "are we going to have a toast?"

Nahla rarely spoke around her father, but she clearly felt confident that Stefan's mood was so good she could risk it. The child was right, for Stefan replied, "A toast is indeed in order, my dear."

"Ooooh," exclaimed the little girl. "What's it about?"

"Have patience, Nahla. Wait until everything is ready."

Nate entered carrying a tray bearing a bottle of wine from the cellar and a silver jug covered with a soft white cloth. Condensation was forming on the outside of the jug.

A tense excitement filled the room as Nate and Olivia filled the family's glasses. Faye felt dread enveloping her heart. Whatever it was that Stefan had to announce, she was sure it would not bode well for her children or herself.

Nate and Olivia completed their task and stood to one side, their hands folded in front of them.

"As Castiel and Nahla so astutely observed, I have something important to tell you. The most important members of the clan met today. Naturally, I was invited. We discussed many things, including the ongoing success in our campaign to wrest control of certain areas from the Dirksens and claim this entire galactic sector. Our family has been part of this increase in our strength, and I was delighted to receive personal praise and thanks from Raith Sherrerr himself.

"We decided today the time has come to step up our bid for control. Business and small-time power struggles are useful, but results come slowly and with plenty of backward steps. Now's the time to press forward with our advantage. So, Faye, children, raise your glasses. The Sherrerrs are going to war!"

Thirty-Eight

The next morning, Stefan announced over breakfast that they had two hours to pack whatever they wanted to take with them, and then they were leaving. He didn't know when they would be returning to the estate, he said, if ever. The children were in a frenzy as they tried to find treasured items they'd misplaced and fill their bags with their favorite toys and clothes. The choices they were making weren't particularly well thought out or practical—Oriana was packing for a hot climate, while Ferne was taking his jackets, cardigans and boots —but Faye didn't bother to say anything. Whatever they lacked, someone would arrange to supply at their destination.

Faye told Olivia to pack a range of clothes and left the maid to it. She went out into the garden and passed the time walking the paths. Despite her terrible situation and the years she'd spent confined and abused there, she could remember happy times in the garden with the children. There had been times when she'd momentarily forgotten her desperate plight and had taken simple pleasure in the company of her girls and boys, before the shadow of the existence of Stefan and his proud, cruel family had covered her heart again.

Parthenia's tarsul loped by, crossing Faye's path. Stefan had told the children they couldn't bring their pets with them, which had caused many trembling lips and silent tears as they absorbed the news while struggling not to anger their father with their reaction. Faye had wondered at the meaning of the information. It wouldn't have been much trouble to bring the animals along in a separate autocar or shuttle. Maybe Stefan's decision had only been a whim, heedless of the effect on his offspring, or a manifestation of his cruelty.

A ripe fruit was hanging down from a vine looping overhead. Faye reached up and plucked it. The sweet, slightly bitter juice dripped down her chin as she bit through the fuzzy skin.

An arm pressed close around her waist, making her start and drop the fruit. She coughed as the juice went down the wrong way. It was Stefan. He'd snuck up on her from behind while she was lost in reverie. He leaned so close to her ear his lips brushed it as he said, "I thought I might find you here, Faye. You always did like our garden, didn't you?"

She pulled away from him. "What do you want?"

"Always the cold-hearted bitch, aren't you?"

"You expect me to be warm toward my rapist?"

"Details, details. You should learn to enjoy it. I certainly do. In fact, I think I prefer it."

Faye smiled.

"That's what I like to see," Stefan said. "I'm glad I could persuade you to come around to my way of thinking. Though, I must say, please continue to scream and fight as you did before. It adds a special frisson."

"Oh, I wasn't smiling at the thought of you forcing yourself on me, dear husband. No, I was imaging the pleasure I'll experience when I see you pay for everything you've done to me and all the other evil acts of your life."

"Enjoy the thought, because a thought is all it will ever be," Stefan replied. "We Sherrerrs are more powerful than we've ever been. It won't be long before we've stamped the Dirksens into the ground. Then, no one will dare stand up to us and we'll have the richest pickings from every business and trade deal that goes on. And when we've secured our hold, we'll begin our move into the neighboring galactic sectors. What do you think about that?"

"Your megalomaniac family's ambitions are of no interest to me nor any other decent-minded person. What was it that went wrong with the Sherrerrs, Stefan? Did a splicer make an absent-minded slip a few generations ago that set your clan on its mad path toward galactic domination?"

Ignoring her question, Stefan replied, "Oh, but you should be interested, Faye. Our declaration of war on the Dirksens has important implications for the mages in the family."

They had been walking along a path as Stefan guided her back to the house. At his words, she halted. "Why is that?"

"I thought that might capture your attention," Stefan replied smugly. "I didn't want to tell the children last night. At their tender ages, it doesn't do to worry or alarm them too much."

She marveled at how he thought that beating their mother didn't worry or alarm the children.

"But the reason that we're moving to another location is due to the fact that they're going to play a major role in the conflict. I talked up their abilities to Raith Sherrerr. He's expecting high things of them."

Her heart racing, Faye said, "But I told you long ago, we can't kill. Mages can't kill. Or else how do you think it was possible to capture Kris and me?"

Stefan turned pale and glowered. "And I told *you* never to mention that man's name."

Her body was rigid and her fists clenched. "We can't kill. You won't make my children into murderers."

"You may not be able to actually kill—and I'm still not sure I quite believe that—but I'm sure there are other ways of causing harm to our enemies. What if you were to move a company of soldiers to the deep ocean, for example? Or make a starship's engine explode? I'm sure you could do it, with a little persuasion." He ran a finger down her neck to the top of her cleavage, making her shudder with disgust.

"No," Faye said. "It doesn't work like that. If Casting might cause harm to someone...it...it doesn't work. We can't do it." Her words sounded unconvincing, and Stefan wasn't slow to pick up on her hesitation.

"I'll soon find out the truth. You were always forthcoming when I threatened the children."

"That won't work. You'll never make me believe you would kill one of our children. Castiel and Nahla are too precious to you and the others are too useful. You've said so yourself."

"You're right," Stefan replied. "I wouldn't kill them. But that doesn't mean I wouldn't hurt them."

Rage exploded in Faye. She lifted her hand to strike him, but he caught her wrist and forced it downward, bending her arm so painfully she thought it would break. She cried out and grabbed at his face with her other hand. This time, she was too fast for him, and her nails gouged furrows in his cheeks before he managed to wrench them away.

He had both her wrists in his powerful grip. He forced her to her knees, his face a mask of glowering hate hanging over her. Her ability to control her reaction to her husband's maltreatment had all but disappeared. She lunged at his stomach and fastened her teeth on it, biting down with all the force she possessed. Through the material of his vest and shirt, she felt his flesh between her teeth.

"Arghhhhh," Stefan exclaimed. He let go of her wrists and wrestled her head away from him. He kicked her so hard she fell to the ground, her head hitting the stone path. Sparks flickered in her vision and blackness encroached. She sat up and put a hand to her head. Her vision cleared, and she saw Stefan striding away.

THIRTY-NINE

Carina was up to her knees in mud. Trees surrounded her, their canopies blocking out the sky. The trees' roots rose as high as her head and the place reeked of odorous brine. She guessed that meant she was in some kind of estuary forest and the tide could come in at any moment. The planet had one close moon and the tides were high, the tidal zones stretching for kilometers.

Her Cast had gone a little awry, unsurprisingly. She wasn't well acquainted with the topography of the planet. Still, she shouldn't be too far from her intended destination—the capital city. At its spaceport she could expect to find some sort of passage on a ship heading offplanet.

She had some elixir left. Should she just Cast again? She was alone as far as she could tell and not in immediate danger. She decided it would be wise to conserve the precious liquid in case she encountered a situation in which she needed it more.

She tried to pull first one leg and then the other out of the mud, but she could only move them a little, and then she seemed to sink lower. As she struggled, she consoled herself that she hadn't Transported into a tree or into the ocean. There did seem to be some kind of safeguard with the Cast so that it wasn't possible to move a solid object inside another solid object, so arriving in the tree would have been unlikely, but she wasn't sure if the same rule applied to liquid.

Something in the mud slithered past her calf. Gulping down a squeal, she jerked her leg upward. It shifted a little and she strained to hold it where it was and retain the little movement she'd managed. She looked around. She needed something to grip. If she could hold onto something solid on the surface, she should be able to gradually ease herself out.

The only thing that looked as though it was within reach was a tree root. Carina put her hands on the mud and walked them forward until she was lying as horizontal as possible. Her knees were bent painfully backward, but she reached the root and grasped it firmly with both hands. As she did so, she noticed a layer of water on the mud grow deeper as she watched it.

She cursed. She gently moved her legs while at the same time pulling as hard as she could on the root. Her right leg lifted a little more, and then her left. The rapidly encroaching water was filling the gaps she was making around her legs, dissolving the mud and making her task easier. At last, one leg was free. She knelt with it gently on the watery mud while she worked on the other leg.

The mud released her left leg with a satisfying *plop*. Relying mostly on the pull of her arms on the root, she slid across the mud to the tree. Its cold, wet, sliminess penetrated her Sherrerr uniform and soaked her to the skin. She quickly climbed the limb-like tree roots until she was balancing on top of them. From the brightest patch of light in the canopy, she guessed the rough direction of the sun and so also the direction of the city, and set off toward it.

She used the roots as stepping stones to prevent her from needing to walk on the muddy floor, which was quickly becoming aquatic. But they were damp from their previous submersion and a black algae clung to them. Her chances of slipping and falling in were high. It was time to quit being so cautious, and Transport herself again to a hopefully more favorable location.

She took out her canister of elixir and unscrewed it, but as she lifted the container to her lips, she spotted a green bank through the tree trunks. She was only a short distance from higher ground, if she could make it without falling in.

Leaning on the rough bark of the tree trunks for balance and for purchase, she continued to tread carefully on the roots until she reached the foot of the bank. Her previous view of it had deceived her. The greenery began at a level higher than she'd thought. Across from the last stand of trees, over a narrow dip, was a swathe of black and brown, muddy foliage. The high tide mark, where the green, drier-looking stuff began, was two or three meters above her head.

Still, she thought she could scramble up it, and she was already covered in mud. She couldn't get any wetter or dirtier. She made the leap across the dip and clung to the slippery stems. At the same time, she dug the toes of her boots into the soft surface. Crawling upward spider-like, she reached the green ground in a few minutes.

After that, the going was easier. The bank sloped at an angle that meant she had to continue on all fours rather than two legs, but the air was fresher after the stench among the trees and she was no longer in danger of being swamped by the incoming ocean.

When she reached the top, she turned and sat down to catch her breath. She was looking down on the tree tops and out across a glimmering ocean. The sun hung low and the large, crater-strewn moon was high in the sky. She had visited many planets in her short time as a merc, and this was one of the prettier ones. It wasn't a surprise the Sherrerrs had chosen it as the base of their operations.

All she had were her skills, her wits, and a three-quarters-full bottle of elixir. The latter meant that she wouldn't go hungry, but she couldn't Transport herself to another planet, more was the pity.

Her breathing had returned to normal, and the wind was drying her sweat, leaving her cold and uncomfortable. A hungry ache had started up in her belly too. It was time to move on if she wanted to reach the capital by nightfall.

She stood and scrambled over the top of the bank. Farmland lay on the other side. Smooth, green, cropped vegetation sloped down from her feet, and animals were lazily grazing it. Hundreds of the knee-high bipedal creatures the locals grew for meat dotted the slope down to the bottom, where a large farmhouse stood. The capital city lay on the horizon.

The animals were entirely uninterested in her as she went across the field in long strides. However, the herders watching them were very interested in her.

"Hey," a voice yelled. "Where do you think *you're* going? You're not allowed here. This is private property."

She turned and spotted the owner of the voice: a youthful man in old clothes and a floppy hat, appearing above a fold in the land.

"I got lost," she called back. "I'm leaving now."

"Oh, are you?" another voice shouted. This person was approaching from below. She was older and her skin was reddened by the sun. "We'll see about that. Stop where you are. I want to make sure you haven't stolen any of our stock."

She supposed it was vaguely possible that she'd broken the neck of one of their livestock and pushed it inside her shirt, but it seemed an unlikely conjecture. "I don't have anything of yours," she snapped, and altered her direction to avoid crossing paths with either of the herders. The woman and youth changed direction too.

Carina was annoyed. She had enough to contend with. She didn't need suspicious farmers added to the mix. She adjusted her path again and began to jog.

"Catch her, Piffer," the woman shouted to the young man. "Show her she can't just wander over our land without permission."

Piffer started to run.

Carina sped up. The situation was ridiculous. She could fight off the man and the woman she presumed was his mother, but why should she? Why couldn't they just let her go on her way? "I told you, I don't have any of your stupid animals," she yelled. "Now leave me alone."

It wasn't until the man had nearly caught up to her that Carina understood what she needed to do. She'd been worried about her Sherrerr uniform being a liability. Any member of the clan or employee who saw her would wonder what she was doing, and perhaps demand to know. Yet everywhere on the planet and for most of the sector, the Sherrerr insignia was known and feared.

She slid to a halt on the moist vegetation and spun to face her pursuer. The stylized blade on her collar was covered in mud, so she roughly rubbed it with the edge of her sleeve. Her chin up, she stared the man in the eye as he drew closer. When he saw the emblem, he also skidded to a stop.

Carina glared.

"Mother..."

"What's wrong?" the woman shouted. "Grab her."

"Er, I don't think that would be a very good idea."

"Why not?" The woman arrived, sweaty and red-faced. "Oh."

FORTY

As far back as she could remember, Carina had known of the Sherrerrs and the aura of intimidation and disquiet they radiated. Like most people, she'd tried to avoid coming into direct contact with any of them or their dealings. Everyone knew the best place to be when Sherrerr—or Dirksen—business was afoot was as far away as possible.

Yet she wasn't prepared for the deference and plain fear the mother-and-son pair of farmers, Bunter and Piffer, displayed when they thought she was working for the clan. She'd only wanted them to let her go on her way in peace, but they insisted on her going back with them to the farmhouse so she could clean up and eat something before she left.

No doubt they were frightened of retaliation for their behavior and were anxious to put things right. She was cold, wet, and hungry enough to not take too much persuasion to agree to their offer. Bunter looked relieved when she said she would go with them, and told Piffer to run ahead and draw a hot bath.

"I'll make a roast," Bunter said, smiling deferentially, her already-rosy cheeks afire. As they went the rest of the way to the farmhouse, following Piffer's disappearing heels, Bunter twice stooped and grabbed one of the grazing beasts. She swiftly twisted the necks then slung the bodies over her back, holding onto their heads. The newly dead animals bounced in time with her steps. "Nice and fresh," Bunter said.

The bath was ready by the time Bunter showed her into the bathroom of the old house. She waited for Carina's uniform as she undressed and promised to get as much dirt out of it as she could while dinner was cooking. Carina retrieved her elixir bottle before handing the farmer the wet clothes.

She sank into the hot water gratefully after Bunter left. Perhaps it was all a trap, but she doubted it. The horror on the farmers' faces when they realized her allegiance hadn't been faked. She felt a little guilty about taking advantage of them, but quickly forgot about it when she remembered they'd chased her and had wanted to beat her.

There was a knock at the door. "I've put a bathrobe just outside," Piffer called, "to wear while your clothes are drying."

She began to soap herself and wash off the grit and grime of the marsh. The soap stung the cuts and grazes she'd gathered along the way. Next, she lathered her hair and used a jug to rinse it with clean water from the faucet. By the time Bunter called to say dinner was ready, she was feeling better than she had in a long time.

She dried herself and put on the bathrobe, slipping her elixir bottle into the pocket. The gown covered her legs to the floor and her arms to the wrists, giving her an idea. On tiptoe, she went across the landing and opened a door. The room held a single bed and a wardrobe. On the nightstand was a picture of a pretty young girl who bore no resemblance to Bunter or Piffer. She guessed it was the latter's room and the girl in the photograph was someone he liked romantically.

Piffer was about Carina's size. She went to his wardrobe and took out a pair of pants and a shirt. They were old and worn but clean. She put them on then covered them with the bathrobe before going downstairs. Her Sherrerr uniform had proven useful but she needed to ditch it before it invited too many questions she couldn't answer.

Bunter and Piffer were waiting for her in the kitchen. Only one place at the table was set. They weren't going to eat with her, only watch her eat. Awkward. She didn't think she would have gotten used to being a Sherrerr guard.

The meal was delicious and she enjoyed it despite the over-zealous attentions of the farmers. Her uniform steamed on a chair in front of the hot stove. Breaking the painful silence, Bunter said, "I got most of the mud out of it. Should be good as new in a few hours."

"I can't wait that long," Carina replied. "I'll have to wear it wet."

The news that she would be leaving soon caused a visible slackening in the tension on the farmers' faces. Then Piffer's positively brightened and he blurted, "I could try putting it in the seed airer."

"Yes, that might help," Bunter said.

The young man grabbed Carina's uniform and sped from the room.

"We have a machine to dry the seeds we keep for next year," Bunter explained. "It stops them from going moldy in storage."

"Oh," Carina said. "Good idea." She was distracted with filling her belly with as much of the roasted meat and other dishes she could. She had a long walk ahead of her tonight.

"It's funny," said Bunter, "we haven't seen Sherrerr troops around here for a while. And you're by yourself."

She nodded and swallowed a mouthful of food. "Surveillance. I can't say any more than that. Do you have anything to drink?"

"Yes, of course," Bunter replied. "Of course. What was I thinking?" She went into a pantry and returned with a jug. "Is beer okay? We don't have anything stronger." She leaned forward and said in a lowered tone, "Piffer can't hold it. Then he's no good for work the next day. I won't have it in the house."

"Beer is fine."

She was trying to think of a way to plumb the woman's mind for useful information, but every subtle inquiry she could think up was guaranteed to raise suspicion. She had no good reason to be asking about starships scheduled to arrive or depart from the capital's spaceport, assuming Bunter would even know, which seemed doubtful. And anything she might ask about the movements of Sherrerr guards or soldiers was definitely a bad idea.

When her stomach really couldn't hold any more, she pushed back her seat and said, "Thanks. I'm done. Can you ask your son if I can have my uniform? I'll be on my way."

"Are you sure you've had enough?" Bunter asked. "There's plenty left."

"Yes, I'm sure. It was very good."

"I'm glad you liked it. What about some dessert? I have some fruit compote in the pantry."

Carina had been in the process of standing up. She stopped and looked the woman in the eye. Bunter looked away. Something wasn't right. The farmer should have been glad to see her go, not trying to delay her.

She ran for the door, but when she flung it open, Piffer was there waiting. He moved to punch her, but Carina swerved. She caught him with an upper cut under his chin, snapping his head back and sending him unconscious to the floor.

When the two farmers had begun to suspect her, Carina didn't know. Probably while she was in the bath, when they had time to think over her presence, which made no real sense. Why would a lone Sherrerr soldier wander the area unless he or she lived nearby? Carina was a stranger with a weak excuse for being in those parts. The farmers must have contacted the Sherrerrs and been told to keep her here as long as possible while they made their way over.

They hadn't yet arrived or it would have been someone in a Sherrerr uniform waiting for her on the other side of the kitchen door. However, she probably didn't have much time.

Carina headed for the rear of the house, leaving behind the cursing and wailing of Bunter, who was tending to her son. The Sherrerrs would approach the house from the road. If she was quick enough, she could slip out the back before they surrounded the place.

With a gasp of frustration, she realized she was barefoot. Her boots were by the front door. She doubled back, ran past the still-prone Piffer and his lamenting mother, snatched up her wet, muddy boots, and scooted back the way she'd come. A thud resounded from the front door. Her heart leapt into her mouth. The Sherrerrs had arrived.

She didn't have time to put on her boots. She didn't have time to take any precautions. She had reached the back door. She threw open the bolts and raced outside.

"There she is," a voice shouted. A hiss of pulse round flew past her ear. Not far from the back door stood a hedge next to the fields behind. She ducked down and forced her way under it.

"Get her," someone shouted.

The bathrobe was snagging on the branches, and it was a pale color, easily spotted in the darkness. She undid the tie and struggled out of it, seizing her elixir bottle before she abandoned the garment.

Her boots in her other hand, she raced along the hedge, using it as cover. It split two ways, and she took the direction that led her out into the farmland, praying the Sherrerrs wouldn't bother to pursue her too far. She was a long way from the mountains. She doubted the local clan would have connected the report of someone masquerading as a Sherrerr soldier with the disappearance of another soldier many kilometers away.

Keeping close to the hedge, she ran on until a stitch in her side forced her to slow down. She risked a glance over her shoulder. The fields were dark. The only lights visible were from the distant farmhouse and a few vehicles clustered outside.

She slowed to a stop and sank to the ground, her breathing ragged. Her feet felt like they were cut to pieces from her run, but she could Cast Heal and in a few moments they would be okay. She was still far from the capital and the spaceport that was her route offplanet, but she'd swapped the uniform that would identify her for civilian clothes and she had a full belly.

She put on her boots. Things seemed to be taking a turn for the better.

FORTY-ONE

When Carina had been a little girl, she'd often wished she could create something out of nothing through Casting. Sadly, she'd found her Nai Nai never taught her that Cast, and eventually, when she'd gotten up the courage to ask about it, her grandmother had explained that though it was possible to create matter from energy, that was a job for top scientists, not mages, and that to create something from nothing was what she would call magic.

Carina could have simply Transported someone else's cash into her pocket. All she had to do was to see it. But that would have been stealing, and, as well as being intrinsically wrong, Nai Nai had told her that you never knew for sure if that person needed the money more than you.

She had Transported herself close to the city's outskirts but she couldn't risk suddenly appearing in busy areas. So, without credits for an autocar, she was forced to walk all the way from the outskirts of the capital to the spaceport. Her belly, which had been full the previous night, was soon empty again. By the time she arrived at her destination, she was footsore and ravenous.

The spaceport was one of the biggest she had ever seen. The field was divided into three sections: shuttles that ferried passengers to deep-space vessels traveling outsystem; shuttles that belonged to interplanetary spacecraft that journeyed to insystem planets or to go asteroid mining; and local shuttles that only went into orbit for fast journeys to distant countries.

She was on one side of the security fence and the vessels were on the other, with an access road running across the center of the field. Multi-person autocars ran up and down the road, ferrying the crew to the buildings at the far end of the spaceport, where their IDs would be processed if they wanted to spend time planetside.

The cargo loading bays and fuel stations were in another part of the spaceport, so once the crews had left, the shuttles stood still and silent. Somewhere above in high orbit, long range deep-space vessels awaited some of them. She hoped she would soon be aboard just such a space-craft—a ship to take her far from the Sherrerr-controlled system and all the sad memories it held.

It was a pity she hadn't gotten to see the little Sherrerr boy, Darius, again. He'd been a sweet, smart kid, and the only mage she'd ever really known apart from Nai Nai. Her parents had been mages too, but she couldn't remember them very well. But it couldn't be helped that she hadn't been able to meet Darius or his family. Her time on Ithiya had been a wild goose chase.

She walked slowly along the fence, scrutinizing the shuttles. The local vessels bore the name of their company. Others were named according to the spacecraft to which they belonged: *Matador, Sandra, Ambition, Colossus, Marchana, Shooting Star, The Falcon, Whirlwind, Nightfall*. Most of the shuttles looked well cared for, even the older models. Failing to keep your vessel shipshape on space flights rarely ended well, and that didn't only apply to the interiors. A clean exterior where scratches were buffed out and holes and scrapes repaired made for a better attitude from the crew. Captain Speidel had told her that.

However, a shuttle that was well cared for was not what Carina needed. Such a craft would have strict protocols for hiring staff, and the crew would follow them or find themselves dismissed at the next planet. But she had nothing to prove who she was. She'd never carried proper papers. Sometime during her homeless period she'd lost them. Either that or she'd never had any. She wasn't sure. It hadn't mattered too much up until now. Merc bands were less interested in that kind of thing than they were in whether you could fire straight and had the guts to kill someone in hand-to-hand combat.

What she was looking for was a seedier kind of craft. A vessel that probably did a little contraband smuggling, like weapons, drugs, or people. If she'd had the gems, she could have sold them to pay for passage on such a ship, but they were halfway up a mountain, and now she had the harder task of persuading the captain to allow her to work her passage.

She saw exactly what she was looking for. It was a squat shuttle, a little small. Too small to be in the deep spacecraft section, yet here it was. A small craft had a small hold. Yet only the large starships could carry sufficient cargo to make the weeks, months, and even years-long trips between systems economically viable. If the shuttle was small, its space-craft was also small, which meant it had to be carrying rare, expensive cargo, or, as was more likely, it was a smuggler.

What was more, it was scratched, scraped, pockmarked, and filthy. No one cared about this ship. They were only interested in making some fast money and moving on.

Someone in overalls was sitting on the ramp cleaning his fingernails with the point of a small knife. He looked like a seasoned space traveler —pale, greasy, and with dark circles under his eyes. His gut pulled his clothes tight as it hung out over his lap. She guessed he was a cargo hand or something similar. Not the person to talk to about being hired, but he would have to do.

"Hey," she called through the fence.

The man looked up at her and looked away again. He started cleaning the nails on his other hand.

"Hey," she shouted again. "What are you shipping?"

The man got up, ignoring her again and went inside the ship.

She cursed. But he reappeared and came over to where she was standing.

She began, "I was wondering—"

He was pointing a gun at her. He held it close to his side so it wasn't obvious.

"I don't mean any harm," she said, backing away. "I'm just looking for a ship to work passage on. I can work security."

"No you can't. If you could work security you would know not to ask stupid questions. Now fuck off." The man turned to walk away.

"I'm an ex-merc. That gun you're holding is a Deacon X5 and if I had to fight you I'd go for your left knee."

He stopped and faced her. "How'd you know about my knee?"

"The way you walked over. You favor your right leg. And knees are weak points anyway."

He rubbed his stubble as he scanned her from head to toe and back again. "You don't look like a merc."

"I started young."

He paused, considering. "I can't deny we could do with another hand aboard ship. The first mate's been arrested and won't be leaving the planet anytime soon. But we're a small operation. You wouldn't only be working security. You'd have to pitch in with everything. Cargo handling, maintenance, cleaning up in the mess."

"I don't mind. I'll do whatever you want. When are you shipping out?"

"Hold on. No one said you were hired. And what's your hurry? Is someone looking for you? Done something you shouldn't?"

"No," she lied. "I'm just sick of this planet. Can't wait to get off it."

"I don't want anyone coming after you. Like I said, we're a small operation. Can't afford to have the authorities breathing down our necks. You get what I mean?"

She got it. He didn't want to attract any attention that might result in a thorough search of the ship. She wondered what it was they were smuggling. "Sure."

"Okay, meet me at the crew entrance in a couple of hours."

"Is it a sure thing? Do I have a job? Or do you have to speak to the captain?"

"I am the captain."

Forty-Two

Two hours was a long time for Carina to waste. She had no money, nothing to do, and nowhere to go. She decided to hang around the departures area of the spaceport. Her work aboard the smugglers' ship was by no means guaranteed and she thought she might spot another opportunity that was possibly more legal. She found a quiet corner and sat on the floor while she people-watched.

It was the usual crowd that passed through such places. Ultra-rich travelers arriving for luxury cruises or to depart on their private vessels. These were easy to identify from their clothes, their bearing, and their retinue of servants, porters, and bodyguards. Carina considered approaching one of these groups to find out if they needed extra security help but quickly put aside the idea. Most of the wealthy in that area were either Sherrerrs or closely affiliated with the family. Coming into contact with the Sherrerrs again was the last thing she needed.

Much more common than the wealthy crowd were the local vacationers off on trips to far-distant countries or even tourist resorts on other planets or the system's moons. These were far less stately, less well-dressed, and louder. They let their children run riot around the place while they waited in line to go through to their gate.

In that galactic region there weren't many aliens, but they were naturally more likely to be seen at a major spaceport, and this one was no exception. She saw quadrupeds with prehensile noses, multi-limbed arthropods, and bipedal aliens in environment suits that protected them from the local atmosphere and possibly air pressure too. Most of the human passengers were polite enough not to stare, but many younger children would stop their play to watch the aliens pass, and sometimes they even went up and prodded them before being hauled away by an embarrassed parent.

Carina had encountered more aliens than most and usually without any problems. Sentient species tended to understand that even when clear communication was possible, the gulf between cultures and thought processes was too vast to be easily crossed, and so each left the other well alone.

The first time she had fought aliens was an event in her life she rarely thought about and would rather have forgotten. She'd been ten years old, and it was the first time she'd killed. The aliens in question were regians, who possessed the odd ability to shift in time. They didn't move far, only a few moments into the future and the past. Yet their ability made them a formidable enemy because they were so difficult to kill. The pulse round, knife or whatever had to hit them at the exact moment that they passed through the present in order to make contact. Otherwise the offensive weapon hit empty air.

She had managed to kill the aliens with a Cast called Split. The name said it all. The Cast tore the aliens apart, and because Casts worked over several moments, the effect was slow enough to hit the regians on target.

She shuddered. She hated using her mage abilities to kill. A shot to the head or a knife to the heart was fast and clean and would be her preferred method to go out with if she ever lost a fight. Casting to kill wasn't only more difficult than regular killing, it was long, drawn-out, and agonizing to the victim. She'd met some bad characters over the years, but she hadn't met anyone who she felt deserved that kind of death.

"Carina," a familiar voice said. "I thought I'd find you here."

Startled from her reverie, she looked up to see Bryce standing over her. "What the hell?" She stood up. "What are you doing here? I sent you back to that town, not here. And I thought I told you we couldn't meet again. Leave me alone." She began to walk away.

Bryce clutched her arm. "Don't go. Please. I came in on the morning shuttle and it's taken me hours to find you. I thought you would be trying to go offplanet. I only want to talk to you."

"Well I *don't* want to talk to you. I saved you, remember? If you're grateful for that, you can pay me back by doing what I ask."

"I understand why you don't want to have anything to do with me after what you did, but you can trust me, Carina. I wouldn't do anything to hurt you."

"Bryce," she said, her tone softening. "I don't think you would do anything to hurt me—at first. But things would change over time. You would see me differently. Eventually, I wouldn't be Carina to you, I would be a mage with all that entails. Understand me when I say I can't afford to have friends who know what I can do. It just isn't safe, especially for me, but also for you."

"Okay, okay. I think I understand. I won't force you. But let me get you something to eat at least. Let me return the favor, just a little?"

Was he being genuine, or was it a trap? Had Bryce divulged what she'd done, and had someone put him up to finding her and capturing her? Her friend's expression seemed open and honest. And she was very hungry. "All right, but I want to go somewhere I can see anyone who approaches us."

"Yeah, of course," Bryce replied, looking wounded.

Cafes and eateries sat at the edges of the departure area, and Carina chose one that had an empty table out front. The site gave her a wide view. Bryce went inside to order some food, then returned to the table with two glasses of the local brew. He put one in front of her and sipped the other as he sat down.

When he was seated, she swapped the glasses. He looked puzzled for a moment then said, "You don't really think I would drug you?"

"I don't know what you'd do, and if my caution upsets you, I don't care. I can't afford to take chances. You don't understand what could happen to me. You haven't thought it through. If you had, you wouldn't be surprised that I swapped our drinks."

He took a sip. "I guess you're right. I don't get it. If I could do what you can, I wouldn't be hiding it, I'd be using my powers to make myself rich."

"You might try, until someone figures out what you're doing and decides to make you make them rich instead. And what do you think they would do to you if you refused?"

"But I would just—"

"What?" she asked angrily. "What would you just do? It isn't easy or simple, you know."

"Okay, calm down. I was only trying to figure it out. If you say the best thing you can do is keep things under wraps, I accept that. You would know better than me."

"Damn right I would."

Their food arrived. Neither Carina nor Bryce said anything until the waiter had returned into the cafe. Then Bryce picked up his fork, dug it into Carina's food, and ate a mouthful. "Satisfied?"

She began to eat fast, glancing at the clock that overhung the departure area. She had an hour until it was time to meet the smuggler captain in the crew section, but she wanted to be done with this meal with Bryce.

"So you're going offplanet?" he asked.

"That's the idea."

"Deep space?"

"If I can. I want to put as much of the black between me and this place as possible."

"Because of the danger that someone will guess what you did at the Sherrerr place, and come after you?"

"That, and other things. I've had enough of Ithiya. It's time to move on. How about you? Have you found a way to afford your treatment?"

"I have, actually. That was why I was looking for you."

"Huh?"

"When I got back to my home town, I found out my parents had returned and they'd been looking for me. After they went away, they opened a business that turned out to be really successful. They came back to find out what happened to me. The first thing we did after meeting up was go to a splicer. I had the treatment overnight and it seems to be working. Another month or so and I should be cured."

"That's great, Bryce. I'm really happy for you."

"Thanks, but there's more. My parents are opening a branch of their business. They want me to run it. That was why I came straight here to try to find you. I guessed you'd be trying to get offplanet. I can help you. You can come with me and help me run the business."

"I appreciate the offer," she said, "but I really can't. Thanks for the meal. I have to go now."

What she'd said wasn't strictly true—she had a while to wait before she was due in the crew section—but she wanted to cut the conversation short. She knew Bryce meant well, but simply by saving him she'd irrevocably cut ties between them forever. It was kinder not to drag it out.

She stood.

"But Carina..."

"Bye, Bryce. It was good knowing you."

Forty-Three

Stefan argued with the spaceport official, but it didn't do any good.

"I am very sorry, sir, but there really is no other way. It isn't far, sir. Just a minute's walk across the public area."

"You *do* understand who I am?" Stefan asked the woman through his teeth, throwing sharp glances at passengers entering the departure area who were lingering, curious to see what the problem was.

Faye pitied the poor spaceport clerk who had been called upon to explain there was no private entrance for exclusive passengers—even Sherrerrs—and they would have to walk across the public departure area like everyone else.

"Yes, sir," the woman replied, looking plain terrified. "As I said, I am very sorry, but it's unavoidable if you wish to board a shuttle at this spaceport."

The autocar had left after depositing them at the departure area entrance. The children stood waiting quietly. Nate had placed their bags onto a trolley. He wouldn't be coming with them aboard the Sherrerr starship, *Nightfall,* and neither would Olivia, Faye had been delighted to discover. Her personal maid wouldn't be spying on her any longer.

The three Sherrerr guards from the estate coming with them shuffled and adjusted their grips on their weapons as they scanned the bystanders. Though the dangers of an attack were slight, they did increase the longer they stood around in public.

"Perhaps we should just go through, Father," Castiel suggested. "I don't like standing here with all these people watching."

Stefan's head snapped around at his son's words, but the storm that threatened didn't arrive. "Oh, very well. But this won't be the last you'll hear of this," he said to the clerk. The relief that had begun to flood her face upon hearing Stefan give up his objection was replaced with tension.

They set off through one of the doorways into the departure area, drawing more attention to their retinue. The clerk hadn't been exaggerating—the entrance for private passengers was less than a minute's walk across the busy space. Stefan had had his temper tantrum over nothing.

They were about halfway to the other door when Faye saw her.

Carina.

She was walking directly across their path.

Faye stopped dead in her tracks.

"Ow," Darius cried.

Faye was holding her son's hand, and she must have gripped it too tightly. She quickly let go and tried to compose herself and walk on before anyone spotted her reaction. But it was too late. Darius had picked up on her heightened emotions and he was looking up at her curiously. Then he turned his attention to the crowd to see what had caused her reaction.

"Carina!" shouted the little boy.

"Darius, no!"

She tried to grab his hand but he was too quick. He sped around Stefan and between the two bodyguards who were walking in front.

"Carina!" Darius shouted again.

This time, Carina heard him.

Faye watched in horror as her eldest daughter turned to see little Darius running toward her, his arms outstretched. Joy filled Carina's face as she too spread her arms. When the little boy reached her, she lifted him into the air and grabbed him into a hug.

All the Sherrerrs and their staff had drawn to a halt to watch the strange spectacle. Carina put Darius down and squatted so she could talk to him face to face.

Faye couldn't hear what they were saying over the general hubbub of the departure area. She only hoped Darius would remember in time that the subject of Carina was prohibited. There was still a chance her daughter would escape her husband's clutches.

Stefan was white-faced and rigid. "Darius," he barked. When his son didn't hear him, he instructed a guard to retrieve the boy.

Faye held her breath. Her heart raced. She thought she was going to faint. Perhaps she should pretend to faint and cause a distraction, but that might excite Stefan's suspicions. She could only hope her husband's rage at being an object of public scrutiny would distract him enough to fail to make the connection.

No!

Darius was dragging Carina over toward them by the hand. Faye let out an involuntary gasp. Her son probably wanted to show everyone the person who had saved him from the Dirksens. Her poor, sweet, kind, thoughtless boy. Parthenia turned to eye her curiously.

The guard met the pair and took Darius' other hand. He was telling him he had to come back to his father.

Please, Darius. Please do as you're told. Carina, leave now. Go!

Stefan had his hands on his hips as he watched and waited for his son to return. Then his stiff posture slackened. His hands fell to his sides. He'd noticed something. He took a step forward to peer at Carina.

Faye willed her daughter to look away so Stefan wouldn't see her face, but it was hopeless. Carina was clearly deeply interested in their group. Her eyes were scanning them. Though the effort nearly killed her, Faye avoided her daughter's gaze like she was avoiding death itself.

In her peripheral vision, she saw Stefan's head turn toward her, then back to her daughter.

"Guards," Stefan said, "seize that woman."

"Carina," Faye screamed. "Run!"

A moment's confusion flitted over her daughter's features, then she got the message. She turned to speed away, but she only made it a few steps. The guard who had gone to retrieve Darius caught up to her. As he grabbed her arm she swung at him with the other and punched him in the side of the head. Dazed, he let go, but the other guard had reached her and kicked her in the back. She fell forward. The third guard fired from a distance, stunning her before she hit the ground.

Faye's legs went weak. She found herself on her knees. Stefan had Carina. He had all her children, even the one he hadn't fathered.

Darius was by her side, sobbing. "I'm sorry, Mother. I'm so sorry. I forgot."

FORTY-FOUR

Carina was aboard a starship. She could tell that much from the slight vibration of the ship's engine through the floor. Slowly the memory of what had happened filtered through to her. She'd been shot and stunned, heavily. Her stomach cramped with nausea and fingers seemed to be digging agonizingly through her skull. She felt like she'd been out a long time.

Swallowing the saliva that was flooding her mouth, she risked opening one eye a slit. All she could see were two pairs of feet in expensive shoes. One was a man's feet and one was a woman's. The woman's feet were tied to chair legs. Carina moved her own feet and hands slightly, just enough to discover she was also bound.

"The resemblance is quite remarkable," the man said. "Even at this angle. I don't know what took me so long to see it. I must have been too preoccupied with our son's disobedience. I should beat him for it, but I can't bring myself to at the moment. I'm too pleased with the stupid brat for bringing me this prize. Hmm. She's taking a long time to come around. Maybe she isn't made of such stern stuff as it seemed when she tackled the guard."

He stood. Carina watched his legs as he walked over. One foot lifted as he prepared to kick her. She swung her feet forward and swept his other leg from under him. He crashed to the floor. In a heartbeat she was on her knees. She scooted over and drew back her head to strike his. If she hit him hard enough in the right spot she could knock him out.

But someone grasped her hair and pulled her upright. The hand then threw her down onto her knees.

"Should I stun her again, sir?" a voice asked.

The man was getting to his feet. "No, that won't be necessary." He straightened his pants. "But some kind of reprimand is in order." He went behind Carina and kicked her in her kidneys. The pain that erupted left her unable to breathe. She drew in a great whooping gasp. Her vision swam.

The waves of pain eventually began to subside, and she could look about her. The man had returned to his chair and was watching her, his hands on his knees. The woman, who appeared to be restrained by her hands as well as her feet, was pale and scared.

"Sit her up, guard," the man said. "Looking at her face while she's lying down is making my neck ache."

Hands grabbed her shoulders and hauled her over to the wall, propping her into a sitting position. Carina gazed at the man and the woman. She realized she'd seen the man before. He was the haughty one who had arrived by shuttle at the Sherrerr stronghold. Yet he hadn't been anything more than a visitor. He didn't belong to the military arm of the Sherrerrs. Was it possible he knew she'd absconded from there? Carina was unsure of why she'd been captured by this family that she'd helped.

The man had to be Darius' father. The little boy had seemed troubled when he spoke of him, and now Carina could see why. Behind his handsome features deep arrogance and cruelty seethed.

The woman was drawing more of her attention. She seemed even more familiar than Darius' father, though Carina couldn't remember where she'd seen her before. Was she ever so slightly shaking her head? The woman had known her name—Darius must have told her, and she'd remembered. She'd told her to run, wanting to protect her from capture. Why?

"I have to say," the man said, "I'm more than a little disappointed. I was expecting a heart-warming family reunion. Yet you two are acting as though you don't even know each other."

"We don't know each other," said the woman. "I've no idea who this person is. She's entirely innocent, and she rescued your son when he was kidnapped. Yet this is how you repay her."

Something was going on that Carina didn't understand. Saying nothing seemed the wisest course of action. The man didn't appear to know about her mage powers, which was her greatest fear. The way Darius had acted, the woman had to be his mother. She was a mage, according to what the boy had said. So it was also probably her who had sent Carina the elixir ingredients, gems, and the polished pebble. But her husband was clearly evil. He'd trussed her up like an animal ready to be slaughtered. Why had she married him?

The realization dawned that Darius' father was holding his mother captive. It was just as Nai Nai had warned. The father was using the mother for her powers and treating her like a slave.

"Oh, Faye…" the man said regretfully, as if a thought saddened him.

Carina's heart froze. She fought to keep her features still. She mustn't show any reaction.

The man went on, "Do you really believe after all this time I can't tell when you're lying?"

Carina's throat was tight. She wanted to scream, to shout, to do anything, but she couldn't. She mustn't. The pieces of the puzzle had all slotted into place at once but she could do nothing. Faye was her mother's name. The resemblance to herself was there, yet she could hardly believe it. Was it possible this woman with the haunted eyes, the gaunt face ravaged with pain and sorrow, this broken shadow of a woman, was really her mother? What had she been through that had done this to her?

This woman had given birth to her. Darius was her half-brother, and that retinue of children in the party were probably her half-siblings too.

The enormity of her realization threatened to overwhelm Carina. Nai Nai had said her father had died and her mother had disappeared. Carina had assumed that, after all the time that had passed, her mother was dead too. But she was still alive. She'd been kept captive all those years and forced to bear children for her vile husband.

Carina wanted to vomit. She wanted to run to her mother and hug her, tell her she would be okay, tell her that she would rescue her. She had to get her away from this evil monster.

Trying to keep her face expressionless, she gazed at her mother. Tears welled up in the woman's eyes. Carina looked away lest her emotions betrayed her. Her mother was right. They had to do everything they could to prevent her husband from confirming their relationship and knowing she was also a mage.

Then she could work on getting her mother out of here.

The man steepled his fingers and brought them to his lips. "Tell them to bring me the wand," he said to the guard.

A message spoken into the guard's comm button resulted in a long, slim, metal instrument being brought to the door a few minutes later. The husband took it and looked up its length before going over to Carina's mother and laying the instrument against her arm. She screamed.

"Good, good," the man said. "Just wanted to make sure it was working."

"I don't care how much you hurt me," her mother said, "you aren't going to make me implicate a stranger."

"But I'm not going to hurt you, my dear. I'm going to hurt *her*."

The man approached Carina. She struggled and lashed out at him with her legs as she had before. He tutted and stepped away. "Hold her still," he told the guard.

The guard pinned her into the corner with a heavy boot to her stomach. Her mother's husband approached again and laid the instrument against her head. White-hot pain blinded her. She tried to go inside herself as Nai Nai had taught her and ignore the signals of her nerves, but she couldn't. The torment was too strong. It beat through all her defenses and she became aware she was screaming. Then the pain eased a fraction. She was on her side, curled up, lying in her own vomit.

The husband tutted again. "Disgusting. I prefer to use the wand because it creates less mess. No blood, you see. And then you go and do that."

"Please, Stefan," Faye said. "Don't do this. She's a stranger."

"Maybe she is," he replied. "Maybe she isn't your daughter and a mage. So what? Then she's a nobody. If I torture her to death, it won't matter."

Carina caught a glimpse of the thin metal bar before the pain descended again and she was lost to it. There was nothing in the universe but her and the agony. When the pain lifted once more, she was in another part of the room. She must have been trying to get away from the torture instrument, though she had no recollection of it.

How often the man touched her with the bar, how long the pain went on, Carina didn't know. She lost track of time. She forgot why it was happening. She screamed herself hoarse. She begged for death. Anything to stop the dreadful agony descending once more.

The man said nothing as he carried out the torture. At least, if he did, it was during the moments when Carina lost all sense of what was happening. It seemed as though he was in no hurry to stop. He was only enjoying himself as the session drew to an inevitable conclusion.

Finally, dimly, she heard her mother's soft, trembling words. "Stefan, stop. You win. You're right. She is my daughter and a mage. Carina, please forgive me."

Laughter erupted from her husband. The man laughed so hard he dropped the torture instrument. "I already knew, you fool. I already knew."

FORTY-FIVE

Carina didn't know how long she drifted in and out of consciousness. Whenever she woke, her surroundings were the same: a bare room, harsh lighting, and the steady, subtle thrum of the starship's engine vibrating the floor. When she could finally stay awake she found she was no longer bound tightly. Restraints around her wrists and ankles were fastened by a line to the wall.

She sat up and was amazed to see no evidence on her skin of the torture her mother's husband, Stefan, had put her through. Her nerves remembered, however. They jangled painfully with every movement she made. Carina recalled her torturer's laughter after he had wrested the admission from her mother through forcing her to watch her daughter's agony. He said he'd known all along she was a mage. But how?

Her hand flew to her side and she felt for her canister of elixir. It was gone. Of course. The guards must have searched her after she'd been captured. They'd given the canister to Stefan and he'd known what it was.

Carina gingerly shifted herself to the edge of the room, where her restraints were attached to the wall. She could rest against it for support, though the pressure on her back made her wince at first. The door to the room was smooth on the inside, with no security panel or other means of opening it. She was in a cell of some kind with no hope of escape. She could only wait until someone decided to check on her.

She had no fear she would be left to die. Stefan would want to make her use her mage powers for his benefit. He would be back soon.

She tried to process everything she'd learned. Darius must have told her mother her name, and her mother would have guessed she might be the daughter she'd been forced to abandon. Nai Nai had told her that her mother had disappeared, but the old woman died when Carina was too young to press her for more information.

Nai Nai had also told her that her father was dead. If her mother had ended up married to that evil Sherrerr, it meant Stefan had probably killed him. Carina shivered then sobbed. She wept for her dead father and in pity for her mother. What had her life been like in the years she'd been gone?

It was no wonder she hadn't recognized her mother at first. She bore little resemblance to Carina's dim memories of the happy, gentle person from her toddlerhood. The poor, poor woman. Nai Nai had warned her so seriously and so often for good reasons. Her mother was living proof of the old woman's words.

And of course, little Darius hadn't told her of his mother's dreadful plight. At six years old, he would have no idea of the true situation of his family. Carina tried to remember what he'd said about his brothers and sisters. She seemed to remember he had four or five. Some of them were mages and some weren't. That made sense. If only one parent was a mage, some offspring would inherit powers and some wouldn't. Stefan had bred at least two or three more mages on her mother. Now he would want to add her to his collection.

Carina recalled her joy at seeing little Darius again. Now she understood the connection she'd felt with him. He was more than another mage to her. They shared the same blood.

The door opened. Carina stiffened. Stefan entered the cell. "Wait here," he said to someone behind him before closing the door. He leaned his back against it, regarding her as he folded his arms across his chest. Amusement crinkled the corners of his eyes.

Stefan's manner was the most disarming thing about him. If he hadn't tortured her within an inch of her life, Carina could have mistaken her mother's husband at first glance for a normal, not-unlikable man. He was very good-looking, and though he was middle-aged he wore the years well. When he wasn't inflicting pain and cruelty on others, his expression was intelligent. The monster inside him was obviously only visible when the occasion merited it.

Years of surviving alone on the streets and then fighting as a merc had given Carina nerves of steel, yet this man scared her. She couldn't imagine what he might be capable of, and neither did she want to find out.

"Ah, Carina," said Stefan. "You have no idea of the joy it gives me to find you at last. I knew your mother had borne a child before she came to me. Though she always denied it, I can tell these things, you know. I knew there was at least one more mage brat running around in this part of the galaxy. But it isn't only your powers that make me so pleased to meet you."

He squatted on his heels so he was at eye level with her.

"As I look at you now," he went on, "I'm reminded so strongly of the first time I met your mother. She was a little older than you then, but just as beautiful. Time has worn her features—strongly as it turns out now that I have the opportunity to compare the two of you, but she was breath-taking then. There's a special beauty to women who are hurt and despairing. I love their vulnerability. It excites me no end."

"I'm glad to meet you too, Stefan," Carina said. "I always promised myself that if I ever found out who had taken my parents from me, I would make them pay. And now I've finally found you."

"Ha! I'm sorry to have to disappoint you on that score, my dear. Your mother has threatened me with her revenge too many times to count, yet here I am. And here you two are, under my control. You won't be harming me in any way. On the contrary, you'll be helping me."

"I'll kill you first." Carina stood up, though her restraints pulled at her wrists and her legs could barely take her weight. The after-effects of the nerve torture screamed at her, telling her to be still.

If only he would come closer.

Stefan laughed. "I believe your mother said the very same words. Yet look where her defiance got her." He also rose to his feet. "Your arrival is as fortuitous as hers was. Through the careful deployment of her powers, my status in my family has risen considerably. I'm looking forward to adding you to my stable of mages now that we Sherrerrs are embarking on our push to destroy our competition and rise to supremacy. I imagine you have abilities that exceed even your own poor, dear mother's."

"I wouldn't fight the Sherrerrs' war for them even if I could," Carina replied. "Not after what you've done to my family."

"Hmmm...so you're also holding to the lie that mages cannot kill. I never believed your mother, and I don't believe you. You will fight for me, Carina, and willingly. Do you think I can't make you? You're mistaken. I have many years' experience of dealing with your mother. I know exactly how to force her to bend to my will, as you found out earlier. I have no doubt the same methods will work on you."

Carina didn't reply. She was willing him to move closer.

And then he did.

His confident swagger as he sauntered across the small space told her what he had in mind. She reasoned that a few moments' disgust was well worth the result.

"I have another reason to be thankful you turned up just now, Carina," Stefan said softly. His pupils were wide in spite of the strong light in the room. "Your mother won't be giving me any more children, but you're young and healthy. I'm sure you could bring seven or eight little ones into the world with my help. Another brood of mages would cement the domination of the Sherrerr clan, and in time, it would be natural for me to lead it. How does that sound? Wouldn't it be wonderful to be the Lady Sherrerr? First woman of this galactic sector."

He was so close she could feel his breath on her skin, hot and humid. But she couldn't act. She had to wait for the right moment. To hide her expression of loathing, she turned her face away. Stefan took her movement for acquiescence. He pressed his body against her, grasped her jaw, and pulled her face around to his. As he kissed her, he squeezed her breast hard while his other hand snaked down between her legs.

Carina twisted her head violently downward and fastened her teeth on Stefan's neck. She bit him with all her strength, grinding her teeth to reach his jugular vein. At Stefan's scream, the door flew open. A moment later, something struck her head, breaking her bite on Stefan's neck and nearly knocking her out.

She sank to the floor, his blood dripping from her chin. Stefan also fell. His hand clutched his neck, and blood ran from between his fingers, but it didn't run fast enough. She hadn't managed to reach his vein.

"Should I stun her, sir?" the guard asked.

Grimacing in pain, Stefan replied, "No." He gasped, "No, leave her be." The blood from his neck dribbled slowly down to his shirt. Though he continued to wince at the pain Carina had caused him, she was amazed and sickened to see a smile form on his lips. "Thank you for that, my dear. I'd almost forgotten what it's like to be with a woman who truly fights. I will enjoy our first encounter very much indeed."

Forty-Six

Several hours after Stefan departed, the door to Carina's cell opened once again. This time, two guards entered. While one kept his weapon trained on her, the other unfastened her restraints and hauled her to her feet. After tying her hands behind her back, the first guard pushed her out of the cell.

"Where are you taking me?"

Neither of the guards answered. They only guided her through the starship's corridors.

It was a large, military vessel similar to the one the Sherrerrs had used to blow up Banner's Moon, no doubt intended to take part in the effort to "destroy the competition" that Stefan had mentioned. She wondered if Stefan had commanded her to be brought to him so that she could Cast in an upcoming battle.

To her surprise, when the guards finally opened another door and pushed her through, she found herself in the entrance to a living compartment. The ties around her wrists were removed and the guards left and closed the door. The low murmur of quiet voices came from the lounge area. Carina followed the sound and found herself looking at a group of children, presumably her new family. A boy and girl of about the same age were playing a 3D game, a teenage girl was drawing on a holoscribe, a younger boy was wrestling with his sister on the floor, and Darius was lying across a sofa, his feet up on its arm as he read from an interface.

He was the first to notice her. "Carina," the little boy exclaimed. He threw down his screen and ran over to her, then stopped. "What's that on your face?

Her mother appeared in a doorway. She turned pale as she met Carina's gaze. She swept across the room to grab her in her arms. "You're hurt," she said. "Come and sit down. I'll call a medic."

Carina finally understood what Darius had meant. "It's okay. It isn't my blood. It's Stefan's." She rubbed away the dry, crusty flakes.

The relief that swept across her mother's features was quickly followed by horror. "What did he do to you? What has he done?" Her voice rose to an almost hysterical pitch.

"He hasn't done anything," Carina replied. "I'm okay. Really."

Her mother covered her face with her hands. "Oh, Carina. I'm so sorry. I'm so sorry. I tried so hard to protect you."

"It isn't your fault. None of this is. It's that Sherrerr bastard who's to blame. I'm not going to let him get away with it."

"What's a bastard?" Darius asked.

"Oh, nothing," said Carina's mother. "A bad man."

"Are you talking about Father? Is he a bastard? He *is* a bad man. He ordered the guards to catch Carina. I hate him."

Carina's mother shushed the child and glanced fearfully into the living room. The teenage boy and his younger sister had stopped wrestling and were watching and listening to everything that was going on. All the children were. The boy and girl had stopped playing their game and the teenage girl was looking at them over her holoscribe. Carina's mother took a deep breath. She took her by the hand and led her fully into the room. "Children, I would like you to meet your sister, Carina."

After a moment's pause, the boy and girl who had been playing the 3D game came over and hugged her around her waist. The girl introduced herself as Oriana, and the boy said his name was Ferne. The teenage girl said gravely, "I'm very pleased to meet you, Carina. I'm Parthenia." She remained where she was. The teenage boy and younger girl ignored Carina and resumed their wrestling.

"That's Castiel," her mother said, gesturing to the boy, "and Nahla."

Now that she heard the names again, bits and pieces of what Darius had told Carina about his family came back to her. She remembered he hadn't particularly liked Castiel, and the boy had no mage powers. She imagined it would be hard growing up among siblings who could do things you couldn't.

Her mother announced, "Carina has had a difficult time and needs to rest. She'll be able to talk to you all and get to know you later." She took her hand to lead her away.

"Awww, Mother," said Darius. "I want Carina to play with me *now*."

"You'll just have to be patient," her mother replied. She took her into a bedroom.

After closing the door, her mother clasped her close and held her so tightly she could hardly breathe. Carina hugged her mother back as sobs wracked the woman's thin body. She felt like if she pressed too hard on the frail back, her bones would break.

Her mother was repeating the same words over and over through her tears. *I'm sorry. I'm so sorry.* Eventually, Carina gently loosened her mother's hold on her and held her at arms' length. The poor woman looked even worse than she had the last time she'd seen her. Carina didn't know how she was still standing. She guided her across to a bed and sat her down, wrapping her arms around her.

"I missed you, Ma," she said.

"I missed you too, darling," her mother replied, her voice thick with bitter sorrow. "When Darius told me a mage had rescued him and her name was Carina, I could hardly believe it. How could it possibly be you? And yet after he described your appearance I knew it *was* you— that by some strange, amazing coincidence it was my daughter who had returned my son to me.

"I knew how lonely you must be. Such is the life of a mage. I wanted to send you a sign that you weren't alone, that someone knew who and what you are. I hoped it would give you some comfort, even if I could do nothing else to help you. But I wish I'd never sent you those the elixir ingredients or one of your grandmother's stones. That was so stupid of me. I would rather have never seen you again than have you end up here with me and the other children."

Carina put her hand atop her mother's. "Don't worry about me. I'm not a child any longer. I can get us all out of this, and I will. I won't let Stefan or any other Sherrerr hurt you or any of my brothers or sisters ever again."

Her mother smiled sadly. "I wish that were possible. I've tried so many times. I've come so close but each time I failed. Stefan is too clever and his control is too strong. Why else do you think you're here? Why hasn't he kept you locked up in a cell?"

Carina had wondered about that. It seemed strange her mother's husband would allow them to be together and give them the opportunity to plot their escape.

"It's because he knows the closer we are emotionally to each other, the greater the hold he has over us," her mother explained. "He wants you and I to renew our relationship and for you to bond with your sisters and brothers. Then, to force us to Cast as he wishes, all he has to do is threaten to hurt someone we love. For a man with a heart that's never known anything but avarice and lust for power, he has a remarkable understanding of love. Like when he was torturing you. I couldn't bear it. I couldn't allow you to suffer that pain, even though I knew you would suffer worse things and for longer, if I confessed what you are." She began to weep again.

Carina hugged her. "You didn't make him do that, and your confession didn't change anything. He knew what I was. He was only enjoying torturing both of us, just in different ways."

"I know," her mother said, "but still, I gave in, again."

"Mother, please don't blame yourself. None of this is your fault."

Carina also felt like crying. Her mother's wretchedness was unbearable. But she wanted to remain strong. Perhaps her mother could draw strength from her own.

"Carina." Her mother swallowed. "I have to tell you, your father... he's gone. Stefan swore that he would let him go free if I would only tell him what mages can do. He lied. When I'd given him the information he wanted, he brought Kris in, and..."

"Please..." Carina sat and gripped her mother's hands until she finally mastered her emotions. "I knew. I already knew about Dad."

"You knew? How did you know?"

"Nai Nai told me he was dead. She said she didn't know what had happened to you, but that Daddy had died. I don't know how she knew. Maybe as she was his mother, she felt it somehow. But that man Stefan isn't going to hurt any of us anymore. It stops here."

"I've wanted it to stop for so long, Carina. I wished for it so hard. I tried everything I could, but he's too smart and too evil. All I hope for these days is for everything to finally end, one way or another."

"Don't give up. I've been in some hard places and I always found a way out. I'll find a way out of this too, for all of us."

"That's the problem. It has to be all of us or none of us. Anyone who's left behind will be made to pay for the escape of the others. That's one of the things that makes it so hard to leave."

Carina suddenly regretted her reckless attempt to kill Stefan. She hadn't thought about what his family might do to her mother if she'd succeeded.

"Besides," her mother went on. "I'm not sure if all the children want to be free of him. Parthenia seems to want to please him. And he isn't mean to Castiel or Nahla. They love him like any child loves its father."

Carina recalled the non-mage children in the family, who hadn't said a word when she was introduced. She hadn't felt the natural emotional closeness she'd immediately felt for Darius, the twins, and even the reserved Parthenia. Yet Castiel and Nahla were her mother's children too. Of course she had to love them just as much as the ones who had inherited her mage powers.

"Castiel and Nahla don't know what their father is capable of," Carina said. "If they did, they wouldn't want to stay with him."

Her mother's wan, grief-stricken face sank further. "I don't know if that's true."

FORTY-SEVEN

Stefan's first move was to try to involve Carina in the upcoming attack on one of the Dirksens' military bases, a planet called Cestrarth. He brought her to the battle planning meeting.

Stefan was taking no chances with her physical freedom. He had her tied painfully tightly to a chair set back a little from the table. Castiel sat next to her. No one had said why. Carina wondered if Stefan was training up his son and her half-brother in his role as a torturer of the mages in the family.

Carina noticed with satisfaction that Stefan's neck still bore the wound of her attack. The ship's medic had applied a healing gel, but her bite mark was easy to see, each tooth distinct. *Ha, Ma managed to keep the Heal Cast a secret,* she thought. She smiled grimly to herself. The next time he gave her an opening, Stefan wouldn't survive.

She considered it oddly over-confident that he was making her attend the battle planning. She would of course become privy to the Sherrerrs' strategies and tactics. Either Stefan's need to show off his new mage to the other Sherrerrs was blinding him to the danger, or she was attending a mock meeting where she was only being fed facts it was safe for her to know.

The attendees filed in. Unlike Stefan, they wore the Sherrerr uniform. The family insignia was reiterated on their collars at a frequency that accorded with their rank. The officers were all older than Stefan. A gray-haired woman called Tremoille took the seat nearest

Carina, giving her only a cursory glance. One of the woman's arms was prosthetic. A portly man with a long face arrived next and sat opposite Carina. He proceeded to stare at her unblinkingly. A short, younger woman sat next to him. When the next officer arrived, Carina stiffened.

It was Commander Calvaley of the Sherrerrs' mountain stronghold on Ithiya. After her special request to visit the men's quarters, there was no chance he wouldn't recognize her.

"Well, I never," Calvaley said as he dropped casually into his seat and got a clear look at her face. "If it isn't Private Lin, who disappeared right from under our noses. This makes a lot of sense."

"What's that?" Stefan asked.

"Your mage is no stranger to me," Calvaley replied. "She served in the attack on Banner's Moon. Served bravely and well. She appropriated a new Dirksen weapon that's designed to incapacitate the enemy with terror. It emits an ultrasonic frequency that resonates with the amygdala in the brain, triggering an uncontrollable emotional reaction. Your mage stole what we believe to be the prototype before we blew up their moon. Or perhaps you spirited it out of there?" He raised an eyebrow.

If only, Carina thought, though she said nothing. Casting Transport on that thing would have saved a lot of effort and stress. Too bad she couldn't sip elixir while wearing a helmet.

"Carina," Stefan said. "I'm impressed. You were helping in the Sherrerr cause even before I met you."

"I was just a soldier doing my job, before I knew the Sherrerrs were rapists and torturers. I won't be helping you again."

"Stefan," the portly man at the head of the table said. "Keep her in check, would you? We don't have much time. I'd rather proceed without interruption."

"Of course, General," said Stefan. "I apologize." He went over to Carina and bent down to speak into her ear. "If you think that my raping and beating your mother was bad," he said softly, "just wait and see what I'll do to her if you speak again."

Carina clenched her teeth. She was already feeling the effect of the power Stefan held that her mother had warned her about. She would give anything to save the poor woman from more suffering. A sense of desperation began to gnaw at her.

At her side, Castiel smiled.

———

Carina had no choice but to listen as the Sherrerr heads of command discussed their tactics to defeat the Dirksens' forces on Cestrarth. They were expecting to meet a vigorous defense and were working on the assumption that their attack was unlikely to be a surprise to their rival clan. As a result, they were bringing a large portion of their firepower to bear with the intention of striking hard and fast. The Sherrerrs wanted to utterly crush the opposing forces on the planet and take it over. Cestrarth's position lent it strategic importance, and losing the military forces would strike a major blow to the Dirksens.

One way or another, it would be a decisive first battle in the war, in space, in the air, on the ground, and at sea on Cestrarth. As the officers talked, Stefan would glance at Carina every so often, as if hoping she was thinking up Casts she could use to aid the Sherrerr cause. She was not.

She was trying to figure out how to get her mother and siblings out of reach of their psychopathic husband and father. It wouldn't be easy. Even if she could get the ingredients and create an elixir—a process she'd discovered Stefan guarded against effectively—she couldn't Transport the family off the ship. They were probably light years from any civilized regions, let alone habitable planets. The Sherrerrs would have gone somewhere remote in order to gather their ships in secret. Though she might have attempted a Transport Cast from a ship in orbit to a planet's surface, trying to move a human being planetside from deep space was highly likely to end in a nasty, painful death.

Even if she had elixir in her hand right now, escape of any kind was out of the question. Her only other option was to take command of the ship—a ship that was carrying tens of thousands of armed troops. It was no good. Escape wouldn't be possible until the ship traveled to an inhabited region. Carina would have to think of a plan that might work when they were near a habitable planet.

As soon as they were free, they could survive and avoid recapture with the help of their mage powers. At least, the mage children could. Carina wasn't sure what to do with the children who hadn't inherited her mother's abilities. Would they want to leave too? She wasn't sure. It seemed that Stefan had never behaved excessively badly toward them. Maybe they would prefer to remain living the rich, highly privileged lifestyle of the Sherrerr clan.

Castiel was watching her too. He was still smiling. He looked extremely like his father. Carina wondered what her mother thought of her eldest son.

The meeting was drawing to a close. The holo of Cestrarth floating above the central table disappeared and the officers began to push back their chairs and leave. The parts of the battle plan that had filtered through to Carina had given her no ideas on how she could Cast to influence the outcome, even if she'd been willing to try. The only time she'd Cast during a battle, all she'd done was Transport troops to another place. Killing took a lot of concentration and power, and it was grisly. She had no desire to do that to Dirksen soldiers, who, like the Sherrerr troops, were only pawns in the game the two great clans played.

Calvaley was walking around the table, heading over to her. "I haven't given up on you, Lin," he said when he arrived at her chair. "You're an excellent soldier, and with your abilities you could rise high in the ranks very quickly. You could occupy an influential, lucrative position where you would not be subject to coercion. What do you say?"

"Now wait a minute," said Stefan, rising to his feet.

"Sit down," Calvaley told him. "I shouldn't have to remind you that you are not an officer in the Sherrerr armed forces, and until you are, your surname counts for little. You are tolerated, Stefan Sherrerr, for what you can offer, and no more."

The rage emanating from the object of Calvaley's scorn was almost palpable.

"I would sooner cut my own throat than work for the Sherrerrs," Carina said. "When you tolerate the actions of scum, you sink to the same level. One of my deepest regrets is that I ever helped you. I won't make the same mistake again."

"Hmmm...shame," said Calvaley. "Not everyone thinks the same as you, you know. Control is the foundation of civilization. Without it, there is nothing but anarchy and barbarism. If you think our behavior is bad, you wouldn't want to see what happens in a society that lives without fear of retribution. A society that lacks a controlling force isn't a society, it's a collection of individuals fighting, maiming, and killing to get what they want. When we have ultimate control over this galactic sector, we will see peace and prosperity on an unprecedented scale."

"Keep telling yourself that, Calvaley, while you consort with rapists, torturers, and murderers. What you think you're fighting is what you are. I despise you."

Stefan drew back his hand to strike her across the face, but Calvaley stopped him with an impatient gesture.

"You're young and confused," he said to Carina, "and I have no doubt that Stefan has put your poor mother through a lot, so I'll forgive you that. In time, when we've won this war, you'll see I was right. Like I said, many see the sense of our actions. That other soldier who disappeared with you saw fit to return to our ranks after his little sojourn."

Calvaley could only mean Bryce. Bryce had rejoined the Sherrerr army? Carina said nothing, but her shock must have shown on her face.

"That surprised you, didn't it?" Calvaley said. "Yes. I spotted him aboard ship this morning. He enlisted under an assumed name of course, but I knew his face. You see? He left with you, but he's seen the error of his ways and come back to fight for a noble cause. What do you think of that?"

Carina's mind was whirring as she tried to think of why Bryce would have re-enlisted with the Sherrerrs when he had a new business to run.

"Consider my proposal, Lin. It stands—for a little while."

FORTY-EIGHT

Ensconced deep within the Sherrerr ship, Carina was shielded from all the effects of the space battle going on with the Dirksen fleets. She had learned they were aboard the Sherrerr flagship, *Nightfall*. While the destroyers, dreadnoughts, and fighter ships of both sides fought for control of the planetary system, all she saw was the interface feed from drones at Cestrarth. The flying spies transmitted vids and data from the planet surface to the room where Stefan had put her along with her two guards.

A jug and a glass sat on the table in front of her. The jug was filled with elixir. Parthenia had made it, and she'd done it perfectly. She had wondered why, when Stefan clearly had a mage who was willing to help him, he bothered forcing her to do his bidding. Perhaps it was because he thought she was better at Casting, or he wanted to assert his power over her.

After guards had taken her to the room, Stefan had told her he would be back soon, and left. She knew that he'd gone to fetch someone he could threaten to hurt if she didn't do exactly as he asked. When he'd reappeared with little, sweet Darius in tow, her horror was almost equaled by her rage.

Stefan had his method of coercion honed to its most efficient and effective. It wasn't surprising he'd controlled her mother so well over the years. First, he picked his victim well. Carina had been expecting him to use her mother, but of course he'd realized they would try to collude and defy him, even at the cost of extreme pain. He'd passed over his wife in favor of another person he knew Carina cared about.

She'd loved the little boy even before she knew he was her half-brother. If she'd even guessed at what went on within Stefan's household, she would never have returned him. But at his young age, the little boy didn't know or understand half of it. Her mother had done a good job of protecting him. When Carina had asked him about his home life after rescuing him from the Dirksens, he had only told her the facts from his six-year-old perspective—his brothers and sisters, tutors, pets, and daily life. It seemed that up until recently, things had been fairly normal on the surface within the walls of the Sherrerr estate.

"Normal" was the last word Carina would use to describe what was happening now. She could hardly conceive of someone so depraved they would hurt a little boy, let alone their own son, in order to get what they wanted.

Darius was holding his father's hand trustingly and looking all about him as the pair entered the room. As soon as the little boy's gaze alighted on Carina he gave a beaming smile and tried to break away from his father to run to her. Stefan held tightly to his son's hand, however, saying, "There will be time to speak to Carina later, Darius. Please sit down here."

Looking a little confused, Darius climbed into the seat his father had indicated.

"We have an important job to do today," said Stefan, "and you're going to help us do it."

"Do you want me to Cast?" Darius asked. He'd spotted the jug and glass on the table.

"No. Carina will be doing the Casting today. She is older than you and her abilities are much stronger."

"Oh, am I here to watch?" asked Darius. "Like I have to watch Parthenia sometimes?"

"You are here to watch, to learn, and to provide encouragement."

"I can do that," Darius said, though without enthusiasm. He was watching Carina sadly.

She was nauseated with disgust and overcome with fury. At the word "encouragement," Stefan had drawn out the torture instrument he'd used on her from inside his jacket. He was holding it behind

Darius, and the little boy couldn't see it. The implication was clear: if she didn't do as Stefan asked, he would use the device on the child.

Her nerves hadn't entirely recovered from the ministrations of the slim metal rod. They still tingled painfully at intervals when she was awake and asleep. Her whole being rebelled at the idea of Darius suffering the same agony she'd endured.

The little boy asked, "What's the matter, Carina?"

She'd been trying to keep her expression neutral. She was clearly failing at the attempt. "Stefan Sherrerr, you're a monster."

"No, my dear," he replied. "I'm very much a man, as I intend to demonstrate to you, to my great delight and pleasure, when I have a spare moment. Now, the situation is very clear, but as this is your first time, I think it wise to make it even clearer. I am well aware of the capabilities of mages, and also the limitations of their Casts. I know the effect is not immediate, that there is a lag, which is fortunate for me and very unfortunate for you. Both of the guards are under strict instructions to immediately retaliate with deadly force if anything should begin to happen to themselves or myself.

"You may wish to take a chance, but will your Cast work before you or your brother are under any threat? I can assure you from experience it will not. Your mother found that out the hard way, if only her poor feeble mind could recall it. Be assured, a pulse rifle fires faster than any Cast can work. If you do try, you will fail. You and your brother will be gone, and I will have four mages remaining at my disposal.

"But I would ask you not to attempt it, nevertheless, Carina, as step-father to step-daughter. Though you and I have yet to become better acquainted, I have grown quite fond of the boy, and I would be sorry to hurt him."

"Father?" Darius asked, looking up at Stefan with wide brown eyes.

His father ruffled his hair. "Never mind. Just sit there and be a good boy."

Stefan's words had been beyond his understanding, but Darius must have picked up on some of what was going on because he suddenly began to cry.

Carina couldn't stand it. "Take him out of here. I'll do what you want."

Stefan raised his eyebrows. "Capitulating so soon? I was expecting more of a fight from you. What was it you were saying? You'd rather cut your own throat? How dramatic. Yet here we are and you cave like a virgin on her first night."

"Done with your gloating?" Carina asked. "Take him away."

"No, I don't think I'll do that. I'd much prefer little Darius to remain present. His presence will keep my threat fresh in your mind, and he might learn something from watching you in action."

Carina herself didn't know what she could do to fulfill Stefan's command that she help the Sherrerrs win their battle. She only wanted to protect Darius. The child had already been tortured by the Dirksens to try to make him reveal his mage status. He'd been through enough without his father torturing him too.

She closed her eyes and gave a heavy sigh. "Has the battle on the ground started? You know I can't do anything in space, right? I can't affect the Dirksen ships." Starships traveling at even slow speeds were impossible for a mage to target, as far as Carina knew. In the handful of times she'd tried, she'd failed.

"Your mother did manage to convince me of that limitation on mage powers, under considerable duress. I remain convinced, for the moment."

"Then what's happening on the ground? And how the hell do you expect me to do anything about it from up here?"

"The battle has begun," Stefan replied. "See the drone feed." Four holograms flickered to life above the table. Each showed a different view of a planet. There appeared to be four separate military encounters about to take place. One was at a vast concrete complex that bordered a stormy ocean, a second was at a plain that lay within a circle of extinct volcanoes, the third was at sea—Carina guessed that the military installation was on the sea bottom—and the fourth was in a polar region. At all four locations, Sherrerr tanks, armored guns, military drones, and soldiers in exosuits were approaching and defensive fire had begun.

Carina thought of Bryce. Was he taking part in any of the battles? Calvaley had said he'd seen him aboard the ship. She hoped that was where he'd stayed. She also remembered Mandeville and the other soldiers who had helped her bring the Dirksen weapon to the Sherrerr shuttle.

For the first time in her life, her distaste for the bloodshed and violence of military combat turned to hatred. Before, when she'd been a merc, she'd seen armed conflict as a necessary evil of human society. It was going to happen anyway, she'd reasoned. She couldn't stop it so she might as well profit from it. Her feelings were different now. Her disgust for Stefan turned on herself when she realized what she had to do.

"Well?" Stefan asked impatiently. "Have you thought of something? Or do you need some persuasion?" He lifted the slim metal rod.

"I can't Cast across the galaxy," Carina said. "You'll have to take me closer."

FORTY-NINE

Carina asked Stefan over and over to leave Darius aboard the ship and not bring him with them on the shuttle to Cestrarth. She promised him she would Cast to help the Sherrerr side even without Darius present, but he refused to even listen to her. He took his son from the room, telling her they would all go to the surface together once a shuttle was prepared.

Powerlessness and hopelessness engulfed her as he left with his son. Stefan was right. Despite all her brave words, she was caught in the same trap her mother had been for all those years. She couldn't see any way out of it. And what had Stefan meant when he said her mother had found out 'the hard way' what would happen if she refused? Her mother hadn't mentioned any events along those lines. Carina wondered if the recollection was too painful.

A short time later, her guards took her to the shuttle bay. The place was nearly empty. Most of the shuttles were ferrying soldiers to the surface and the fighter ships had left to take part in the battle. Stefan and Darius were waiting for her, standing outside a shuttle at the far end of the bay.

When she arrived at the vessel, she repeated her request. "Please, Stefan. This is incredibly dangerous. We'll be flying right inside the battle zone. Anything could hit us and take us down. Drones, ground-to-air missiles, defense rockets, even well-aimed sniper fire. This isn't a military craft."

"We won't be as defenseless as you suppose," he replied. "We will have a support team. Let's go."

They went up the ramp and into the cabin. Stefan had brought the elixir along, only this time it was in a canister rather than a jug to prevent it from spilling during what promised to be a rocky flight. The shuttle's cabin windows were wide, providing an unusually good view. As well, a holo feed from the surface had been set up. She had all she needed to wreak death and destruction on the Dirksen troops with her powers.

Carina said, "What if I can't do this? I've never tried this before. This isn't how mages use their abilities."

"If you can't sway the course of the battle with your efforts," Stefan replied, "you'd better do a damned good job of convincing me you tried." He directed his son to a seat. "Fasten your safety belt, Darius."

The little boy did as he was told, giving Carina a look filled with fear. He hadn't spoken a word since his fit of crying. Her heart ached at the harsh introduction he was experiencing to his father's truly evil nature.

The pilot boarded, and the shuttle took off. "Which battle site do you wish to go to?" Stefan asked after an hour or so. "We're approaching the planet." He wore a headset enabling him to comm the pilot.

Carina still had no idea. She'd only decided she had to try to do something to sway the fight. Now they were on their way down, her mind remained a blank. Oceanside, a plain encircled by volcanoes, a sea bed, or the subzero, icy environment of a polar cap? The Dirksens had chosen the locations of their military installations well. All presented challenges to the attackers that their own troops would be trained to turn to their advantage. She was wracking her brains for a Cast that would dispose of Dirksen troops. She had to think of something.

"Which is it to be Carina?" Stefan asked again, a hard edge to his tone.

She had to pick. Which one? "The sea bed."

Stefan relayed her choice to the pilot.

"No, wait," Carina said. "The one by the ocean. Or..."

"Which one? Make a decision," Stefan snapped. "You're wasting time."

"The ocean, I guess. Yes, the ocean." She had the germ of an idea.

"Where are we going?" Darius finally piped up.

"Never mind," Stefan replied. "Be quiet."

"We're going to a place where soldiers are fighting," Carina answered.

Stefan frowned but said nothing. He gazed out of the shuttle window as if he had a lot on his mind. They were entering the upper atmosphere. A large, copper-yellow landmass spread out beneath them, stretching to the curved horizon, surrounded by blue ocean. They were sunside, and the border of the atmosphere was clear to see, shimmering as it faded into the blackness of space.

"Why are the soldiers fighting?" Darius asked.

Carina wished she could have gotten to know her little brother in better circumstances. "It's hard to explain. But, Darius, can you do something for me?"

"Yes, of course, Carina. What do you want me to do?"

"Soldiers fighting is a horrible thing to see. You're too young to be watching something like that. Can you promise me that when we arrive there, you'll close your eyes and keep them closed the whole time until I tell you it's okay to open them?"

Stefan rolled his eyes but again he chose not to interfere. Carina imagined he thought his son's welfare wasn't worth bothering about.

The landmass was drawing closer. The pilot was flying them to an area of coastline. As they got nearer, Carina could see the battle was well underway. Specks that were fighter pinnaces were circling the site, jinking to avoid missiles. Puffs of smoke and fire from bombs and other air strikes rose from the military complex they were rapidly approaching. Carina doubted the Sherrerrs were doing much real damage. The structure she'd seen close-up before had been wide but only one story high. Most of the installation had to be underground.

Three fighter planes were zooming up toward them.

"We're being attacked," Carina said.

"No," replied Stefan. "They're Sherrerr planes. They're for our protection."

"What's the state of the battle? Is there a chance this place will be nuked from above?"

"Didn't you listen to anything at all at the planning meeting? We want to *use* the planet, not destroy it. There's not much point in having control of an uninhabitable disaster zone, is there? We just need to gain control of their military sites and put down their defenses. So you need to help us overthrow this site. I have given my assurance you can do it, so my reputation in my family is riding on your success. You'd better deliver, or you, your mother, and all your new brothers and sisters will regret it."

No pressure then.

"You can do it, Carina," Darius said. "I know you can."

"Darius, this isn't what mages are supposed to do. We aren't about hurting people. I want you to understand that."

"Shut up and concentrate on your task," Stefan spat.

The military installation was clear to see now. It reached for two or three kilometers along the coast. The Sherrerrs certainly had their work cut out for them. The Dirksens' guns were firing back at their ground and air attackers, and though the Sherrerr rockets and missiles were hitting their targets, the damage seemed minimal. It was a battle that would take days and massive amounts of firepower to win, if it were winnable at all.

She needed a way to destroy the installation without also causing thousands of Sherrerr casualties. Carina's germ of an idea had grown as they were flying down. It could work. It really could.

FIFTY

"Tell the pilot to fly up and down the coastline," Carina told Stefan. She didn't really need to survey the area. She'd made her request just to buy some time as she marshaled her thoughts and feelings. What she was planning wouldn't hinge on the lie of the land, but on whether she could actually manage it. She rarely had occasion to Cast Rise, and she'd never done it on such a large scale before.

A Cast of that magnitude would require very deep concentration. If she allowed the things most prominent in her mind right now—concern for Darius, fears for her mother and the rest of her new family, worries about what Stefan would want her to do next—to dominate her thoughts, she would never succeed.

And she had to succeed. She simply had to. Stefan had been correct when he'd said that all her brave words had flown out the window the minute he threatened to harm her little brother. Darius had already been through so much when he was kidnapped. He'd had his tracker chip cut out of him by the Dirksens and they'd tortured him to try to discover if he had mage powers. He also had a monster for a father. She couldn't bear to see the little boy hurt again, even if it meant taking part in a war that was none of her business.

One day, hopefully soon, she would help Darius, her mother, and her other sisters and brothers escape from Stefan's clutches. Until that moment she had to do as Stefan asked. Her heart sank as she realized her mother must have told herself exactly the same thing many years ago. She wondered when Ma had finally given up hope.

She would never give up hope. She *would* find a way out.

They were flying at an incredible speed and jerking erratically as the pilot fought to avoid the fire targeted at them. A brilliant flash of light shone through the windows, an ear-splitting *boom* rent the air, and the shuttle rocked and spun upside down. They'd been hit!

Then the pilot righted the vessel.

"Lost one of our fighters," Stefan remarked, almost casually. "You must begin soon. Are you ready?"

Their remaining two guard pinnaces were shooting down the missiles, but they were in great danger of being hit at any moment.

"You'll have to tell the Sherrerr troops to evacuate. Now."

"What? I have no authority to do that."

"If you don't want them to be destroyed, you have to make them stop attacking and withdraw. It's the only way."

"I'm telling you—"

"Then take us back to the ship. I'm a mage, Stefan, not a miracle worker. I can't wave my hands and make the installation disappear or kill all the Dirksens with a nod of my head. You should know this. You've lived with mages for fifteen years and seen what they can and can't do. We aren't murderers. I hardly ever Cast when I was a merc. This isn't easy for me. So do as I ask or forget it, because no matter what you threaten, I can't help you." Despite what it might mean, she had to try to save some troops from what she was about to do. Bryce and Mandeville could be down there. Also, she knew how much this meant to Stefan. She wanted to exploit what leverage she had.

Stefan's brow furrowed in anger. He seemed about to give a retort, but thought better of it. He asked the pilot to patch him through to the Sherrerr command. A moment later he stated Carina's request. He was speaking with Calvaley. After some back and forth, he received the man's agreement.

The shuttle retreated to the upper atmosphere while the Sherrerr troops withdrew from the shoreline. Carina hoped they were moving sufficiently far away to be out of the danger zone.

As the shuttle hung in the upper atmosphere, she saw the fight for control of the planetary system space. Though the starships themselves were too far away to see, flashes and shooting stars signaled the space battle. She hoped that *Nightfall* and her family would remain safe.

After a while, Stefan said, "The troops have retreated. Are you ready?"

No. She would never be ready.

She nodded. Stefan told the pilot to return to the oceanside military base. He reached across the aisle and gave her the bottle of elixir. When they were in sight of the shoreline, she took a large gulp, swallowed the disgusting mixture, then took another gulp. She drank the whole bottle. Would it be enough? She had no idea.

Closing her eyes, she took mental steps down into her mind, disappearing into herself. She shut out the outside noise entering through her ears, the feel of the shuttle seat beneath her, and, with the greatest difficulty, her fear about what she was about to do. She both did and didn't want the Cast to work. Her pulse and breathing slowed. She was alone in the darkness.

In slow strokes, she wrote the character. Each stroke perfect, each in the correct order. *Rise.* When the character was complete, she sent it out. Now she could harness the power of her emotions. She let out her rage at her mother's long captivity and rape, her father's murder, her brothers' and sisters' confinement and abuse, and her own capture and exploitation. She gathered the raw feelings and flung them along the path of the character, speeding in its wake, propelling it to its destination.

Everything was gone. Her mind was blank. Her feelings spent. A terrible weakness overwhelmed her. She could barely open her eyes.

When she did and the shuttle interior swam into view, the first thing she saw was Stefan peering closely out the window. Darius was at his side, also looking downward with great curiosity.

"Darius," Carina said weakly, "get back in your seat. I don't want you to see this."

The little boy did as he was told. "Are you okay?" he asked as he fastened his safety belt.

She was not okay. She was definitely not okay. "I'm fine."

She didn't want to look out the window, but if the Cast had worked, she could guess what was happening. The ocean would be retreating. The waves that had lashed the rocks and concrete buffers of the Dirksens' installation would be gone, and the ocean bed would be laid bare for a kilometer or more from the shore.

If the Dirksens understood what was happening, and if they were quick, they could save a lot of their troops, though their installation would be ruined.

She hoped the Dirksens were quick.

Stefan was nodding. "I see. Very impressive." His back straightened. "Here it comes."

Once, when she was a little girl, before Nai Nai had died and she'd become a street brat, Carina had seen a vid at her friend's house of a natural disaster. Though humans had the technology to avoid many forms of death, they hadn't found a way to prevent eruptions, landslides, earthquakes, hurricanes, or tsunamis.

She had watched her friend's vid in horrified fascination as the water at a beach had disappeared then returned with terrible force, inundating everything in its path. She had watched the terrible weight of water destroying whatever it touched, swamping, crushing, drowning. As a little girl, she'd never imagined she could ever or would ever want to use the power of a tsunami herself.

The enormity of what she'd done settled over her like a suffocating gauntlet. She'd become a weapon of mass destruction.

She closed her eyes.

"Very good, Carina," Stefan said. "Well done."

Fifty-One

When Carina and Darius returned after the battle, the atmosphere in the family living quarters was subdued. Carina's mother greeted her sadly and the children looked up from their occupations momentarily, one or two of them murmuring greetings.

"Carina defeated the Dirksens," Darius said as he went into the living area. "She made a huge wave..." He mimed it with his arms. "And then she sent it crashing down on the Dirksen building. It was amazing." He threw his arms down. He hadn't seen the tsunami but Stefan, in a jubilant mood, had told his son what had happened.

"Shut up you little creep," Castiel said. "Carina only did what Father told her to do. It was Father's victory."

"No..." Darius said, confused. "It was Carina who did it."

Castiel got up from the sofa where he'd been lounging and stalked across to his young brother. "Who brought us here?"

"Father."

"Who took you out in the shuttle?"

"Father."

"Who told Carina to Cast to defeat the Dirksens?"

"Father did, but—"

"Then it was Father's victory. Carina was just Father's weapon."

"But—"

"But nothing," Castiel shouted, and he pushed Darius to the floor.

"Castiel," Carina's mother admonished. "Don't do that. Apologize to your brother and help him up."

Castiel snorted derisively and went back to the sofa. He threw himself onto it and lay down, his hands behind his head.

Ferne had run over to his brother and was helping him to his feet.

"You're a very bad boy," Darius shouted at Castiel, who only smirked and made a rude gesture.

"Stop it, please," Carina's mother said.

She looked worse than ever, Carina thought. She was pale and skeletal, as if something was eating her from the inside out.

"Well done, Carina," Parthenia said.

"Thanks," Carina replied bitterly. "Like Castiel said, it wasn't my idea." She went to her room, closed the door, and sat down on her bed. She couldn't bear the terrible tension that existed constantly between the family members. In her years of solitude after Nai Nai died, when in her darkest moments Carina had wished with all her heart she had her parents and a family, she'd never imagined it would be anything like this. Stefan's abuse had worn down her mother so much she looked like she was at death's door, and the children were split into deeply divided factions.

On one side were the non-mages Castiel and Nahla. The girl wasn't unfriendly while she was away from her brother, but in his company she mimicked his bitter, scornful attitude toward the others. In the other camp were Oriana, Ferne, and little Darius. They played together in quiet games where they pretended to Cast. Carina could remember playing such games herself when she was younger.

Parthenia kept herself apart from the two groups and was quite solitary. In some ways, she reminded Carina of herself, minus the growing-up-on-the street influences on her character. In other ways, Carina found her difficult to read. She'd noticed her looking at their mother with great sadness, yet at the same time she seemed to love Stefan very much and want his attention. Carina hadn't figured out Parthenia yet.

A knock sounded at her door. Carina's mother came in and sat down next to her. She took Carina's hand.

"It's hard when he forces you to Cast, isn't it?" she asked. "I'm sorry you had to go through that."

"I'm okay," Carina replied, a catch in her voice. "It isn't like I've never killed before." Her words were little more than lies intended to protect her mother from guilt and anguish. Nothing Carina said could have been further from the truth. She was constantly fighting to ignore mental images of thousands or even tens of thousands of Dirksen soldiers drowning in their underground bunkers.

She also wanted to spare her mother the details of how Stefan had threatened to hurt Darius. The woman could probably guess well enough, though, and didn't need her husband's methods spelled out to her.

Carina looked into Ma's sad, thin face. She sat up. "Is there something wrong with you? Are you sick?"

The woman took in a deep breath and let out a long sigh.

Her mother's face was filled with such despair, Carina saw her question had struck a nerve. She grabbed her hands. "You are sick! What's wrong?"

Ma swallowed before replying, "I guess I should tell you. I have Ithiyan Plague. I stopped taking the preventative some time ago."

"What? Why did you do that? Have you been to see a doctor?"

"No. I haven't told anyone. I wanted to become so sick that Stefan would have to take me to the capital, to a medical specialist. He would have brought the children with us. I was hoping that once we were outside the estate, I would have a better chance of escaping him." She smiled wryly. "Things didn't quite work out as I planned."

"You need to see a doctor right away. There has to be an army medic aboard the ship."

"I guess I should do that, now that my plan fell through. I just can't seem to get up the motivation. I've lived with this illness so long, I feel like it's part of me and my destiny."

"Don't talk like that," Carina said, filled with alarm. She'd learned from Bryce how quickly the disease became serious once it took hold. She clutched her mother's hands. "I only just found you." Her throat constricted and she couldn't speak. It was no surprise her mother looked so bad. She suddenly jumped up. "Come with me." She pulled on Ma's hands to try to encourage her to stand, but she remained sitting.

"Where? We can't leave these quarters."

"You have to see a doctor. You're seriously ill."

"Oh Carina, I don't know that I want to."

"You have to, Mother. If not for yourself, then for the rest of us. For me." Carina sank to her knees and laid her head in her mother's lap.

"Please. As bad as things are, I can stand it. I finally found you. It was so hard being alone for all that time, always hiding what I was. I hate Stefan and I hate the Sherrerrs and everything they're doing, but I can bear it. We'll work out a way to escape together. But if I lose you, I don't know what I'll do."

Her mother stroked her hair. "I missed you so much, Carina, but it comforted me that you were safe with your Nai Nai. I knew she would take good care of you. I didn't think she would die so soon and leave you all alone. I'm sorry for that, but better a life spent alone on the streets than growing up in Stefan's luxurious slave camp."

"Maybe that's so," Carina replied. "But that's the past. I'm here now, and I'm strong. That evil monster hasn't worn me down. And I can fight. I'm determined to get us out of here, more so than ever now that I know how sick you are. I want to give you a reason to live, Ma. I never had you for so long. I want us to be together for many more years."

"I want that too, Carina. I just don't think it's possible. I tried to keep you safe from Stefan, but he caught you in the end. I guess I've given up hope." She sighed. "But if you want me to see a doctor, I will."

Carina jumped up and ran to the main door of the living quarters. She told the guards her mother was very ill and needed to see a medic immediately.

Fifty-Two

The ship's doctor spent only five minutes with Faye in her bedroom before contacting Stefan to ask permission to take her to sick bay. With her husband's say so, she went with the doctor to the medical center. No one was allowed to go with her. Carina argued for permission but Stefan wouldn't grant it.

After spending another hour examining her and running tests, the doctor left the room, saying she would return soon. Faye waited alone on the narrow examination table, naked under her medical gown. She hadn't looked at her body properly in weeks, and even she had been shocked at how thin she'd grown and the extent of the bruises that covered her skin.

The doctor returned. She sat on a tall stool next to the bed and folded her hands in her lap. "I'm sorry to leave you like that. I had to speak to your husband first. I'm sure you're well aware of how things are run around here."

"I understand. So, what did you tell him? What's the news?"

"Faye," the doctor said, "why did you stop taking your preventative? You must have been aware of the risks."

"I was fully aware, but my reasons for my actions aren't your concern. Are you going to tell me what you found out or not?"

"I also wanted to speak to your husband to ask permission to have you evacuated to the nearest friendly planet so you could begin medical treatment immediately." She paused and looked down. "That permission was refused."

"I see."

"If I had the equipment and the drugs, there might be a chance I could..." The doctor paused again. "The disease has progressed so far, it's now in its final stages. You have maybe one or two weeks left. I'm very sorry."

Faye nodded. It would be hard on Carina. Very hard. She regretted that. And little Darius. He loved her so much. But despite her regrets, she couldn't help but feel a tiny bit relieved that her long suffering would soon be over. If there were an afterlife, she would see Kris again. "I think I'll go back to my family now." She climbed down from the table and picked up her clothes.

"I'll prepare some medication for you to take with you," said the doctor. "It'll help ease your symptoms and make you more comfortable. I imagine you've been feeling some bone pain and tenderness and are having night fevers?"

"Yes, that's right."

"I thought so. I wish I knew why you didn't seek help earlier. What you have is entirely curable with the appropriate treatment even in its late stages. Maybe if I could get you to a hospital within the next week or so you might have a chance, but that seems unlikely in the circumstances."

Faye locked eyes with the woman. "You examined me, didn't you? You saw the scars. That's what he's done to me. For years. In my position, would you want to carry on?" When the doctor looked away and didn't answer, she said, "Please leave. I want to get dressed."

In the empty examining room, as she slowly put on her clothes, Faye wondered why she'd waited and done nothing while the disease ravaged her body almost as badly as Stefan had. She'd told herself it was for the same plan that she'd related to Carina, but the words she'd just blurted out to the doctor seemed to ring truer. She could have told Stefan how sick she was weeks before, but she hadn't. Perhaps, deep down, she'd never intended to go through with her plan. Perhaps she had only been trying to find a way out.

The guards escorted her back to the living quarters. It was late. All the children had gone to bed. Only Carina remained awake, waiting for her in the lounge. When she went inside, her daughter stood up. "What did the doctor say? Have you started treatment?"

She went over to the beautiful, strong, courageous young woman and took her in her arms. She could hardly believe the little girl she'd left behind had turned into such a wonderful, good human being. It hurt so badly to know the time she had left with her was painfully short.

She kissed her daughter on her cheek. How could she tell her? She couldn't find the words. Not now. Not yet. "Yes," she replied. "She's given me some medication."

Carina hugged her tightly. It hurt, but Faye didn't say anything.

"You're going to be okay?" Carina asked, her face buried in her mother's shoulder.

"Yes, I'm going to be okay."

Fifty-Three

Carina was sleeping soundly, relieved that her mother's illness could be cured, when guards woke her. They'd come directly into her bedroom. The two women watched impassively as Carina dressed, then they escorted her through the dark living area. The rest of the family were asleep. Carina didn't know what time it was but she felt as though she'd slept only one or two hours.

Tiredness tugged at her eyelids as the guards took her through the ship, one in front of her and one behind. Neither would answer her questions about where they were taking her or why. She could only hope she wasn't being permanently separated from her mother and siblings.

"Carina," Stefan said expansively when she arrived at her destination. "Glad you could join us." The guards had led her to a wide auditorium. Tiered rows of seating against one wall faced a window that took up the entire opposite wall and looked out on the local starscape.

"You mean you're glad your guards woke me up and forced me to come here," she retorted. Senior Sherrerr officers who had been at the pre-battle strategy meeting were also present, but she didn't care about embarrassing Stefan in front of his family. She would take every opportunity to demonstrate to them exactly what he was.

Stefan frowned in anger. "Come and sit here." He gestured to the seat beside him.

Other officers were here too. Twenty to thirty men and women in uniforms bearing the Sherrerr insignia were taking up most of the seats that faced the view of the galactic expanse. Carina recognized Raynott, who had orchestrated the assault on Banner's Moon. Calvaley was absent for some reason. A pair of guards stood at each entrance, though whether they were there for her she wasn't sure. She started. One of them was Bryce.

He didn't react when their eyes met, and Carina was thankful that no one seemed to have noticed her shocked reaction. She didn't think Stefan would want her to have friends among the guards. Once more, she wondered how Bryce had ended up aboard the Sherrerr flagship.

She sat next to Stefan. A guard stood on her other side. Stefan immediately leaned closer to whisper something in her ear. Certain he was going to communicate some nasty remark or an even nastier threat, she stood up and briefly pretended to straighten her clothes. When she sat down again, she propped her elbow on the armrest farthest from Stefan and rested her chin on her hand, so her mother's husband would have been forced to lean comically far across her seat to speak in her ear.

It was a petty gesture but Carina was taking whatever she could get. Stefan tutted under his breath. She wished she could reach over and break his neck. Only the knowledge that her mother and siblings would suffer the consequences prevented her.

Tremoille, the senior female officer Carina had seen at the strategy meeting, began. "Now that we're all here, finally, I'll play the vid data sent back by our drones. As you'll see, the intel we gathered on Cestrarth has proven to be correct and not planted information."

The window on the stars went black as it became a screen. A different starscape appeared.

"We sent out around three hundred drones," the older woman said. "This vid is has been compiled from all the recordings we received."

The starscape shifted, the lights in the room dimmed, and the area between the audience and the window became a room-wide holo of a field of stars. The stars were subtly moving, or rather, the drones had been traveling into them at high speed, faster than the fastest starship.

"So, where exactly is this?" a voice asked.

"Sacrasi Region," Tremoille replied.

"What?" someone exclaimed. "Right on our doorstep. The arrogant bastards."

"Last place we'd think to look," another audience member remarked.

"Exactly," said Tremoille. "If it weren't for the intel we got from invading their planet, we would never have thought to look here."

The stars in the holo continued to shift. The drones seemed to be heading toward a dark area of space at the center of the scene. Carina's curiosity had been piqued, but she was damned if she was going to ask Stefan to explain what they were watching.

A few moments later, she saw it. Or rather, them. The drones had sent back telemetry on heat signatures their scanners picked up. The specks of red were artificial structures in the depths of space.

"At this point," said Tremoille, "we began to lose drones." Tiny flashes of light peppered the holo. The red specks grew quickly larger and began to assume the rough outline of starships. "The Dirksens had spotted them and were picking them off. The volume and quality of data decreases until the last drone is taken out. Around..." The officer paused. "Here."

The hologram blinked out, and the window reverted to being a plain window again.

"Are we sure that was what we think it is?" someone asked.

"It would be a difficult fake to construct," Tremoille replied.

"Nevertheless, it could be a decoy," the questioner persisted. "The information we found on Cestrarth could be false after all. The whole thing could be an elaborate trap. If we send the strength of our fleet there, we would be leaving our own planets inadequately defended."

"On the other hand," said Raynott, "if it is the Dirksen shipyard and we destroy it, we will have struck a decisive blow. They would find it hard to recover and fight back after that."

"Agreed," the first officer said, "but the same applies to us. Even if it is the shipyard and not a trap, it will be very heavily defended. More so now they detected our drones and they know we know where it is. The battle to destroy it could cause us great losses we'll find difficult to recover from."

"What if we could take out the shipyard without expending vast amounts of firepower?" Stefan asked. "What if we only needed to get one heavily defended ship close enough for my mages to take out the entire place?"

Carina turned and stared at him. So this was why he'd had her woken up in the middle of the quiet shift.

"You're suggesting your mages could destroy the entire Dirksen shipyard?" Tremoille asked incredulously.

"I'm certain of it," Stefan said. "It's stationary, unlike starships, which they find difficult to target. Starships move too fast. We have the schematics of the place. I'm sure my mages could cause significant damage with a Cast."

Carina noted he didn't ask her for confirmation. She had no idea how to do what he was promising his clan.

"Aren't you being a little over-confident?" Tremoille asked. "I mean, the destruction of the military installation on Cestrarth was impressive, but attacking the Dirksen shipyard will be an order of magnitude more difficult. And it isn't as though there's an ocean handily nearby. What do you imagine they would do?"

"I suggest you give them a chance," Stefan said. "It won't only be Carina here. The others are ready to take part in a battle. Even my youngest son." Someone in the room made a sound signaling disgust. Stefan ignored it and went on, "Working together, I'm sure they could destroy the place."

"We don't plan battles according to vague notions and possibilities," Tremoille remarked acidly. "I ask you again, what do you imagine they would actually *do?*"

"I've seen my wife move things with the power of her mind many times," said Stefan. "I'm sure that by combining their powers they could move a strategic ship or piece of equipment that would create a great deal of damage."

"Not in any shipyard I've ever seen," a voice murmured.

"Then if we could get something to connect them with a member of personnel," said Stefan, "they could control their actions and force them to activate a self-destruct."

"Why in all the galaxy would a shipyard have a self-destruct capability?" Raynott asked.

Stefan was beginning to look flustered. Carina was sorely tempted to leave him to flounder in embarrassment in front of the Sherrerr officers, but she had an idea. If she and her family really could destroy the Dirksens' shipyard, it might work to their advantage.

"I think we could do it," she announced. "I'm not guaranteeing anything, but I think we could. If you give us a chance."

"Hmmm..." Tremoille looked suspicious. She clearly didn't trust

Carina, and she was quite right. Carina wasn't remotely interested in helping the Sherrerrs, but she would do anything to free her mother and siblings from captivity.

"Tell us then," Tremoille said. "What would you do?"

"If you can get us in close enough, and if you do have the correct schematics, we could Cast Fire into their fuel stores."

Fifty-Four

After a long debate among the Sherrerr officers, they agreed that Carina and her family would be given the opportunity to try to destroy the Dirksen shipyard. They decided to commit their largest and most powerful ship, *Nightfall*, to the attack. Defended by most of the rest of the Sherrerrs' fleet, *Nightfall* would bring the mages within Casting distance of the shipyard. The flagship could sustain a lot of damage before she was put out of action.

The practical and strategic aspects of the attack were out of Carina's control. She would have to trust the Sherrerrs' military arm to do their job. Destroying the Dirksen shipyard with the Fire Cast was up to her and her family. That part worried her. She didn't know how effectively her mother had trained her siblings in their Casting, but she suspected it was not very well—deliberately so. In her mother's position, Carina would have taken every opportunity to downplay her abilities and limit those of her children. She doubted her sisters and brothers were at anywhere near the proficiency she needed them to be. Yet if they were to escape, their Casts had to be successful.

"I confess I'm surprised at your congeniality," Stefan remarked to her as the meeting broke up and his voice wouldn't be heard over the hubbub. They were getting up from their seats. "What's brought about your change of attitude?" He turned and fixed his gaze on her, as if he were trying to bore into her mind.

Carina shrugged. "It doesn't benefit us if the Sherrerrs lose. You would only make our lives harder, wouldn't you? I'm not so stupid as to refuse to do something that would help my family."

Stefan looked unconvinced, but he said, "I'm glad to hear you're coming to your senses at last. It's a shame your mother has never been so sensible. Her life could have been much more pleasant if only she had been equally compliant. I only hope your new approach is genuine. If it isn't, the punishment I will inflict on all of you will be swift and merciless. You're aware what I'm capable of. Do you understand me?"

"I understand. But I think you'll be surprised at what we can do when we really make an effort."

"I hope I will be." Stefan paused, his gaze searching her face. He stepped closer.

Carina fought the urge to push him away from her, violently.

"Perhaps I misjudged you," he said. "I'd thought you were going to be as difficult and uncooperative as your mother, and I would be forced to exert the same level of control as I had to with her. Not without enjoying a certain amount of pleasure, I have to confess. But if you're of a different mind, I see no reason why we couldn't work together to rise to a preeminent, if not primary, position within the clan. *Together*. You couldn't do it alone as that idiot Calvaley suggested, but if we joined forces we could be a formidable couple, you and I."

"You seem to be forgetting something," Carina said. "You're already married. To my mother."

"Yes, but not for much longer. Didn't she tell you?"

"Tell me what?" An icy steel vice fastened around Carina's heart. What did Stefan mean? He must have heard about her mother's illness, but she was going to get better. "I know she's sick but..."

"Yes, she's very ill. The stupid woman. What possessed her to stop taking her preventative, I'll never know. The doctor informed me it was too late for her to receive treatment. She only has a week or two left."

"What?" Carina's legs gave way. She collapsed into her seat.

"So she didn't tell you."

"She told me she was going to start treatment and she would be okay," Carina replied, shock entirely disarming her.

"No, that isn't the case." Stefan was looking down at her impassively. "I don't know why your mother would want to mislead you on something so important, yet she has. Odd. Anyway, after a respectable period of mourning, we will marry. Think on it, Carina. You could repeat your mother's unhappy experience or you could be more agreeable and enjoy your life. Though I would, of course, expect to father another brood on you. Our marriage will give our children legitimacy. Those mage powers are too useful to waste."

Stefan's words barely registered with Carina, disgusting though they were. Why had her mother lied to her? Why had she given her false hope? She was adrift. She held her head as if it might halt the spinning of her mind. Her mother was going to die after all, and there was nothing she could do to prevent it.

"Stand," a voice said.

Carina looked up into the expressionless face of a guard. Stefan had gone. The briefing room was almost empty. Minutes must have passed without her noticing.

Numbly, she rose to her feet. She'd been assigned two guards to return her to her quarters. This time, both of them were male. As she glanced at the other guard, she froze. It was Bryce. His eyebrows flicked up as an almost-unnoticeable acknowledgment.

"Move," the other guard said, motioning her toward the door. When she reached it, he went in front of her as they walked down the corridor. Bryce was behind her. Carina glanced over her shoulder a few times as they went along, but she didn't dare risk speaking to him while the other guard could overhear.

They took her back to her family's living quarters. The place remained quiet and dark, her mother and siblings still sleeping. The two guards escorted her inside the door, then left.

Carina stood motionless in the entrance area, still reeling from the news that her mother was going to die. Moments later, the door opened again and Bryce slipped inside. He closed the door.

"I told the other guard I had a message I'd forgotten to give you," he said. "I can only stay a few seconds."

"What the hell are you even doing here?"

"I saw what happened at the departure area at the spaceport. No one did a thing as the Sherrerr guards dragged you away, and neither could I. Not then. But I found out where you'd been taken. When I heard it was the flagship, I joined up."

"Yes, but why? What about your parents? They must be waiting for you. You said you were going to run a branch of their business."

"Why? I'm here to rescue you of course."

"What?!"

"You rescued me from the Sherrerrs' mountain stronghold. Now it's my turn to help you out."

"I've never heard anything so ridiculous. How do you propose to do that? You're going to get yourself killed, and probably me too. Stay away, Bryce. I've got a handle on this."

"Hmmm, yeah, looks like it. Let me help you."

"No. Don't you see? I can't trust you. Mages can't afford to trust non-mages, or *this* is how they end up. I helped you because I felt sorry for you, but that's it. My connection to you is over. Please do me the courtesy of leaving me and my family alone. I have to do this by myself. It's the only way."

"You think I can't be trusted?" Bryce exclaimed, trying to keep his voice low. "Carina, everyone on the ship knows what's going on in your step family. You think I'm like Stefan Sherrerr and I'm going to rape and torture you to make you do what I want?"

"No, but..." Yes. That's exactly what she thought. It didn't matter how nice her friend was. Knowing her would turn him into her mother's husband one day. "The knowledge of what I can do would change you. You think it wouldn't, but it would. It's natural. That's why mages always have to live in secret and keep their powers hidden. You might not understand but that's the way it is."

For the first time since Carina had known him, anger flashed in Bryce's eyes. "You know what your problem is? You want to help others, but you won't let anyone help you. You've got so used to living in fear it's damaged your judgment of people. Not everyone is your enemy. We aren't all like Stefan Sherrerr."

"I'm sorry, Bryce. I can't take the risk of trusting anyone else. I have to do this myself."

"You think that's the answer? How has that worked out for you so far? How did it work out for your mother?"

At the mention of her mother, the memory of the recent news flashed into Carina's mind. Sobs welled up in her chest and her eyes filled with tears.

Bryce's expression softened. "I'm sorry," he said, mistaking the cause of her distress. "I have to go. But I'll be around. I'm here to help you, Carina. Don't forget that. I'm not out to hurt you."

He left. Carina sank to the floor, grief washing over her.

FIFTY-FIVE

The Sherrerr flagship was a hive of activity as the crew prepared for the attack. After successfully invading Cestrarth, destroying the Dirksens' main shipyard would be a hammer blow that would resound across the entire galactic sector. The Sherrerrs' enemies would struggle long and hard to regain their military strength after such a defeat.

Carina was also busy preparing her brothers and sisters. She avoided her mother, which wasn't difficult as her illness confined the woman to her room. The morning following the briefing meeting on the Dirksens' shipyard attack, she had coldly told her mother she knew she had lied to her about her illness.

Her mother had touched her arm and gone to speak, but Carina had walked away. She couldn't bear to listen to the woman's explanation of her deceit. She didn't want to hear any more lies. Her feelings were beyond anger and hurt. As far as their relationship was concerned, she was in a place she didn't think she would ever be able to leave. Unable to understand why her mother would treat her so badly after their many years of separation, she tried to avoid even thinking about the subject. The tension in their relationship was intolerable and a distraction from her work.

When they made their escape, she would take her mother with them so that she could die in peace, free at last. She deserved that. But she wasn't the person Carina had imagined her to be, and she didn't think her mother had really loved her as much as she thought she did. The whole thing was so confusing and hurtful, she simply had no idea how to deal with it.

Since her mother had proven herself untrustworthy, Carina didn't tell her about the escape plan. Neither could she trust her siblings with the secret. Darius was too young and not in control of himself, and she didn't know Parthenia or the others well enough to feel confident confiding in them. As for Castiel and Nahla, she wasn't even sure they wanted to escape or whether she should bring them along. As Sherrerrs who weren't also mages, they would probably fare best if they remained with the family, providing they weren't suspected of conniving in the escape. Carina was particularly averse to bringing along Castiel, who gave off the same nasty vibe as his father.

The first Casting lesson was hard. Carina and the four children with mage abilities sat on the floor in a circle. Four guards had rifles constantly trained on them. The children were accustomed to the set up, but Carina was not. She wished that the effects of Casting were instantaneous. If that had been the case, she could have taken out the guards within seconds and maybe even taken control of the entire ship.

The first thing Carina discovered about her siblings' Casting ability was that she was correct in her guess that her mother had taught the children badly. Only Parthenia had any real proficiency in simple Casts like Transport, Locate, and Split, and Carina had a feeling that it was in spite of, not due to, her mother's teaching. When she realized the children had noticed her disappointment in their skills, she had them practice Enthralling each other, which lightened the mood.

As the lesson progressed, Castiel and Nahla stopped their playing and watched. Carina guessed that Castiel was probably bitter and jealous that most of his brothers and sisters had a very special ability, but she didn't know what to do to make him feel better. She couldn't confer mage powers upon him. You were either born with it or you weren't. Nahla sat with him, mimicking his sour looks.

Darius was joyful about being taught by her, though his age made him like a puppy, willing but excitable. Oriana and Ferne were steady and industrious. Parthenia had an almost pathological need to do things perfectly the first time.

Carina taught the children for two hours before stopping for the day. Casting, even small Casts, was mentally tiring. She felt she'd done as much as she could to sharpen her sisters' and brothers' skills, and she'd gotten to know them all a little better as mages. Parthenia's Casts were steady, exact, and reliable. Darius's Casts were the most powerful, but he was unpredictable. One moment he would Cast quickly and effectively, another moment he wouldn't be able to Cast at all. Oriana's and Ferne's Casts were weaker than the others' but they didn't display Darius's momentary lapses in ability.

At the end of the session, when the children left the circle and Carina began to tidy up, Darius crawled over on all fours. Carina sat down to speak to him, and he climbed into her lap and rested his head on her shoulder. "Why are you sad, Carina?"

"Am I sad? What makes you say that?"

"I can feel it."

Carina had been expecting her brother to say she had a sad face or something similar. It seemed a strange remark from the little boy, and one that reminded her of something Nai Nai had once told her. "You can?"

"I know how everyone is feeling."

Wow. "That must be uncomfortable for you sometimes."

His little brown-haired head nodded like the most ancient and wise sage. "It is."

Carina recalled her grandmother had told her about mages who felt others' emotions, but she couldn't remember exactly what the old woman had said.

"I'm sorry you're sad about things," Darius went on. "Mother is always sad too."

"I guess she must be. She's very sick."

"I know."

Did Darius know how close their mother was to death? Was it Carina's responsibility to tell him? She hugged the child. "I am sad, but having you around makes me feel better."

"I know that too," he said as he hugged her back.

———

The next day, Carina moved on to her siblings' preparation sessions. *Nightfall* was fast-burning her way to the Dirksens' shipyard. Other Sherrerr ships were also on their way there, ready to defend their flagship as she maneuvered the Sherrerrs' secret weapons close enough to Cast. Stefan had told Carina they would be within range to make the final approach within seventy-six hours.

Her plan on what exactly she would do after they'd accomplished their mission wasn't clear. She was hoping for a lapse in concentration from their guards in the excited aftermath of victory. They would have elixir on hand. All they would need was a few moments. She hoped she could cause enough disruption to get her mother and the children off the ship.

But first they had to destroy the shipyard.

"You can all Cast Fire, right?" Carina asked. When her brothers and sisters nodded, she said, "That's great." Fire was one of the first Casts she'd learned. All the essential survival Casts were taught first. She'd hoped her mother had stuck to that custom. "So if you can already Cast Fire, what we're going to concentrate on now is distance. What's the farthest you've ever Cast?"

"I've Cast from our estate to the capital on Ithiya," Parthenia replied. "Mother said it wasn't possible to Cast any farther than that."

Castiel was present again. He lay on his stomach, resting his head on his hands, watching with hooded eyes. Acutely conscious that he would probably report whatever she told them to his father, Carina to tried frame her words to avoid directly contradicting her mother. "Actually, I might be able to teach you to Cast even farther. What do you think about that?"

"That would be wonderful, Carina," Darius replied, his gaze adoring.

Parthenia and the other two nodded.

"Okay," said Carina. "We're going to start practicing Casting really far today. You know how to use coordinates, right? I arranged for small tanks of fuel to be sent to these locations." She showed them the figures on an interface. "In a few days, we'll be helping in the war against the Dirksens by Casting Fire into their fuel stores at their shipyard."

Ferne's eyes grew wide. "Whoa," he breathed.

"Yeah," Carina said. "Boom. My point is, the Dirksens' tanks are going to be a lot bigger than the canisters we have to practice on. They'll be easier to hit. Our challenge with the canisters is going to be hitting them at a distance. I don't expect you to succeed at first. I want you to know that because I don't want you to feel discouraged if you miss.

What I'm asking you to do is hard, but we have plenty of time to practice, and on the day it should be easier."

"How do we know if we hit?" Oriana asked.

"The ship's scanners will pick up the explosion. The bridge will comm us."

"Bet I hit it first," Ferne said, his face alive with excitement.

"That would be cool, but this isn't a competition," said Carina.

Under the watchful gaze of their four guards, the children began to practice. The task wasn't easy even for her. She'd seldom had a reason to Cast at great distances. Without being able to see the effect of the Cast, the practice was either ineffective or highly dangerous.

She took a sip of elixir, closed her eyes, and made the Cast. Just as she was beginning to wonder if she was going to embarrass herself in front of her siblings, and be forced to inform Stefan that her plan wasn't going to work, she hit the fuel tank. She felt the Cast strike home, then a few seconds later the confirmation came through the ship's comm.

After an internal *Phew!*, Carina said to her sisters and brothers, "Now it's your turn. Who's first?"

Ferne's hand flew into the air.

Fifty-Six

Stefan had sent guards to bring Carina to him. She was disappointed to see that Bryce wasn't one of them. In spite of their argument the last time they'd met, his familiar face would have been a welcome sight. On top of all her other problems, Carina was feeling anxious. After two days of trying, she hadn't been able to teach any of the children how to Cast the distances required to blow up the Dirksen shipyard.

That had to be why Stefan wanted to speak to her. Castiel must have reported their lack of progress. She didn't particularly care about Stefan's anger—she'd agreed to help in the attack on the Dirksen shipyard for her own benefit, not his—but she hated the idea of being alone with him. She gave an involuntary shudder as she went along. He'd made his sexual intentions clear and she couldn't stomach the idea. Externally, the man wasn't unpleasant. Internally, he was barely human.

The guards took her into a small office. When neither of them left, Carina relaxed a little. She doubted he would want to try anything serious in front of two onlookers, even loyal Sherrerr guards. Her earlier attack must have made him frightened to be alone with her. *Good.*

Her mother's husband was sitting at a desk, looking unusually haggard. The strain of worrying about fulfilling his promise seemed to be getting to him. That was also good.

"Sit down," he said as she went in.

She sat opposite him and the guards took positions on each side of the doorway. Carina estimated she could get over the desk to Stefan before they had time to react. She might even be able to kill him before they killed her. She fought her desire to avenge her father's death and her mother's torture. It would be a pointless victory while her siblings remained held in captivity.

She gazed at the man levelly, waiting for him to speak.

"I hear you haven't been successful in teaching the children how to Cast at great distances."

"That isn't true."

"Really?"

"I haven't been successful *yet*."

"Don't play with me, Carina. You know how important it is that the children and yourself make the Cast successfully. Are you going to be able to do it or not?"

"Make the Cast or teach the children?"

"Both, you idiot!" Stefan half-rose to his feet and leaned over the desk, pressing his fists into the surface.

His inner self showed most strongly when he was angry, Carina noted. His face had contorted with such fury he looked like a demon. She looked up at him coolly. "I will make the Cast. As to my sisters and brothers, I think they can do it."

"*Thinking* isn't good enough. It's vital we blow all the fuel storage tanks at once. We'll only get one chance. There are hundreds of Dirksen ships there. If we only cripple the station, we'll have a cloud of bees on our tail."

"Wasps."

"What?"

"You mean wasps. Bees only sting once and die. What's really scary is wasps. They'll sting you over and over again. Or you could say hornets. They're twice the size and ten times as mean."

Stefan thumped the desk and yelled, "Stop trying to be clever. Do you think you can make a fool of me by failing to destroy the shipyard? Is that your plan?"

"There wouldn't be a lot of sense in that, would there? Like you said, we'll be in a much more dangerous position if we don't make the Cast."

"I'm warning you, Carina. If you have some trick you're planning to pull, I'll make you regret it for the rest of your long, agonizingly painful life."

"I'll bear it in mind." She regretted not including the murder of Stefan in her escape plan. Maybe she could make an adjustment.

He sat down. "Is there anything you need to assist you in teaching the children?"

Carina's eyebrows lifted at his uncharacteristically civil question. "Well it's hard to teach when you have a gun aimed at your head. If we could lose the threat of imminent death that might help."

"Out of the question. The guards stay."

"Why? What do you think we would do? Like you said, it's in our interests that we perform the Cast. And do you really think one woman and a bunch of kids could take over the entire Sherrerr flagship?"

Stefan's flinty expression broke into a sly smile. "Not as stupid as you like to make out, are you? Neither am I, sadly for you. I repeat, the guards stay. Anything else?"

"The crew has been good at placing fuel canisters at the right distance from the ship. I don't think there's much else I can ask from them."

"And you have plenty of elixir?"

"Yes. Where's it from? I thought I would have to ask one of the children to make it for the lessons."

"We have a plentiful supply aboard the ship. Your mother made it. And, no, I'm not going to tell you where it is."

"Then, no. I can't think of anything."

"You know you only have thirty-five hours before the attack?"

"I'm aware of that, yes."

"You need results, and soon. Or things won't turn out well, especially for you."

"Is that it?" Carina asked. He was right. She had little time left. Too little time to sit around while he threatened her.

"You can go."

She rose and went to the door. A guard opened it. Before she went out, however, she turned to Stefan. "Mother's sinking fast, you know. I don't think she has long now."

Stefan had already turned his attention to his interface screen. He didn't look up. He only flicked his hand at her, gesturing that she leave. The guards escorted her away.

It had been too much to expect the brute to give a second thought to the woman he had held captive and tortured for fifteen years. And it wasn't like her mother wanted to see him, but Carina couldn't help feel a deep despair over the situation. Her own feelings regarding Ma were too powerful to face right now, though she knew one day she wouldn't have a choice about it.

A line of troops were also in the corridor, heading toward them. Carina didn't take a lot of notice. It seemed like the corridor was always full of soldiers on their way to exercises. *Nightfall* was packed with them to defend it from boarders and to board enemy ships.

Then she thought she heard someone say her name. She looked up and caught a glimpse of a familiar face. The next moment, the person she'd seen was past her but looking back, smiling, as she turned to stare.

It was Mandeville. The next second, he faced front and the troops marched away.

The sight of her former fellow soldier momentarily lifted her mood. She wondered what he thought she was doing aboard the ship and being escorted by two guards. He hadn't seemed surprised to see her, as if he already knew she was being held captive. Did the Sherrerr' troops know about the mage powers of her family? Was it common knowledge? Or did only the officers know?

She realized that if the entire ship knew what they could do, they weren't only at risk from Stefan and the other high-ranking Sherrerrs—everyone else aboard might be interested in capturing them too.

FIFTY-SEVEN

The officers wanted a dummy run. They wanted a demonstration that Carina and her sisters and brothers really could do what she'd promised. It made sense. The mage strike was a prominent step in their battle plan. It was probably the most important step. They needed an assurance, if not a guarantee, that the plan stood a reasonable chance of success. Carina wasn't sure herself if they could do it.

A test site had been set up and drones sent out to record visuals of the result. The officers were back in the briefing room, and this time the children were here too. The room was filled with quiet conversations as everyone waited for the tanks to be maneuvered into position. Carina spotted Calvaley, sitting at the top of the ranked seats, speaking with Tremoille.

The children still hadn't succeeded in hitting the tanks with their Casts. Their problem was, the only feedback received during practice was a no-hit. All they knew was that the fuel tank they'd been aiming at hadn't exploded. They didn't know where their Cast had appeared, whether it had fallen short or gone too far or veered too far up, down, left, or right. So they didn't know what corrections they had to make. Essentially, the mage children were shooting blind.

Carina couldn't bother her mother about the problem. The poor woman was so ill she hardly seemed to notice anything anymore. Carina also couldn't tell Stefan about it even if she could bring herself to voluntarily speak to the snake. He would only become furious and suspect that her failure was deliberate. And apart from the guards, her mother and Stefan were the only people she saw.

She began to regret her argument with Bryce. He'd meant well, and he couldn't be expected to understand her position. Perhaps he'd even been correct when he'd said that not everyone would want to exploit her as soon as they found out about her abilities. Perhaps Nai Nai had been wrong after all and there were people she could trust with her secret. It wasn't like she had a whole lot of friends.

Calvaley stood and addressed the room. "The test tanks are in position. Private Lin, you may proceed."

"Do we have the coordinates?" she asked. A guard appeared, carrying an interface. He handed over the screen, which displayed six sets of figures.

"Six sites?" Carina exclaimed. "We can only make five Casts."

"No," Stefan said, "six. We received additional intel and we need you to do six. That shouldn't be too much of a problem, should it?"

The children looked at her nervously.

"There are only five of us, Stefan. Five mages, five Casts. What do you expect me to do?"

"I'm sure you can handle it," Stefan replied smugly. "I have complete faith in you."

She would have to Cast Fire twice, simultaneously, at two different locations. Did Stefan know that was possible? It would make her job even harder, but she could probably do it. She had to do it if she wanted the other steps of her plan to fall into place.

Turning from Stefan, Carina asked Calvaley, "Can I say something, sir?"

"Go ahead, but don't make a long introduction. We all have plenty else to do."

"I didn't want to give an introduction. I just wanted to say, these are very difficult conditions for my brothers and sisters. Being observed like this puts them under a lot of pressure, and that makes it hard for them to Cast."

"We're at war," Stefan retorted. "What kind of conditions would you like? A tea party? A soiree?"

His response drew some muted giggles from the audience.

"They're children," Carina said. "*Your* children, and they're attempting something that's extremely hard for them."

"They're mages, and they're here to do a job."

"Stop it," Calvaley interrupted. "Get started, Lin. Your words have been noted."

Carina took a breath and turned to her sisters and brothers, who were seated on the floor in a square, facing each other. A jug of elixir and five beakers sat at their center. She showed them the interface and assigned a different set of coordinates to each child.

"There's no need to hurry," she told them. "It doesn't matter whether we hit them all at once. We only need to try to hit them, okay?"

"Carina," Oriana said quietly, "I don't think I can do it."

Oriana knew she was the weakest at Casting of all of them. Her ordinary Casts were often feeble, let alone the difficult Cast she was now required to do.

"Just try your best," Carina said. If Stefan hadn't suddenly sprung a sixth site on her, she could have tried to cover for one of the children's failures with a second Cast of her own. But now there was no chance of that.

The starscape view out the window turned black, and a holo of the test site appeared. It was a merged image, showing the six barrel-shaped fuel tanks in close proximity, though in reality they were kilometers apart.

"Which one's mine?" Darius asked.

"It doesn't matter," Carina replied. "Don't worry about it. Only concentrate on the coordinates." At six years old, Darius was in danger of becoming confused and Casting at the visual, not the tank itself. The Fire he Cast would quickly go out as there was nothing but the air in the room to sustain it. It would be an interesting display for the onlookers but a failure nonetheless.

The audience were shifting in their seats and murmuring as they grew impatient.

"Are you ready?" Carina asked the children.

They nodded with an attitude that showed they weren't feeling remotely ready.

"Okay. Let's do it." She poured each child a measure of elixir and handed out the beakers. Then she poured some of the mixture for herself. "Remember, shut out everything. It's you, the character, and the destination. That's all there is."

After waiting for the children to drink their elixir and shut their eyes, she downed her own, the bitterness of the liquid barely registering in her worry about what might happen if the children failed the test.

Would the Sherrerrs abandon the plan of using them as weapons in the attack on the shipyard? Would they call off the entire attack? She thought that was unlikely. Destroying the Dirksens' main starship manufacturing yard was essential to crushing their strength. But if the Sherrerrs were unsuccessful, she and the others were at risk of capture or death. And she needed the vast debris field the explosions would create. If they weren't allowed or able to blow the shipyard to smithereens, she had no plan B.

Silence had fallen as the spectators waited and watched for the mages' Casts to take effect. Carina closed her eyes. She could provide them with somewhat of a spectacle at least. Maybe that would be enough.

She sank down into the darkness of her mind. The sounds of breathing, shuffling feet, and shifting bodies disappeared. The red tint behind her eyelids retreated to blackness. She was alone in the dark. The first stroke cut across her inner vision, silver-light and glimmering. The second followed, sweeping down from the first. A third appeared to one side, short and tapering. Its mate appeared on the opposite side. The character was complete. *Fire*.

Now came the difficult part. She had to Cast Split into Fire, severing the character longitudinally, creating a perfect mirror. This took great concentration. Dimly, she became aware of a trickle of sweat running down the side of her face. She forced her mind back to the character, Fire. A touch of mental effort, and it slid into two images.

It was time to Cast the characters to their destinations. The fuel tanks were large. She didn't have to hit the exact coordinates. Pinpoint accuracy wasn't the problem, it was the distance involved. She gathered up all of her mental and emotional strength into one powerful bundle, and flung the Casts far from her, out into space, across the distance to the fuel tanks.

She opened her eyes and held her breath. The tanks hung above her, spinning lazily under residual momentum. Her sisters' and brothers' eyes remained closed, their faces strained with concentration.

A tank exploded, quickly followed by another. The silent spectacle filled the room with dazzling light. After the flash had departed, however, four tanks remained untouched. The audience watched them. Carina watched them too. Might Parthenia manage it finally, in her slow, steady style? Or might Darius hit lucky with an unpredictable burst of mage power?

No. There was no change in the tanks. Carina might have drunk more elixir and destroyed them herself, but what she was doing would have been obvious. The officers wanted to know that all the children could perform the Cast. In the heat of the battle, they might not have time for her to destroy the tanks one by one.

Oriana opened her eyes and looked up at the holo. "I'm sorry," she said. "I missed."

"I missed too," said Darius, also opening his eyes. Parthenia was shaking her head. Ferne looked glum.

"Idiots," Stefan hissed. "Carina, can't you teach them any better than this?"

"Be quiet, Stefan," said Calvaley. "That was you who destroyed the two tanks, Lin?"

"Yes, sir."

"Then it seems to me that we should only rely on you in the upcoming attack. We can leave out your brothers and sisters, for now anyway."

"No," said Carina. If she was the only one to take part in the battle, the chances were she would be separated from her family. It was vital they were all together when the shipyard blew. "I mean, no *sir*. I think they can do it. I really do. I just need to give them some more practice. If I might say so, it's the pressure of all these people watching that's the problem. Casting is much easier in private. If we were alone, I'm sure they could be successful. We can blow that place to pieces if you give us the chance."

Tremoille spoke in Calvaley's ear. He listened, nodded to her, then said, "You've got your chance, Carina. We've seen what you can do. Anything else your brothers or sisters can manage will be a bonus. We'll arrange a private room when the time comes."

"And guards," Stefan said. "The children must be watched at all times."

"Yes, of course," Calvaley replied. "Guards will be assigned."

Fifty-Eight

Faye heard the soft snick of her bedroom door opening. Beyond her closed eyelids, her room brightened. She opened her eyes. Light from the living area was spilling through the open doorway, silhouetting Carina in its frame.

"Come in," said Faye, pulling herself painfully to a sitting position. "I wasn't asleep. Just resting."

Carina stepped inside and closed the door. Faye activated the light, telling it to dim to fifty percent when the brightness hurt her eyes. Carina came over to the bed and perched on its edge, not meeting her gaze.

Faye drank in the sight her daughter. Though they looked alike, she could also see Kris's face in Carina's. The fact that a part of him lived on gave her some small comfort.

Without speaking, Carina took her hand. She looked both sad and angry. It wasn't hard to guess why. She knew she'd betrayed her daughter's trust when she'd lied to her about the state of her health. She'd only wanted more time to try to find the right words and the right moment, but neither had come until it was too late. It was only that she'd been unable to bear the thought of telling her daughter that, fifteen years after abandoning her, she was about to abandon her again, and it was her own fault.

"Carina," Faye said gently, "I'm—"

"Sorry," Carina interrupted. "I know." She sighed. "Ma, I need your help. I need to teach the children to Cast at a great distance. They can't seem to do it, no matter how much I try to teach them or how often they practice. They just can't hit what they're aiming at."

"I'm not surprised. I didn't teach them well. I wanted to limit Stefan's exploitation of them as much as I could."

"I get that. But now I really need them to do it. Can you help? Nai Nai taught me what she could until she died, but after that I was on my own. Everything I learned from then on was guesswork."

"There is a way," Faye said, "but why is it so important that they do this task you've for set them? You know the more they demonstrate what they can do, the more Stefan and the rest of the Sherrerrs will ask of them. Aren't their lives going to be miserable enough as it is?"

"No," Carina replied. "Not if I can help it. I have a plan, Ma. We can all escape. I only need them to do this thing, and it should give us our opening."

"Oh, Carina," Faye said. "I used to make a plan every week. I used to dream of the time when I would finally manage to escape. But look what happened. Here I am and here are your sisters and brothers. And whenever Stefan caught me, his punishment was severe. Do you want to go through that? What if he decides to punish the children too, in your place? Could you bear it? What about Parthenia? You know he has his eye on her?"

"I've noticed," said Carina. "His perversions are disgusting."

"Like everything else about him. I admire your fighting spirit. I wish with all my heart you and the children could escape the dreadful monster, but it isn't possible. I realize that now."

"It *is* possible. You're ill and tired and Stefan has broken you. You've given up. But it is possible for us to escape. And, Ma, if you come with us, we might reach a planet in time to save you. You might still respond to treatment."

Carina's expression belied the hope in her words. Faye saw the reflection of her own death in her daughter's eyes, and she accepted it. But maybe there was one last gift she could give her. Maybe she could summon a vestige of hope that there could be a different life for her children than the one she'd been forced to lead.

"I don't think that's likely," Faye said. "When I go to sleep I don't even know if I'll wake up again. But you know, Carina, I don't mind.

Stefan pushed me so far, I don't think I can ever find my way back. And who knows? Perhaps I'll see your father again."

Carina's hand gripped hers and her eyes shone.

"I'm sorry," Faye said. "I don't want to make you unhappy. You said you don't know how to teach the children to Cast at a great distance? That isn't so hard to answer. If you can do it, then Nai Nai must have taught you. Don't you remember how?"

Understanding dawned in Carina's eyes. "Of course! It's so simple. How could I have forgotten?"

Faye smiled. "The children will pick it up quickly enough, I'm sure. Especially Darius. His ability is very strong when he puts his mind to it."

"Yes. Ma, is there something different about him? He says he can feel others' feelings."

"I think he's a spirit mage. Your Nai Nai would have been able to explain it better, but as I understand it, he draws his power from other people. It doesn't come from the stars like yours and mine. And as he draws in others' energy, he also draws in their emotions. He doesn't know what he is yet, but one day you can tell him."

"I will. I wish I could tell him more, but I know so little. Nai Nai tried to help me memorize information about mages, but I was so young when she died. I think I forgot most of it."

"The prohibition on recording anything to do with mages makes it hard to retain information. Perhaps I should try to tell you everything I know, while we still have time."

"I'd like that," Carina said. "Then I can pass it on to my sisters and brothers as they grow up."

"Okay," said Faye, "make yourself comfortable."

Carina moved over so she was sitting fully on the bed. She crossed her legs.

Faye began with the Elements, the Seasons, and the Map, but Carina already knew these. Nai Nai had taught her well. She also told her all the Casts she knew. There were a few Carina had never heard of—difficult Casts that Nai Nai might have been waiting to teach her when she grew older.

She also told Carina her understanding of the history of mages. She said that when she was young, her mother had explained that mages had first appeared thousands of years ago in a country on a planet called Earth. The first mage was a scientist. How she stumbled upon the correct ingredients in the correct proportions to make elixir, and performed the first Cast, no one knew. However, it was generally accepted that not long after, the first mage told her secret to friends, but when they tried to do the same thing they failed. The first mage wasn't believed until she performed a Cast to prove what she could do.

The word of her ability spread. Many attempted to repeat her performance. Most could not, but a very few could. Scientists speculated the ability was due to a random mutation in the first mage's genetic code, though at the time they couldn't discover what it was. They said the mutation might have appeared at intervals throughout human evolutionary history, but it was only the first mage finding the key to unlocking the skill that had brought it to light.

The self-discovered true mages banded together to share their experiences and knowledge, and to hone their craft. They retreated to a remote mountaintop where they would not be disturbed or scrutinized. Others who identified they were mages sought out the isolated place and were welcomed. The curious and avaricious, who nursed ambitions of profiting from the mages' ability also sought them out but, after their long, hard journeys, they were turned back.

"My mother told me the mages gave a test at the door to the compound," Faye said. "Any visitor would be offered elixir and an object they had to move from one side of the entranceway to the other. If the visitors couldn't perform the Cast, they would be refused entry. It didn't matter how low on supplies they were, or how cold and desperate, only mages were allowed inside."

"I bet that didn't make them many friends," Carina said.

"It didn't, but what choice did they have? If they didn't have that policy, they would be forced to house and feed every wanderer who appeared at their door. They only wanted to be left alone to work on their abilities. But their rule was their downfall. A few of the people they rejected died or were never found again. The public, who already feared them, grew to hate them, calling them murderers. General opinion also said they should be using their powers to cure everything that was wrong with the world, not hiding themselves away and selfishly hoarding the profits of their ability."

Faye told Carina how humankind had invented deep space travel at around the same time, allowing journeys far beyond the narrow confines of one planetary system. Realizing that if they didn't escape soon, they would be forced to do the bidding of governments or powerful corporations, the mages gathered all their folk together, stole one of the new starships, and traveled as far from Earth as they could.

In time, however, the rest of humanity caught up with them. As the memory of what had happened to them on Earth was still fresh in the mages' minds, they decided to hide their ability and remain anonymous but secure within the societies that were springing up all around.

Faye paused. As she'd been speaking, her little remaining strength had drained from her, and her voice had grown quieter and quieter.

Carina reached over and touched her mother's knee under the coverlet. "That's enough for now, Ma. You can tell me the rest another time."

Faye smiled, the effort hurting her face. "That's about as much as I know anyway. But I have another story I need to tell you, and soon." It was the most important story of her life, and she'd never told it to anyone. It would give her peace to tell it, and Carina needed to know.

"I'll hear it later," said Carina. "You should sleep now."

Faye's eyelids were already closing.

FIFTY-NINE

The two guards who had appeared to escort Carina once more to Stefan's office were grinning. She stood in the entrance to the living quarters and stared. It was Bryce and Mandeville. How in hell they had *both* finagled their way into pulling guard duty for her?

She had just left her mother asleep, or more likely passed out, after listening to her story of the history of mages. The woman's skin was so thin and pale her veins showed through, and each breath she took seemed an effort. Carina didn't know how anyone could look as she did and still be alive. It was like she was clinging on for a reason. Carina had hoped the reason was because she wanted to escape with them, but though it hurt her deeply to admit it, she was sure that wasn't the case.

Her mother was going to die and she wasn't sad about it. Maybe she was only hoping to see her children free at last before she went.

The corridors were busy. Carina, Bryce, and Mandeville couldn't risk speaking openly or delaying the journey to Stefan. The man was like a bird of prey in his exact, watchful habits. He would notice if they were late and would want to know why. But they could talk quietly as they went along.

"What's going on?" Carina murmured. "How did you manage this?"

"You've got more friends than you think," said Mandeville. "Not everyone aboard ship thinks what the Sherrerrs are doing is right. Not even all the officers. When I found out your family were being held captive, I couldn't believe it. Certainly changed my opinion of them."

"You mean you had a good opinion before?" Bryce asked.

"Kinda neutral."

"Mandeville here told me what you did on Banner's Moon, Carina," Bryce said. "What did you think you were doing, helping the Sherrerrs?"

"I was trying to help you, you idiot," Carina replied defensively. "How do you think I got permission to visit the men's quarters? Besides, that was before I knew they were holding my mother and half-sisters and brothers hostage."

"I guess that put a different spin on things," Mandeville remarked.

"Just a bit."

"So, Carina," Bryce said, "we don't have a lot of time. I wanted to tell you we're gonna help you escape."

"Really? How?" Though she appreciated the sentiment, Carina was skeptical.

"You need to drink that stuff to do what you do, right?" Bryce asked.

"Er, yeah."

"Mandeville found out where it's stored. They keep a pretty tight watch over it, but I think I can sneak some out for you."

"You can?" Her own supply of elixir could make a huge difference to her chances of success, but then she realized the implications. "Wait. I don't know if that's such a good idea." If Bryce was caught trying to steal elixir, it could throw all her plans into disarray. The Sherrerrs would conclude she had something to do with the attempt and they would cancel all plans to use her and the children. They wouldn't take a risk of things going wrong at such an important moment in the battle. It would be safer to keep them all confined until it was all over.

"What are you talking about?" Bryce asked. "Don't you want to get out? If I get you that stuff, you can just move yourself out of here like you did at the Sherrerr stronghold."

"There's a limit to how far I can Transport. I can't just fly across the galaxy, especially not with all my siblings in tow. If I tried that out here in deep space, I'd be moving us all to a freezing, airless vacuum."

"All right," Bryce said. "But you could use the stuff for something else."

She *could* use it. If she had free access to elixir, there were all kinds of things she could do to smooth the path of their escape. Only she still wasn't sure if she wanted Bryce's or Mandeville's involvement. It would complicate things.

When she didn't answer, Mandeville seemed to guess what was on her mind. "You're wondering if involving us is going to make things harder for you, right? I can see why you might think that, but you're wrong. Remember when we were on Banner's Moon? Would you have gotten that weapon out without the help of me and the others?"

She did remember. She recalled how she nearly got left behind, and it was only because Mandeville hauled her aboard the ramp of the departing shuttle that she got away before the moon was destroyed. Besides, was she in a position to turn down any offer of help? Though she'd tried to pretend to herself that she really could pull off the escape, deep down, she had her doubts.

"Okay," she relented, "I accept your offer."

They had arrived at Stefan's office. Before Bryce pressed the comm button, he gave her a wink. "Glad to hear it. It's about time you understood who your friends are. You won't regret it."

They went in. It was the same format as previously. Carina sat opposite Stefan and her guards stood on each side of the door. She felt a little better about spending time in Stefan's company knowing that Bryce and Mandeville were here, watching everything that went on. She hadn't forgotten Stefan's various threats, including the one he'd made that he would demonstrate to her he was a man. Knowing that neither Bryce nor Mandeville would stop her, the urge to put a final end to her mother's tormentor was strong. She gripped the chair's arms.

"That performance you put on at the test session was pathetic," Stefan said. "You embarrassed me, and I won't forget it."

"I told you the children weren't ready. What did you expect would happen? If you want to avoid embarrassment, pay attention to what I tell you."

Stefan glowered. "How are the children coming along with their practice? Will they be ready in time?"

"Yes, I think so. They don't have any problems with Casting Fire, only with hitting the target. I was reminded of something I'd forgotten. I think I can teach the children how to aim better now. When that obstacle's out of the way, I don't see any reason they shouldn't succeed."

"Good. I wanted to talk to you about something else."

She sat back and raised her eyebrows, wondering what Stefan's latest depravity could be.

"I don't want you getting any ideas about trying to escape during the battle," Stefan said. "If you're anything like your mother, you'll try to take advantage of the distraction. I'm not stupid, Carina. You haven't deceived me in the way I've noticed you deceiving Calvaley and the others. I know exactly what you want and what you can do, and I'll make sure you're watched like a hawk every moment during and after the battle. Any attempt to get away will be met with a severe response. Do you understand me?"

"I understand." Her hopes about the success of her scheme wavered. Stefan, as always, presented the largest barrier. But she wouldn't let his threat stop her from trying. Whatever punishment he had planned, she had to try. She couldn't live the life her mother had lived, and she couldn't allow her brothers and sisters to spend their lives in captivity, work animals to fulfill their father's desires.

"I'm not sure that you do," said Stefan. "You remember what I did to you when you were first captured, to force your mother to admit you were her child? That's nothing compared to what I'll do to you if you attempt to escape and take my children from me. But it isn't only you who'll suffer. You realize that?"

"I do, but—"

"Don't insult me with your assurances, Carina. I see through you. I read your mind as clearly as if I too had mage powers. I haven't brought you here to listen to your lies. I've brought you here to let you in on a secret that only I and your mother know, except she's managed to blank the fact from her memory. I'm telling you now so you understand what I do to the people who defy me.

"When I held your mother and father in captivity, it was the first time I had ever encountered mages. I suspected they existed, of course. Everyone knows the old tales. But I was the only person smart enough to set a trap to catch them. I played upon their compassion, and created a situation where only someone with supernatural powers could help. That was how I caught them.

"But when it came to forcing them to use their powers for my bene-fit, I was a novice. They refused. They denied their abilities, in spite of the evidence I had of what they had done. I had to think of a way of bending them to my will. Something that would be effective and leave a lasting impression. They were impervious to torture. It was then I hit upon the idea of using their love for each other against them. I threatened to kill one if the other refused to do my bidding.

"I threatened to kill the male—your father, because the female was more useful to me. Even as early as then I had conceived the idea, if you'll excuse the pun, of breeding a brood of mages all of my own. Parthenia had already rounded out your mother's body. To cut a long story short—and believe me, it's a very long story full of weeping and pleading and bargaining—your mother did not do as I asked, and so I killed her husband in front of her. It was a large sacrifice. I had only one mage instead of two, but I think it was worth it." Stefan paused, his eyes twinkling, as he watched the effect of his story.

She was struggling to breathe. Her mother had told her something entirely different. She'd said that Stefan had killed her father after she'd given away their mage secrets. She'd said Stefan had promised to set her father free in return, and he'd broken that promise. Who was telling the truth? Was it possible her mother's tortured mind had invented another story?

"So you see what I am capable of," Stefan said, a smile playing about his lips. "When the time comes to perform your task and destroy the Dirksens' shipyard, I want you to bear my tale in mind. You may go."

Numbly, she stood. Bryce opened the door and she went out. Mandeville followed. In silence, the three returned to her living quarters. Just before they reached the sentry guards, Bryce whispered, "Carina, don't worry. If you don't manage to take that fucker out, I will."

Sixty

At the beginning of the next teaching session, and the penultimate one they would have time for before the flagship arrived and the battle began, Darius ran up to Carina and flung his arms around her neck.

"I'm sorry you feel so bad," he said. "Why do you feel so bad?" His big brown eyes stared into hers, their noses nearly touching.

Where to start? Carina wasn't sure if her mother would last out the remaining time before their escape attempt. The threat of Stefan's appalling retribution hung over her. Would he murder one of her siblings to punish her? She'd unfortunately clearly demonstrated to him that she had the strongest, most reliable mage powers of them all. Would Bryce or Mandeville get themselves killed trying to help her? And if she succeeded and did manage to get them all to a shuttle, could they escape the ship and get to a habitable planet without being recaptured?

Her resolve was wavering. She knew she would rather die than live the life her mother had, but the alternative put many more people than herself at risk. She hadn't asked her sisters or brothers if they wanted to be rescued—she still hadn't decided whether she should take Castiel and Nahla with her—and she didn't dare mention her plans to them in case word got back to Stefan. Was it really fair to take them out of the situation, considering all the dangers involved?

"Are we going to start?" Parthenia asked impatiently.

Carina jolted out of her ruminations. "Yes. I thought of a way to teach you to aim better. That's what we're going to practice today."

"What's that?" Oriana asked. "My aim is terrible."

"Well today it's going to get a lot better," Carina replied. "Trust me. When I was a little girl, my Nai Nai—"

"What's a Nai Nai?" Ferne asked. "Was it your pet?"

Carina laughed. It was the first laugh she'd had for a long time. "No, Nai Nai means your father's mother."

"Oh," Darius said. "Is she nice? I never met my father's mother."

"She was very nice," Carina replied, "but she died. My Nai Nai taught me to Cast long distances by using Transport and Locate. You take something and Transport it—"

"I get it," Parthenia exclaimed. "Then you Locate it, and see if it went where you sent it."

"Exactly," said Carina. "You can find out how far off target you are and adjust your aim accordingly the next time."

Ferne said, "Yes! I want to practice. I know I can do it now."

Carina had brought along some squares of cloth. The children would only have to hold them a moment to make the necessary connection, then Transport them to a set of coordinates. After the piece of cloth arrived, they would then be able to seek it out using Locate and match the coordinates with its actual position.

The session was informative. They discovered that Darius was Casting roughly twice as far as he should have been, and that Parthenia had only been missing the coordinates by a short distance. If the tanks had been as big as the ones they would be aiming for at the Dirksen shipyard, she would have hit them without any problems. Oriana and Ferne were erratic in the distance and direction by which their Casts missed, but by the end of the session their accuracy had improved enormously.

Throughout the two hours she taught her sisters and brothers, Carina felt herself growing closer to them. She'd begun to acquire the same ability to forget about the guards aiming rifles at them while they practiced as her siblings had. In turn, the girls and boys seemed to feel a closer bond to her as their Casting ability improved and the mood of the session lifted. There was a sense of shared achievement. It made Carina reflect on what her life might have been like if Stefan hadn't taken her mother and father from her. It would have been fun to be a big sister to the children who came after her.

There was still a chance she could have that, she reminded herself. She could put right the wrong Stefan had committed, and give the girls and boys the life they should have had, free of coercion and the constant threat of violence.

By the time Carina ended the session, Castiel had finally stumped off to another room, Nahla trotting in his wake, and slammed the door, probably sick of the constant attention on the other children. She was satisfied that the mage children would be able to send Fire accurately at the final practice before they arrived at the shipyard and the battle started.

The guards collected the unused elixir and beakers and left. For the first time, Carina was alone with her mage siblings without Castiel to spy on them. Dared she mention something of her plans? If they knew what was happening, it could make things a lot easier.

"You all did really well today," she said. "You worked hard and you never gave up. I'm proud of all of you."

"Thanks, Carina," Darius exclaimed, his eyes shining.

"Thanks," said Ferne. "You taught us well too. It's easy to understand when you teach us."

Carina guessed his subtext: better than when Mother taught us. But of course the boy had little idea of the reason behind the difference. "When we reach the target, I'm sure you'll be able to blow it up."

"I hope so," Parthenia said.

Carina checked the door to the room where Castiel and Nahla had gone was completely closed. She leaned closer to the circle of children. "What do you think will happen after the battle?"

"The Sherrerrs will win the war and then we'll control the whole galaxy," Darius said, and threw his arms in the air.

"Maybe not the *whole* galaxy," Carina said. "What I mean is, what do you think will happen to us?"

"I thought we would go back to our estate," said Parthenia. "Aren't we going home after this?" She looked confused and troubled.

"Yes," said Oriana. "Aren't we going home?"

"Is that where you want to go?" Carina asked.

Parthenia replied, "I do. I miss my tarsul. I don't think the servants are looking after him very well."

"How about if you went someplace else?" Carina asked. "How would you feel about that?" It was as much as she dared to say. If word of the conversation got back to Stefan, it could easily be passed off as idle speculation and not introducing the children to the idea of escape to a new life.

"I'd love to go somewhere else," Ferne said. "It's so boring living on the estate. We hardly ever go anywhere or do anything. I want to live in a city and do exciting things. I want to have my own friends and not have to play with my brothers and sisters all the time."

"Hey!" Oriana objected.

"I love you, sis," said Ferne, "but I'm tired of playing girls' games. I want to play with boys my own age, like I see other kids do in the vids. I want to go to school."

"I don't think Father would like to hear you say that," Parthenia said gravely.

Not for the first time, Carina had a weird sense about the girl. She didn't know how to take her. She seemed to always hide her true opinions.

Then again, Carina thought wryly to herself, *so do I*.

"You are coming back home with us, aren't you?" Darius asked. "Then when Mother gets better, you can sit with her and watch us play in the garden."

A shadow fell across Carina's heart, and the other children also looked sad and downcast. The little boy didn't know their mother was barely clinging to life. For the second time, Carina wondered if it was her responsibility to tell him. If she didn't, who would? To Stefan, Darius was only an instrument.

Parthenia was watching her. Then she turned to her brother and said, "Mother is very sick. She might not get better."

"Don't be silly," said Darius. "Of course she'd going to get better. That's right, isn't it Carina?"

She couldn't answer him.

SIXTY-ONE

The doctor bent down and pressed a cold metal pressure syringe to Faye's neck. A brief sensation of uncomfortable tightness was replaced by a pleasant numbing sensation as her blood carried the medication around her body, alleviating its aches and pains. Her breathing grew easier and her head began to clear. Her vision also sharpened, bringing the doctor's concerned expression into focus.

Faye wet her dry lips with her tongue. "How long?" Her low, cracked, whispery voice sounded unfamiliar to her ears.

"I think another twelve to twenty-four hours. Your organs have begun to shut down, which is what's causing your discomfort. I'm giving you as much pain relief as I can without knocking you out, as you said you didn't want that. What's your pain level like? If you've changed your mind, I can ease the path for you, reduce the wait if you see what I mean."

"No," Faye replied. "I want to hang on as long as I can."

"Then the treatment I'm giving you will help. I'm sorry there's nothing else I can do to prolong the time you have left. If we'd been able to get you to a medical facility, it might have been a different story. But at times of war such things aren't always possible, even with the best intentions."

Faye could almost hear Stefan's voice as the doctor parroted his words. Explaining, justifying, and rationalizing his abhorrent, disgusting behavior. What tales was her husband spinning to the officers and members of the Sherrerr clan aboard the ship? Yet despite his facade, she was sure they all knew what he was like. They knew what he'd done to her and was doing to his own offspring, yet they chose to do nothing. As long as it didn't affect them and they profited from his actions, they would let him do whatever he wanted. She wondered who was worse—psychopathic Stefan or the people around him who winked at what he did.

"Is there anything else I can do for you?" the doctor asked. "For instance, would you like me to explain to your children what's happening? I don't relish the task, but I believe that sometimes it helps to hear the news from someone outside the family. And it is a large burden to place on, say, Carina's shoulders."

"I think most of them already understand, except maybe Darius. I'll tell him myself. I'd prefer it that way I think."

"Whatever you say." The doctor paused. "I'm sorry, but I have to ask you this. What would you like to happen after?"

It took Faye a moment to understand the doctor's subtle meaning. "After I die? I haven't thought about it, oddly enough. I'll let you know."

"The usual thing when someone dies aboard a starship is to hold the funeral ceremony and then eject the body into space. But I'm sure, given your standing as Stefan's wife, that the ship's company would make every effort to fulfill your wishes, whatever they may be."

Faye was sure the Sherrerrs would happily shower with every pomp and ceremony the woman they'd refused to help while she was alive. "I'll give it some thought."

"Right. Well, if you're feeling more comfortable now, I'd better go. I have lots to do. I have to prepare the sick bay for the upcoming battle."

"Are you anticipating lots of casualties?"

"On a ship this size, no. We're all pretty well protected behind the shielding. If the Dirksens manage to penetrate that, a few casualties will be the last of our problems. I doubt they'll show any mercy after what happened on Cestrarth. They'll probably do their best to destroy the ship." She smiled sadly. "You never know, you may even outlive me."

"You seem very calm about the idea of your life being in danger."

The doctor shrugged. "Life is strange. On the one hand, it seems so vital and indestructible. On the other, it can be snuffed out by the simplest thing. An awkward fall, a weak artery suddenly bursting, an overindulgence in the drug of one's choice." She snapped her fingers. "Gone. And there's nothing I can do about it. Seeing such things happen time and time again has given me a fatalistic outlook, perhaps. Everyone dies in the end. Perhaps it's insensitive of me to say so, but you have been given time to make your peace and say goodbye. Not everyone gets that."

"It isn't insensitive. I appreciate what you've done for me." Though the doctor was loyal to the Sherrerrs, Faye had found her compassionate and diligent.

"I wish I could have done more, but it wasn't to be." The doctor stood up. "If you need any additional medication, just let me know. At this stage, there's no point in worrying about long term effects."

After the doctor left, Faye thought over her words. She'd long accepted that her life was coming to a end, but she'd only thought about what to do with the time she had left. She hadn't considered what should happen to her body afterward.

Mages had certain funeral rites. The details were hazy, but she could remember the central idea. The five Elements were supposed to be used to send off the body. It was believed then that the mage's soul would immediately join the universe and blend with the souls of all the other mages who had ever lived. Ejecting her body into space wouldn't fulfill the requirements. She needed wood, metal, water, earth, and fire to ensure her spirit would find Kris's out in the deepness of space. She had had to beg Stefan to allow her to perform the necessary rites for her dead husband. If the Sherrerrs ejected her from the ship, her body would float frozen among the stars forever, never degrading. Her spirit would never escape and she would never see Kris again. She couldn't bear the thought.

Yet how could she arrange the correct funeral? Asking Stefan would be pointless. He had already almost forgotten she ever existed. The only person she could ask was Carina, but her daughter had enough on her plate.

The minute Faye thought of Carina, the door opened a crack and her daughter peeked in. "The doctor said it would be okay to come and sit with you for a while."

"Yes. It's fine. Come in. She's given me something potent and I'm feeling much better."

Carina stepped into the room, closing the door behind her. She sat at the end of the bed. "Ma, I wanted to tell you something. I know you don't have long, and I wanted to let you know what's going to happen. I hope it will make you feel happier."

"I'm listening."

"I wanted to tell you my escape plan."

Her daughter went on to explain how she planned to take advantage of the turmoil after the upcoming battle to steal a shuttle and get away.

When she'd finished, Faye said, "Oh, Carina."

"What's wrong?"

"I'm just so worried about you all. I don't have long left. It would be wonderful to see you all free, but I find it hard to believe it could ever happen. What will Stefan do if you fail?"

"What could be worse than living like this?"

At Carina's words, Faye saw herself through her daughter's eyes. She'd gotten used to seeing herself, empty of everything except despair, but to her daughter she must look shocking. She realized that when Carina saw her, she was seeing herself after a similar period of time with Stefan, and that she would rather die than turn into the shadow of a person her mother had become.

"But the children," Faye protested. "Little Darius..."

"Ma, I understand it'll be dangerous, but I'm doing my best to protect them. Can't you see that?"

"I don't know, Carina. I don't know." They seemed to be steering toward another falling out. She didn't want to start an argument, especially not now she had so little time left. Was this how it would have been if she and Kris hadn't fallen into Stefan's trap? If they'd remained a family, and Carina had grown up with them would the two of them have been at loggerheads? In the years she'd so deeply missed her firstborn, she'd imagined an entirely different scenario. A too-sentimental one, perhaps.

"Why are you smiling?" Carina asked. "You don't think this is funny, do you? Are you feeling okay?"

"Don't worry. I'm not suffering the effects of my medication. I was only thinking that life rarely turns out as you expect it. If that's what you want to do, that's what you must do. I understand. It's just that the thought of my children being hurt is unbearable to me."

"There's more than one way of hurting people," Carina said, "and your husband knows it only too well. Maybe I can do it—I mean, maybe

I can take the risk—because they aren't my children. I didn't give birth to them. Maybe it's easier for me. But I have a question. What about Castiel and Nahla? Should I take them too? Do you think they'll want to come?"

"Nahla will want to go wherever Castiel goes. As for him, I don't know. Maybe you should ask him when the time comes."

"I don't know that I'll be able to. I might not have time, or..."

"Or?"

"Ma, I'm worried he'll betray us. He might alert the guards, or even try to stop us himself."

"I don't think he'll do that. I don't think he would hurt his sisters and brothers. I know how he acts, but I think he feels a connection to them, deep down."

Carina looked doubtful, but she dropped the subject.

Faye said, "Carina, I have to talk to you about something. I only have hours left, according to the doctor. I need to talk to you about what I want to happen when I'm gone."

Sixty-Two

Although *Nightfall* was hours from her destination, the ship was at battle status. At any moment, Dirksen surveillance probes could detect their approach, along with the approach of most of the Sherrerr fleet that was accompanying them. As soon as the Dirksens saw what was coming, it was inevitable that they wouldn't waste time in parley. The number of ships the Sherrerrs were committing to the battle made clear their intent. The only rational response the Dirksens could offer was an immediate, aggressive defense.

The mages were on round-the-clock lockdown. No one was allowed out of the living quarters for any reason whatsoever. Someone—probably Stefan—was taking no chances that they wouldn't be exactly where they were needed at the crucial moment. Even the doctor had had to argue with the guards for admittance. Carina heard the raised voices outside the main door. When the guards finally allowed the doctor inside around half an hour later, she appeared harassed and angry.

I only have two minutes, she'd said to Carina as she pushed pre-prepared syringes into her hands. *These are for your mother, to ease her symptoms. I'm not allowed in to see her until after the battle, so you'll have to give her the shots.* She hastily explained the procedure, continuing in spite of the guard poking his head around the door and telling her that her time was up.

Take care, Carina, the doctor had said as the guard pulled her out of the entranceway by her arm.

Now, all Carina and the children had to do was wait. The minutes dragged into hours as the moment of their deployment edged nearer. The children played simple games like hide-and-go-seek for a while. Then they began to tease each other and fight until Carina, mindful of their sick mother in the next room, told them to play quietly or not at all.

The tension was getting to them, she knew, as if their feelings about losing their mother weren't enough. But arguing with each other only made the situation worse. The children then lay morosely on their beds or the sofa, reading, drawing, playing screen games or staring vacantly at nothing.

Carina hadn't seen Bryce or Mandeville since the last time she'd been to Stefan's office. She'd begun to have her doubts that they would provide her with elixir as they'd promised. Looking back on their most recent conversation, Bryce's confidence and optimism seemed ill-founded. She didn't even know if he or Mandeville were still aboard the ship. Troops might be moving between vessels as the fleet approached the Dirksens' shipyard.

After her initial reluctance, Carina had warmed to the idea that they would be around to help. Allies were a new phenomenon to her, but she'd been prepared to make an exception. Had she been too optimistic? Perhaps things were the same as they'd been for a long time—her alone against the universe.

She still hadn't decided what to do about Castiel and Nahla. She didn't trust Castiel at all and thought that her mother's love for the boy had blinded her to his true nature. When their mother had gently explained to Darius that she wasn't going to get better and that she would be leaving them soon and forever, Carina was sure she'd seen Castiel smirk while his brother sobbed his heart out.

She was hoping that Castiel would elect to stay and then Nahla would want to stay with him. Could she force him to remain if he wanted to come along? She was sure he would contact the Sherrerrs the first opportunity he got. She could just imagine his little evil smile when Stefan arrived to collect them from whatever hiding place they reached.

The door to the living quarters opened. Carina's heart leaped. The guard delivering their meal was Bryce. She struggled to maintain her composure. She couldn't let her joy be observed by the guards outside or Castiel or Nahla.

"Your meals, ma'am," Bryce said, maintaining the subterfuge. Smart guy. He guessed that the children might not be aware of her escape plan.

"Thank you," Carina replied, taking the packaged meals and drinks from him and putting them on the table. "Have you heard any news about the attack?"

"Only another hour or two at most," Bryce replied. "That's what we've been told. I was released from duty to bring you these."

"We appreciate it. Thanks."

Bryce looked like he wanted to say something but he hesitated. Finally, he said, "I hope you enjoy your meal, ma'am. The cook's given you a new kind of cordial to try. I've heard it's an acquired taste."

An acquired taste? Carina had never heard Bryce use such formal language. Then his meaning hit her. The elixir! He'd managed to sneak them some elixir. But if Castiel or Nahla tasted the drink, they would know immediately that something was going on.

"Oh. Maybe it isn't suitable for the children," she said.

"I would say not."

"I want some," Darius exclaimed, jumping up. "I want to try it."

Darius, no!

"Don't be stupid," Castiel said. "You won't like it. I bet it's like that wine that Mother and Father drink."

"That's what I heard, sir," said Bryce.

"See," Castiel sneered at Darius. "You're such an idiot."

"Don't be rude to your brother," Carina admonished.

"Can I have some?" Darius pleaded. "I promise I won't spit it out."

"No, you can't," Carina replied.

Castiel pulled an I-told-you-so face at Darius, who pushed his face into his folded arms and began to cry again.

"You," one of the door guards barked at Bryce, "out."

He nodded at Carina.

"Thanks again," she said as he left.

"Dinner's here," Castiel shouted, ignoring Carina's order to be quiet so as not to disturb their mother.

The children who were in their bedrooms emerged while Carina was hastily sorting through the drinks to find the elixir. They all seemed identical. How was she supposed to tell them apart without tasting each one? Bryce must not have had the opportunity to mark the one that contained elixir.

"I want a drink," said Nahla, holding out her hand.

"Wait," Carina replied. "One of them is different."

"Actually," said Castiel. "I'll have that one. Father says I'm nearly grown up. I'll probably like it."

"No," Carina replied. "You can have the same as the others."

"But I want the special one," Castiel said through his teeth. "Give it to me now."

"No. You can have this one." Carina had been quickly opening and sniffing the drinks. She held out one she knew didn't contain elixir.

Castiel dashed it from her hand. The liquid splashed across the floor and the container rolled to a stop. The other children, who had been opening their food packages, stopped what they were doing and stared. They'd seemed used to Castiel's behavior, but they were watching Carina to see what she would do.

"Well it looks like you're going without a drink, Castiel."

The teenage boy stamped his foot like a toddler. "No I'm not. *You* are. Give me yours."

Carina ignored him, continuing to sniff and then pass out the drinks to the other children.

"If you don't give me yours," said Castiel, "I'll tell Father, and you know what he'll do to you." His eyes narrowed and his expression grew vicious.

Carina got the impression he knew exactly what he meant. Castiel stepped up to strike her face, but she caught his arm in midair. The boy was strong but he wasn't as strong as her, and he had no idea how to fight.

"Parthenia," Carina said, "take these." The girl stepped forward and took the remaining two containers while Carina held onto Castiel's arm, their gazes locked. When she had a hand free, she slapped the boy full across his face twice, not as hard as she could have, but hard enough to teach him a lesson.

Castiel was clearly unused to corporal punishment. His defiant expression dissolved into one of shame and defeat, and the arm Carina was holding relaxed. She let go of it and was about to say something to mollify the boy when his vicious look returned. He ran at her. She stepped to one side and punched his jaw as he sped past. Castiel staggered and fell. Before he had time to regain his senses, She grabbed him and dragged him over to his bedroom before pushing him inside. She closed and locked the door.

Nahla was wide-eyed with shock and outrage. "You can't do that! Father's going to be so angry with you, Carina."

"Father can do what he likes," Carina muttered as she retrieved the drink containers from Parthenia. She sniffed one and returned it to the girl. She sniffed the final one. Bryce had done it. He'd brought her elixir, and his small favor could make all the difference.

SIXTY-THREE

Faye was slipping away. She could feel it. Her feet were mired and a shadow was creeping over her. The struggle to hang on was hard. If she could remain alive a little while longer, she might see her children free, finally. If she could only witness that, she would be content to leave and seek Kris again among the stars.

But it was so hard. The medication the doctor had given her didn't seem to work as well as it had. The pain and dreadful lethargy didn't go away when Carina gave her the injection. She no longer had the strength to even lift her head from her pillow. All she could do was lie still. All she could concentrate on was the sound of her own breathing.

She thought she'd heard shouting from the living area, but she couldn't be sure. Perhaps it was a dream. Her dreams and her waking life were melded. One moment she would be young again and in Kris's arms. The rest of her life was an un-imagined nightmare that would never come to pass. Then she would be back in her dimly lit room aboard the Sherrerr starship, waiting for the minutes to tick down and release her. She drifted away again, lost in avenues of time.

She was home. It was late afternoon, and she'd just come in from the garden. She'd harvested the roots that Po Po liked so much. Kris's mother spent all day caring for little Carina while she and Kris worked in the fields. The old woman was kind and gentle with her granddaughter and spent hours entertaining her and teaching her the beginnings of Casting. Faye was happy to cook for her in the evenings, tired though she was. She couldn't have wished for a better babysitter.

When she went into the kitchen, Kris was there stirring the soup she had set to simmer. Faye put the gathered vegetables down and her husband turned at the sound.

"You're back early," Faye said. Kris usually stayed at work on their farm until the sun went down.

"Did you hear the news?" Kris asked. "There's been a landslide."

Faye picked up her ear comm, which she'd left in the kitchen. She liked to cut herself off from the outside world sometimes. She pushed the comm into her ear at the same time as saying, "Where did it happen? I hope no one's been hurt."

"East Mountain Province. A whole village disappeared, they say."

The news report Faye heard through the comm was relaying the same information. One hundred and eighty-seven estimated missing, feared dead. "That's terrible," she said. "Those poor people."

"Faye," Kris said, "East Mountain isn't far from here. I want to go and help."

"What? Now?"

"Yes. If I leave immediately, I can arrive by late evening. I might be able to save some lives. There must be people still alive under the mud, trapped in their houses."

"But..."

"I only need to be gone a few days, just until there's no hope of reaching anyone alive. Will you come with me?"

Faye pulled out a chair and sat down. "I want to help too. But what do you mean exactly? Do you think we should go and help dig people out?"

Kris came over to her. "I mean that we can Cast. We can Transport things out of the way. We can Locate people if we have something that belongs to them. You know how I feel, Faye. How I've felt for a long time. There's so much good we could do in the world with our abilities. But we do nothing. We sit at home, practicing our powers, keeping the skills alive, but for what? What's the point of possessing the talent we have if we never use it? Meanwhile, people die in terrible circumstances, suffering pain and anguish, and we don't do anything about it."

"People die all the time, in their billions, across the galaxy," said Faye. "We can't help them all."

"No, but we can help some."

It was an old argument they'd had many times. Kris was bright and talented as well as being an excellent mage. Yet his mother's caution had confined them both to eking out a living as farmers, where she hoped their isolation from most other people would keep them safe. It was the way of mages, the older woman had told them. It was the only way they managed to survive.

To Kris, it felt like a prison sentence. Not only because there was so much more he could do with his life, but because he was so kind and compassionate. He yearned to do good and to help people. He didn't suspect others' selfish, cruel motivations like his mother did. Faye had been caught between the two, trying to appease both. She'd always known that one day their lifestyle would become too much for her husband. She only wished the moment hadn't come so soon. She'd hoped for a few more years of contentment and safety.

"What do you say?" Kris urged her. "I'm going there, Faye. I have to. It's like the opportunity was created for me to finally do some good with my powers. I only came back to see if you would come with me. I want you to, but I'll understand if you'd prefer to stay with Carina."

"Oh, Kris," Faye said. She was torn. She didn't want to leave her toddler daughter, but Po Po would take good care of her. She also didn't want Kris to leave, but his mind was made up. If she went with him, she could prevent him from being reckless or too trusting. He would have to Cast in absolute secrecy if he was going to help the landslide victims.

Her husband was watching her. "Three days," she said. "Only three days, then we come straight back."

He grinned. "Three days it is. I've packed our things and told my mother what we're doing."

"I bet she wasn't happy about it."

"No, and you probably don't want to hear what she said, but I brought her around to the idea in the end. It'll be good to help people. It's what we should be doing."

"Not if it means sacrificing ourselves."

"That isn't going to happen," Kris assured her. "You'll see."

"Wait. What did you say?" Faye asked. "You packed *our* things? You mean mine too?"

He winked. "I knew you'd agree."

The light in the kitchen was quickly turning darker, as if the sun were speeding to the horizon. Kris was still, frozen. He began to fade.

"Kris," said Faye. "Where are you going? What's happening?" It was like her husband had Cast Transport on himself. "Kris, don't leave me." But he'd faded almost to nothing. The kitchen was dark and hazy. "Kris, please, don't go. I'll come with you. I said I'll come with you."

Suddenly Faye was lying down in a bed. Someone was bending over her. It was a woman, a young woman who looked similar to herself. It was Carina, but she'd grown up. What had happened? How had the time passed so quickly? Faye couldn't remember anything after that conversation with Kris.

"It's okay, Ma," Carina said. "Don't worry. I'm here. I'll look after you."

"Carina? Where's your father? He's gone. I was going to go with him, but he left without me."

"You're sick. You've been dreaming. But I have some elixir. I can make you better for a little while."

"You're going to Cast Heal? Don't do that. Cast Locate. Find your father for me. I miss him so much."

But her daughter was already sipping the liquid. Her eyes closed. Her hand lifted and Faye felt its soft warmth on her forehead. The effects of the Cast began to wash through her, clearing her mind of its fog, easing the ache of her muscles and bones, lifting the veil on reality.

Faye exhaled, a catch in her throat, as her memory returned. Her daughter's face came into vivid focus, lines of care and worry etched on it that made her look older than she was. Faye struggled with the tormenting facts of her life as they returned to her. All she could muster to say was, "You have some elixir? Did Stefan give it to you?"

"No," said Carina. "A friend got it for me. I'm going to use it to set up our escape."

"You're going ahead with it then?"

"What choice do I have?"

"You're right. I hope with all my heart that you manage it."

"You changed your mind?"

"Nothing is too much of a risk to free yourself and the others. You have my blessing, and if anything goes wrong, I want you to promise me that you'll never blame yourself. Not ever. Understand?"

Carina nodded. "Thank you. That means a lot to me."

"And don't waste any more elixir on Healing me. You know the effects won't last more than a few hours. I'm ready to leave now. It's what I want."

"I know, but I need some more time if I'm to do what you asked. I need my plan to succeed."

"I'll try to hold on a little longer." Faye hadn't told Carina the story of how she and Kris were captured. She wanted to tell her. It was important that she knew, but Faye was too weak and the past seemed far distant.

"We're nearly at the battle site," Carina said. "It shouldn't be long now."

Sixty-Four

It had taken all the elixir she had remaining after helping her mother, but Carina had put in place the Casts she guessed she would need to get her and the children to the shuttle bay. Casting into the future was extremely difficult and she was long out of practice. She'd also used a considerable amount of guesswork to decide when and where she needed the Casts to begin, based on her understanding of the timing of the attack and her knowledge of the layout of the ship. She could only hope the Casts would work when the time came.

She wished she could have saved even a mouthful of elixir to Cast Heal on her mother one more time, but there was nothing left. To effect their escape, she would have to rely on the elixir that would be provided when they attempted to blow up the shipyard. There had always been a plentiful supply, so she didn't worry too much in that regard. Carina was more worried about her mother.

With luck, she would cling onto life just a little longer. Carina desperately wanted give her at least a few moments of freedom before she passed on, and she wanted to get her away from the Sherrerrs' ship. That would be the only way she could perform the rites her mother believed would commit her spirit to the universe, where she would be reunited with Carina's father.

Carina's bitterness over her mother's imminent death threatened to swallow her up at times. Stefan Sherrerr had torn them apart so long ago, she could barely remember her as she'd been when Carina was young. Now they were finally reunited, death was set to sunder them once more. Her memories would be of a tortured, broken ghost of a woman, not the happy, loving person Carina dimly remembered. It seemed so unfair.

Stefan Sherrerr's crimes against her mother, her siblings, and herself were abhorrent. Carina was determined he would meet justice one day, but she knew she couldn't allow her desire for revenge to get in the way of her escape plan.

While they waited for the moment they would be called to join in the battle, Carina remained with her mother, performing what small tasks she could to help keep her comfortable. She seemed to barely exist in the living world. Her gaze was distant, as if she were looking out into the stars, and her voice sounded as if she were speaking from another world.

From time to time, when her strength temporarily rose, she would tell Carina anecdotes from the time when they'd lived as a family. Short, inconsequential stories that held no significance to anyone outside of the two of them, tales that warmed Carina's heart with the realization of how much she had been loved by both her parents. Knowing she was hearing the stories for the final time was upsetting, but she was also grateful for the opportunity to hear them at all.

It was in the middle of such a reminiscence that the moment Carina had craved and feared arrived. The guard didn't knock. He came straight into her mother's room. "Bring the mage children and come with us."

Carina let go of her mother's hand and got up from her bed. She kissed her before motioning the guard out of the room and following him. "Only the mage children? What about Castiel and Nahla?"

"They are to remain here. The rest of you are to come with me at once." He laid a hand on his weapon, as if anticipating her resistance. Stefan must have warned him she might cause trouble. He was right, only not about the kind of trouble she would cause.

"We're coming," she said. "There's no need to threaten us."

Parthenia, Ferne, Oriana, and Darius were already waiting. Castiel and Nahla watched on.

"Let's go," she said to her mage sisters and brothers. Three more guards awaited them in the corridor, along with the two who would remain outside the living quarters. Already, Carina was calculating how she would tackle them and the many other obstacles that would soon stand in her way. Neither Bryce nor Mandeville had reappeared. Even one guard on her side would have been extremely useful, but it looked like she would have to do without.

One guard leading them, another following, and one on each side, the party was guided to the bridge. When Carina realized where they were going, she grew troubled. For her purposes, the bridge was the last place she wanted to be. Too much scrutiny. Too many people. Too many possibilities for something to go wrong.

When she stepped inside, a whirl of light and movement greeted her. The battle was underway, playing out in streaks of color on the holo that occupied the center of the room. Tucked away in the heart of the massive ship, Carina hadn't even been aware of it. The shipyard hung in the middle, Dirksen ships surrounding it, dwarfed by its massive size. Sherrerr ships were advancing upon them. Pulse cannon flashed out from both sides as the starships drew closer.

The activity was reflected in the behavior of the crew. They were intent at their consoles, hastily swiping and pressing their screens or holding one hand to their ear comms, concentrating on the information being fed to them.

Tremoille occupied the central console just in front of the holo, gazing into its depths, following the progress of the battle. She barely glanced at Carina and the children, only flicking her hand to one side to indicate where they should sit.

A low table and five stools had been set up on one side of the space.

"That's no good," she said.

"What?" exclaimed Tremoille, whirling around to glare at her.

"We can't possibly Cast in here. It's too noisy, too distracting. I said we needed somewhere private. You have to put us somewhere quiet or we won't be able to help you."

"What's that?" a familiar voice barked from behind her. Stefan had arrived.

"We have to go someplace else," said Carina. "Somewhere peaceful, or we won't be able to Cast. You know that."

"Is that right, Stefan?" Tremoille asked.

"Of course it's right," Carina said. "Why would I lie about it? You all agreed to it at the dummy run. Did you forget?"

"Stefan?" Tremoille repeated.

The admiral's question to Stefan remained hanging in the air.

Carina stared at him, boldly daring him to contradict her over the issue. He needed this victory, this example of what he had to offer the Sherrerr clan, and she knew it.

"It would be better for the children to be somewhere quiet, Admiral."

"Why didn't you tell me that before?" the woman said testily. "Find them somewhere. Fast. We'll be within range in five minutes."

Stefan ordered Carina and the children to pick up the tables, chairs, and elixir and follow him. They went through the corridors quickly as he urged them on.

Carina's feet lifted from the floor momentarily before sinking down again. The children let out gasps and cries of shock. Parthenia snapped down the lid of the jug of elixir she was carrying.

"What was that?" Oriana asked.

"The a-grav went out for a second," Carina replied. "We must have taken a hit. If it happens again, use the bars to pull yourself along." On each side of the corridor, narrow bars were set into the walls, as was standard for military vessels, but the children couldn't have been expected to know.

"Are we going to be blown up?" Darius asked nervously.

"No, we're the ones who are going to be doing the blowing up, right?"

"Right," he replied, a determined expression settling on his young face.

"Will we be in trouble if we can't do it?" Ferne asked.

Carina was about to answer, when Stefan interrupted. "Yes. If you don't do as you're supposed to, you will all be severely punished. Do you understand?"

The children immediately looked down and murmured, "Yes, Father."

Carina didn't reply. *Just a little while longer. Just another ten or fifteen minutes, Stefan Sherrerr, before you say goodbye to us forever.*

He thumped a door access button. They were at the briefing auditorium where they'd been tested before. As they went inside, Stefan started up the holo display. The image of the battle blinked into life above their heads. The shipyard was larger, and the Dirksen ships nearer. It seemed to Carina that the number of starships on both sides had decreased, thousands of lives sacrificed to the battle between the warring clans.

Stefan ordered them to set up the tables and stools, elixir and beakers, ready for Casting. He was listening to information arriving via his ear comm. "Sit down and get ready," he ordered. "You have two minutes. You'd better make this happen, all of you. Believe me, if you fail, you'll regret it." He glared at Carina.

Just a little while longer.

SIXTY-FIVE

The Dirksen shipyard had drawn so close it nearly filled the entire holo image, though in reality it was still distant and beyond Carina's range for Casting. She guessed that Darius might have been able to reach it. But the distance was closing rapidly. Carina estimated they had another thirty seconds or so.

The plan was that the Sherrerr flagship would halt when they were just within range. Remaining stationary would make it vulnerable to attack, but Carina had emphasized that to Cast while the distance was constantly decreasing might be too hard for the children.

They were all sitting in position, full beakers of elixir on the table in front of them. The four guards stood close by, their rifles trained on them as always. Stefan was too smart to take any chances, but Carina clung to the hope that their success in destroying the shipyard would provide that little bit of distraction she needed. Taking out four guards and Stefan was a tall order, but she didn't think it was impossible. Stefan wasn't armed, so that was a bonus, and the guards seemed young and poorly trained. No doubt the best troops had been reserved for ship invasions.

As the final few seconds counted down, Carina's heart threatened to burst from her chest. She might never have a better chance than this to escape her stepfather's dreadful yoke. She had to make it work. She had to succeed. If she didn't, she would be condemning her sisters and brothers to slavery and herself to a life like the one her mother had endured for so many years.

"Nearly there," Stefan said. "Get ready."

"You've got this, kids," Carina said. "You can do it." She went to pour out the elixir, but the a-grav failed again. Her stomach lurched and she floated from her seat before sinking down with a bump.

The ship jerked, sloshing the elixir in its lidded jug. They must have taken another big hit. The shielding had to be failing. Darius was watching her, a worried expression on his face. She smiled confidently and poured out a couple of mouthfuls of the precious liquid each before carefully replacing the lid on the jug. It was all they needed for the Fire Cast. She wanted to use as little as possible. They would need all the elixir they could get later.

"Now," Stefan barked.

"Right," she said to the children. "Go ahead." She took a sip of elixir and closed her eyes, shutting out the kaleidoscope of colors playing out over her head. She steadied her breathing and her heart rate, shutting out her fears and worries, and sank deep into the inner darkness of her mind. The pre-prepared coordinates were carved into her memory. She quickly but carefully wrote the Fire Cast, Split it, and sent the two Casts speeding away from her, across the abyss of space. They would hit. She was confident of it. It was what was supposed to happen next that worried her.

Carina opened her eyes and focused on the shipyard. Her targets were out of sight, hidden somewhere within the colossal structure. Long seconds passed. One by one the children also opened their eyes and gazed at the heart of the holo where the shipyard hung, defiantly intact. What if the intel had been wrong? What if it had been deliberately planted to mislead them?

Nightfall was now at the center of the battle and being mercilessly pummeled by the Dirksen forces. What if it had all been a trick to lure them in? Stefan's expression was shifting to fury, his hands balled into fists.

Then the first fuel tank blew.

The flash was blinding. It filled the image with an impossibly bright glare, searing Carina's retinas for a split second before it was gone. Through the after image, she caught a glimpse of the shipyard, now distorted as it began to break apart. A second blaze of light erupted. "Close your eyes," Carina shouted.

She looked away from the scene, seeing the reflection of the brilliant flashes on the briefing room's walls. She couldn't afford to close her own eyes. The moment the explosions were over, she had to act, fast. The sixth and final fuel tank blew. She returned her attention to the guards, who had kept their focus downward on her and the children. *Damn. Stefan must have warned them.*

Like snow in a heavy blizzard, the holo showed the debris of the shipyard spinning around them. The flagship was in full reverse in the aftermath of the explosion.

"We did it," Darius exclaimed, leaping up.

"Yay," cried Ferne, waving his arms in the air.

The guards' holds on their weapons began to relax, and they smiled, also enjoying the Sherrerr victory. Now Carina had her chance. A split second before she made her move, however, Stefan barked, "Guards. Watch your charges."

The men and women resumed their focus, training their muzzles on Carina and the children once more. *Damn. Damn. Damn. Damn you, Stefan Sherrerr.*

He had robbed her of that small moment of distraction she needed. Her stepfather seemed to read her mind. The corner of his lip lifted in a triumphant half smile. "Good. You all did as you were—" The door chime sounded, drowning out his words. Irritated, he went to the door. When he opened it, Carina's heart leaped. It was Bryce. She couldn't hear what her friend was saying, only Stefan's side of the conversation.

"Calvaley? Why didn't he comm me himself? Hmpf. I see. Where?" He stepped out into the corridor and turned to say, "You're all to remain here until I return. Guards, keep them covered at all times, do you understand?" He went out and the door slid shut.

Carina didn't waste a second. One of the guards was watching the shipyard debris expanding across the holo and speeding toward them. Immediately, Carina was on her, driving her elbow upward into the woman's chin. She knocked her out cold. Before the guard hit the floor Carina had torn her weapon from her hands and shot another guard in the face. There was no point in aiming at any armored part of their bodies. A single shot probably wouldn't penetrate, but luckily they had their visors up inside the ship. She spun to aim at a third guard, betting on the moment of confusion caused by her actions. But her luck had run out. Before she could take aim, the other guard fired.

Something exploded in her chest. She was out.

———

When Carina came to, she was still in the auditorium. Only a few short moments seemed to have passed. She thanked the stars that the guard's weapon had only been set on a light stun. Stefan clearly valued them more highly than he made out.

She was looking at the wrong end of a pulse rifle. The guard she'd knocked out remained sprawled, unmoving, on the floor. The guard she'd shot was sitting up and rubbing his face. The one who wasn't aiming at her was speaking into her mic.

The situation looked hopeless. Stefan and the rest of the ship would soon hear what had happened. Within minutes, they would be hurried back to their quarters and locked inside for who knew how long while Stefan meted out his punishments.

But Carina was determined not to give up. Her mind whirred as she tried to figure out how to turn the tables on the three remaining guards. Search as she might, however, she couldn't come up with an answer. Desperation began to take hold.

Then Parthenia made her move.

None of the guards were watching the children. The one Carina had shot was distracted by the stinging, burning after-effects of being stunned, which Carina could also feel. One was focused with a laser-like intensity on her. The other was looking down as she murmured in her mic, half-turned away from Carina's brothers and sisters.

From the corner of her eye, she saw Parthenia take a sip of elixir. She could hardly believe it. What was her sister doing? She struggled to show no evidence on her face of her sister's behavior. Whatever it was she was planning, Carina had to take the opening her sister was giving her. They were all out of second chances.

She saw it. The unconscious guard's gun had fallen to one side of her body. It lifted, hovered, and began to slowly float toward Carina. Parthenia had Cast Transport and was sending her the weapon. Yet it would be of little use to her if she was looking down a muzzle.

The guard who she'd shot in the face uttered an expletive. He'd seen the floating rifle. The one who was watching Carina shifted his gaze for a split second to see what was happening. It was enough. Carina grabbed the muzzle of his gun and leapt up, wresting it from his grip. At the same moment, the weapon Parthenia had Transported arrived. Carina let it slide under her lifted arm and quickly fired off two pulse rounds. The previously stunned guard fell, unconscious once more. The one who had been speaking into her mic also hit the ground, face first.

As the remaining guard made a grab for his weapon, Carina squeezed the trigger a third time and sent a round into his stomach. He staggered backward. She lifted her weapon and aimed better. The fourth round hit him in his forehead. His eyes rolled upward as he toppled.

"Thanks," Carina said to Parthenia. "Grab the elixir. Come on, everyone."

"Where are we going?" Darius asked.

"I think we're going to escape," said Ferne.

"Not just yet," Carina said. "We have to collect Ma."

Sixty-Six

In the corridor outside the briefing room the lighting slowly flashed and an acrid stink hung in the air. *Nightfall* was on high alert. Somewhere on the ship, a fire was raging and the air filters were struggling to clear the smoke. The place was in chaos. Crew rushed through the corridors, only taking enough notice of Carina and the children to avoid colliding with them.

They ran.

Each time Carina had moved through the ship, she'd taken mental notes on its layout. On such a large vessel, signs were necessary, and she'd taken care to read those too. She knew exactly how to return to their living quarters and how to get from there to the shuttle bay. The only question was, could they do it without being recaptured? She didn't know who the guard in the briefing room had been speaking to over her mic or what she'd said, but they had only minutes of freedom at the very most.

The running children drew plenty of curious glances, but everyone appeared too busy or distracted to challenge them, even though Carina carried two weapons loosely hanging down by her sides. She guessed that the crew identified them as Sherrerrs, and the aura of the family was their protection. It would be a very temporary reprieve, she was sure.

They reached the corridor that led to their living quarters. The short dead-end was empty save for the two sentry guards. Carina had turned her weapons up to full stun. She quickly dispatched both the guards. They would be out for around half an hour.

She burst into the living quarters. Castiel and Nahla were in the living area, and they looked up, their eyes wide and their mouths gaping. Ignoring them, Carina ran into her mother's bedroom and over to her bed. The woman's heavy eyelids lifted.

"Are the children free?" she whispered. "Did you do it?"

"Not yet," Carina replied, "but I'm going to."

She threw her weapons' straps over her shoulders in order to lift up her mother, but then she had a better idea. "Ferne, Oriana," she called. The twins, along with the rest of the children, were already peering through the doorway. Carina said, "Do you think you can handle these?" She held out the two pulse rifles.

"You bet," Oriana said excitedly as she came over and grabbed them. She handed one to Ferne, who gazed wonderingly at the weapon.

"Just don't point it at anyone you don't want to kill," Carina said.

Castiel marched over too. "What are you doing?" he asked angrily.

"We're leaving," Carina replied. She pulled back her mother's blanket. The woman's body was wasted to little more than skin and bones. Gently, she lifted her into her arms. She was pitifully light to carry.

"You can't leave," Castiel said, outraged. "I'm going to tell Father."

"You do, and I'll shoot you," said Ferne. He aimed at Castiel.

"Are Castiel and Nahla coming too?" Darius asked.

Carina hesitated. *No* hung on the edge of her lips.

Her mother spoke. "Yes. You must all go with Carina."

Castiel's eyes hooded over. "Yes," he echoed. "We're coming too."

Foreboding tingling, Carina said, "Okay. Let's move then."

They flew through the ship. The twins ran in front, their weapons at the ready. Darius, Castiel, and Nahla came next, followed by Carina, carrying their mother. Parthenia brought up the rear, clutching the jug of elixir to her chest.

Carina expected Castiel to try something at any moment. He had some plan in mind, it was obvious. What it was and when he would make his move wasn't clear, but he seemed to be biding his time.

If Carina had Cast correctly with the elixir Bryce had stolen for her, each of the doors on their route that could be locked to bar their way should have quietly opened, and without alerting the security system. *If* her Casts had worked. If any of them hadn't, they would be sitting ducks.

They arrived at the first door. It was shut. The group halted. Perhaps the door had been locked as an emergency measure due to the fires and risk of depressurization, or perhaps the bridge knew they were attempting to escape. The effect was the same. Ferne turned to Carina. "What do we do now?"

"We'll have to Cast Open," Parthenia said.

"There's no time," said Carina, inwardly cursing.

The door slid to the side.

"Go," yelled Carina. The Cast she'd sent into the future had finally worked.

They sped through. The second door they encountered was already open. Carina had set a delay between each one. After her first miscalculation, her timing was perfect.

The sound of running, booted feet came from behind, constricting her chest. They were being pursued by guards. "Faster," she shouted, but the children were already running at top speed and they were beginning to flag. A life of luxury had left them physically unfit and quickly tired.

The running feet drew nearer, and the group had nowhere to hide. "You have to run faster," Carina urged. She looked over her shoulder. The guards had entered the corridor. Only Oriana and Ferne were armed and they were running in front. She considered telling them to fire at the guards, but it would be hopeless. They were kids against trained adult men and women.

They were going to be shot and there was nothing she could do about it. She only hoped the guards' weapons were set to stun. What was she thinking? Of course they were set to stun. Stefan wouldn't allow his precious commodities to come to serious harm. Carina looked down at her mother, who was clinging to life by a thread. Tears filled her eyes.

The guards began to shoot.

"I'm sorry, Ma," Carina whispered. "I tried."

She waited for the rounds to hit. She could see that the third and final door—the entrance to the shuttle bay—stood open as a result of her Cast, as if waiting for them. They'd been so close.

Pulse rounds were hitting the walls, searing and scoring the surfaces.

So far, no one had been hit. More rounds flew past, above and around them. Carina became confused. The guards should have brought them all down. They had to be terrible shots, or very badly trained, or...

Holy shit!

The guards were deliberately missing them. They were allowing them to escape.

They ran into the bay. "Lock the door," Carina called. "Parthenia, Cast Lock." The guards might have given them a chance by being the worst shots in the galaxy, but she doubted their commanding officer would let them get away with not trying to enter the shuttle bay.

Four shuttles were inside the bay. Carina scanned them. She would have to fly one, but she thought she could manage it. When she'd been a merc, a pilot who she'd had a brief fling with had shown her the basics. She picked the shuttle that looked the most familiar.

"Come on, kids," she said. "This way." She had a short time to figure out the controls and fly it out of the bay before the Lock Cast would wear out. Carrying her mother in her arms, she set out toward the small vessel.

Then she noticed no one was following her. Carina looked back.

"Carina," piped Darius, "is Father coming too?"

Chilled with disbelief, Carina saw why all the children had stopped. Stefan was in the corner of the bay, next to the door. He had Bryce. His arm was around Bryce's neck and he was pointing a gun at her friend's head.

Stefan's smile was ghastly. "The minute I heard that you and the children had gone missing, I guessed where you were headed. Guards will be here any minute."

As if on cue, a helmeted head appeared in the small window of the shuttle bay door.

"Nice try, Carina," Stefan said, "but you lost. I'm going to have such fun teaching you the error of your ways."

"I did what you asked, Carina," Parthenia said quietly. "I Cast Lock."

Carina gave a slight nod, acknowledging her sister's words without taking her eyes off Stefan.

"Parthenia," she said. "Please help Ma."

She gently lowered her mother's feet to the floor. Parthenia helped the woman weakly stagger to one side of the bay. Carina was watching Bryce.

Her friend was sweating, but he didn't plead for his life. "Go," he said. "Just go."

Dull thuds came from the door as the guards tried to open it, but nothing would work against Lock. Nothing electronic or mechanical. Ten minutes. The Cast would work for around ten minutes. She had time to get everyone away before the guards would break through the door—everyone except Bryce.

It was an impossible choice. Should she save her friend's life and consign her sisters and brothers to a lifetime of slavery? Or take the children to freedom but allow her friend to die?

Blood was rushing through her ears. The hammering from the door seemed to be pounding through her head. From the corner of her eye Carina saw Castiel standing with his hands on his hips. Nahla clung to his side, appearing confused about what was going on. The weapons the twins were holding hung loosely in their hands. Even if they stood the remotest chance of shooting Stefan before he killed Bryce, Carina could never ask them to fire at their father.

Darius had sunk to the floor, his arms wrapped over his head, as if the turmoil of emotions in the room was too much for him to bear.

She'd nearly saved them all but, as always, Stefan's ploy was working. All he had to do was threaten to hurt a person his victim cared about. Carina couldn't see a way around it. She couldn't let Bryce die, not even to save her brothers and sisters. How could she spend the rest of her life living with her decision?

"Thinking it over, Carina?" Stefan asked. "The question is about to become moot. I know that Lock doesn't last forever. Soon you won't have time to get away. That door will open and the guards will round you up. I might as well blow your friend's head off whatever you decide. Usually, I'd rather not. I don't relish the idea of his blood and brains all over me. But I'm prepared to make an exception."

Carina's jaw clenched. She couldn't bring herself to say the words. She couldn't allow her siblings to return to this monster, but what choice did she have?

"What's it to be?" Stefan asked. "Your idiot friend or my children? I'm not waiting any longer."

Carina went to speak, but a movement off to the side of the bay caught her attention. From his position, Stefan couldn't see Ma. She had collapsed by a wall with Parthenia by her side. Her daughter was removing the jug of elixir from her lips. Ma's eyes were closed, and she was Casting.

"You're right, Stefan," Carina said coolly. "You won't have to wait any longer."

He frowned. "So you're giving up? Of course you are. But I changed my mind. I'm going to kill him anyway."

He dragged Bryce around and pushed the end of the muzzle to his forehead. But as he went to press the trigger, Stefan cried out. The gun fell and clattered on the floor. Stefan shuddered, and Bryce moved quickly away. Stefan shrieked and gripped frantically at his back, his face a white, rigid mask of agony. His legs buckled, and he dropped down onto his side. Blood began to spread from his back, creating a widening pool.

The children were fixated on the spectacle of Stefan's ordeal.

"Children," Carina shouted, "go to the shuttle at the end of the bay and get inside." When they didn't move, she said, "Bryce, please, take them to the shuttle." Her friend obliged, ushering the twins, Nahla, and Darius away and across the bay. Parthenia wouldn't leave her mother, but she faced the wall, her forehead pressed against it, her hands gripping her ears. Castiel refused to go. He was mesmerized, appearing fascinated as he watched his father die.

Carina recognized the Cast. She'd used it herself, long ago. Out of horror of its effect, she'd never used it again on a living being. As Stefan had been gloating and threatening to kill Bryce, Ma had Cast Split. Her husband was now slowly tearing in two.

While Stefan writhed and screamed, begging for mercy, Carina's gaze turned to her mother. She was moving, crawling bit by bit, grimacing with pain, toward him.

It was a horrible scene to witness. Though Carina had seen many fellow soldiers injured and killed in battle, she'd never heard the almost inhuman howls that issued from Stefan Sherrerr's throat. The pool of blood around his body spread wider, but still he didn't die.

In spite of everything he'd done to her father, her mother, and her sisters and brothers, Carina pitied the man. She hoped the end would come soon. His body was grossly distorted. His clothes seemed to be the only things holding him together.

As his cries became weaker, her mother reached him. Her hands slid through the pool of blood. Her nightdress soaked it up. When she looked down on what remained of Stefan's face, he was still breathing. She said, so weakly Carina could barely hear, "I told you I would have my revenge, Stefan Sherrerr. I lied. Mages *can* kill."

Then he was gone.

Sixty-Seven

They had no time left.

"Parthenia," Carina shouted. "Get to the shuttle." She ran over to her mother and scooped the blood-soaked, fragile woman into her arms and raced with her to the other side of the bay. Parthenia arrived at the shuttle right behind her, carrying the jug of elixir.

The door opened. Bryce had seen them coming. As soon as they were inside, he thumped the button to close it again. "I hope you know how to fly this thing."

"So do I."

Carina went into the passenger area and gently placed her mother in a seat before going into the pilot's cabin. As she strapped herself in, she ran her gaze over the console. She guessed she knew what most of the controls did, but as she glanced up, a bigger obstacle confronted her. The shuttle bay doors were shut. They could only be opened from the bridge.

Except that wasn't the only way. "Parthenia," Carina called back into the passenger cabin. "Cast Open on the shuttle bay doors."

While she waited for the Cast to take effect, Carina checked the other end of the bay. The door there was already opening. The Lock Cast had worn off and the guards were pouring through. They began firing at the shuttle. This time, their commanding officer was at their heels. The shots they fired hit their target. Their weapons weren't powerful enough to disable the shuttle right away, but neither could Carina afford to wait any longer. If only there were a Cast to fly a shuttle.

She activated the screen. It lit up. *Yes!* A pulse round hit the window, scoring a hazy gash across the outer shell. Carina started up the engine, giving the approaching guards a quick glance. If they didn't take the hint and get out of the bay, they were about to be fried.

The bay doors were opening, revealing a black expanse littered with stars, vapor, and flying debris from the shipyard explosion. They still had a chance of escaping into the confused mess of heat signatures.

Carina silently thanked her sister. She scanned the console, trying to find the take off mode. Another opaque gash appeared on the window. She thumbed the console, and the shuttle lifted up, wavering in midair. The bay doors had nearly opened wide enough.

Hesitantly, she attempted to maneuver the shuttle out of the bay. As she flew the vessel through the gap, she hit the edge of the upper door and winced as the screech of metal echoed through the ship. Then they were outside, but that was only the beginning of their flight from *Nightfall*. She had to fly the shuttle into the debris cloud and then hope the flagship's scanners would lose them.

Of course, they would be shot at all the way. The only thing they had in their favor was the fact that it was a military craft. She quickly found the jinking command and activated it as they cleared the ship.

"Carina."

Bryce was standing at the pilot cabin entrance.

"Kinda busy right now."

"I know. I'm sorry, but..."

When Bryce didn't complete his sentence, Carina guessed what he'd come to tell her. "No," she exclaimed. She stood halfway up before sitting down again. Sorrow and despair overcoming her, she said, "I can't leave the controls."

The shuttle window was filled with flashes of light—the remains of the shipyard speeding past. She had the shielding on full, hoping nothing large hit them. The shuttle's speed had to match the velocity of the debris if her plan stood a chance of succeeding. Some of those flashes were pulse cannon fire from *Nightfall*.

She had to focus. She checked the shuttle's scanner readings on the debris. Desperation was gnawing at her. Her mother was dying. That was what Bryce had come to tell her. But she couldn't go to her. She was the only one who could get everyone to safety. If she didn't do this right, the Sherrerr flagship would vaporize them.

She steered the shuttle out of the shadow of the Sherrerr ship and toward the debris cloud, setting a matching speed. The craft juddered and the scent of frizzled electronics invaded the cabin. They'd been hit. The control screen winked out.

"Carina." It was Darius this time.

"I can't speak to you right now," Carina said. The poor kid. He'd witnessed his father's horrible death and now his mother was dying. But she couldn't help him. She had to save their lives.

"Do you want me to Cast Cloak?"

Carina's gaze was still fixed to the pilot's screen. It had reappeared but it was flickering. The shuttle was nearly at the debris cloud's velocity. *Nightfall's* scanner would have a tag on them. It could read the heat signature of their engine, but the debris was also hot. It was time to deactivate the jinking function.

Darius's words finally sunk in. "Do I want you to Cast what?" Carina had never heard of Cloak.

"I can hide the shuttle if you want. Just for a little while."

She stared at her little brother. "What the hell? How?" But it wasn't the best time for explanations. "Yes. Yes. Whatever it is, do it, Darius. Do it."

The ship shook again. The pilot's screen went black. Carina glanced at the pilot cabin entrance but Darius had gone. She tried to reactivate the controls. After a few seconds, the screen returned to life, listing the damage to the ship. Their primary power was offline. The shot must have hit their main fuel tank or severed the lines to the engines. They were lucky the tank hadn't exploded. The shuttle was running on auxiliary power. Would it be enough to get them to the nearest planet?

Try as she might, Carina couldn't work the controls. But they were running at the speed of the explosion remnants. She'd done all she could do. For the moment, it seemed to be working.

She unfastened her harness and went into the passenger cabin. A strange scene confronted her. Castiel was tied to his seat and so was little Nahla, sitting one seat away from him. The other children were crowded together around the spot where she'd put their mother. Ma's bare, blood-stained foot poked out into the aisle.

When she went over to her, the children stepped away a little, making room.

Parthenia was utterly distraught. "I tried Casting Heal but it didn't work."

Carina said sadly, "It won't work at the very end. There's nothing we can do."

But for the slight rising and falling of her chest, Carina would have thought her mother had already left them. Her face was still and calm, a peacefulness resting on her features that Carina had never seen before, except maybe when she was very young. She stroked her mother's hair. It was fine and soft. One of the few early memories she had of her mother sprung into her mind. She remembered being carried in her arms and burying her face in her mother's hair.

At Carina's touch, the dying woman's eyes opened. They were dark and warm and sad as she fixed them on Carina. "Look after your sisters and brothers for me, will you, Carina? Especially Darius. And Castiel. They need you."

Carina looked up at Bryce, who was watching over the back of her mother's seat. He shook his head slightly as if to signal that her mother didn't know about the altercation that had resulted in Castiel's being restrained.

She swallowed. "I will."

"I love you all," Ma whispered. "I'm sorry. I have to go to Kris now." Her mother exhaled deeply, then her gaze was still.

SIXTY-EIGHT

For a while, no one spoke. Though Carina had long known her mother's death was inevitable, now that it had actually happened, she almost couldn't believe it. A gulf had opened inside her.

For a painfully short time, she had felt whole. Now she didn't think she would ever feel the same way again. Rage and anguish battled within her. The injustice of it all was overwhelming. Ma had done nothing to deserve what she had suffered. Her children had been born into slavery through no fault of their own. Nothing could justify what had happened to Carina herself. And now they were finally free, nothing would bring Ma back.

Carina became aware of the sound of weeping. She looked up from her mother's unmoving face to see that it was the twins and little Darius. The three children were standing in a huddle, quietly crying. Parthenia stood apart, pale and still, as if frozen with shock.

She took a deep breath. She had to be strong. She had to get them all to safety. She was about to return to the pilot's cabin when Bryce put a hand on her shoulder.

"I'm so sorry, Carina."

She nodded numbly. "Could you try to find something to cover her up? I have to set a course for the nearest planet. Then I have to arrange some things for the funeral. Why are Castiel and Nahla tied up?"

"The boy made a grab for the jug of that liquid you guys use, but the big girl— Parthenia?—she was too quick for him. They started fighting and I dragged him off her. He started saying some stuff... I didn't really understand but maybe he'll tell you himself. Parthenia seemed to think it was very bad news. Tying him up was all I could think to do in the circumstances. And the other one—the little girl—she's like his puppet. I don't trust her either."

Dealing with Castiel would have to wait. Carina returned to the pilot's cabin to find the ship's autorepair had kicked in. The controls were slowly flickering back to life, but they were still running on auxiliary power.

Whatever Darius had done appeared to have worked. The Sherrerr flagship had ceased firing and wasn't on their tail. Its scanners couldn't locate them, though she didn't know how long the situation would last. Either her tactic of escaping into the debris cloud had worked or Darius had hidden the shuttle with his mysterious Cast. If the latter were the case, she hoped they would be far away and undetectable when it wore off.

Auxiliary fuel tanks wouldn't take them a great distance. They had to land somewhere before the fuel ran out. Carina located the nearest planetary systems. Only one was within range, and then only just. She selected the destination, and the shuttle maneuvered to the new heading. Then she turned down life support systems to the minimum for survival. Even so, they would barely have enough power for the rest of the trip.

She hadn't heard of their destination, which was good. An insignificant, quiet, backwater system was exactly what they needed.

Now she had to face the unpleasant task of speaking to Castiel. Carina didn't relish the prospect. She was barely holding it together as it was. She didn't think she had the strength to deal with the evil little worm right now. She wished she'd gone against her mother's wishes and left him on the Sherrerr flagship. Perhaps she could have taken Nahla away from him, but she doubted the little girl would have allowed herself to be separated from her brother. She was already heavily under his influence.

As he gazed up at Carina, Castiel looked more than ever like his father. His eyes were deep but they were soulless. There was nothing inside.

"Release me," he spat. "I demand that you untie me at once. I am a Sherrerr."

"You certainly are from the sound of it. Why were you trying to take the elixir?"

"Because I'm a mage too. I can Cast. I insist on my right to Cast like the rest of you."

"No, you're wrong. If you could Cast, you would have been able to do it from a young age. Mother would have taught you like she taught the others."

"She didn't teach me because she didn't want me to be a mage. She hated me."

"No, Castiel. She loved you." *Too much.*

The adolescent boy struggled against his bonds. "I *can* Cast. I know I can. I could feel it in me when I watched the lessons. I can write those characters in my mind. The only reason they don't work is because I don't drink the elixir."

Carina watched Castiel as he grew red-faced from futilely fighting his restraints. Could what he was saying be true? She didn't think so, but he seemed so certain. She didn't think it was possible to develop the ability to Cast later on childhood, but her main source of knowledge about magehood had been Nai Nai. Her mother might have known about the phenomenon, but now she had also passed on.

Castiel rested from his struggles and looked up at her from beneath hooded eyes. The color of the boy's hair was a mixture of her mother's black and his father's light brown. Faint, fine hairs grew on his upper lip. Had his mage powers been triggered late, as he entered puberty?

The thought that Castiel might be a mage was horrifying. All his father's cruelty and malice plus the ability to Cast would make for a truly terrible, extremely dangerous human being. She hoped he was wrong. On the other hand, if he was right, it was probably a good thing that she had taken him away from the Sherrerrs. What might they do with a mage of Castiel's personality working for them? Though perhaps he would find his way back to them soon enough.

One thing was certain—she would have to watch Castiel and his little sidekick very carefully.

"Carina."

Parthenia was behind her. Carina hadn't had a chance to speak to her sister since she had helped her escape the briefing room on *Nightfall*. The girl looked exhausted.

Carina took her sister's arm and moved her away from Castiel before enveloping her in a hug. "Thank you so much for helping. We wouldn't be here if it weren't for everything you did."

Parthenia's eyes were dazed and her lips trembled. "I gave Mother the elixir. I didn't know what she was going to do. I helped her kill Father. I helped my mother kill my father." Her voice had an edge of hysteria to it.

"Oh Parthenia, you didn't know. You couldn't know. It wasn't your fault. Ma had many reasons…" But Carina didn't go on. The life of rape and torture her mother had endured at the hands of her father would be something Parthenia would struggle with for the rest of her days. "None of it was your fault. You mustn't ever think that. And you did nothing wrong. Please don't blame yourself."

"And I never had a chance to say sorry," Parthenia choked. "I didn't have time to explain that I was always on her side. As I got older and I understood what Father was doing to her, I wanted to help her. I wanted Father to turn his focus onto me and leave her alone. I thought maybe then she would have some peace and freedom. I even protected her from him one time in the garden. She'd made some elixir, but I saw that her maid was looking for her and she was about to find her. I ran out and got rid of the elixir before her maid saw it. I didn't want her to be beaten again, Carina. I wanted to tell her I'd been trying to protect her, but there wasn't enough time. You can't imagine what he would do to her."

Carina could imagine, too well. She hugged her sister, not knowing what to say. What could she say? There were no words that would take away her pain. She hoped that with time and the love of her brothers and sisters—with at least one notable exception—Parthenia might come to terms with the events of the last few hours and in fact her entire childhood.

Bryce appeared. "I wrapped your mother in emergency blankets. It was all I could find."

"Thank you," said Carina. "Can you help me with some other things?"

"Of course. What do you need?"

She was about to answer when a little hand tugged at hers. She looked down at Darius. His face was blanched and grimy streaks ran from his eyes to his jawline. When he spoke, it was so quietly Carina couldn't hear his words. She squatted down to his level. "What did you say?"

"I said, I did it, didn't I?"

"You..." Carina had almost forgotten his offer to Cast something called Cloak. "You did, I think. Did you Cast to hide the ship?"

The little boy gave two brief nods, tremulous confidence hovering in his eyes.

"I've never heard of that Cast," Carina said. "Is it hard?"

"No. It's my own Cast. I made it up."

She had never heard of Casts being invented. They either existed or they didn't. Nai Nai had tried to teach her them all before she died, but maybe she'd run out of time or forgotten one or two. Ma must have taught Cloak to Darius and he'd forgotten that he learned it.

"It was really hard to think it up, though," Darius went on.

"To think it up? Darius, are you sure you don't mean it was hard to remember?"

"No. I had to imagine it, and that's really hard. I only tried Cloak once or twice before, when I was wishing I could hide better when we played hide-and-go-seek. We were trying to get away, weren't we? And I thought it would be best if we could hide. I tried it, and it worked, right? I hid us."

Carina could hardly believe it, but it seemed that what her little brother was saying was true. If it was, he was truly a special mage. "I think you might be right, Darius. You hid us. You saved us."

He smiled shyly, but then his mouth turned down. "I wish Mother hadn't died."

"Me too, Darius. Me too."

Sixty-Nine

Ma's funeral was short and simple and bittersweet. Though Carina ached with the loss of the mother she had barely gotten to know as an adult, she couldn't help but feel relief at the knowledge that she was finally, utterly, free.

She had asked Parthenia if she wanted to help her wash their mother's body. She wasn't prepared to send Ma out to the stars besmirched with the blood of the man who had tormented her most of her adult life. When her sister agreed, Carina was glad. She would have felt lonely performing the task by herself, and she thought it might help Parthenia overcome her sense of guilt if she gave her mother this final demonstration of her love and care.

When Ma was clean, they poured elixir into her mouth. Traditionally, four of the five Elements would be placed with the body of a mage before it was consumed by the fifth, Fire, but Carina hadn't been able to find all four aboard the shuttle. She'd expected wood to be difficult to find, until Oriana remembered that her brooch was carved from a hard, black wood called ebony. There was plenty of Water and Metal aboard, but in the end it was Earth that stumped them. Where could they expect to find soil aboard a space vessel?

So Carina had chosen to sacrifice some of the precious elixir, which contained all the Elements, in the hope the stories were true and Ma's spirit really would live on and find her first husband somewhere out there in the universe.

As she was about to wrap her mother in fresh blankets, the sight of the disease-ravaged, scarred body seemed to remind Carina of something. It was something to do with mages and scars. When she remembered, her hand flew to her mouth.

"What's wrong?" Parthenia asked.

"Tracers," Carina replied. "Have you all been fitted with tracers?"

Her eyes widening in alarm, Parthenia nodded.

When Darius had been kidnapped by the Dirksens, his captors had misled the rescuers by cutting his tracer chip out of his body and using it as bait. Stefan Sherrerr hadn't had the opportunity to fit Carina with a tracer, but it looked like all the other children had them. As long as they carried the chips, the Sherrerrs would eventually hunt them down and recapture them.

"I'll have to Transport it out of you," Carina told her sister.

"Are you sure you can do that?"

"I think so. I haven't tried anything like it before, but I don't think it should be too hard if I know where the chip is." The Cast wasn't the problem. Carina was worried about using up more of the elixir. Until they landed on a planet, they wouldn't be able to make any more. They had to save it for essential Casts, but removing the tracer chips was vital.

Parthenia didn't know where her chip was. She only knew that one had been inserted into her when she was very young. Carina was forced to ask Darius about the chip's location. She went into the passenger cabin.

"Darius."

"Yes?" Darius replied through a mouthful of food. Bryce had found the emergency rations and was handing them out.

Carina went over to him. "I'm sorry to have to ask you this, but when the bad men took you and cut out your chip, do you remember where it was?"

The little boy put down his cookie, his contented expression turning glum. "It was here." He pointed to the top of his right buttock.

"Thank you," said Carina. "Just one more question. Did someone put another one in the same place after you returned home?"

"Uh huh." Darius took a bite of his cookie.

"Right. I'm going to take it out again." Carina's little brother looked alarmed. She added, "I'm going to Transport the chip out. It won't hurt. I promise."

"Okay."

Carina removed the chips from all the children including Castiel and Nahla, though the older boy objected and warned Carina to not come near him or she would regret it. She placed the tracers with Ma's body.

After each of the children had an opportunity to say goodbye to their mother for the final time—Castiel laughed when Carina offered him the chance, and Nahla echoed her brother's scorn—they placed Ma in the airlock.

Carina watched the still, wrapped figure for a long time through the airlock window. She tried to put from her mind the dreadful torture her mother had suffered and to remember the sweet, loving woman of her youth. Somewhere within her mother, that woman had still existed, and she had borne her love for Carina through the long years of pain. It gave Carina some comfort to know that, and it also comforted her to know they had been reunited for a short time, no matter how hard and painful that time had been.

Finally, when she was ready, Carina opened the outer airlock door and watched the small, slim bundle lift and float out into space. She went into the passenger cabin, where the atmosphere was quiet and pensive. The shuttle was growing colder by the minute on the bare life support the vessel was running.

"Are you going to Cast Fire now?" Darius asked.

"No," Carina replied. "Fire won't work by itself in space, and we don't have any fuel to spare. But don't worry, I'm going to send Ma off in the right way."

She went into the pilot's cabin. The scanners told her where Ma's body was floating, a short distance away. Carina adjusted the shuttle's course to the necessary position. As it came around, the flare from the engines caught her mother's body, instantly disintegrating it. Carina then returned the shuttle's course to its previous setting.

Relief washed over her. She lay back in her seat. Though her gaze was on the starscape through the shuttle's window, Carina didn't really see it. Her focus was turned inward. Her mother was free, and providing she could get her brothers and sisters to the backwater planetary system, they would be free too, though she still had no idea what to do about Castiel and Nahla. She would have to put them somewhere they wouldn't be in danger and then separate the rest of the family from them. Castiel would probably try to return to the Sherrerrs, but there wasn't a lot she could do about that.

Life would be hard for the children now. They'd been brought up in luxury and had no concept of how to survive day to day when you were nobody and had nothing. But Carina could teach them. That was certainly a life she was familiar with.

"Everything okay?" Bryce was looking into the cabin.

Carina had almost forgotten about him. "Yeah. We don't have anything to do now but wait. We should be at the place we're heading for in about eight days."

"What's the planet called?"

"Err..." Carina couldn't remember. She checked. "Ostillon, in the Floria system."

"Never heard of it."

"Me neither. But it's inhabited, so that's where we're going. It's more than we could have hoped for. In a crippled shuttle, we're lucky to be within reach of anywhere that supports human life."

"Are we still in Sherrerr territory?"

"I don't think so. I think this is a disputed district. One of the areas they want to take over when they beat the Dirksens into submission."

"Hmm. Okay. I guess we'll have to settle in for the wait." He paused. "Do you remember when I told you I wanted to leave Ithiya and travel the stars?"

"I do."

"This wasn't exactly what I had in mind."

Carina laughed, and it felt like it was for the first time in a long time. The mirth helped to ease her anxiety and grief. Then she remembered what Bryce had left behind in order to try to rescue her. "I'm so sorry, Bryce. Your parents and your brothers and sisters must be worried about you. Did you get a chance to tell them where you were going before you signed up aboard *Nightfall*?"

"I sent them a quick message. It's all right. They know I took the treatment for Ithiyan Plague and I'm not going to die. That must be a big weight off their minds. As soon as I have the opportunity, I'll let them know I'm safe."

When her friend turned to leave, Carina said, "I wanted to say something."

"What's that?"

"I wanted to apologize for mistrusting you. Without you helping us, we could never have escaped. I'm glad I accepted your help in the end."

He smiled. "No problem."

"And it wasn't just you, was it? Did Mandeville help you steal the elixir?"

"He did."

"When we were running to the shuttle bay, the guards who came after us were firing over our heads."

"It's like I told you, Carina. There were plenty of people on that ship who didn't agree with what the Sherrerrs were doing to you and your family. It's one thing to pick a side and sign up to fight for them, but it's another to be forced into service, especially using the methods that bastard used. I'm glad he died, and I couldn't think of a better way for him to go."

Bryce's expression had turned uncharacteristically angry. Carina decided she wouldn't like to be on the wrong side of him in a fight.

"I'm glad he's gone too," she said, though she didn't think she could ever use Split to kill someone unless she had no choice.

The cabin had grown so cold, her teeth were beginning to chatter. "Are there any more of those emergency blankets?" she asked. "It's going to get colder than this."

"I handed most of them out to the kids, but there are a few left."

Carina returned to the passenger cabin with Bryce. The shuttle would take them to their destination with no more help from her. In the cabin, Castiel and Nahla were asleep. Bryce had put blankets over them. The twins were also nodding off, wrapped in each other's arms under their blanket. Parthenia had Darius on her lap and she was whispering in his ear. No doubt she was telling him a story to help calm his fears.

Bryce handed Carina a blanket. "You know, two bodies are warmer than one."

She lifted a corner of her lip, but he was right. She searched for and found the weapons. She wanted to keep them close in case Castiel managed to escape his bonds. Carina and Bryce sat together and tucked the blankets around themselves. The cold was biting deeply. Carina's head was so cold, she laid it on Bryce's shoulder and lifted the blanket right over herself. After another adjustment of the blankets, they were both ensconced in darkness, the warmth of their bodies contained within the space.

She couldn't remember the last time she'd been close to another person in this way, not as a casual hookup. Though the warnings of her grandmother would probably haunt her forever, she thought she could get used to it.

Bryce's breathing was steady and regular. He'd fallen asleep. She felt herself drifting off too. The terrifying, harrowing events of the day were slipping away from her. Her mind was shifting to the future. It was uncertain, but at least they were free.

———

The days that followed as the shuttle crawled toward its destination were both boring and tense. Military craft were not fitted out to entertain children, and even if the vessel had contained toys and other distractions, the atmosphere wasn't conducive to play. Castiel's seething hatred of them all seemed to grow stronger every hour, and Nahla was morose and withdrawn. Carina would have loved to entice the little girl away from her brother but she wasn't interested, preferring to dwell in his overbearing shadow.

Even eating didn't provide any momentary interest. The rations stowed aboard the shuttle were enough for a much larger group of adult men and women, but they were bland, nothing more than calorie input.

The death of their mother and the excruciatingly painful murder of their father had thrown a pall over the children that Carina worried might never lift. She also felt especially ill-equipped to help them. She had lost her mother too, and she didn't think she had ever gotten over the death of Nai Nai or the loss of her father many years ago. She hadn't recovered, only moved on. She didn't know when or if the children would ever move on from the tragic events of their early years.

As the days wore on, she was grateful for Bryce's warm, friendly, calm presence. He would make sure the children were well covered in blankets during the sleep periods. The shuttle was so cold, an exposed foot or hand would soon chill and wake the sleeper. Carina and Bryce slept together as they had that first night aboard, sharing the warmth of their bodies.

On the final night before they expected to arrive at Ostillon, Carina was awoken by someone shaking her shoulder. She opened her eyes to darkness, then remembered she'd put the blanket over her head. When she pulled it down, Darius was standing in the aisle, looking cold and scared.

"What's wrong?" Carina asked. The rest of the children were sleeping. Bryce woke and sat up.

"The shuttle wants to tell you something," Darius said.

"What?"

"The shuttle was talking, but no one was listening to it, and it stopped."

Carina stared at her little brother for a moment as she came to her senses and tried to figure out what he was talking about. "The shuttle...? Oh, you mean there was a message broadcasting in the pilot's cabin?"

When Darius nodded, she leapt out of her seat and ran into the cabin. A message could mean many things, most of them bad. The shuttle might have been reporting a critical failure, or that someone had fired on them, or... The vessel juddered. Carina cursed. Then she saw where they were and her heart rose a little. Perhaps they weren't screwed after all.

"What is it?" Bryce asked, coming into the cabin.

"We're about to be boarded."

"Shit."

"I know. But the good news is, we're at Ostillon."

She ran out into the passenger area and found the jug of elixir. Metallic scrapings sounded along the hull. The children were waking up. She only had a minute or two at most. Carina ran back to the pilot's cabin and looked at the image of Ostillion on the screen. They were over a large landmass, thank goodness. She had no idea what the conditions were like down there. She just had to hope they weren't too harsh to survive.

"Carina," said Bryce. "What are you doing?"

"I'm going to Transport everyone down to the surface." She pushed past him. The distance to the surface was great, but she could manage it, providing she had enough elixir. She took a swallow, closed her eyes and focused. She couldn't send everyone together, but she could send them in pairs so they wouldn't be alone.

"Where are we?" Castiel said. "Unfasten these straps!"

Carina wrote the character and sent it out. When she opened her eyes, empty straps hung where Castiel and Nahla had been sitting. They were gone.

"Oriana and Ferne," Carina said, "get ready. You're next."

The twins held each other and nodded.

"Wait," Carina said. "Take something of Parthenia's. When you're on the planet, make some elixir and Cast Locate to find her."

Parthenia removed a bracelet and pushed it into Oriana's hands. Carina took another large swallow of elixir. She wrote the character, and the twins were gone. Wrenching sounds were coming from the airlock.

"You take one too," Parthenia said, giving Carina her other bracelet.

She put it in her pocket and gulped down some more elixir. She was feeling faint with the non-stop Casting. "Darius, go to Parthenia."

"But I want to—"

"Now!"

A jolt rocked the ship. The boarders had to have the outer airlock open.

Darius threw Carina a sulky look and stomped over to Parthenia, who held out her hand for him. Carina closed her eyes. When she opened them, her oldest and youngest siblings had disappeared.

Brilliant lights shone from the direction of the airlock.

"Get ready, Bryce," Carina said. She looked down into the jug of elixir. There was only a little left. Not enough to Transport two people safely.

Bryce registered her expression. "What's wrong?"

"Nothing," she replied, upending the jug to tip the remaining drops into her mouth.

"Carina, wait," said Bryce. "Don't you dare—"

He was gone. The cabin was empty. She put down the jug and picked up the weapons.

CARINA'S STORY CONTINUES IN ...

DARK MAGE RISES

Sign up to my reader group for your exclusive copy of the Star Mage Saga prequel, *Daughter of Discord*, and the rest of your free J.J. Green starter library at

https://jjgreenauthor.com/free-books